SEX AND GENIUS

CONRAD WILLIAMS

BLOOMSBURY

To Fiona

First published 2002
This paperback edition published 2003

Copyright © 2002 by Conrad Williams

The moral right of the author has been asserted

Bloomsbury Publishing Plc, 38 Soho Square, London W1D 3HB

A CIP catalogue record for this book
is available from the British Library

ISBN 0 7475 6152 4

10 9 8 7 6 5 4 3 2 1

Typeset by Hewer Text Ltd, Edinburgh
Printed by Clays Ltd, St Ives plc

Chapter One

BAD LUCK CAME IN threes. An unlucky person magnetised misfortune, became soft and sappy and attractive to body blows which were dealt in a cluster: kidney-jab, upper-cut, finishing rib-kick.

He sat bleary and tired on an Italian train.

They had stalked him in the station, a quick shuffle of bodies, a girl and a man, two others somewhere; he buckled into himself, keeping the wallet in the pit of his jacket and clutching his suitcase like crazy; but the mobile got swiped, along with his ticket, yanked from his trousers by flurrying hands.

He was not surprised, and that was part of it. He was wearing a good suit and looking easy to pick off, foreign, not outwardly assured – not since that morning on the Gatwick train when his solicitor mugged him. A verbal assault, followed by a payment deadline (strong language, red faces); and now as he sat on the hard seats of the Circumvesuviana, his knees projecting beyond his Neapolitan neighbour's, his hands pressed flat on his suitcase, his heart grimly thudding, he knew what the third blow would be. The man he had come all this way to see would say no.

'Your favourite author's a recluse. And a purist. I can't imagine he's ever owned a television set.' Hilldyard's elderly agent had been sceptical. 'If I mention the word documentary he'll have tummyache for a week, and that will be that.'

'Snotty about television,' advised the *Profile* editor. 'He sent the Beeb guy packing like a fourth-form twit.'

'Which he is.'

'Yeah, but London Weekend got stuffed, too. Lord Crusty Shit' – he was referring to Hilldyard's agent – 'wouldn't let them near the old boy. He's seriously uninterested, Michael.'

1

'I'll get him.'

'That author is not a people person.'

'I actually know something about his writing.'

'I'll believe it when I see it.'

'Unlike some people.'

He had waited an age for the train to move. And then it moved silently, drawing into daylight under a thicket of power-lines in the direction of Portici, Torre Annunziata, Castellamare di Stabia, evocative place-names denoting a coastline of asphalt and concrete. The sky was overcast, Vesuvius somewhere close, lost behind vapour.

The solicitor had mauled him; an extraordinary outburst. They stood in the buffet car after a chance encounter on the slow Gatwick train.

'Are you real or just leeching off the system?'

'I'm . . .'

'You spend it on the lunches, the elegant scripts by bankable writers, but never a dime for your poor old brief.'

'Can I explain?'

'What are you? A fly-by-night?'

'It's a short-term cashflow . . .'

'Shove cashflow. I've heard cashflow till I'm blue in the face. I walk into Terry's or The Place I count as many cashflow fuck-ups as ponytails.'

'Jack, please . . . I'm working on a documentary about James Hilldyard.'

The solicitor shook his head. 'I don't want your pitch. I want ten grand.'

'I'll pay.'

'The Bloomsbury office, the intelligent slate, the *Brains Trust* dad with highbrow connections. One minute you're the renaissance of British broadcasting, the next you're a clotheshorse with no chequebook.'

'Listen, will you! The fuckheads cancelled my series!'

He was exhausted now. A long-haul weariness suffused his limbs and joints, the rhythm of the train inducing stupor. He was in no state to meet Hilldyard.

He had not been so nervous since dating Christine. Everything depended on how they got on and the onus was so heavily on him to ask the right questions, set the right tone, be on the right kind of good form, just to be liked by the old man.

His solicitor had been tough at first, moderately vexed, justifiably so. Michael owed him money. But then he became furious, because Michael, on his own admission, turned down a documentary series which the BBC offered him as an alternative to *The Western Canon*.

'Why the fuck?' said Grossman.

'*Sex and Genius*! You must be joking!'

'You've got debts, liabilities!'

'I left the BBC to stop making tabi-pop arts garbage aimed at the Café Rouge audience!'

'Christ, Michael!'

'I couldn't do it. It was a trashy idea.'

He had the case behind his calves and a book on his lap. He gazed through the window of the train as though there was something he did not understand. If Hilldyard turned him down, he would go bankrupt and lose his house.

For this situation he had only himself to blame.

Seven novels, written over thirty years from the mid-1950s to the mid-1980s; two short-story collections; three non-fiction volumes (essays, travel pieces, journalism): the corpus of work was not large, nor the novels long. But Hilldyard had won the Somerset Maugham and Booker Prizes, the Whitbread and Hennessy awards, and as if these were insufficient, a dozen other honours and fellowships, and innumerable nominations. It was an order of achievement that Michael tried to assimilate as he sat staring at the face in the paperback photo. In his suitcase he had a sheaf of reviews and articles, a critical bibliography; he had the novels themselves, jumbled in memory; he had scant information on the author's uneventful life, reported in the articles as leaping from birth in the West Country, to teaching at a prep school, to a spell with the British Council where he met his wife. (He had no children.) Michael's only inside knowledge, and the thing that gave him courage and the hope of success, was the fact of his own appreciation – he would even say veneration – an enduring asset, acquired in his twenties, when he had read everything the novelist had published with a kind of alarmed marvel. For Michael, Hilldyard was the Master, a contemporary genius. To meet him was more of a pilgrimage than a triumph of access. Maintaining one's cool as a television producer would be hard on a good day; and these days were not good days.

The author's literary agent had vetted him with gusto.

They had sat opposite each other on Louis Quinze chairs, a decanter between them, Michael petitioning at the Court of Versailles. Basil Curwen was a beady mid-century type, fastidious, crisply spoken.

'I'd like to discuss the possibility of a documentary about James Hilldyard,' he had begun.

'For whom would you make such a programme?'

'*Profile* are interested.'

'Ah . . . *Profile*.'

'A seventy-five-minute special.'

The agent exhaled cigarette smoke. 'Hasn't that strand become rather fatuous of late?'

'Yes. This would be different.'

Curwen smiled inauthentically. 'I think I would find that hard to believe.'

'Probably. Arts programming is uneven these days. But I would persuade you.'

His face muscles shifted in response to Michael's presumption. 'Would you, indeed?'

'I know every novel he's written. I know his non-fiction backwards. I'm sure that Mr Hilldyard would be interested if I could just speak to him.'

The agent was amazed. 'One doesn't just speak to him!'

'Why not?'

'Heavens! We are talking about a very great novelist.'

He stared hard at Curwen, at the implied belittling of his status in the industry.

'I make films about very great novelists.'

'Lawrence Friedmann and Phil Barry have approached us. We have said no to them, and they are both well-known broadcasters.'

Curwen was notoriously tricky. A doyen in his time, six years of lung-cancer had made him brittle, over-determined to assert his temporal power as an agent. Despite having cancer, he worked hard and smoked harder. He refused to be outlived by his clients.

'I want to tackle Mr Hilldyard on his own territory.' Michael had fastened on to his train of thought. 'I want to talk to him about what concerns him most. Writing fiction. My aim, if I have an aim, is to give the viewer a sense of the intensity with which a great writer engages with his art form. I'm not chasing a story. I've no axe to grind. I want Mr Hilldyard to communicate the aesthetic, cognitive and moral possibilities of the novel as he sees them. I want to capture at source the thing that enthrals me when I read his prose. A sensibility. A vision of life. I want to know how he does it! What he goes through to produce a work of fiction. His seventy-fifth birthday is a perfect hook for the programme. We might not get another chance.'

Curwen held his cigarette aloft, giving him a veiled look.

On a fine day sea light glimmers on the coastline tower blocks. Capri floats on the horizon like a vast galleon. The autumn sun casts a nostalgic haze over the edifices of the shipping yard, suffusing cement walls with seaport luminosity and the glow of a glorious past. Today the horizon was indiscernible, the shoreline wreathed in cloud.

As the train ran along the southern side of the Bay – under the mountains of the Sorrentine peninsula – he realised he was entering Hilldyard's world, his landscape of retreat. Michael gazed at the peaks above with their summit crosses vaunting Christ against Vesuvius. He glanced at his fellow passengers: girls with enormous eyes and eagle noses, men with tattoos and long eyelashes, a teenage Nero fatly hanging from a strap. He, in return, was noticed, but not watched. The events of the day had collapsed his aura. There was nothing for people to latch on to beyond the visible fact of his being tall, dark-haired and not badly dressed for a foreigner.

Bankruptcy would be bitter. All the more so for bumping into Nick Adamson two weeks ago. He had spotted him by chance in a Soho media club. Nick was throwing a party in celebration of his thirty-fifth birthday, and The Place had let him have both floors and all bars. Non-invited members were turned around in the lobby and propelled on to the street. Michael, who was uninvited, stood at the threshold of the ground-floor bar, gazing at the sparkling crowd and champagne buckets, and saw his old college contemporary in a white jacket, straddling a chair-arm and donating fluorescent smiles to admiring females. The room was buzzing. A-type movie males elbowed around at cleavage height. Famous actors stood chatting to bedazzled film critics. Exquisite women were touchably close: Adamson's 'friends' – the talent aristocracy – drawn to his circle by the astronomic success of *Castles in the Air*, which budgeted at five and a half and grossed a quarter billion.

Michael made his way over to him with a sinking heart. He had to say hello. The handshake with Adamson consecrated failure. Envy shot through him like a sudden sickness, something his maturity could neither refute nor shrug off. The gap between his own future and that of Adamson was irrecoverable now. Failure was not enough, he realised. One had to endure the success of one's peers.

'I've heard the hard-luck story so often it makes me fart.' Grossman was in his face, seething with contempt. 'Go to pops, get the stash, pay the bill.'

He shook his head miserably. He was thirty-six but felt like a twelve-year-old.

'I get nothing from him.'

'Except credibility, which you've squandered.'

The solicitor was ridiculing him as a dilettante, a poseur.

'I'll give you a month.'

The two men stood facing each other.

'If I don't have a good cheque four banking days before time, I'll smack a winder on your company.'

His heart was bashing away in his chest. There were too many deadlines now.

'Putting me into receivership won't pay your bill.'

Grossman came up close, breath hot, eyes switching aggressively back and forth.

'I'm not sacrificing my business to your artistic pretensions.' He stared harshly, seeing out the charge of contempt. 'Cheerio, Michael.'

The train terminated at Sorrento. Already the light was failing, an inky dusk spreading from the eastern sky over the Bay. He transferred to a coach, and by the time the vehicle had completed its slow climb to the crest of the mountain, the southern side of the peninsula was in darkness. The coach descended on to the windy corniche that ran above the sea, and all he saw in the gloom was the road's parapet spooling out in the headlights. It shot onwards, cut sideways, squiggled off into the pit of a cove where already the remote eyes of a lorry could be seen pursuing their slow convergence with the headlong coach; and as his gaze fastened on the low shelf stripping away into black, here cracked, here obliterated into a gaping tooth-hole by some doomed car, it was as if consciousness only existed within the realm of the headlights, and beyond that realm there was nothing.

In Positano he took directions and made his way down the Viale. The town hung about him, lights twinkling at different elevations, roofs scattered in the ravine below. He was bewildered by the topography of a place that gave on one side to the night sky and invisible sea, on the other to the indefinite mass of the mountain.

Blackness hung on the veranda of his hotel. He crossed to the entrance and went in. The *Signora*, plump and bespectacled with beehive hair and dangly earrings, acknowledged him impassively. After the filling in of a form and the submitting of a passport he was led to his room. She noisily unlocked the door. There was a low bed, side mats and rug; a picture per wall. The shutters were fastened behind brown curtains. It was a basic room, adequate for sleep. He thanked her and began to unpack.

He lifted out his laptop, printer and stationery and put them on a desk. He placed a sheaf of TV trade magazines on the chest of drawers. Christine's photo he took from its nest among shirts and socks and set on the bedside table. After hanging his trousers and taking a pee he sat down at the desk and fiddled with an adapter for the laptop. Soon the screen was aglow and he was typing in questions for his meeting with the author.

Later, he sat on the bed. He held a collection of Hilldyard's essays and criticism. The volume was broken-spined and frail, maimed by frequent use. He had recalled a particular passage. His eyes skated over the text, scanning page by page, and suddenly it was there, right by his thumb, and he found himself dog-earing the corner and marking the margin with a pen; and before long he was absorbed, his fingers delicately containing the will of the paperback to separate; and as interest became involvement, and involvement restored him to himself, he barely noticed the damp air, or the noise of a cistern in a neighbour's bathroom.

He lay on the bed, eyes ringed with tiredness. He was fading now, feeling drowsy, numb, and the thoughts that passed through his mind were less worrying than before. And as he lay, head on the pillow, gazing at the blank whiteness of the wall, he remembered what Curwen had told him.

According to the agent, James Hilldyard had turned down three-quarters of a million for film rights to a novel.

'He had second thoughts about the book, which of course is superb, and probably will be his last.'

'Three-quarters of a million?'

'And Shane Hammond. Who wanted to star and direct.' Curwen coughed, his eyes were watery.

'This is something new?'

'His first novel in fifteen years. It'll never see the light of day.'

He had been fascinated to be privy to such information; and now, as sleep pulled at his eyelids, he allowed himself a smile. Hilldyard had rebuffed Hollywood; and Michael had disdained *Sex and Genius*. Renunciation connected them, and appropriately so. If in his twenties he had not read Hilldyard he might never have realised why in his thirties he should turn down *Sex and Genius*. Great writers fortified one against triviality, and it was good to know that Hilldyard was still worthy of Michael's high principles. Three-quarters of a million pounds had not broken his iron hold on perfection.

* * *

I would advise people to write fiction; not necessarily for publication, far less as a living; but as a means to apprehend their lives. There is no better way to possess life than to recreate it through the writing of a novel . . .

It was four in the morning. He held the paperback in his right hand.

A great novel simultaneously illustrates the human condition and the possibility of perceiving it. However awesome the achievement, however excrutiating the sense of a genius beyond one's own, one is always inspired. An alchemy has occurred, an interaction of subject and structure that makes everything work, beyond craft, beyond calculation. Someone has played with narrative and the form has suddenly engaged memory, insight, passionate sympathy. Form is an instrument of thought and the form of the novel liberates intelligence, and in certain combinations, genius.

In a great writer, Michael realised, there was a Christ-like quality. To render the human condition a writer must not only imagine but also endure that condition. He must feel in imagination as people feel in life, and thus restore to the reader the reader's own life, aesthetically crystallised. Hilldyard, it would seem, had suffered Michael's condition. His work encompassed and surpassed Michael's specific intelligence, his particular sensibility. And in the months after

Christine's death Hilldyard's were the only novels that Michael could read. The writing reassured him. It was comforting to be in the company of a sophisticated but humane intelligence, of a writer whose need to describe and discriminate and view the human scene with such care reinforced life. His prose was restorative; and for that Michael would always be grateful.

Chapter Two

'SIT DOWN. MAKE YOURSELF comfortable.'

'Thank you.'

Michael reclined in an easy chair, squinting at a bright but overcast sky. He put on his sunglasses, but then removed and repocketed them. Eye contact was essential. He drew slow breath. The air was close and the long climb up to the author's villa had made him sticky under the arms.

'Kronenbourg or Peroni?' The voice was light.

'Peroni, please.'

'Beer for you. Orangina for me.'

He had a few seconds to get bearings, to calm down. He was sitting in the heart of a public figure's private world. He breathed deeply, put his hands on his lap.

The first glimpse had been a shock. The face that had peered around the front door was blighted with wrinkles. Hilldyard's eyes were pink-rimmed, his expression almost ravaged. He looked as though he had just got out of bed, and stood for a moment frowning at the visitor on his doorstep. Michael introduced himself and the author licked his lips. 'Come in,' he said.

There was something mole-like in his aspect, as if he had difficulty facing daylight, the outside world. He guided Michael through to the balcony, apologised for the untidiness of his living room, dithered a moment and then offered him a drink. Michael was directed to a group of wickerwork chairs whilst the old man shuffled off to his kitchen. When he came back, with a tray and glasses, he seemed slightly more with it, as though the need to be decently hospitable had begun to revive him. His haggard face, Michael realised, was the essential face of the artist; a face that displayed the wear and tear of an intensely felt life; and when the author regarded Michael, even glancingly, one saw in his gaze a certain resilience. He did not look well, but he saw clearly, and it was the fixity of that look that established a link in Michael's mind between the master novelist and the old man in front of him. However disorganised their opening chatter, Hilldyard's strength of perception was present in those fastening eyes.

He placed the tray on the table and backed carefully into his seat. With a glance he gave Michael to understand that they had rather well accomplished stage one of the proceedings: introduction, drinks, seating. He squinted at the light, and then reached for his glass. 'Where are you staying?'

Michael drew himself up.

'I'm at the Montemara.'

'I hope the beds are serviceable. She has three pregnant daughters!'

'Oh . . . My one was fine.'

Hilldyard cleared his throat, as if to say something important. 'You like it here?'

Michael nodded with more fellow-feeling than certainty. He had barely noticed the town.

'Don't worry about the weather. The *Camora* will intervene. Somebody will be bribed. Perhaps God. The sun will then shine.'

Michael managed a smile. He was still uneasy, unsure of his voice. 'It's a great improvement on Soho.'

'Especially the Maiori restaurant. Did you ever have the misfortune to go there?'

'The one in Frith Street?'

'Spam for antipasto. Spaghetti you could eat with your gums. My publisher's favourite haunt, sod's law!'

Michael swallowed. 'Where's good to eat here?'

'Virtually anywhere. La Cucina is excellent. To avoid Americans you might give Black's the slip. Unless you want to see the antipasto trolley camcorded by a Texan in a ten-gallon.'

Michael laughed appreciatively, though the sound of his laughter was not quite normal. He was a few split-seconds behind spontaneity, and although the nerves were less attacking now, he was not himself, not in confident form. On the way up he had felt shaky, intellectually unprepared, his adrenalin drawing up nothing useful. It was almost as if the meeting were doomed to fail because he was not himself this morning.

'You've been coming here for years?' he said.

'A month every autumn. The town has a spell, and the steps are good for my heart. Sooner or later I'll expire with a bag of salami in the one hand and a bottle of beer in the other. Ideally, on the cusp of a keen appetite and a deep thirst.' Hilldyard smiled. 'But not just yet, if you please. Would you care for an olive?'

'Oh . . . thank you.'

The elderly man rose and went back into the villa.

Michael took the opportunity to glance around at the potted plants, the side-table with periodicals, the view (framed by tapering cypresses) of a grey sea and hazy mountains.

He had no sure sense of the author's frame of mind. He seemed straightforward, not overly impressed by his standing as a great novelist. If his face were more ruined by age than Michael had expected, his manner was solid, his address keen. He wasn't too old to be the subject of a documentary film.

When he came back from the kitchen, his hand around a dish of olives, Michael said unaffectedly, 'I'm so grateful for the chance to meet you. I do hope it's not an intrusion.'

'Of course not.'

'It's a great privilege for me.'

'I doubt it. I'm just an old gaffer, as you see.' He eased into the chair, holding on to his knee as he sat.

'I don't know what Basil told you.'

The old man stared at him. It was a look that both waited and evaluated.

'He said that you wanted to make a programme about me.'

'I do.' Michael nodded quickly. 'A seventy-fifth-birthday tribute. Half interview, half retrospective.'

Hilldyard glanced anxiously into the light, took his glass of Orangina carefully.

Michael could feel his heart beating hard. 'Is that something you'd be willing to consider?'

Hilldyard leaned forward and cleared his throat. He seemed for a moment mildly distracted, as if absorbed by a physical sensation. 'Actually, I'm very keen not to be interviewed or filmed.'

Michael started.

'I'd prefer posterity to have all of the work and none of the life.' He blinked. 'When posterity comes, that is.'

Michael felt himself losing colour and control. He held on to his glass of beer and struggled to think of a response.

'I . . . I can imagine your misgivings.'

The author looked at him with sudden severity. 'I doubt it.'

'You see, I think it's important to get you on the screen.'

'One doesn't need advertising.'

'No, I mean . . .'

'Seven novels in countless editions. Braille, large print, audio cassette. I'm not in short supply.'

'And that should be celebrated.'

'Go ahead. Have another beer.'

Michael's mouth was dry; he was not feeling well. He could not accept that he had come all this way for nothing. 'I want to make a programme that conveys your idea of the . . .'

'I've no message.' Hilldyard scowled.

'Yes, but . . .'

'And I'm hideous to look at. Grossly untelegenic.'

Michael smiled nervously. 'No message, but you do have views.'

The author was intrigued. 'What views?'

He shook his head. It sounded trite, but it was only what he meant. 'On how you reckon your contribution to the novel.'

'I'd have thought that pretty obvious.'

Michael frowned and then spoke with some fervour. 'Nothing is obvious in an era of multi-channel television.'

Hilldyard's eyes narrowed.

'What about your idea that writing can't be left to the professionals?'

'I've had second thoughts about that. I now think it can be.'

He swallowed. 'Your doctrine of a duty to subject matter? An ethical imperative that disciplines literary imagination?'

The author was consumed with impatience. 'I regard myself as an utter failure and I think it would show.'

'A failure!'

'A failure.'

'You're a great novelist!'

'I can't put myself before a camera and speak with authority on anything.'

Michael's gesture of appeal froze. He was baffled.

Hilldyard tapped his chest. 'I'm hollow inside and may have been for years.'

'But . . .'

13

'A documentary would be one long obituary. I want to look forward, don't you see? Or, at the very least, sideways.'

Michael was dumbfounded.

'One needs to suffer,' said Hilldyard, with abject sincerity. 'Suffering is a writer's best friend. One regenerates through pain and I'm grimly familiar with that torturous process. But to lose fecundity at this stage . . . at a time when bones are aching and friends are dropping off . . . You can't imagine how dismal that is. I haven't published in fifteen years. I couldn't look a camera in the eye without feeling utterly bogus.' His eyebrows arched as if to apologise. He pulled a hanky from his trouser pocket and wiped his nose. 'I'm sorry. I can't do it. I won't do it. There's nothing more to say.'

Michael was overcome and could not speak.

'Nothing is hollower than the voice of the dead artist in a man. Your viewers would not be inspired.'

Michael was aware of an out-of-body sensation, as though shock had displaced him. The documentary had been summarily dispatched, and he felt the termination of a cause that left no spectrum for his thoughts, nothing but the odd fact of his sitting here in the presence of the writer. He looked askance, sensing the breeze in his hair, the near smell of pelargonium leaves. He could not begin to understand why Hilldyard had agreed to see him.

Hilldyard looked at the glassy brightness of the sea, his expression vacant.

Energy drained from Michael. He knew where he stood and could think of nothing to say. From this moment on bankruptcy was inevitable. He was not embarrassed by the lengthening silence. His capacity for awkwardness was completely exhausted.

'It's hard to be a literary institution,' said Hillyard slowly, 'when one's last novel is loathsome.'

Michael looked up. His heart was beating hard. 'Loathsome?'

'Rotten to the core.'

He tried to react. His voice was tight. 'Has anybody read it?'

'The opinions of others are of no use to me.'

Michael wondered if this were the manuscript Curwen had mentioned.

'When one has been a writer all one's life, it is impossible to believe that something as mysterious as your own creativity can be seen into by another person. It's not a neurosis that can be unravelled. More a process of necessary pain.'

Michael received the old man's gaze directly.

'You're wondering why I've asked you here.'

'Well, I . . .'

'Basil says you've read all my novels twice and know them better than I do.'

He shrugged. 'I'm . . .'

'I need a literary secretary.'

There was a moment's silence. Michael stared at the old man.

'Sounds like a *non sequitur*? Or perhaps not. When Basil told me all about your knowledge and appreciation of my work, it occurred to me that you might be intrigued by a different kind of relationship to the one you envisaged. I know you're a veritable *homme d'affaires*, and my notion will seem impractical and distinctly forward.'

Michael's astonishment betrayed him. He coloured at the directness of the overture.

'But I need the perspective of a stranger who likes my work and would be interested to help its creator . . . muddle through a few things. There'd be research, admin, correspondence. I have an omnibus edition of the novels to prepare, occasional pieces to compile; and there are a couple of ideas that I'd like to incubate in Positano, which might benefit from a well-disposed interlocution or two. I know it sounds mad. You get to my age and you just say these things because there is so little time. But that's what I need, you see. Not a television documentary.'

Michael sat up awkwardly in his chair.

'I've embarrassed you.'

'No, I . . .'

'You think I'm naive or senile. Both?'

He found it difficult to take in what Hilldyard was proposing. A moment ago he had been turned down as a documentary maker. Now he was being offered a closer relationship with a man he had just met.

'We hardly know each other!'

'You know me very well. You've read my novels and liked them. And, of course, being a writer I'm very well disposed to like someone who likes my work.'

'I'm not sure how . . .'

'Neither am I.'

Michael regarded the author with amused consternation. He had come all this way to secure Hilldyard's co-operation and now Hilldyard was soliciting his.

15

'Well, I'm honoured to be asked.'

'May we discuss it?'

He shrugged. 'Of course!'

'Over a bowl of pasta?'

The old man stood up suddenly, so that Michael was also obliged to stand up and meet him directly. 'Let's nip down to the Cucina and have a drop of *vino locale* and a bowl of *vongole* and talk it through.'

'OK.'

'I'll get my wallet.'

He stood in a trance of bewilderment, gazing at the view. He brought out his sunglasses and pushed them on to his nose. His fingers danced on the balcony rail as he re-examined the tinted town sinking down to the sea.

'You'll need those,' said Hilldyard, referring to his shades, as he returned with his parasol, and Michael removed them as they went back through the villa; and when they came outside into the alley, and Hilldyard staked out the route with a directional thrust of his parasol, Michael followed him in a slipstream of light-headedness. They reached the top of a flight of steps and the author turned on him zestfully.

'I could eat a horse!' he said.

Chapter Three

THE WEATHER WAS UNSETTLED for two more days. Banks of cloud sat on the hills; vapour blurred the outlines of the town; a greyness and flatness and dullness oppressed visibility, and between the hours of sea mist rising from the horizon to a cloudy vault above Positano, downpours spent themselves in withering bursts. It was not until the third day that he saw Hilldyard's Positano, and by then he was at the beginning of something new, which needed little encouragement, but received an electrical jolt.

He was lying in bed, in the shuttered gloom of his room. He had emerged from a bottomless sleep and had no idea of the time. Pale lines formed on the wall; eddies of light played on the ceiling. He rolled on one side, wondering if the weather had improved. An oval shape, projected through a crack in the shutters, flickered on the bedspread. A line of yellow intensified into a bar of gold. He flung the sheets back and sprang off the bed, opening the shutters and turning on a blaze that flooded the room, colouring in everything. He pulled a towel around his waist and went on to the balcony, where brilliance overwhelmed him. He looked up at the sky, but was hopelessly dazzled, his eyes tickling and watery; so he came back inside, tripping through a nebula of dots, to the bathroom, where he grasped the taps and set the day running.

He later returned to the balcony, and found himself entering upon a vision: a coruscating prospect, in the middle of which the sun torched across the sea and unfurled on the white villas below a quivering radiance. Positano had been switched on; placed before him in its glory.

Banked up ahead were the shoulders of the mountains, dropping into the horizontal glitter of the sea. In the middle distance hundreds of buildings staggered down the slope, a helter-skelter of balconies and arcades set off by pines and cypresses, and endless bougainvillaea. It was a breathtaking spectacle, and it made him succumb at last to the town's extraordinary beauty. He could almost believe he had departed the real world for a seaside Eden. Everywhere vine twined along wires and up railings; convolvulus blossomed over gutters; walls were embellished with Virginia creeper and arrows of ivy.

On the morning of that third day he discovered something else. The *Signora* came to tell him at breakfast that she had been called on by a Signor Correggio, a local solicitor and friend of Hilldyard's, who had instructions to pay Michael's hotel bills on the author's behalf. Michael could stay for as long as he liked. She would even move him to a bigger room on the second floor, if he wished. She relayed all this with new femininity and warmth, as though he were now an important guest.

Michael was greatly surprised. Hilldyard had said that he wanted to pay for his 'services', but after two days of agreeable conversation, the logistics of employment were most unclear. He was still flummoxed by the old man's proposition, which seemed impractical and inappropriate. Hilldyard knew he was a producer, and producers do not really have time to be literary secretaries, or even to sit around discussing literature on wickerwork furniture; except that he of course did, and was inclined to; but that was a fluke. And what puzzled him even more was that Hilldyard took the fluke in his stride. There was something lordly in his view of practicalities, his attitude to time, his *force majeure* assumption of Michael's hotel bill, as if they were bound to work things out and get on famously.

He did have time. Perhaps the rest of his life. There was certainly no point in going back immediately. He had to talk to his bank. He had to find a new solicitor and liquidate voluntarily; but there was nothing positive he could do. Nobody was going to lend him money. He had asked his father, who said no, and had already borrowed from his brother, who was a director of the company and, being a barrister, would blow up horribly if he knew the real situation. Three set-backs had turned a viable business into a chasm of debt – and there was nothing on the horizon. So he baulked at the *Signora's* announcement, but he would not protest. With Hilldyard's support he could stay on for a few more days; and if, back home, there were grim realities to face, it was all the more reason for submitting to the temporary accident of an Italian holiday.

After breakfast, he strolled on to the veranda, sat down at a table and gazed across the lit ravine of the town. He was warmed by the gentle heat of the sun, and, as he sat there letting the colour and light come at him, he began to relax. The stress in his joints and eye-sockets eased. He looked at the curlicues on the table legs, at the tubs of myrtle and geranium, at the terracotta pots and mosaic tiles, and for the first time in ages felt open to pleasing sensations. He was suddenly tranquil, and when his second *cappuccino* arrived, and he began to settle in to the view, taking as much from its sparkling detail as possible, he realised how much he needed a break. In recent weeks he had been frantic, strung out, narrowly obsessed by worrying things. The chance to experience an emotion other than stress was enough of a reason not to rush back, in addition to the bonus, intriguing and bizarre, of being courted by Hilldyard.

Whatever specifics were involved in Michael's 'helping' Hilldyard, the author's primary goal was apparently neither administrative nor editorial. He wanted to introduce Michael in stages to his cherished retreat, to its views and walks and extraordinary light, and to encourage the deepest relaxation, as if nothing laborious should happen until they were fully acclimatised. Hilldyard wished him to be calm, rested and at ease; and if this were indeed required, he would not object. Hilldyard was, after all, a genius, and geniuses must set the pace. And so they went on walks, and drank in *caffè*, and took the scenery very seriously; and as Michael began to unwind so Hilldyard took pleasure in being his guide.

Their first walk had been along the Viale Pasitea, which made its way from the top of the town, down and around the hillocks on which Positano's multicoloured villas clung, descending on its hair-pin meander past *alimentari* and *pasticceria* and projections of rock to the church at the base of the town. At every turn the light seemed to modify; the plumb-line of the sea became a backdrop one moment, then the mountains; and gradually the two men descended through the different strata of local life: policemen at the top, reviewing the junction for signs of work; mistresses of the *pensione*, airing rooms, stacking laundry; and way down, in the town's crowded basement, the boutique bazaar, relatively quiet in October, but still purveying to the more opulent visitors clothes in the Lucrezia Borgia style.

If the involutions of the town were a temple to the visual sense, Positano's beach prescribed sensual abandon; and it was here that Hilldyard insisted, to Michael's amusement, that they rent deck-chairs, position themselves at the water's edge and 'stake out the scene'. Hanging out on the beach was a major pastime for the Booker Prize winner. He juggled three pairs of sunglasses, seeking the best tint for the view, and presented himself to the October sun with abandon. He snoozed off, sat in silence; and he summoned waiters to ply Michael's thirst. It was here on the beach that their first strolls culminated and where new ones were planned. 'We have to get you up to Montepertuso and over to Capri. There's also the corniche, Via Whatsit, which scoops around the ravine. That's a great walk.' All this was training for the ultimate experience, the view from a garden in Ravello, 'Where I like to have epiphanies if I possibly can.' The plan was to work up to that moment, 'Because,' he gravely said, 'if that doesn't jump-start me, I may as well jump off the belvedere.'

To Michael's mind Hilldyard had been jump-started. Since his arrival there had been an acceleration in the old man's vitality. The grizzled figure of their first meeting had turned into a spry elder statesman, sociably keen to escape his intense inner world. Determined to court Michael and secure his 'assistance', he flourished precisely those qualities that a fan might hope to see in his idol. He was wise and witty, deep and paradoxical, always innumerable steps ahead. He improvised generously on all subjects of literary interest, without hesitating to halt gold-dust disquisitions on the art of the novel if something caught his eye.

'D'you see the way those briefs, which are only a line of red, have the power to transform that pendulous dough-sack of a gut into two skinny legs?'

He also asked questions, drawing Michael out with tact and curiosity; and thus it emerged that Michael had been in television for ten years, first at the BBC, then as an independent; that he had produced films about Henry Miller and Sylvia Plath, plus a drama for *Screen One*, and an interview for *Profile*, which got the lowest rating in arts-programming history. Michael spoke of his recent difficulties; the grim fate of *The Western Canon*, the demise of *The Great Pianists*, the subjugation of all programme proposals to the quest for the Pinot Grigio-post-wine-bar-twenty-something demographic. He explained how he had been forced to cut a sequence in his documentary about Gina Ginsburg, and how that had depressed him; and how, gradually, he had lost the ability to adapt to whatever *Zeitgeist* was prevailing in the multi-channel era; and how monkeying around with ratings-obsessed corporate stooges 'totally devoid of passion or culture' had come to seem futile; unworthy of Christine, who had been a real painter, a proper artist. And in this way Hilldyard learned that Michael's wife had died six years ago.

Hilldyard was sensitively alert to this information, though tactfully more focused on Michael's girlfriend deficit. 'I'll keep my eyes peeled. There must be someone more toothsome than the ladies we saw this morning, heaven help them, and us. Even Rubens would have drawn the line. Why will such venerable dears wear cut-away bikini bottoms? . . . Neapolitan women are, of course, dramatically feminine. The longest lashes. The sultry upper lip. And can you believe it, even in this day and age their hips sway when they walk!' He would cast an eye around. 'Any pulchritude ahoy?'

On the whole there was not. Michael abandoned himself to other pleasures. He lay in a crucifix position on the pebbles, his ribs becoming dry and hot, the gust of the sea breeze stroking his chest hair, the sun appearing through eyelids like a magnified version of itself, a swarming brightness against which the familiar dot grew hyperactive, bouncing up and down, aside and across, slowing down and then pinging off as though kicked. He listened to the open echo of voices, the feet of nearby pigeons crunching around in search of food, the martial super-crunch of bathers traversing the shale; and when he became too hot, and opened his eyes to a scene that was bleached in the foreground and watery in the distance, he would lean on his elbows and gaze at the blue-grey level openness of the sea until his head was cleared by the antics of the surf, pouring itself on the pebbles in perpetual somersaults, never quite gaining, but crushing out a wave now and then that teemed forward, foam boiling all the way to his feet, before flattening to a hiss and dispersing.

One morning someone beautiful did appear. Michael caught sight of her over his book. Thirty feet away a beach boy arrived with a deckchair, which he settled on the pebbles. The newcomer following behind him was a young woman with swept-up hair and a cotton skirt. Michael's attention mellowed into soft regard as she came on the scene, dropping her bag and perching on the edge of the seat. In due course she pulled a book from the bag and arranged herself more comfortably. He noted the evocative line of her profile. He was very happy to receive the impression as an extra caress to relaxation, as something rippling in sensuous space, but after a while he appreciated he had not seen her before. She was a newcomer to the beach, apparently alone. Her straw-gold hair was far more English pastoral than Riviera Italian. She lay back, book on her knees, without seeming overly warm in seventy degrees; though after a few minutes she was kicking off sandals and reaching for the sun-tan lotion.

On a beach scattered with supine bodies any activity is oddly mesmerising to the recumbent sunbather; and thus Hilldyard's attention drifted from his book and sharpened on the middle distance when the same girl made her way to the water's edge. She had peeled off skirt and T-shirt and now made lurching steps across the pebbles. She balanced with lithe inflexions of hip and hand, carrying herself flexibly over each step, showing taut thighs and graceful arms and the side of a bikinied bosom. The men looked on seriously. She entered the water, hips shuddering. Surf fizzed around her, waves slapped at her tummy, but she waded on, rinsing her wrists and bending forward until the agony of the rocks unbalanced her, and she toppled into the sea. The water was warm, and soon she was flourishing, flicking the hair from her face and floating on the waves.

Hilldyard turned to Michael and raised his eyebrows. Here at last was pulchritude; both of form and movement, and something in his gaze evinced the deepest fulfilment. It was almost to confirm, such a vision, which the author likened to Venus reversing her birth, that physical beauty was artistically complete, untrammelled by desire, because, as a novelist, his sensory possession of it was already total.

On this and other occasions Michael felt something valuable transferring, something he would not have noticed as a documentary maker. Through Hilldyard he was learning not just to see things more particularly, but to steal them into his imagination. The mastery of one's sensory life, its being seized and registered, was an act of willed consciousness. It became rewarding to look at things in this way and to discern how an impression struck Hilldyard – not as he would write it, but as he encountered it, with reactive vitality. And yet Hilldyard's superiority in this department, which represented a whole technique of being, made him doubtful of his own value. Beyond and around their amiable conversation Hilldyard was living at a higher pitch than Michael, noticing things, processing and retaining them, bringing to experience a matrix of intentions. He had an angle on every detail, a view on every subject, the fuel of temperament driving his intelligence. And despite his kindness to Michael – he was solicitous to a fault – Michael's value to him seemed intellectually minimal. Certainly there was 'work' to be done when the sunbathing stopped (if ever it did), but Michael sensed that such work as there was was not of the essence. Hilldyard, he began to understand, needed an intelligent companion more than a literary secretary; and although there was talk of admin and editing, Hilldyard had seen fit to solicit a 'busy' television producer precisely because secretarial support was not what he needed. He needed an ideal reader by his side, a devotee, someone whose sense of the best in his writing would help him regenerate; and if this person came in the form of a producer, the complications of that were immaterial to him. Hilldyard had found his man, knew what he wanted, and everything else would just fall into place.

This realisation was a relief to Michael. In his current straits it felt good to be useful, especially to a novelist. Indeed, there seemed rather more value in facilitating the work of a great writer than making programmes about great writers for the extremely bored and totally indifferent. And besides, he had come close to the thing that interested him, the life of an artist, the enterprise of writing, the implicit belief that novels mattered. Just by staying in Positano, in a haven of sensation and memory, he was recovering contact with an old passionate self that years ago had impelled him to a career in the arts, because that was what seemed important – the reflection of one's inner life, the registration of philosophical, aesthetic and spiritual responses in forms that contained and interpreted life, as opposed to the life that one necessarily lived, full of compromise and tired superficiality. If he could forget the pass which that life had brought him to, something valuable might result.

Hilldyard's spirits continued to improve, and a pleasant routine established itself. In the mornings, Michael would sit in the villa's walled garden under the spires of the cypresses, reading an A4 Xerox copy of the author's first novel, and annotating the pages against editorial discussion. Hilldyard might attend to correspondence upstairs, or read in his chair, or make the odd telephone call. Before lunch they would walk a little; and after lunch they might bathe or take their books to the hills. The author, despite his years, was hale. To Michael's surprise he climbed the hundreds of steps from Positano's second beach without losing breath. His physical willpower was as marked as his creative resolve, and Michael took this as a hopeful sign that his company was helping. He was confirmed in this view a few days later by a telephone exchange with Basil Curwen.

'You two seem to be thriving,' he said. 'James is singing your praises.' Curwen expressed disappointment at the fate of the documentary. His hopes had not been high. The business of the vetting, all that awkwardness, was behind them and Michael admired the way Curwen switched on the charm with shameless inconsistency now that it was necessary to do so. 'We may have some arrangements to draw up. In this matter I'll be led entirely by James and yourself. Perhaps you can give me your hotel details.' Cerberus himself had turned nice. His next call did not come too immediately, of course.

The day after Curwen's call someone else telephoned. Michael saw the old man's face fall as he took up the receiver and he decided to make himself scarce. When he returned a few minutes later Hilldyard had gone to his bedroom. He didn't disturb him and simply made a sandwich and sat on the terrace with a bottle of beer, continuing his reading. But when at teatime the old man had still not surfaced he took the precaution of knocking on his bedroom door.

There was a groan from within.

'Would you like something to eat?' he said.

'I'll never eat again.'

The tone was theatrical, cueing Michael to enter the room in the same grave spirit. Hilldyard lay prostrate on the double-mattress, blankets pulled up to his chin.

'Are you officially ill?'

'Don't switch the light on.'

'Sorry, I'll go away.'

'No, stay!'

Michael left the door open, lighting his way to a chair by the wall, which he drew over to the bed. The author's eyes glistened. Age had caught up with him again. He was really quite old, a fact belied by his recent vivacity; and now he seemed pathetic, too. An expression of baby-like distress puckered his brow.

'Something absolutely awful has happened.'

'What?'

He breathed in deeply, rehearsing the pronouncement.

'My niece wants to visit me.'

Michael was unfamiliar with Hilldyard in this vein. 'Is that absolutely awful?'

'Catastrophic.'

'Oh! Where is your niece?'

'In Rome, God help us. And she wants to come down here.'

Hilldyard's eyes widened as though he had uttered something terrible.

Michael took in the situation to the best of his ability. 'Is she . . . ?'

Hilldyard sighed tremendously.

'Is she . . . ?'

'I don't know what she is.'

'You obviously don't like her.'

'Like? I'm terrified of the woman!'

'Terrified of your niece?'

'I'm supposed to be a writer, not a hotelier.'

Michael nodded uncertainly.

'Now her mother, bless her, dies this year, leaving Frances with two ugly half-brothers and a cad of a dad who lives in America, and it's awfully incumbent on yours truly to be kind, and I want to be kind because I am her relative, but not now!' He gazed at Michael in misery. 'And maybe not for a very long time. I don't have the strength of character when I'm writing to be nice to highly-strung women of a certain age.'

Michael understood only too well how much Hilldyard needed to work.

'Can't you put her off a bit?'

'I'm wrestling with my conscience.'

'When did you last see her?'

'Don't make it worse!'

'Perhaps I could look after her, show her around. Who knows? She might like me.'

'Of course she'd like you!'

'Any pulchritude?'

Hilldyard gave out a snort. 'Frances doesn't deal in pulchritude.'

'Is she good company?'

'Oh God,' he groaned, 'she cut her wrists two years ago. She's a tragic, agonised creature, at times quite potty. And to be blunt, she'll try to kill herself again and she'll probably succeed.'

Michael was distressed by the idea. 'Then let her come.'

'I don't want to be responsible for anybody ever again.'

'Offer her a weekend. Say you have to work.'

'She's going to claim me as her guardian. I'll be latched on to like a drizzling titty.'

Michael held his eye.

'You don't know Frances. She affects me. We affect each other.'

He replied by offering to make some tea, which Hilldyard accepted, and then left him to his dilemma.

By now the sun had passed behind the mountain, and Michael

leaned momentarily on the balcony to follow the ochreous glow on the spits of cliff to the east of Positano. Twilight had passed its bluey tint across the shapes of the town, now speckled with streetlamps, and a light hubbub issued from reopened shops on the Viale. A car in low gear eked its way round a bend; a scooter, weighed low on its springs by two teenage boys, whined stoically down the hill. At this early-evening hour life gathered in hidden elevations and secret niches of the town: kids mingled on corners, men drank in *caffè*; in hotel kitchens chefs' knives were being sharpened. A singer in Chez Black would be tapping a microphone, testing her eye on the backdrop of grand piano and drums. A preternatural calm lay on the town, a stillness coming in from the deep reaches of the darkening sea, so that for any one person, taking the air on his balcony and looking into the dusky hues of the twilight hour, a delicious ease of solitude enveloped thought, softening existence and lifting one into the sky's pale reverie.

Michael decided to walk to the *alimentari* for a bottle of wine. He returned at six-thirty. Hilldyard was sitting on the balcony smoking a cigarette.

'I didn't know you smoked,' said Michael, adding his bottle to the scene.

'Special celebration.'

'How come?'

'Got shot of Frances.'

'Oh.' He was startled. 'And how is your conscience?'

'Conscience! I haven't had one of those in years.'

Frances had apparently called back, and Hilldyard had said something about Michael being his special editor, and being tied up with work, and having doubts about the weather and how long he would stay.

'Was she disappointed?'

'I don't really care.'

He was intrigued. 'I'm sure you would have noticed.'

'Didn't notice a thing.'

'You're supposed to notice everything.'

'One can read too much into people's telephone manner.'

Hilldyard had changed his tune.

'I hope she's OK,' said Michael.

'I'm not her only friend in the world, you know.'

There was a pause.

26

'You're her only uncle.'

Hilldyard blushed but was instantly on top of it. 'She's got two half-brothers!'

'But . . .'

'I haven't written seven novels by availing myself to the world as an agony aunt. I have to be selfish and I'm on cracking form when I remember that fact. It's more than my right. It's my duty to whatever I have left. Open that bottle.'

He found a corkscrew in the kitchen. 'A complex man,' he mumbled to himself, as if that would contain his perplexity.

But later, when Hilldyard had retired to his bedroom, leaving him on the balcony with the red wine and the evening air, he heard what he thought was coughing. The sound was muffled by piano music, a transcription of 'Jesu Joy of Man's Desiring', ushering from the gramophone at the end of Hilldyard's bed.

When, after a knock, he entered, he found Hilldyard sitting on the edge of the bed in his pyjamas. Tears glistened on his cheeks. He jabbed a thumb towards the record player as if to suggest that the music had got the better of him; but as Michael withdrew, Hilldyard smacked his hand down. 'You think I'm a monster.'

'No. I . . .'

'A pig. A fucking shite!'

Michael flinched at the vehemence.

'I mean, don't you think it's despicable at my age, putting work before family? The rotten thing is, I have to do it. Even when I can't write. Because I'm a pusillanimous creep. I've got nothing to give, no ounce of human charity, unless I write. People call this dedication self-discipline. But self-discipline would mean trying to help the lives that cross this earth, which I have triumphantly failed to do because I am so utterly preoccupied with my own gifts. I should never have married my wife.' He cleared his throat. 'I refused her children. When she died, she left nothing of herself. And this, you know, stopped me when I could write. When I was free.' His face was strained.

Michael stood in the middle of the bedroom; his head inclined sympathetically.

'I have to redeem fifteen years of sterility. And how can I attempt that in the company of a girl who nursed my dying wife?' He shook his head emphatically. 'Frances is a seriously unstable person. You do appreciate?'

He understood better now.

'Let me assure you. I have duties to family, but I haven't a hope in hell with Frances under my nose cooking up all sorts of stuff and nonsense when I need peace and seclusion.'

'Then you've done the right thing.'

'If only I knew what the right thing was!'

Michael wanted to reassure him. He came to the end of the bed. 'Start work. Recover your powers. See Frances when you're ready.'

Hilldyard's eyes were wide with listening, as though he were soothed by the considerateness of the advice. His old fingers plucked at the bedsheet, pressing its fold.

'You're a writer,' said Michael. 'You have the highest calling.'

'You don't seriously think I'm going to write another book!'

He was astonished. 'Of course I do!'

The old man gave him a level look, assessing the protestation for sincerity. He found what he was looking for and tilted his head back, looking at the ceiling. 'Don't leave me now.'

'I'm right here,' said Michael.

'But you can't stay for ever. You're a young man with plenty of wild oats up your sleeve.'

'I can stay as long as you like.'

'I bet you've got a hundred better things to do in London town.'

He checked himself. 'They can wait.'

'You're a man of the world. There are women to woo and businesses to run. Don't pretend I'm more interesting than all that. Please. I won't believe you.'

Michael smiled. 'I don't have a girlfriend, so that's not a problem, and as for business . . .'

'I'm an old fart, Michael. You're young. You don't belong here.'

He laughed, not knowing why.

There was silence for a while.

'As for running a business, I'm bust.'

It had been good to say the words, to deal them out as survivable fact.

'Bust!'

He nodded.

'Then you must go back! Right away!'

Michael shook his head. 'It's too late. The damage is done.'

'It can't be that bad!'

'I want to stay here and make myself useful.'

28

Hilldyard was appreciative and incredulous at the same time. 'You're giving up your business for me?'

'I'm giving up nothing.'

Hilldyard was perturbed and astonished.

There was a moment of silence. When Michael at last spoke his voice was strange. 'There's nothing to give up.'

The author frowned.

'Nothing and no one.'

'Michael, I . . .'

'You see . . .'

'I think you should . . .'

It was like a dagger grinding in, a point of searing pain.

'My wife died six years ago! I have no children! My company's a write-off!' He exhaled from the bottom of his lungs, a venting of sudden anguish; and then he gazed abstractedly at the old record player. He would endure these emotions. It was his fate to endure them.

Hilldyard contained his surprise with a look that registered everything.

'I'm all yours,' said Michael, throwing it off with abrupt self-control. At least he had come clean.

The author raised a hand and then let it drop. He was strangely silenced.

Everything since her death, Michael realised, had been a failure; but that was his life; and for the person who fails, vanity dies and life continues anyway, returning one to essential reasons for living.

'Well,' said Hilldyard, with an odd sense of occasion. 'I really will have to write a novel!'

'You will!'

'Then we'd better get ourselves off to Ravello. As a matter of urgency.'

Michael's concentration took a moment to clear. He had no idea what Ravello might signify to the old man. It was the place Hilldyard had most wanted to visit, and the place he had most wanted to show Michael.

'Pass those pills.'

The pills were on the shelf. Two packets of aspirin and a set of sleeping tablets, kept in reserve for bad nights and backache.

'Let's go in a couple of days.'

Hilldyard was suddenly tired. There was nothing more to say, so

Michael shortly took his leave. He slid out of the bedroom, pulled the shutters in the lounge and, after turning off lights and slipping the door latch, made his exit. It was a five-minute downhill walk to his hotel.

The evening air was soft; darkness hung thickly on the higher levels of the town, where shuttered villas and *pensioni* gathered against the mountain. He walked past the watchful proprietors of restaurants, the bright windows of a *tabaccheria*, showing postcard carousels and Kodacolor signs; the silent, strolling figures of couples stretching their legs along the Viale before opting for the Cucina or the *pizzeria*. He stopped by an open gallery. An elegant woman waited at a desk. He gazed through the window, half smiling at the gaudy array – the work of a local artist with a psychedelic palette and an operatic brushstroke. They were familiar scenes: the waterfront, the church, villas gift-wrapped in bougainvillaea.

His smile faded slowly.

He always remembered her first show in Cork Street. He remembered arriving like one of the public and seeing her paintings in new frames, mounted on white walls beyond a scented crowd. He had watched her threading her way towards him between the pin-stripes and academy elders, barely daring to look at the epidemic of red dots speckling the walls. Her smile was full of disbelieving excitement, exceptional tension. Christine stood beside him in a glow, catching his eye with a look that attached him to her success. He had seen her paint these pictures in Devon and Rome, in Hereford and Andalusia. He had been with her all along.

He dallied in the hotel terrace, inhaling the night air. There were a couple of messages folded in his keyhole. He took the key and fetched out a slip of paper and an envelope. His heart beat a little faster.

He was not being responsible. He should really go home. The envelope reminded him of the reality beyond Positano, and the possible intrusion of that world into this one. He opened the letter quickly and saw that it was handwritten and signed by someone called Adela Fairfax. The name was strangely familiar, but he could not at first place it. She was staying in Positano and wished to meet him as soon as possible. She needed his advice on a certain matter, apologised for her forwardness, and asked him to telephone her the next day.

Michael was perplexed and curious as he mounted the stairs. He entered his room and something came back to him. He pulled a copy of *Screen International* from the pile of trade magazines by his bed – an edition he had read on the outward flight – and flipped a few pages till he came to a photograph. It was a still from the BBC's production of *Gwendolyn*, an adaptation of a minor Victorian novel transmitted the previous year. He gazed closely at the picture. He was amused at first, but then he frowned in consternation.

What struck him, as he sat on the bed staring at the bonneted face, was not so much that an actress he had never met wanted to meet him in Positano, but that the face in the picture recalled the girl he had seen on the beach.

He held the magazine close to.

Adela Fairfax was Hilldyard's retreating Venus.

Chapter Four

HALFWAY DOWN THE VIALE Pasitea is a restaurant, da Vincenzo's. Next door a *caffè*. Both establishments stand at a bend in the road, and from the tables on the terrace opposite one has the perfect coastline view. Michael had chosen the *caffè* as a meeting point, and now found himself sitting face to face with Adela Fairfax, his *cappuccino* in front of him, the wide sky all around them.

Until this moment they had not yet spoken. He had responded to the letter by calling her *pensione* and leaving a message with the hotel-keeper, who took down his suggestion for a time and place. But when the time and place came, he was still unprepared for the sight of a woman in a blue frock, with fair hair and a good figure, rising from her table to greet him.

He had speculated, of course. She had heard perhaps about *The Other House*, was pursuing him for a role. The scripts had gone out to casting directors and talent agents and there were good female parts, or would have been, if the production had not been cancelled.

He had approached the *caffè* with controlled amusement. It was something of a novelty to be meeting an actress.

His instincts seemed right at first. Adela was wearing Ray-Bans and flipping through a glossy magazine. Her posture was extremely considered, frock flowing, arms draped, as though she had noticed the view and placed herself before it to best effect. Up close, however, he appreciated that she was giving a cool shoulder to the men on the neighbouring table, whose cleft chins and mirror shades panned off when he arrived.

She was relieved, delighted. She pulled off her Ray-Bans with a smile, eyebrows arching in grateful surprise at the sight of the man who had produced himself so obligingly. She rose from the seat and offered a hand.

Her face was unbelievably fresh. Adela Fairfax had the fairest complexion. The irises were green and when she looked up at him, her eyes seemed to follow him into himself. Already she was concentrating, getting a sense of the person she was so keen to meet and whose privacy she had intruded upon. When she pulled off her band, loosening her hair, it seemed a glamorous gesture, but a nervous one, too, as if she were anxious to make the best impression. They sat down and she caught her sleeve on a coffee cup. But then Michael arranged his legs under the table and, as he did so, she allowed him to take a longer look at her, and to register, before a word was spoken, the reality of this curious meeting. The mutual expectation was almost comic. A smile crossed her face. Despite fair skin, she had dark eyebrows, which suddenly converged.

'I'm really sorry to have disturbed you.'

'Not at all.'

'You're so kind to meet me like this.'

She had a natural speaking voice, warm and clear.

'I'm not trying to be mysterious or anything.'

He laughed away his awkwardness. 'Of course not!'

'I could have put more in the letter, but there's so much to explain and – as they say in my trade – I wanted to take it from the top.'

'Well, it's very nice to meet you.'

She smiled broadly. 'What an imposition!'

'Impose, impose,' he smiled back, catching her perfume on the breeze.

She was easier now, elbows propped on the table, wrists floppy. She noticed a waiter coming out of the *caffè* and raised a quick arm, drawing him across the road with a smile.

'Have you been here long?' she asked.

'Oh, ten days or so.'

This seemed to please her. 'Isn't it wonderful!'

He nodded easily. The waiter stood over him and he ordered a coffee.

'Are you on holiday?' he enquired.

'No . . . I . . . I desperately need a break and I'd love to stay—' She flung her hair back. 'But things at home are hectic, and my only excuse for coming here is to see you.'

He raised a humorous eyebrow.

'All will be explained.' She smiled, enjoying herself. She had recovered her confidence. 'Promise me that you'll tell me to shut up if any of this gets tedious. You see, there's lots to explain.'

'I promise,' he said solemnly.

'Can I ask another favour?' She was suddenly concerned. 'Would you treat this in confidence?'

He shrugged, covering his curiosity. 'Of course.'

'And for your trouble may I buy you dinner?'

'Oh!' He was pleasantly surprised. 'Well, I hope I can justify it!'

She set her hands on her lap, repairing her comportment for the next stage. 'I'll tell you about myself first.'

He noted again her fineness of posture, which made best use of table and chair, and gave her some force of address, as though bearing were itself part of a process of thought. She gazed at him directly as she spoke, telling him what he needed to know, but making no assumptions about his knowledge or interest. She was twenty-eight, young and ambitious with much before her, but already distinguished in her field, and by Michael's standards extremely successful.

She had trained at RADA, then gone to the RSC. In her early twenties she played Charmian at Stratford, and Desdemona in a West End transfer, but her first big break was in Jack Unswick's *Lothario*, a production that Michael remembered from its saucy posters and commercial aura of lust and wit. Television followed. She was Belinda in *The Bartholomew Saga*, Cissy in *First Daughter*, and a year later, at the fair age of twenty-seven, her features appeared on the cover of the *Radio Times*; she had landed *Gwendolyn*, eponymous heroine of a primetime mini-series. The role had an establishing effect. It defined her particular appeal and gave to the audience an old-fashioned demeanour, of beauty emboldened by courage and quickened by pain, and the exquisite expression, lost to the modern world, of sublimated passion. Michael had seen it in the *Screen International* still, and he saw it now very well. Adela was fair and glowing, but the quick lashes and dark eyebrows created an impression of acute inner life. She smiled, but she smiled in different ways, and he realised as he sat listening that there was an engaging transparency in the range of her looks, and those eyes – so candid in their clarity of colour – were very suggestive of feeling. She spoke her own script, told her own story, but every word located the source of a particular emotion, precisely remembered, carefully conveyed.

There had been many offers after *Gwendolyn*. Many dud scripts. The American networks desired her; the National beckoned. West

Coast talent agencies were taking an interest, keeping her in sights. She wanted movie roles but had no bankability; the only concrete breaks were for dubious projects, erotic thrillers, subsidised Euro films stitched together by a dozen financiers in too many languages. The BBC had another classic in the offing, but that was to be typecast.

'I don't want to be stuck in the heroine ghetto. I mean, I think those characters are fascinating, beautiful in a way, and I can reach them quite well. I don't know, perhaps they still express a great deal of what it is to be a woman. But before I become terminally typecast I want to play something ambivalent, more modern. That must be the next thing. And I think I've found it.'

He was intrigued.

'Or rather, it's found me.'

She frowned again, as though digesting something.

'A really big movie,' she said quietly. 'Fully financed, fully pack-aged. The lead's a huge star.' She gazed at him earnestly, as though still moved by that fact. 'Shane Hammond. He's approached me to play the main female role.'

Michael nodded appreciatively. 'That's wonderful.'

'Yes, and it's a project you know something about.'

'I do?'

Her face was a picture of seriousness. 'The Shane Hammond project.'

Michael had to think quickly. Hammond was of course a house-hold name, but it took a moment to make the connection. He was curious and then slightly nonplussed.

'Shane and I were in *Uncle Vanya* at Chichester,' she said.

It was a *non sequitur*, but he nodded.

'He and my older sister were at RADA. We go back.'

He sat quietly, letting this information settle on his mind.

'You're a friend of his?' he asked.

'Probably less than a friend and more than a colleague.' She was suddenly lit up. 'We hadn't spoken in years. I never thought I'd see him again—' She sighed admiringly. 'He's so mega.'

He smiled.

'Humungous,' she gleamed. 'According to my agent, Shane's number-one bankable. Not to mention incredibly good-looking and a brilliant actor.'

'He's big, all right.'

Her eyes were wide with marvel and mirth. 'His head must be enormous.'

Michael nodded. 'I dare say.'

Shane Hammond had gone from Harold Pinter revivals, Shakespeare stagings at the National, and low-budget art-house movies to an Oscar and film stardom in about three years. He had acting kudos and box-office clout. *Thinking Time* did three hundred and fifty million world-wide; *Charisma* took a Palme d'Or and six Golden Globes. Hammond was in the almost unique position of being a star who was a real actor, a good-looking man who could inhabit very different roles. He had gone to Hollywood and retained his independence, mixing genre hits with art-house fare, action thrillers and Shakespeare remakes.

'I thought he was out there being God, and then I got a call.'

Michael refused to anticipate. He was very engrossed.

'In the middle of the night. Shane's on location. I'm in bed. A weird call. There's a voice, which I don't really recognise. A few pleasantries, 4 a.m., you know. Then, will I read a book, please. No explanation. Much implication.'

'What was the book?'

'*The Last Muse.*'

He nodded slowly.

'By James Hilldyard. Bernie – my agent – bikes the manuscript from Basil Curwen. I've read it by teatime the next day.' She shot him a clear, green-eyed glance. 'It really knocked me out.'

'A manuscript?'

'It hasn't been published yet.'

She was referring, it seemed, to the very novel that Hilldyard had suppressed.

'It knocked you out?'

'Oh,' she shrugged. 'Incredible.'

Hilldyard had described the work as loathsome.

'At 6 p.m. Bernie's heard from Coburn Agency. They rep Shane. I'm offered the part. Female lead. What Bernie describes as Shane's love interest.' She smiled. 'I have to say, this was all very exciting and rather ridiculous.'

'Was there a film script?'

'No script.'

He was surprised. 'They financed a film with no script?'

'Well . . .' She glanced poignantly to the side. 'A script would have been written, I suppose. What really maddened me was they didn't have the rights.'

Michael remembered the story: Curwen's movie deal, Hilldyard's second thoughts, three-quarters of a million nonchalantly repulsed.

'What a mess!' she said, spreading her fingers. 'Shane's suits completely blew it. The negotiation was fine. I think the deal was agreed. Then there's a hold-up and some creep from Coburn goes behind Curwen's back and calls Hilldyard in Italy.'

'Someone phoned Hilldyard?'

'An agent – Rick Weislob.'

Michael was amazed. 'Curwen gave out the number?'

'Weislob told Curwen that Shane wanted to speak directly to Hilldyard, but then he went and called him himself. Hilldyard was horrified. He blew them out.' She touched her bosom. 'Shane is so distraught. His heart was set on this book. And can you imagine Coburn Agency? Shane's been signed there for six months. They do packaging, get distribution deals, virtually exec movies, but now they can't even deliver an option agreement. And what really upsets him is that he reveres Hilldyard. He thinks the book is a masterpiece.'

He nodded in slow assessment. It was strange to be sitting in a *caffè* in Italy talking to an actress about film rights and movie stars. He sipped his coffee and glanced out to sea.

'Which is why I'm here.'

There was a pause. Adela galvanised herself.

'We have a stalemate,' she summarised. 'Shane's people are power-less. Curwen can't help.'

He waited for elucidation.

'It's down to me, I realise, if anything is to happen.'

'D'you mean . . . ?' He involuntarily smiled.

She stared at him uncertainly.

'You've come to persuade James Hilldyard?'

'Oh no!' She was taken aback. 'I wouldn't presume. I mean, who am I?'

There was a durable pause in which he declined to respond.

'I've come to see you.'

He stared at her.

'According to Basil you have a wonderful relationship with James.'

There was much that might have been implied in such a remark. Michael remained silent.

'I know this is presumptuous.' She raised a hand, was pained. 'I have never done anything like this and it looks like disgusting self-interest, which it probably is, but I've come here because I genuinely think it's worth trying. There's something important at stake.'

He shook his head, equally pained by her agitation. 'Tell me. What d'you want?'

'Your help.'

He was surprised. 'My help?'

'I'd be eternally grateful.'

'But to what end?'

Her face lightened, encouraged. 'I want you to persuade James Hilldyard to change his mind.'

Michael blinked.

'And to grant the film rights.'

There was an interval in which he merely stared.

She merely waited for him.

He thought he was blushing and raised a hand to his lips. He had no inkling she was coming to this. He was surprised, embarrassed, at a loss to know what to say. He pinched the bridge of his nose, playing for time. Adela had proposed something which to him was unthinkable.

Her eyebrows converged, as if to meet his seriousness. 'I am very presumptuous.'

The waiter jackknifed between them, speeding cups on to the table, posing himself for further instructions. She waved him away.

'I think you're very enterprising,' he said quietly.

'Basil has nothing to do with this. I went to him because I thought I could approach Hilldyard personally, which he said was pointless. Then he told me about you. It was my idea to contact you. As far as Basil is concerned I'm here on my own initiative. Shane knows, of course, but this is all my doing.'

He nodded reasonably, noting that Curwen must nonetheless have given her his number. He might well have put her up to it.

'I can't possibly help you.'

To his surprise she blushed. She was not ready for a turn-down.

'Please tell me why.'

'Well . . .' He was uncomfortable now. 'For one thing, the novel's been withdrawn.'

She was really quite distressed. 'It should be published. It should be filmed!'

'Not in his view.'

'How can he? It's so wonderful.'

He smiled tightly.

'Why give a manuscript to your agent if you think it's no good?'

Michael shook his head. 'He must have changed his mind.'

'Then his mind is changeable!'

He was almost impressed by her insistence. To entertain hopes of persuading a famous novelist against his better judgement took a mixture of bravado and stupidity.

'I think no means no.'

She clasped the air, wringing her wrist. 'No means no to a Hollywood movie. And this was never going to be a Hollywood movie. This was going to be film for grown-ups, something intelligent.'

He smiled awkwardly. 'It's hard for you to be disinterested.'

'That's why I've come to you,' she pleaded. 'Read it and form your own opinion. You're the only person who can persuade him.'

'Read what?'

'The manuscript. I have a copy!'

He was startled. There was a moment of silence as he digested the information.

'Please!' she said.

She was going to be insistent and he wondered in a vague panic whether he could make her back off without seeming discourteous. She had gone out on a limb for a project that appealed to her and that took some pluck. Unfortunately the matter was more delicate than she realised, so much so that he had doubts about receiving the manuscript without the author's knowledge.

'Listen,' he said, with kind firmness. 'I have a very new and rather special relationship with James Hilldyard. I'm not his agent. I've no interest in where he sells his work. Other people do that job, and if they can't convince him, I wouldn't try. My responsibility is simply to help James with his work. He finds it useful to have me around. So I need to be sensitive, and I know for a fact that *The Last Muse* is a book he doesn't like, and won't want to hear about. To lobby for it on someone else's behalf would be an abuse of my position.' He paused, unsure how much else to say. 'The essence of my role is, actually, not to question him. It is to go along with him. And if he trusts me, it's because I've worked that out for myself.'

She nodded slowly. She had listened carefully and seemed to understand his position rather better. She looked at him with renewed interest.

'If he trusts you so much—' she was suddenly admiring – 'you must have very good judgement!'

There was no need to acknowledge the assertion.

'He relies on your judgement?'

'He relies on my tact.'

'But then aren't you the one person who can make him think twice?'

It was odd to hear this from a person he had only just met. She gazed at him steadfastly.

'And if he has any taste for the truth your views won't upset him.'

He frowned at the stealth of her logic. 'What truth?'

'That the book is wonderful.'

He shook his head.

'And should be made into a film.'

'Oh please!'

'Surely you can raise it with him!'

He groaned. She was relentless.

'He must do himself justice,' she declared.

'Why should I force him to defend an artistic decision?'

'He can't be that touchy!'

'He's a writer, Adela!'

'So impatient with the human race?'

He didn't like the inference or its tone. 'What you're asking me to do is just not on the cards!'

She tossed her head, shaking the hair back from her face in a spirited manner. 'You see, it's not just my opportunity. It's everyone's.'

There was something in her switched on to maximum, not entirely charming, but somehow impressive. Her commitment was focused, moving around obstacles and objections, which made it more important that she should understand him. She needed to absorb his concerns and make sense of them. He wanted her to feel Hilldyard's best interests more keenly than her own.

'Look, Adela . . .'

'You'll read the book and you'll agree with me. It's incredibly involving, amazingly written and definitely adaptable. But there's something else here. I've read hundreds of scripts, Michael. I'm sure you have, too. What I mostly get offered is corny rubbish that's made into worse rubbish. And then I read a book which is emotionally satisfying and subtle and I can hardly believe it when somebody comes along and says they want to make a film of it, because films like this are hardly ever made any more. It's an opportunity to do something really special. Can I tell you,' she said, moving to the edge of her chair, 'what it feels like to want a part? It's a hunger. You just have to have it. You know it will call on everything you have and that you can do it. And that's what I live for. What makes it worthwhile being an actress. And the reason I'm out here pleading with you and embarrassing myself is because I really believe there's a character in this book that I was born to play!'

Michael nodded with an uneasy half-smile on his face. When she switched it on there was little he could say in reply.

'Shane's wedged into Hollywood. He can get money, best writer, best cast, and really control quality. It's a major opportunity. And I can't bear that it might not happen because James Hilldyard spoke to some jerk in a Hollywood agency.' She exhaled suddenly, fanning her face and falling back in her chair. 'Gosh, it's warm!'

He sat pensively. Adela, he could see, was a force. She was intelligent and ambitious, a natural persuader. She had enough self-belief to fortify her against the contrary views of great novelists.

'You'll never take no for an answer,' he said.

'I live by my instincts. I have to believe them.'

This he did not doubt. And he also saw that she was more extended by having come to Positano to beg his assistance than he would be put out by talking to Hilldyard. Her interest was a fact, a force, a human need; and although Hilldyard's views were totally negative, it was no great sin for Michael to check them again, delicately and discreetly, and make sure that the matter was indeed closed.

'I hope you'll accept Hilldyard's verdict?'

'If I have no choice.' She smiled equivocally.

'Then I'll ask him for you.'

'Oh, thank you!'

The immensity of her relief was embarrassing. He was a stranger to her, and yet in this matter she was utterly dependent on him.

In a single movement she produced a plastic carrier bag from under her seat and set it on the table. 'Here you are, then.'

He gazed at the carrier bag with some alarm. This was the manuscript, praised by two or three people in the world, reviled by Hilldyard.

'When can you read it?'

If he asked Hilldyard's permission to read the book, the author might decline.

'Um . . . As soon as possible.' He would read first and deliberate later. It was not the ideal way to proceed, but that's what he would do.

'Oh thank you!'

'Can you stay a little longer?' he asked.

'Oh certainly. I'll explore. I'll go to Capri.'

'You don't mind being alone?'

'I don't feel lonely here. And anyway, I hope we can have dinner. Not that I want to pester you.'

'Not at all,' he said. 'Of course, if Hilldyard says no, you may not want to see me again.'

Her lips twisted in appreciation. She was amused by this imputation. 'I'll want to see you.'

He laughed at the determined graciousness of her reply.

'I've been very curious about you, actually. You're a producer, but somehow working with Hilldyard. That's very interesting.'

She was astute.

'I don't know if I really am a producer.'

'Basil said you were distinguished and discriminating.' She shivered grandly.

'Did he say that?' He enjoyed the irony but kept a straight face.

'I had an image of you.' She smiled provocatively. 'Rather older, a mature operator. A businessman-cum-connoisseur. Man of the world, confidant to artists and writers. Swann in Proust.'

He duly noted the reference. 'The jealous Swann?'

'But you're different.' She dwelt on his face so that he felt studied, sampled even, as though something of his essential self were being extracted for classification.

'I certainly feel different.'

She caught him instantly. 'It must be extraordinary.'

He saw that her interest was genuine. 'It's the best thing that's ever happened to me.'

She launched forward on her elbows. 'What has happened? What is this relationship? According to Basil, James thinks you're marvellous.'

He was innocently pleased by this. 'I'm not sure why.'

'You must have something special.'

'Oh well . . .'

'To command the respect of a man of genius is my ultimate ambition.' Her eyes glittered at the frivolity of the statement, which however silly was likely to be true, a paradox she could relish.

'Oh yes?'

She tossed her hair back, raised a refined profile. 'I'd love to be a muse. The source of inspiration. God knows what he'd think of me. Does he like women?'

He remembered Hilldyard's reaction to her on the beach.

'He does.'

'Well, anyway, you will have dinner with me? I want to hear all about this.'

Michael rose from his seat. He took up the carrier bag in his arms. 'Shall we try to meet the day after tomorrow?'

'Will you call me?'

'Of course.'

'Or come to the beach? We could do lunch.'

'I'll call.'

She rose to see him off, and as he turned to take his leave he thought it better not to shake her hand. And as he could not kiss her, he simply bowed and smiled. She stood there with a hand on the chair, and smiled back.

Chapter Five

MICHAEL HELD THE TELEPHONE receiver in one hand and Nick
Adamson's card in the other. The line had gone dead, but now he
knew where Adamson could be reached in forty-five minutes. He
replaced the receiver, lay back on the creaking bed and yawned. Too
much had happened in a day. Tomorrow they were going to Ravello,
and tomorrow was already today.

At night-time his room was just a cuboid cell. Four white walls, a
ceramic floor, a blank ceiling. There were no human sounds at this
late hour. Only the tone of the pine outside, keening in the breeze,
and the obscure pulse of the sea thumping the mountain a hundred
yards below. Positano at night was eliminated by darkness, an empty
warren of hotel rooms and villas hanging in the black.

He rolled on to his side. He felt a mixture of hollow hunger and
mental indigestion. Consuming a novel in a sitting had a disconcert-
ing effect on one's frame of mind. The real seemed less present than
the fictional. Aroused and disturbed by the book he now returned to
the limits of his consciousness, a strange transition, disheartening.
For the last several hours he had been overwhelmed by a superior
intelligence. Something extraordinary had passed through his mind,
and all he knew in the drained aftermath was that he wanted to call
Adamson. It was a strange impulse. Nick meant nothing to him any
more; they were old acquaintances whose lives had diverged since
college, leaving only the fact of their student past in common. But the
meeting in the club had given him a pretext, which was all he needed.
To Adamson, of course, he was just a piece of dying memory, briefly
rekindled by the Soho encounter. If Michael were to call him, he had
better get on with it. The impulse couldn't wait to be acted on.

The manuscript lay fanned out on the bedspread. He had spent the
evening clutching his way through the novel, shifting from a chair on

the balcony to a supine position on the bed, neck stiffening over the last hundred pages, which he read in a posture of tense involvement. After finishing the book he strolled around the room feeling rather wilted.

He had been conscientious. He had done a good deal of work for Adela, though he could hardly believe in this actress now. She had passed across his day and through the Italian scene like a vision, and although, in the course of his reading, he intermittently remembered her sitting at the *caffè* table imploring him to help her, their meeting seemed an age away. When he tried to picture her face he found the image blurred, as if she were too personable to memorise in one go. She had certainly appealed to him. And he had certainly obliged her.

He was uneasy. He had decided to tell Hilldyard everything. His conscience required it, but it was also his duty. Because Adela was right: the novel was magnificent.

Whatever the author's scruples, everything worked on the page. All the usual felicities were there: the familiar enveloping tone of voice, the control of material, scenes broached and characters set just so on the stage of one's imagination; the pages of high style and transparent description; the charged situation that brought every-thing to a terrible clarity, a beautiful emergency of interest. There were no *longueurs*. No failures of coherence or intensity. Quite the opposite. He was reminded of his idol's supremacy, of the vibrant fusion of his craft, intelligence and humanity, a manifold that struck him as even more miraculous now he knew Hilldyard personally. In the quantum leap between the author's intelligent conversation and his best writing lay the mystery of genius, the mystery of a writer being able to do so much more on the page. To recover the sense of that was almost shocking. There could be no equality with such a man, merely courteous parallel existence. However friendly, he lived for an intensity of thought beyond ordinary minds – a humbling realisation for Michael.

He could see at a glance that the book was adaptable. There were scenes, dialogue, events; beginnings, middles and endings, though not happy ones. It told the tale of a middle-aged man wrong-footed by love. The action was contained, the story concentrated, the plot mercilessly focused on the ambiguity of love as pathology or cure, fulfilment or curse; it was a book that resuscitated the sense of a categorical morality, whilst rendering love as a beatitude, an experi-ence of transcendental éclat. More than any Hilldyard novel he had read, it penetrated another's reality, a man crucified by his failure to integrate living and loving. As with all his work it treated familiar themes with unfamiliar truthfulness.

Hollywood wouldn't want this story. Adela's claim was thus corroborated. Shane Hammond was evidently committed to a challenging film in the European art-house tradition – a commitment that was not unimpressive. Here was a film star who liked good prose.

He did not expect his admiration to move Hilldyard. The author would have more finely tuned reservations than he could imagine: the stratospheric vetoes of the absolute perfectionist; but Michael's admiration could not be ignored. A reader's response was a fact, and the more informed and discriminating that reader, as Michael hoped himself to be, the more likely it was that Hilldyard would soften a little. And if Hilldyard softened, Michael would say more, letting his marvel flood out of him; and possibly, it was not inconceivable, the author would change his mind. It was a possibility – however remote – which he would need to anticipate.

He felt a nervous tingle at the prospect of talking to Adamson. He had seemed so easy in London, self-consciously friendly, as if success had granted him reserves of casual charm for people like Michael. Hey, if you were positive, anyone might be useful. One gave out the karma of pleasantness to ordinary folk, and it came back to you in the world's admiration. But beneath the fixed smile lurked a harder energy. All his life Adamson had made it. Even as an undergraduate, when raising money for student films, he was clinching contacts, toning CV, pushing towards his destined incarnation as Hollywood producer; and even if in those days he were all things to all men, one sensed his desire to go beyond what friends and contemporaries could offer him. Accordingly, Michael had distrusted him. Ambition was a suspect quality in an undergraduate. Though if Adamson personally were the shallow coefficient of his own ambition, he had nonetheless achieved his goals and reaped the harvest of his will. However single-minded he had been at twenty, he was incalculably more so now – a man with the capital of success behind him and the drive to build on it. Michael was drawn to the idea of someone who succeeded where he had failed. He was curious to encounter the qualities he lacked, curious to see them lived out in another.

He hoped Adamson would manage courtesy.

The ringing tone opened a vista on to daytime Los Angeles. He pictured the fog hanging on biblical hills, vaulting palm trees, the view from Adamson's poolside condo. He had no idea whether he lived in Santa Monica or Beverly Hills, but wherever he was based he would be true to the clichés.

The housekeeper answered: Japanese.

'Michael Lear for Nick Adamson, please.'

'Thank you, sir. Hold the line, please.'

Michael held on, listening hard. He heard footsteps, a resonant voice, footsteps returning.

'Nick Adamson.' The tone was peremptory.

He wondered if his name had been mentioned.

'Nick, hello. It's Michael.'

'Michael?'

'Michael Lear.'

'Oh! Michael! How ya doin'?'

'I'm well.'

There was a pause.

'Is this a bad time?'

'You caught me in the gym.' He sounded matter-of-fact, economical with the pleasant. 'I'll switch on to mike.'

Michael hesitated, waiting for Adamson to make the necessary adjustments.

'Hear me?' The voice was suddenly echoey, cavernous.

'Yes.'

'You in LA?'

'No, Italy.'

'OK.' He was neutral. 'That was some encounter last week.'

'It was good to see you.'

'You, too.'

He probably took a lot of calls like this, now he was hot; names from the past shooting him a line, hustling projects.

'So what's new?' he said.

'Nick, I'd appreciate your advice.'

He let out a hollow laugh. 'I charge by the second.'

'I won't make a plea for old time's sake, but I'll owe you a favour.'

'Just don't tell me you've got this incredible script about a social worker from Harlow New Town who gets cancer and commits suicide.'

There was a Californian tang in the voice now, as if Adamson had arrived at his true hip and no-nonsense self.

'Not quite.'

'Well, I'm here on the exercycle doing forty miles an hour and I can hear you loud and clear.'

Michael strove to be succinct, even at the risk of seeming naive. 'I've an author friend who's been approached for film rights on his latest novel. It's a literary novel.' There was no need to tell him everything. 'He's worried that the film version will, I don't know, bastardise the book.'

'He should be so lucky,' said Adamson, panting slightly. 'But yeah, if it can be bastardised, it will be.'

'Is that a universal law?'

'Pretty much.'

He could sense that Adamson was already bored. 'We're talking about a major novelist.'

'Doesn't help when you're trying to finance a picture. You need a hot script, bankable stars, an ace director. And literary novels are a fuck to adapt. If your friend gets a decent offer, he should take the moolah and run. Chances are the thing will never happen.'

These generalisations were unobligingly perfunctory, but then Michael had not played his card. It was as if Adamson could not be trusted to believe him when he said 'major writer'.

'You'd give the same advice to James Hilldyard?'

There was a light hesitation. 'As in James Hilldyard the famous novelist?'

'Yes.'

'That's your friend!'

Michael hesitated. 'Yes.'

Adamson paused, adjusted tone. 'Major bard. I can see he's concerned.'

He sensed that Adamson, though still noncommittal, was listening harder.

'I need to advise him on the hazards of adaptation.'

Adamson cleared his throat. It was not something he found easy or rewarding to think about. 'Kind of story?'

'English characters, forbidden love, beautiful landscape.'

'Like what genre?'

Michael allowed himself to smile. 'Nick, it's a literary novel.'

'Equals art-house picture.'

He remained poised. 'I expect so.'

'Great way to lose money.'

'What would be the impact of American financing?'

He grunted. This was hard work for Adamson. 'American distribs won't touch this without a star – a face that'll play in the flyover states – and that kind of talent will be wrong for the material. I'd forget American money.'

Michael had always found the financial pragmatism of the commercially inclined producer an ugly thing. It was so sure of itself. So smugly bottom-line.

'You really think so?'

'Without a doubt.'

'That's interesting.'

'It's called reality, Michael.'

He bridled. Adamson was patronising him. 'Actually, Nick, the project has money attached.'

'Oh yeah?'

'Oh yeah.'

There was a moment's silence.

'Like what money?'

He paused for effect. He was beginning to enjoy the call. 'Like twenty million dollars. Shane Hammond to star and direct.'

There was a click. Adamson's voice was suddenly close, immediate. He was on the cordless.

'This is a Shane Hammond picture?'

Michael smiled to himself but kept the smile out of his voice. 'That's what's on offer.'

There was silence, the sound of a man checking his surprise.

'Actually . . . Hilldyard turned them down.'

'What!'

'Coburn Agency made an offer for the rights. Hilldyard declined.'

Adamson was aghast. 'He declined!'

'He did.'

'That's like pissing on God. What did they do? Pull his chain with some low-ball offer?'

'Three-quarters of a million dollars.'

'Jesus! Why?'

'He wasn't interested.'

'He walked on the offer?'

Michael did not want to complicate matters by describing Hilldyard's attitude. 'He's a serious novelist.'

'Allergic to money or what!'

'Allergic to Hollywood, I expect.'

Adamson broke into nervous laughter. 'Coburn Agency must be in shock.'

Adamson was in shock, too. In a bizarre way it was flattering to have astonished him. His cool so quickly switched to avidity. He was experiencing a paradigm shift. In Adamson's scheme of values nobody turned down film-star interest and serious dollars for reasons of principle. There were no principles that huge or inflexible. Except there were, and he was going to hear about them.

'D'you know Rick Weislob?' asked Michael.

'Mickey Mouse meets *Jaws*. Guy with a conk like a dorsal fin. He's a tough little fucker, and we call him the turd bullet.'

'He phoned Hilldyard at his home in Italy.'

'Oh shit!'

'He didn't make a good impression.'

There was a dry laugh. 'Hey, listen. I'm waging war with Weislob on a Mike Carnegie project. If he suffers, I open champagne.'

'It's not just Weislob. Hilldyard has misgivings about any kind of film.' Michael noted his easy assumption of Hilldyard's viewpoint.

'I can understand that.'

'What I wanted was your opinion on Shane Hammond's clout. On the reality of the financing, which hasn't been checked out. On the prospects for the integrity of a film set up like this.'

'I'm hitting the study. Just hold it.'

There were background noises, the slamming of a door. He pictured Adamson throwing himself into a swivel chair, bringing himself into focus on the project, picking up a different phone.

'It's interesting. Let's break it down.'

Adamson's voice became steadier, truer, his accent less mid-Atlantic. His speech was studded with American slang and movie-biz patois, but the cruiser intonation fell away, revealing an executive edge, as if he had plugged himself into a socket on the desk and were now offering acumen on stream. Michael sensed the real Adamson ticking over: someone who could talk the language with its flaky equivocations and bullshit phrases while seeing through to the bottom line. The sensibility was wide, the delivery fast, but the mind dealt in hard terms with the available data. Adamson's was the style of the entrepreneur in love with his job.

'Basic questions are easy. Is Hammond bankable? Yes, he's roof-liftingly hot. He's flavour of the month, maybe the year. He's the lolly everyone wants to suck, and there isn't enough to go round.

Second question: Can he raise cash for an extreme art-house picture? Yeah. I have no problem with that. Right now he points to something, it's greenlit. Your third question's more difficult. Will it be any good? Two sub-questions. Will the money give him rope, director's cut, all that bullshit? Depends on who the patsies are. If it's some nichey distributor, yes. A studio, probably not. If it's European consortium money, God fucking knows. But if Coburn Agency's hooked into Japanese credit lines, some kind of yellow peril chequebook, those guys can be burned for trillions without batting an eyelid. And maybe there's a trade. In return for a twenty-million-dollar write-off on the art-house flick they get Hammond's next blockbuster. If so, he'll have rope. Now if he gets rope will he make a Palme d'Or meisterwerk or a piece of shit? Hammond, OK, can act. That's if you throw him a Shakespeare script. Hammond as director is untested. Let's say the guy has the best intentions in the world, the fruitiest vision of a beautiful movie, what happens when the script freaks out? What happens when the accountants get the jitters and start walking over the set? What happens when some boardroom ego-features wants to fuck with our star? Will he kick arse, hold to a course, or return to his caravan for a sulk? You understand what I'm saying? Hammond is a talent entity, not a producer entity. And what this project's going to need is a strong creative producer to see his vision through the system and on to the screen.'

Michael cleared his throat. He was amused by the heaviness of the hint. 'I assume Coburn Agency will exec produce.'

'They're agents, Michael. They eat old coins for breakfast.'

'Maybe Hammond has a choice.'

'Evidently not. No producer worth his salt would let Weislob near Hilldyard. And if Hilldyard's sticky your producer's got to be English, in tune with literature and streetwise here.'

There was a significant pause.

Michael had the sure feeling that Nick Adamson was not in tune with anything Hilldyard would call literature.

'Frank Coburn screwed up. The right producer is the guy that can reassure Hilldyard, deliver the rights and work with Hammond.'

There was no need to respond to such arrant self-promotion.

Adamson had the bit between the teeth, but he let the line run open for Michael's reaction.

'Thanks for your advice, Nick.'

'What's your role, Michael?'

'I don't have a role.'

'You represent Hilldyard?'

'No!'

'You're a producer, right?'

Adamson could have no idea, not the faintest sense, of his situation, and it amused him to hear the word 'producer' raised as an attempt to fix him with certain motives and attitudes.

'You guys are buddies?'

'I'm working with Hilldyard. I have more access to his concerns than Rick Weislob. There's been a fresh approach.'

'From whom?'

'Indirectly from Hammond.'

'OK. Right.'

'Which I'm sure he'll turn down. But just in case, I want to know what the considerations might be if he were interested. In order to advise him. I have absolutely no personal interest.'

'Am I reading you? On one side of the ring we have *el* supremely bankable movie star and a shitload of spons. On the other side is one bruiser of a novelist, like Nobel time, every word eternal, and in the middle with the whistle in his mouth, you.'

'No!'

'You're the ref. You have to be satisfied?'

'Hang on, Nick. I'm acting on my own initiative.'

'But you're in there, which means he trusts you.'

He flinched at the crassness, the intrusiveness. 'I have no position on this project.'

There was strangeness in the silence.

'I'd say you have a great position.'

Michael controlled his annoyance. 'My responsibility is to Hilldyard.'

'That's semantic.'

'I'm acting on his behalf!'

'Absolutely.' Adamson changed gear. 'And I respect that.'

'I'm trying to protect him.'

'Which you must.'

He glanced at the manuscript on the bed. 'I will.'

There was an enduring silence on the line.

'What I said before. Don't misunderstand me. There's authors and authors. I think we all know the diff between some marginal Booker Prize literary bullshit scribe and James Hilldyard. We're talking about a contemporary classic writer. And if anybody wants to do a Hilldyard title, it's not because they want to nick the plot, whip the characters and save themselves effort on a story, it's because they want Hilldyard's feel onscreen. A different ballgame. A labour of love. I think we're into a special category right from the start, where fidelity is the watchword. And you need someone with integrity to push that through. Somebody who has a cultural link with the material. Yeah, but can also keep the suits out of the editing room.'

Adamson could switch on the lip-service with all the alacrity of a DJ parleying in a chart-buster. He was all vision, all salesmanship, and as such was an interesting manifestation of what happened to an Oxford education when dropped in pure commercial waters. He had adapted himself into alignment with the market and its rhetoric. Content for him was just an extrapolation of product; 'integrity' a buzz word; 'artistic truth' a brand tool.

Michael decided to push harder. 'Hilldyard would get script approval?'

'Um . . . I wouldn't go that far.'

'You'd want him to approve the script?'

'Oh, most certainly.'

'What's the problem?'

'There's no problem. Scripts are difficult to read.'

Michael frowned. 'I think he can read!'

Adamson cleared his throat. 'James Hilldyard can read. But see it in context. We'll need a screenwriter. He'll cost two hundred and fifty thousand dollars for two drafts and a set. He'll take six months. Everybody'll roll up sleeves. A huge effort will be made bottling the spirit of the book. There'll be lots of behind-the-scenes prep. Thousands of dollars will be spent getting key players on contract, lining up completion bonding, negotiating net profit definitions. Even before pre-production the money's sunk half a million greenbacks, maybe more. Can you really see the corporate accountants switching on that kind of dough if a little old author halfway across the planet can pull the plug? No. There'd have to be trust. And we have a word for it. Consultancy. The right to express an opinion. The great man can read each draft of the script and if he hates what he reads we hunker around, listen to the oracle and pay attention because we want to satisfy. He makes notes. Doyen scriptwriter dwells on the notes. Quality achieved by collaboration not prescription. It works when the elements are first class, which they will be.'

Apart from Adamson, thought Michael, if he were involved, which he wouldn't be.

'Hey, you'd be the perfect person to mediate that process.'

'I'm not mediating anything,' said Michael.

'I think it's very exciting.'

There was a durable pause.

'What happens now?'

Michael sighed against the stress of an incompatible mind.

'What's your telephone number?'

He hesitated a moment too long.

'Michael, I understand your position.'

'I don't have a position.'

'I understand that, too. I hear that.'

'I have a special relationship. For good reasons I need to remain uninvolved.'

'Hey, look. While you're thinking it through let me use my network over here. We got the British mafia to tap into. Plus an insider contact at Coburn's. I mean, let's just see how real this project is on the ground.'

He made a rapid calculation. 'You'd need to be discreet. And it has to be a favour.'

'Cool. I like people to owe me.'

Michael gave Adamson his phone and fax details.

'I'll make some calls and get back to you.'

'OK.'

'Then we work out the plan.'

He wondered how to phrase it. He wanted to be forceful. He was deeply put off. 'No we won't.'

Adamson laughed. 'Listen, buddy. If this picture's real, it's the biggest break you'll ever get.'

'I beg your pardon!'

'You'd be leap-frogging into the bigtime.'

He was appalled.

'Think about it.'

'I don't want to think about it. I'm not interested!'

Adamson rang off.

Michael stared at the phone in a kind of marvel, almost exhilarated by Adamson's opportunism. He was worse than the worst clichés, a two-dimensional parody of Hollywood greed. Michael sprang off the bed and walked round the room with a strange smile on his face. And then he laughed. He knew why he had called Adamson. It was not really for advice, though he needed that pretext. The honest reason was that he wanted to know what had happened to Adamson's soul. Because Adamson was his anti-type: wealthy, successful. And if success had turned him into this, it meant that Michael could at least pardon himself for being a failure.

It was good to be sure of such things at last.

Chapter Six

HILLDYARD HAD SUGGESTED A nine-thirty rendezvous at the bus stop, at a point where Viale Pasitea diverged from the coast road, and Michael was nearly late because he had not gone to sleep until 5 a.m. and then woken to such a drugged and drowsy head that he could only dress so fast, and was positively disabled in his efforts to gather things for the trip: sunglasses and raincoat, sunblock and pullover, notepad but not camera (which he was ordered to leave), all of which inclusions, exclusions or double-checkings overlapped a dizzy sock-hunt and fretful shave.

He hurried up the road to the top of the town, dry-mouthed and unwell. The air was close, the sky overcast. There was a blanket of cloud over the sea and vapour in the folds of the mountain.

Hilldyard sat on the parapet by the T-junction. He was watching the scene at the *pasticceria*, where under the awnings two old men with cloth caps and cavernous eyes looked out on the world. They sat on metal chairs, sipping espresso. They were imperturbably absorbed, deadpan, silently wise to everything an Italian street could offer. Beside them a German cyclist with veins running over his legs like electric cables chomped through a pastry.

Michael greeted the author, shrugged at the weather.

'Don't worry. It'll burn away.'

'In October?'

'This isn't British cloud. It's Italian fluff. No staying power. No grit.'

He asked if he could run for a coffee at the bar.

'Look sharp. Our carriage is due.'

Up here a coach seemed impossible. The corner was too tight, the kerb too cluttered by grocery stalls. Locals sauntered across the junction as if it were a pedestrian zone and old boys sat on the parapet, looking at the view as if nothing had ever happened here or would. And yet, when the coach did arrive, looming at first-floor height, and barely squeezing round the corner, everyone took an interest. The old men called out hoarsely. A Tweedledum personality in braces and cords stood at the vehicle's rear sizing up traffic flow. A bescarved *signora* dug Michael out of the bar and directed him to the head of the coach, where Hilldyard waited with a feeble queue of three people, and whence the high-booted driver now made his disembarkation. The driver was portly, Napoleonic. He strolled along the flanks of the coach allowing passengers to drag their own bags from the hold. The locals hailed him like a returning general, a hero of the corniche, a herald from the outside world. He crossed to the bar to give something to the proprietor and allowed the crowds a thirsty glimpse of his leather boots and high bearing.

The two men, aware of their dutylessness, stumbled on to the coach, which was almost empty. As the bus hovered, sundry others ascended and took up places, none of them bothered by a sense of expectancy. There was nobody much from the rest of the world here and Michael felt the extreme unseasonability of their trip.

'This ride,' the author said solemnly, 'is a cavalcade of vertigo.'

Michael eased into his seat.

'Machismo in a bus driver,' said Hilldyard, 'is a terrible affliction.'

'Yes.'

'Keep your eyes on the horizon and relax into the G-force.'

'It's all right,' he said.

He was not feeling too good.

An old man with a stubbly chin and sunken eyes sat across the aisle. He watched the figure of a mama, who heaved herself on to the coach, trailing four children and making an obese entry down the aisle. Michael was transfixed. The woman's belly was inflated, her breasts had subsided into pendant tubers, the arms were of mighty girth. She bore an authority as great as her size, as if the eruptions of her corpulence were a kind of sovereignty. She commanded the children into their places, quashed a hair-pulling outbreak, and then yanked up an armrest and sat across two seats. Her innocently pretty six-year-old looked down the aisle and found a full stop to her curiosity in the smile of the old man. He bared his tooth gaps and caught Michael's eye in a round-up of good will. Michael smiled at the unblinking *bambina*, and then at the man who shook his head sadly. These little innocents, he seemed to hint, would soon face the world's cares, some of them indigenous to Italy: the problems of corruption, of political incompetence, of over-eating and excessive talkativeness in women. The little ones – they were not the cause of all this – but one day they would perpetuate it.

The bus honked its horn and pulled away. The ride had begun, and all eyes went to starboard, towards the spiralling view of Positano.

The coffee had done something to Michael's stomach. He felt odd, unsettled. He folded his hands and forced his attention. He would not speak unless spoken to. This was Hilldyard's excursion.

The view, even in dull weather, cast its slow spell. Positano was soon removed behind projections of rock. The road curved ahead, now leading to the grey spread of the Tyrrhenian Sea, now burrowing back into the cleft of a cove, past netted escarpments of rock. One saw waves impacting on honeycombed spits of limestone, water bursting from pockets, the docile bulk of the sea swaying against the gums of cliffs. The ride was hard on vision, a constant challenge to bearings. The body tensed with each hairpin turn, braced itself against the swerves and lurches. After several headachy zigzags the road straightened out for a mile, tendering at last a steady view and a stable speed so that he could gaze in relief at the far reaches of the sea, which was partly glaucous, and in the distance, under spokes of light, partly sparkling.

He was still in a kind of pain. He did not know from where it came. It was not fatigue; it was more like a rent in the soul, an inner breach. He held on to the arm of his seat possessed by the idea he should not be here. He should be at home, organising his life; except that he had no life. There was only nothingness to be organised, things that could not be shaped or squared. He swallowed, trying to calm himself. He had to let the mood evaporate. He would have a second coffee in Ravello and catch up with himself there.

'Look at that,' said Hilldyard, pointing through the window at a blow-up dinghy with an outboard motor buffeting across the sea.

'Bonking the waves like a disembodied phallus.'

Michael laughed and looked for himself. 'Zooming along.'

'I just hope it isn't mine.'

'Probably a sea god's.'

'Damn thing's going to beat us to Amalfi.'

He needed a pee in Amalfi. They had anyway to change buses and Hilldyard sprang from the first vehicle on to the tarmac, running between lines of parked minibuses and shouting, 'You've got a hundred and fifty seconds. Run!'

He did not admire Amalfi. Half the waterfront was a bus terminal. The tree-lined promenade throbbed with traffic. He made his way back from the *gabinetto*, trying to walk off a headache before climbing back into the atmosphere of a bus.

He discovered the Ravello bus, not by its sign, but by the striking sight of Hilldyard sitting in the front passenger seat and gazing through the bubble of the windscreen as if the convex glass were an amplification of his power of vision. Michael sat down across the aisle from him. They exchanged nods, signifying the happy execution of his trip to the loo and their satisfactory transfer to the Ravello bus. This was the last leg of Hilldyard's pilgrimage and whereas the old man had seemed on the coast road slackly interested and in fact rather glazed by the reeling spectacle, and was equally casual about serviceable Amalfi, once the bus got moving and began its long, slow climb he sat up for a better view and his expression began to change. A threshold had been crossed, a point at which sensation was quickened by memory. The view opened out. The cold sea and gnashing rocks fell behind them, as did the shuttered, off-season villas along the coast, and the bus hoved into upland scenery, through valleys of turning colour. As their altitude increased, the mountains receded to a proper serenity of distance, tracing a wavy line against the sky. Sunlight impinged gradually, imperceptibly. Smoke from a bonfire became an electric flash. A hilltop basilica was momentarily touched off. Warmth lurked in the airy heights around them.

Hilldyard sat meekly, rocking with the motion of the bus as it braked and turned. He scanned the wide view, as though listening for something, pressing his cheek against the window. Michael felt his own attention quickening as if, even now, on the winding approach road that scooped under Ravello's mountainous plinth, way beneath the leafy level of the town, he sensed the beginnings of an exaltation that would build over the next hour or so to its point of climax in the Cimbrone Gardens, on the famous balcony; and he knew now that, however jaded he was, he felt the renewal of a longing for that unimaginable prospect. Hilldyard's insistence on the place was a challenge. Ever since his arrival in Positano Hilldyard had been relaying him this impression and pointing out that sight, detailing the topography of his inspiration, as if he attached high importance to the existence of such impressions. In showing Michael something that moved him he was demonstrating what he himself was, what composed him. And if Michael realised that the author was returning to the locus of an emotion which he had consciously deposited at Ravello for future redemption, he also understood that Hilldyard offered the chance of Michael's own initiation in the enchanted garden. Hilldyard was asking him to become an artist. He was offering a tonic against worldly cares. He was drawing him into the secrets of solitude. He had mentioned before that Ravello taught him the self-sufficiency of experience. 'I write, of course, like a devil possessed, and for years it bothered me how people could live, have their experience, and leave it unwritten. You see, in my case, I felt I'd not really seized life until I had it down in words, although it struck me at the time how tyrannical that feeling was: that life couldn't just be lived, allowed to pass through the senses and enjoyed, like iridescent sand through fingers. And then I perceived that writing itself was only an agreeable form of awareness, induced by procedures and disciplines specific in my case to the novel, and that this state could be had without writing, by a form of noticing in which one's subject matter is painted on memory there and then. It's as if by noticing things one becomes them. By noticing the details of life one has one's life to the highest degree. Writing is then the form you choose, but not the *raison d'être*. The *raison d'être* is an awareness of detail behind feeling. And that anybody can have.'

The bus terminated in the Piazza Duomo, and the two men edged out into the daylight, finding their feet on the tarmac square.

Hilldyard fluttered a hand vaguely. 'The cathedral.'

Michael nodded. 'Do we go there?'

'No thanks.'

'Is that the Villa Rufolo?' He pointed at an avenue of cypress trees behind a gate.

'After lunch, probably.'

'Do you want to go to the garden straightaway?'

'I think so.'

'May I—' he had spotted a *caffè* – 'catch up with you?'

'You're all waterworks today.'

'I'm parched for a coffee.'

'Coffee's no substitute for sleep.'

'I can't sleep here.'

'I'm sure there are some excellent hotels round about.'

'A coffee might be cheaper.'

'Meet me on the belvedere at one o'clock.'

'The belvedere?'

'The Panorama. Then lunch. Food, wine, all the coffee you can drink.'

Their paths diverged, Hilldyard drawn off by an invisible current across the piazza, Michael moving through empty chairs and tables to another *pasticceria*. He drank his espresso quickly, not wanting to fall too far behind. He was curious to see how the garden affected Hilldyard and concerned to stay in the author's slipstream, as if Hilldyard's rediscovery of the place needed to be chaperoned. Michael felt strongly his duty of response and participation. He had been brought to Ravello for something special and he needed to stem the uneasy feelings, the edginess and upset, the whatever it was that unsettled him, and ready himself for the important thing.

He made his way around the edge of the piazza, turning at the corner where Hilldyard had disappeared a few minutes before and finding himself on a pedestrian concourse of no particular charm. More than one sign urged the way to Villa Cimbrone, as though the summer hordes needed extra persuasion to get out of the square and away from the souvenir shops. The walkway was crazy-paved, inauspicious. It took him past the walled properties of three-star hotels, swimming-pool compounds, the gate of a monastery and the backs of low sheds. A hundred yards later he halted and glanced at his wrist-watch. It was noon on a Friday morning. What was he doing? He was following an old novelist along a footpath in southern Italy.

He thought of Adela Fairfax. She was on the beach, perhaps, waiting for the sun to blossom, waiting for him to get back to her. He thought of Nick Adamson asleep in Los Angeles. The business of the film, he realised, was an intrusion. It weighed on him uncomfortably that he had to raise it with Hilldyard. Around the world people were planning their futures, working out how to profit and get ahead, and Michael, on this footpath in Ravello, wanted no part of it.

Just when he thought he was lost, he realised he had arrived. Before him rose a wooden door in a garden wall. A handbell dangled on a piece of string. A Gothic tower oversaw all who arrived. The effect was like a frontispiece, an invitation to enter.

He pulled the rickety doorbell and heard nothing. There was no entrance sign; there were no visitors to follow. After a wait he tried the doorlatch, which clicked easily, and found himself following the door on its hinged swing into a cloistered courtyard. Above were the mullioned casements of a Moorish villa, pale sky. In the middle of the courtyard a sundial momentarily acquired a diagonal line. There was a brochure on a wooden chair and a barrow of potted plants under an arch. He passed through the arch into full daylight and found himself standing on a flagstone drive that separated the northern aspect of the villa from the tower, now resembling a prop from a Pre-Raphaelite picture. No one came to point the way or sell him a ticket; the villa's windows were opaque, indifferent; and despite the barrow there was no sign of a gardener anywhere. If Hilldyard were here, he had slid off surreptitiously. Michael strolled to the middle of the pathway and had his first look along the avenue that ran all the way from the villa, under stone bridges and between atomic mushroom pines to a distant point of light: the fabled panorama. He patted his pockets. He had the garden to himself.

He cast a backward glance at the panes of the villa, as if to ensure some absent host of his good intentions, and, in an attempt to escape the self-consciousness of being the garden's only visitor, he left the avenue up a flight of steps. The higher path was narrower. He went carefully at first, almost testing the scene with the soles of his shoes and sinking into concentration with each slow step. He let his ears adjust to the points of birdsong, which came at him mysteriously from lost tiers in the spectrum of sound. He took the hint of pine needles and dew into his lungs, the scent of greenery and mould. He enjoyed the crowding vegetation. There were rhododendrons here, ilex trees, resinous conifers.

There was much to see: a sequence of gardens, some formal, others rambling and overgrown. The first had classical parterres billowing with salvia and tobacco plants. The second was an Egyptian terrace, with temple and bronze goat and the suggestion of pagan worship, through which he drifted to the ramshackle expanse of the rose garden, a grassy opening backed by cedars and surrounded by statues. He strolled easily across the space, taking in the shadow on an amphora, the fan-vaulted upper branches of a pine. He knelt before the blossom of a late pink rose, heard a bee's wing buzzing within its petals, looked through thistles at the far elevation of the mountains. The ground was matted with the furry hulls of sweet chestnut, dashed open, and the red fruitballs of the strawberry tree. Purple anemones were scattered in the grass.

Further down, where the hill dropped through the rising stems of chestnut trees, Mercury sat in his pagoda, his profile clear against far vineyards. Walking along an avenue of cypresses that towered to mystical heights, Michael came to a temple to Bacchus, with a stone bench before it, on which he could sit and rest and stare at the lissom figure of an adolescent boy holding a beaker to his lips and tensing his buttock into an eternal hemisphere. Michael placed his hands between his legs. Light gilded the branches. Sun warmed the dusty earth. Nothing stirred except the fluctuating dapple on the temple's fluted columns and the trail of smoke in the valley. He relinquished himself to a slow joy, a depthless relaxation. The garden was immeasurably suggestive. It opened one up, salved the eye. Every vista stirred imagination; and as one lingered beneath the cedars or by the speckled beds of the rose garden one felt the pang of one's pure self, the soul's emotion.

He waited on the stone seat, gravely gazing at the valley, and felt this emotion as a kind of knowledge. It sowed in him a strange compassion for his life, its losses, its peculiar beauty. Things had gone wrong and it was good to be here, alive to the garden, as though it were the first place on earth to be warmed by the sun and as though one could return, after all, to Eden.

He held his chin between forefinger and thumb; was struck to think of what he had come through.

Later, after the stone's coldness had gone through the seat of his trousers, he rose and made his way along the avenue of cypresses. He was poised. He almost felt he had wept. He was ready for the walk to the belvedere.

Hilldyard had shared the garden with him and now, even in his solitude, he felt the impulse repeat itself; as though the blessedness of the place called out for more souls. It was so romantic here: romantic for the young man with his book of verse, romantic for the Italian girl on her tour of the Riviera, romantic for hitch-hikers and back-packers, who in the hot months would teem over Ravello, fighting the sun and swigging from plastic bottles until they found a bench on which to flop and gaze at the aery pines and violent blue sky.

When he returned to the main path all he could see ahead was a formal arch and through the arch brightness. He glanced to his side, taking leave of the garden, as though preparing for something inordinate, which suddenly began as he went under the arch and on to the balcony and saw the sky stretch ear to ear across space. He crossed to the rail where another dimension plummeted to a yonder of minute roads and pink roofs, as though the famous coastline had sunk in prostration at his feet. He murmured at the sight of it. Ahead, the vast expanse of sea and sky was seamed at the horizon. Beneath him, a kingdom of warped fields and miniature basilicas rolled off to the shore. He was caught in the element of light and strained to encompass its impact on vision, as if everything in creation were laid out before him and could only be known by the shock of its magnitude. The view could not be reckoned. Its immensity over-whelmed the senses. He stood by the rail, suffused with the spectacle, as if the worries and sorrows of an average human life were here to be dazzled off; and as he realised that the view had always been here, waiting for him to arrive and succumb to its awesome grandeur, he felt something subside within him, and in his eyes the sting of an agonising gratitude.

He stood by the rail for several minutes and let the breeze cool his cheeks. When in due course he was brimful, he turned away, looking for a seat, and found Hilldyard behind him, crossing the balcony and preparing to conclude his own pilgrimage.

He stood back, allowing the older man his moment.

After a minute, the novelist turned round, blank-faced.

Michael went to his side and together they silently strolled in the planned direction of lunch, Michael thinking lightly, warmly, that she would have liked it here. Christine would have loved it.

Chapter Seven

HILLDYARD COCKED AN EYEBROW. Between forefinger and thumb he had received the edge of a menu; and to his adjusted ear he learned the specials of the day, amiably recited by their waiter. His expression conveyed the near indecent serendipity of finding 'this' restaurant after visiting 'that' garden. The setting could not have been bettered. The hotel garden was itself a belvedere, cut into the hill, and giving on to a view that was scarcely less beautiful than that from the Cimbrone balcony, but less dizzying, and thus a gentler résumé of the morning's sights for the purpose of accompanying lunch. They sat by the rail, contentedly gazing at the folds of the valley. Hilldyard's forehead had caught what rays there were, showing a flushed pink against the grey urn behind him. He seemed extremely pleased. Silver glinted on the tablecloth. Waiters in white jackets came in relays from the hotel, serving diners under the cover of pollarded poplars. Ice buckets were positioned, side-tables drawn up, bottles of wine proffered and uncorked. The two men had been greeted by a maître d'hotel who treated their arrival as inevitable and their gratification as imperative. He instinctively led them to the right table, fastidiously decked them with napkins, and allowed the setting to complete his welcome, whilst bringing at easy intervals the accoutrements to their pleasure. They dawdled over the menu, peeked at neighbouring tables, and were soon cheered by the sight of a bottle of rosé.

The service was no doubt always good, though Michael sensed the waiters quickening in the presence of Hilldyard. In his linen jacket and white shirt he seemed very much the Riviera veteran. His venerable bearing lent cachet to a place. He let them seat him with dead-pan dignity, as if to show that their ministrations might be taken as invisibly discreet – the essence of good service.

Michael viewed Hilldyard's self-containment with care. He had little certainty of the sort of things that might be playing in the author's mind. This had been an important excursion, a pilgrimage of sorts. Much seemed to hang on the trip, and the garden was manifestly affecting, absorbing, evocative. He could see why the old man returned here – for inspiration and restoration. What he could not see, because talkative Hilldyard was at root so inscrutable, was the nature of his memories, his inspiration, the personal nostalgia of the visit. Reading the novel had made him more curious. Over the past two weeks they had discussed art, artists, writers; Hilldyard had descanted on the beauty of Positano. There had been much play of mind, a good deal of quick candour on a variety of topics and almost nothing on Hilldyard's personal history. He was very much the observant writer winding up his awareness of things, and very little the reminiscing sage. Michael was left with the sketchy sense of a man who had lived thirty years in Italy and whose greatest adventures were fictional and in the third person. Hilldyard was no Graham Greene or Somerset Maugham. He was not a man who had witnessed famine, war, foreign regimes and whose life was defined by those experiences. On public issues he could improvise; he could do politics, and he was not untouched by the human-interest clamour of current affairs. Hilldyard was not uninterested in what could happen. He was simply more interested in the data of eventuality. He wanted reality's fabric, the details that made you believe a story rather than the story itself. These he could use. And thus his creative requirements formed the slant of his conversation. What he said was a function of how he wanted to look at things artistically. What he wanted out of life was almost a warm-up for the act of recreating it, or so it appeared; and yet, behind the gauze of his disciplined awareness, was the life that had been lived, and Michael suddenly felt a solicitude for that life, its incompletenesses, its losses. When all was said and done the author had ended up alone, exiled from friends and relatives by the needs of his muse, on anonymous terms with his Italian neighbours, at several removes from the world of agents and publishers, his place in the literary scene. He had known many people in his day, spoke lightly of the famous and fondly of the obscure, but those names were no use to him now. All those relationships were a finished book, its continuities expired. Hilldyard had to support himself on one thing alone: the will to write. He had to press on, looking for what was new, and the thought of him restlessly seeking, in his seventy-fifth year, a way of extending his life through the life of a novel was stirring to Michael, and terrible, too. If he found inspiration, there was still the struggle of composition. He would be striving at the most difficult thing in his late years. And although this kindly man was desperate to write again, there was no guarantee his next novel would work. He had already jettisoned one manuscript. Fifteen null years could turn into twenty.

Michael regarded his companion, sitting across the table, with fondness and trepidation. He looked so thoughtful, so full of the day. With the October sun on the side of his face and the stem of a wineglass in the crook of his thumb, he was a picture of contented seniority. He played the dignified patron with the waiters, ordered his meal in Italian, and sat back with a certain acumen as if posing himself for maximum enjoyment.

Michael gazed at the valley below. It amused him to recall that a fortnight before he had wanted to interview Hilldyard, get him on television. The idea seemed meaningless now. He wanted the interview to continue, of course, but unrecorded. He wanted to be sure that Hilldyard the historical man was OK. He raised his eyebrows and then his glass.

'Cheers,' said the author with an equivalent nod. 'Isn't this dandy!'

'It certainly is.'

'Sorry I'm not a beautiful damsel for you to be wining and dining.'

Michael laughed. 'Lunch with a genius will have to do.'

'Very gracious. But I'll bet you'd prefer a genius with long hair and beautiful eyelashes.'

He smiled. 'Today I prefer your company. Besides, that kind of "genius" wouldn't be dining me.'

'What!'

'I doubt it.'

'That's an odd thing to say!'

'I'm not in the mood at the moment.'

The author laughed gently. 'Actually, d'you know, the setting is so romantic, romance itself might be distracting.'

'Distracting?'

'The scenery might tend to upstage one's escort.'

Michael was not too sure about this. 'That would depend on the escort.'

'But then she would upstage the scenery. Which would be equally unproductive.'

He thought for a moment. It was something he could aver. 'I'd want to come here if I were in love with someone.'

The author coughed into his hand. 'Bit dire if she didn't like the scenery.'

'Of course she'd like the scenery!'

'How could one love anybody who wasn't moved to distraction by the scenery?'

There was a moment's pause.

Hilldyard nipped a bread roll from the basket and gazed directly at him. 'I take it you liked the garden?'

He was struck by the keen concern in the author's eyes.

'I feel baptised.'

Hilldyard nodded. He wanted more.

'I feel much better, actually.'

'Baptised. Yes. Precisely!'

There was another silence.

'How was it for you?' Michael smiled.

Hilldyard glowed humorously. 'Oh, the earth moved!'

'Did it?'

'I feel stroked like a cat. I feel as if somebody had manipulated my soul.'

Michael was pleased.

' "Struck with deep joy." I pick it up, God bless me. I'm more riven by that place with every gliding year. It sucks the love out of you.'

He was steeply curious. 'Do you feel jump-started?'

Hilldyard's attention wavered. He pointed over Michael's shoulder.

He turned and saw that the terrace had been invaded by a party of monks, who were filing in from the wicket gate. All of a sudden there were more men in sandals and brown tunics in the restaurant than ordinary diners. They spilled between chairs and trolleys in the direction of two long tables in the shady part of the terrace. The tables were laid and ready for them, and as they milled along waiters sped anxiously among them, ushering them to their seats.

It was a pleasing spectacle. The men had come from the local *convento*, a few minutes down the path, and although proximity was as good an excuse as any for dining in such a beautiful spot, Michael assumed they were marking an occasion and wondered what that might be. The prospect was somehow captivating.

The faces were varied, as were the figures. One saw the gaunt

Father taking his place at the head of the table, setting the tone with sober profile and moderated spirits; an antique elder drooling over a place-mat; the standard-issue Friar Tuck, porcine, jovial and not entirely promotable. Some of the faces were refined by their calling, others were desiccated by piety. The last to be seated was a young man, a novice, who went to his place with the solemnity of a person newly committed to a course in life. He looked like the young Rachmaninov, strong-featured, crop-headed, finely serious.

It was a sight that held the attention: pious profiles and quarter-profiles under jigsaw leaf-light. He took it in thoroughly, particularly the novice, until anxiety got the better of him.

Hilldyard was entranced; an impression was being taken. Michael stared at him enquiringly.

'Jump-started?' The author was at some remove from the idea. 'Inspired?'

He smiled. 'If anything has inspired me, you have.'

This seemed like an evasion.

'I beg your pardon!'

'Yes. I think you believe in something.'

Michael was nonplussed. 'I believe in your writing.'

'That's not what I mean.'

He had not got an answer. He sipped his rosé. 'What are you talking about, James?'

'That you live according to values generated by a deep response to life. That you are emotional, intelligent, sympathetic, and you invest the things that touch you with a sense of significance. You conform to my view that the felt life brings one closer to reality. The knowledge of one's senses and feelings is the essential knowledge for an artist, and the more one cultivates a sensibility of response the more one perceives. I see that faculty in you. And I see someone who ardently believes in awareness as the predicate to a civilised life. You are the writer's true friend.'

Michael was completely unprepared for the eulogy, utterly astonished to hear himself described in such terms.

'I wish my dad could hear you say that!'

'Oh really! Why?'

He shrugged, looked thoughtful for a moment. 'He wanted me to be an academic, not a television producer.'

'I'll gladly put it in writing.'

Michael laughed. 'Please do.'

'I would! You've been very kind to me!'

'Nonsense. You've been far kinder.'

'You deserve the highest endorsement.'

Hilldyard had certainly changed the subject and Michael felt himself blushing.

'Of course, I know you've had difficulties.'

This surprised him, too.

'You've been in creative tension with commercial life.'

'With the whole of reality.'

'A healthy condition.'

'Oh sure,' said Michael. 'It's the condition of failure.'

'Failure!'

The waiter arrived and inserted between them a bowl of mixed salad and two plates of *crespolini*. Hands freed, he moved round to top up their glasses.

'If this is failure,' said Hilldyard, reaching for his fork, 'I'd like to try success.'

Michael raised his fork likewise and felt strangely apprehensive. He was unsheltered. Hilldyard was thinking about him directly.

'You believed in television?'

He ate and dabbed his mouth. He was disappointed if this was the belief Hilldyard had referred to.

'That's like asking me if I believe in the present tense. One has no choice.'

'You wanted to disseminate your interest in the arts to a wider public?'

'I conned myself into thinking all kinds of grand ideas were possible. I must have been mad, or totally naive. The trouble is, nothing else seemed important. I mean, if the important things were irrelevant, what else was there? Money, I suppose. I couldn't grasp that.'

'Excellent.'

'I doubt it.'

'It's called integrity.'

'I call it stupidity.'

'The age is stupid. A century ago your talents would have been welcome, rewarded, esteemed.'

Michael laughed outright. 'I'm a century too late. Great.'

'The world is hardly crawling with people like you.'

'My type don't make the world go round.'

'Who cares about rotation? Bicycle wheels go round.'

He smiled. It was nice to have someone stand up for him. Hilldyard was very fatherly all of a sudden, unlike his real father. His real father had never rated Michael's cast of mind, preferring intellect to sensibility. And as a result, perhaps, he had lacked faith in his own view of things. He had been waiting for a mentor like Hilldyard to approve of the very qualities he thought were short-comings, and launch him as a legitimate model of a man.

'You reckon I'm washed up in the wrong century?'

'I think we all are. This is the age of commercial exploitation. In the public field aesthetic experience has no place. The only type of ecstasy comes in pill form. No one knows or avers the spiritual importance of the arts. From the political standpoint the arts are a sub-set of tourism or nightlife. Those with spiritual needs are viewed as consumers of a certain type of product. The culture is amenity- and leisure-driven and all insight, all passion, all moral illumination is treated as private stuff, non-transferable and therefore irrelevant as public value. Few people would consider the properties of a great painting or symphony sacred. But for those who feel the arts as you do, their beauty and mystery are as sacred as life itself. And that feeling of reverence finds no wider echo in the way our age has expressed itself, and much that it does express diminishes feelings. Certainly. You're born out of time if you feel that passion signifies. That it's more than just a thrill, a chemical experience in the brain.'

Michael was quiet for a moment. Hilldyard had drawn inferences about him. He did believe in the sublimity of the arts; and in the sanctity of the forms which embodied such experience; of course he did, though Hilldyard's terminology seemed somehow dated.

'Doesn't that make me an anachronism?'

'Or a prophet!'

Michael shook his head.

'You have a grasp of the aesthetic,' insisted Hilldyard, 'which is timeless, of course.'

It was strange indeed to hear these words, and to be reminded of something known previously, and then almost forgotten. He had discovered it with Christine beside him in an art gallery in their first year at university. Looking at a painting by Veronese he had felt for the first time the still concentration that takes you into every detail of a canvas and allows you to experience it in all dimensions simulta-neously, to the point where noticing becomes a current, a circuit

71

between viewer and artist, sparking sensory delight and dramatic involvement and producing an emotion of aesthetic rapture, which he decided right away was extraordinarily precious.

To hear it come back at him now, re-presented to him by the old man, was strangely affecting. Hilldyard had been very sympathetic, and Michael was touched. He was also distressed. They were talking about a life; his life. 'Surely, in any age, the only criterion is survivability. One has to adapt. You have to be the thing the age requires. Otherwise you go mad or broke. And what use is a sense of the aesthetic' – he spoke half ironically, half believingly – 'if it leads one to financial martyrdom? The boring fact is that I haven't succeeded, James. And without success and influence what use are my values?'

'You are not extinct,' said Hilldyard, breaking his bread.

He had to laugh. 'You're a great careers adviser.'

'Well, put it like this. You are certainly enjoying your food.'

'I am. This is wonderful.'

'And you have survived because you still have feelings. Your feeling life is intact. Whereas if you'd sold out you might be viable, but the sentient, original Michael Lear would not exist any more. The thing you have struggled to be would have withered. And what use,' said Hilldyard with sudden contempt, 'is a man who sacrifices the instrument of his original self for status or money? Where does that get the human race?'

Michael gazed into the middle distance. He seemed for a moment painfully close to the history of his own emotions, a swelling or gathering of feeling, as if everything he had suffered had risen to the surface from a deep distillation.

He looked up. 'But then . . . what does one do?'

'You know the answer.'

'I'm not a novelist. I have no great talent.'

'My friend, your talent is the innate inability to sell out.'

The agony of it welled up. 'Everyone thinks I'm a fool!'

'You crave an absolute. A meaningful purpose in life. Your unconscious has rebelled against compromise. There is nothing foolish in that.'

He recovered from the anguish, laughed as lightly as he could.

'The decks have been cleared,' said Hilldyard vibrantly. 'Lop off the old life. Start afresh.'

'And do what?'

72

'Remain true to the finest part of yourself.'

The proposition was so deplorably straightforward.

'Let fate take you where it will.'

He looked down at his hands.

'Once you have grasped the precious thing, you're free.'

'The precious thing?'

'What comes to you in that garden.'

There was a moment.

'What comes, James?'

'Oh!' He frowned with true grandeur. 'An absolute reason for living!'

Michael stared at him.

'Against which no loss, however great, can compete.'

They had both lost their wives, he realised. His mouth was dry.

Hilldyard averted his eyes and swallowed. He blinked fast, mastering feeling.

'James?'

The old man came back at him, a strangeness in his eyes; and then he shrugged.

'What comes there?'

'The miracle of human consciousness. Death's antithesis.'

Michael squinted against the growing brightness of the day. He could feel the sun's heat on the side of his face. He brought the wineglass to his lips, sipped and swallowed, as if washing down Hilldyard's words.

'The kernel of all courage, of all endeavour.'

'What can I achieve?' he said abruptly, softly.

Hilldyard was intense. 'You've achieved it. You've stood for something.'

Michael met his companion's gaze uncertainly. 'What?'

'You've had an influence.'

'On whom?'

'My dear fellow, you've inspired me!'

'I have?'

'You have.'

He did not know what to say.

'I owe you everything.'

Hilldyard loomed before him. His eyes were illuminated. They sought Michael out, wanting to know his gratitude had registered. He wanted to penetrate Michael's modesty.

73

'Are you . . . ?'

'I'm going to write a book.' He touched the table lightly. 'Bring on the dancing girls.'

A smile lit itself on his face.

'Thanks to you.'

His heart leapt.

'I'm dedicating it to you. Your bank manager won't give a toss but posterity might.'

Michael blushed with pleasure.

Hilldyard tapped his glass with a fork. 'This is my third phase. I think we can say, biographically speaking, that the florid Indian summer of James Hilldyard's literary career, the majestic late period, commenced formally at the Giordano restaurant, between courses, in the enlightened company of Michael Lear, two dozen monks and a bottle of rosé. Make that two. Waiter!' He raised an arm. 'And the conversation was more than usually inspired. *Signor!*'

Michael laughed. He found it hard to contain the emotion.

The waiter was in attendance immediately. Already new courses were arriving, and as the plates of *melanzane* and *fritto misto* slid into position another waiter was dispatched inside to the cellars. Michael marvelled at the clockwork concordance of the stages of their appetite with the promptitude of service. Everything was now more perfect than before. The sun was shining, the table was covered in food; monks were eating fiercely nearby, chomping through the deluge of salads and side-orders, bread and spaghetti that kept three waiters in a relay of perpetual motion from the kitchen; and Hilldyard was going to write again.

The author rose from the table and silently mouthed the words 'Excuse me'. Michael watched him make his way to the hotel entrance and allowed himself his moment of elation. He was completely mystified by the notion of his 'influence', but to receive the compliment, to feel the gratitude, was unutterably good for him. If he had inspired the writer there was no greatness in it, just sympathy, appreciation, the value of his being unconditionally 'for' Hilldyard. And Michael, in his turn, had felt nourished by propinquity. To be around such a man was to absorb the energy of his awareness. Genius was a higher degree of being human, and although Hilldyard's gifts transcended his individual character as a man, to see the man whom nature had vested with such gifts, who was only a man, was to sense the preciousness of those gifts anew. All he had done was grasp the beauty of that. And however, whyever, he had had his effect.

He inhaled, glanced at the other diners. Life was beginning. A new bottle came down on the table. The waiter spun off the cork; smiled.

The young novice he had seen before was now eating. He turned spaghetti on his fork and listened respectfully to his elders. His eyes were downcast, as though he were keeping hold of a seriousness of feeling. He seemed in his bearing more ideally pious than his brethren, more seized of religious emotion, more committed to whatever impulse had drawn him in his early twenties to the cloth. Michael allowed the head and shoulders of the young man to rest on his eye like an icon. He had in his sights the vision of a person who had renounced the world, a man who had quit the party of modern life for a calling that seemed, in this casual age, astonishingly regressive: the love of Christ. But the image soothed Michael, and the line of robed men leaning towards each other, reaching for wine, receiving platters from penitent waiters, their ecclesiastical faces and hands flickering under poplar leaves, was like a painting, a natural work of art, and this in itself was a gift, a blessing, which enabled him to take possession of something new: the unity of himself with the world around him. It was all here for him now, present, tangible and beautiful, and if he had been given eyes to see it by Hilldyard, it was to Hilldyard that he owed his life; what more could he find anywhere else? The notion that Hilldyard had put to him was indeed incredible: that what really counted was the nurturing of something tender and exquisite, the heart of himself, the passionate core that he could feel again, a feeling to be valued in itself. It was a sensation that ran to the tips of his fingers, like a reaction to beauty, an overwhelming gratitude, still to be expressed.

Hilldyard returned and they toasted in the new bottle, officially celebrating. Michael expressed his great delight. They moved on to a general toast, the view, the restaurant staff, the wine itself, the bliss of sitting above the valley and further sea in the afternoon sunlight. Michael became fluent at last, finding words to describe the Cimbrone Gardens. Hilldyard nodded and smiled, and between the impromptu odes of relish, directed a wagging finger at neighbouring diners.

'Three o'clock.'

'Is it?'

'Three o'clock over there.'

A young couple sat by the balcony's edge. She read *Elle* magazine. He took a picture with an automatic camera.

'English, no doubt.'

Through the filter of his happiness he remembered there was something to be dealt with.

Once or twice during the morning he had thought better of raising it. He had many forebodings on the matter. Hilldyard's answer he already knew. What kept him curious was the form the answer might take. Besides, he could not let down Adela. For her sake he had to tell Hilldyard what had happened, and submit to the reaction. It was better to render honesty to a mentor at the risk of irritating him than to conceal secret knowledge.

They ordered coffee, and when the cups arrived Michael felt the moment was ripe.

'I have a confession to make. I don't think the sin is very serious. But it needs confessing.'

Hilldyard dandled his wineglass. 'Sounds good.'

'I read your last novel.'

'Which novel?'

'*The Last Muse.*'

Hilldyard replaced the glass, looked at him expressionlessly.

'Someone gave me a copy. I know you have misgivings about it.'

'A copy?'

Michael wavered. He had to get it out. 'I should have asked permission, James. I . . . curiosity got the better of me.'

Hilldyard's face paled.

'Am I forgiven?'

'Did Basil give it to you?'

'Would that make any difference to the degree of forgiveness?'

'I'll fire the shite. Damn him!'

'James . . .'

'What on earth have I done to deserve such treachery from an agent? How can he do this to me!'

Michael was shaken. He thought quickly but not quickly enough.

'I ordered him to destroy the thing. Since when half the world has read it. You've read it? Outrageous! Ghastly!'

'It's not Basil's fault.'

'It's infernally his fault. He's a tarnished, deceitful leper.'

'Someone gave me . . .'

'All copies lead back to his beastly Xerox machine. I gave him specific orders.' Hilldyard threw his face into his hands, a gesture utterly mortifying to Michael, as if he were out of control. Michael held his coffee cup whilst his insides turned to stone. He could not think what to say.

'You've read it?' The tone was attacking.

'I'm sorry.'

Hilldyard was pierced with pain. He squinted and blinked, on the edge of tears. 'That heinous wanker.'

'Maybe his judgement's gone.' He knew this was not true. 'He has cancer.'

'Poor tumours.'

'He's a sick man.'

'Basil is more malignant than any cancer. God, I'm cross.'

'But not with me!'

The ledges of his eyes showed their pink rim. He looked more stricken than angry. He shook his head slowly, as if to wind down vexation and detach himself from the strength of his feelings. Eventually, he gasped, looking at Michael glumly. There was a moment of unpredictable silence. He scratched his ear. His anger was subsiding into lethargy. His eyes closed for a moment, a prayer, and then he was direct and alert and challenging. 'So what did you think?'

He took in his breath. 'Of the novel?'

Hilldyard nodded.

'I thought it was brilliant.'

It was a reaction Hilldyard could not absorb. He gazed at Michael blankly.

'You understand my agony?'

Michael neither understood his agony nor the sense of the question, which only heightened the embarrassment.

'I don't think I do.'

'Oh, come on!'

'What should I understand?'

Hilldyard was incredulous. 'It's obvious!'

Michael frowned, lost.

'You didn't realise?'

He was floundering.

'Oh, good heavens. The entire novel's based on fact.' Hilldyard stared at him, seeing out the charge.

'Fact?'

'It's my story.'

'Your story!'

'My life!'

The revelation was Hilldyard's, but it was Michael who blushed. So many things were implicit in the confession – it was a confession – that he was at a loss to know how to react. He had trespassed into the author's private world and been caught red-handed.

Hilldyard watched the declaration sink in with an expression of bitter triumph. And then he sighed, as if suddenly depleted. His expression changed, becoming softer and sadder. He looked engrossed for a moment and then started to speak with slow care.

'My wife stood by me from the beginning, you see. She sacrificed everything for my work, cooked and housekept, typed my novels. She soothed me through the bad days and supported me with love. And for all that I betrayed her. Once with "Anna" . . . the "Anna" . . . that . . . And twice by writing the novel. While Joan was in her last months, I was writing a love story about my affair with another woman. Joan died with the unalterable conviction she was unloved. She lay in bed thinking her fund of love in life had been wasted. She died of grief for her own life. Whereas I loved her deeply. But I had to write that book. And after she died, I realised it was not a novel I had written but the agony of our lives together ending in this. And then, the madness over, I realised I had done in her life. The guilt of that is ineffaceable. For her sake alone the book can never be published, because I can't bear to advertise the possibility that my wife's life was in vain.'

His hands became active tools of distress, working up a dry lather of anguish. 'Every writer gads along, feeding off life, his own feelings, the feelings of others, bending and shaping it to his purposes, until something happens that just can't be stolen into fiction. I can't take Joan's suffering into the life of a novel. I won't. It is my penance to be silent. Her agony, my posterity. Too hideous. If it were in my power I'd snap my fingers and see all copies incinerate spontaneously. And not just for her sake.' He broke off, grimaced at the view.

Michael was held fast. The information given to him was dense with significance.

' "Anna"—' The voice was croakier now, interfered with. 'She died last year.' Hilldyard managed a swooping-up glance, blinked. 'She was sixty. They are both dead, you see. Brings the whole business to an end.' He cleared his throat, aiming for control.

'And I don't want it survived by any kind of record. Which is not to deny that I loved "Anna". No. I loved her as if I had never loved before, as if all previous loves were mere preparation. I was totally remade by her. I became a different person. And there again is unbearability. Because one view of my life is that the highest reality was the space between two minds and that reality I experienced and then lost. Like discovering a musical talent one day and losing the use of your hands the next. And since that extraordinary summer I've been haunted by the sense of something unconsummated, as if I needed to go to another stage before I could write again, and the means to that progression was stolen from me. What could I write? In the name of what? I couldn't start a book when my own life was incomplete! That agony has cost me years, Michael.' He gasped. 'I have to find a new way, a new source for what I need to do. And I have to forget the self that branched towards "Anna", blossomed, and was lopped off. I have to forget her as though she never existed.' He touched his temple, as though pressing a point of pain, and then looked at Michael with heavy eyes.

The pause was interminable. In Hilldyard's story Michael recognised his own life.

'Can you forget her?' he said softly.

There was no answer.

He was struck by many things, a complex of realisations, and the strange emotion that accompanied an insight like this into the structure of another person's life. Later, he fastened on the paradox of a novel that worked artistically while embodying something unacceptable to the author's moral sensibility. He understood Hilldyard's shame, but that which was part of life was surely part of the novel, and in disowning this particular novel wasn't he suppressing the truth of his experience? Or was it perhaps that this bleak fiction, while based on fact, was inconsistent with Hilldyard's view of the novel, expressing something outside the moral compass of his own behaviour which although it had happened could not signify? He had written it and decided it was not worthy of his better self, the self that would not, as an article of faith, hurt a fly.

He let out his breath, exhaling tension. 'I can see why you didn't want a film.'

Hilldyard slapped his forehead and screamed silently: a gesture that recapped the horror of the idea whilst saving him the effort.

Michael spared a thought for Adela. She would be disappointed, but he looked forward to telling her. He was, in a sense, the bearer of good news: in the conscience of an artist the huge publicity of a feature film meant nothing.

'What applies to the book applies a thousand times to the film.' He made a ghastly expression. 'Just think what they'd do to it.'

'Well, that's the answer I'll give her.'

'Give whom?'

'The girl who lent me your book.'

'A girl?'

He already knew that he had to go into this. 'An actress whom Basil's film people cast as Anna. When you turned down the offer she thought there'd been a misunderstanding.' He shrugged. 'So she came here.'

Hilldyard was appalled. 'She's in Positano!'

'She is.'

'Why on earth?'

'To ask you to reconsider.'

'My God. These people are shameless!'

As he feared, Hilldyard was over-reacting. 'Basil told her about me. So instead of doorstepping you, she contacted me.'

'How atrocious!'

Michael smiled awkwardly. 'She wanted to be sure you weren't misled by the American agent.'

'That twit.'

'She says Shane Hammond is committed to a faithful adaptation.'

'Who?'

'He's a film star.'

'God!'

'She assured me of their best intentions.'

'I'll bet she did.'

He hesitated. He was giving the facts for the sake of completeness, not to seem naive. 'I think she's perfectly sincere.'

'Actresses are always sincere.'

This seemed ungenerous. 'She had interesting things to say.'

'And ambition is always eloquent.'

'Maybe.' He frowned. 'But so is conviction.'

'She obviously convinced you.'

It seemed silly to argue about the bona fides of a woman Hilldyard had never met. Michael had no great mission to stand up for her, but he needed to defend his judgement. 'That should be a recommendation.'

'Is she very beautiful as well as persuasive?'

The tone did not please him. And then he remembered something. 'You seemed to think so.'

'What!'

' "Venus reversing her birth"!'

Hilldyard flinched. 'That girl!'

Michael nodded and watched carefully.

'She's a young woman!'

'Twenty-eight.'

Hilldyard inhabited the state of astonishment very physically, eyebrows knitted, fingers wandering. With his open mouth he seemed to be drinking in the information as though there were now a lot more to the matter. He had been struck by the sight of a nameless bather, had taken his impression, preserved it in memory, only to find the owner of the impression turning up at his back door as a real person demanding something in exchange.

'What's her name?'

'Adela Fairfax.'

Hilldyard needed a few moments. 'She wants to play Anna?' he said softly.

'Yes.'

The mouth opened, breath going out.

Michael sensed something.

'Is there a resemblance?'

'Resemblance?' The laugh was ugly, a bark of contempt. 'Oh God, you'd never want Anna's double on the screen.'

He felt himself colouring.

'Her face had been lived in, Michael. She had lines under her eyes. Experience had written on her face, her body. Time was attacking her. But she was the full person, Michael. Not some corkscrew blonde. Not some nubile clone any beachload of adolescent strummers could fancy.'

Michael tried to absorb the contempt. He had set himself up for this.

'I think there's more to her than that.'

'Do you? You think she can play the woman who stopped me in my tracks for fifteen years, the creature I've bathed in the best words I could wring from my pen?'

He hesitated. He felt the full heat of Hilldyard's integrity, his passion for the truth bearing down on the issue.

'She's an acclaimed Shakespearian actress.'

'She's fluff.'

'She's talented, James!'

'She's twenty years too young for the part!'

'Then they'll age her!'

'Don't you see! They don't want my character. They want a lovely young fresh woman for the audience to fall in love with, and to hell with the book, they'll recast the story round her. And there goes the point of my novel. A total bastardisation!'

Michael frowned. Hollywood's blandishments had affected even his judgement. The glare of interest from famous actors, the production millions, the flattery of all that focusing its beam on a particular book dazzled away obvious objections.

'Fine. That makes it easier for me to tell her.'

'Easier for you?'

'I obviously agree with you.'

There was a pause. The author was incipiently dissatisfied. 'She'll be awfully upset.'

'That's her problem.'

'There are difficult scenes ahead. She'll make it your problem.'

Michael shrugged. 'I can explain it to her.'

'She'll make you take pity on her.'

He was irritated. 'James, you haven't met her. She's intelligent. She'll respect your decision.'

'You're very taken.'

The insinuation frustrated him. 'Not with the idea of a film! To be perfectly frank, what I liked about her was her enthusiasm for your writing!'

'I see. Soul mates.'

'We've only met once.'

'All the more testimony to her allure.'

'Or her intelligence!'

'Intelligence!' he spat. 'Nobody with intelligence would suggest the idea.'

It was like a blow that at one strike disposed of Adela, her talent, her integrity, the reality of her view of things, and to Michael it was terrible to think so harsh a verdict might be true. Because if Adela were tainted by the vulgar urge to turn books into films, he too had been crass in offering to help her. He could suffer the criticism if it came from Hilldyard, but he saw, in a flash, the loneliness such rigorous standards implied.

'Michael.' Hilldyard was worked up, forceful. 'I can't expect you to relay my feelings to this girl.'

'You can!'

'She won't let up. Until she's seen me. Exerted her wiles.'

He shook his head. 'She's not like that!'

'Don't you see? This eloquent actress. She's using you as a stepping stone. She won't take a no until she's had a crack at me.'

'You make her sound hideous!'

'Then prove me wrong.'

'What?'

'Bring her to the villa.'

He felt oppressed. 'That's not necessary.'

'I'd like a word with this young Venus.'

'James!'

'Especially as she's so intelligent and discriminating.'

'Please don't!'

'And then we will see.'

'See what?'

Hilldyard tossed his napkin on the table. 'Which of us is right.'

The old man rose from his chair, and Michael waited a moment before getting up and following him out of the restaurant, glancing distractedly at the remaining diners as he went. A waiter nodded him goodbye as he moved to the wicket gate, giving him to understand that Hilldyard had paid the bill on his return from the lavatory. He caught up with him on the footpath outside and they walked off in silence.

In his heart he felt the lightness of his own will, of his own meanings, which travelled meagrely next to the solemn figure of Hilldyard.

After a few uncomfortable moments, Hilldyard took him by the sleeve. He came to a halt, inhaling deeply. The leafy smell was sweet, evocative: a poplar tree.

The tight clasp eased.

Hilldyard smiled and for a moment rested his hand on Michael's back, as if to pat him along the path.

Later, in the bus, Michael sat swaying with the movement of the vehicle as it lurched around tight bends. The author had sunk heavily into his seat; he seemed pensive, full of the things they had touched on over lunch. Michael noted with tired admiration the old man's ability to go on thinking about things, refining experiences that Michael had only felt, and which were passing in his case over the edge of memory, feelings that he had not known what to do with, feelings misused, unchannelled, frustrated. He had not managed any kind of memorial for Christine in the end. And now she too was passing over the horizon, the sense of her almost lost to remembrance, her spirit slowly parting as the pain eased.

He gazed up at the leaves overhead, and at the fading sky.

Chapter Eight

HE SAT IN THE late-afternoon cool of his room, glancing through the shutters at the rose-light on the mountains, and dialled Adela's hotel number. He could already feel how intensely she would listen. The hotel number was engaged and after three successive attempts he decided to have a bath. He set the taps running and sauntered around easing off his clothes, entering into pensive nudity. He stood in front of the mirror considering his angular shoulders and pale arms and the flurry of hair on his chest.

He must disappoint her and then prepare her. It was almost impossible to convey the hazards of the meeting without alarming her, and yet hard to brief her without pre-empting Hilldyard. Hilldyard's reasons were for him to convey. Michael would just tell her that the answer was no, the reasons were personal, and that the author, as a courtesy, had invited her for a drink. He would invoke her tact discreetly. Too much information and she would become curious, and whilst he wanted to do justice to her curiosity, he wanted her to take the hint. The difficulty was that in his relationship with Hilldyard he wanted everything to succeed. He had stood up for Adela, and the onus was on him to deliver to the author's scrutiny a woman of intelligence and discretion whom he would find it impossible to dislike. Adela must be that person; and she must be it because that was her nature, not because Michael had warned her.

He strolled naked across the floor tiles to the balcony. The light had shifted its tint. The upper reaches of the sky were indigo. The suddenness of dusk brought cool smells into being. He folded his arms and breathed in the sea air and with the inhalation came relief. He had the piercing sense that life was OK. While he could stand here beholding the fairy-lit mountains and the partnered mauve of sea and sky, all human worries could be resolved. He wanted to remain in the afterspell of his lunch with Hilldyard, to set things down as if fresh from a vision. He had written in the past, but never considered himself a writer. Perhaps he could come to it late. And perhaps writing was a question of necessity rather than talent. Certainly, in this setting, working with this novelist, to write was a natural extension of things. He had begun to crave the intimate connection that language could give him to his own past. He wanted to commit himself to paper, and he had to accept that Adela's disappointment and Hilldyard's irritability would soon be water under the bridge. If he felt a final concern for her, it was really a desire to be good to someone still in the world, pitting her desires and ideals against the grinding commercial machine, trying to have a career and a value. He wished her well, and he wanted to be remembered kindly, as part of an experience not entirely futile. In that frame of mind he picked up the receiver and dialled again. The tone rang and he was put through instantly.

She was dignified when he broke the bad news. If the result were a disappointment, at least it was final.

He was impressed. She was obviously upset but her self-control was instant. Perhaps their first conversation had prepared her. Despite her former impatience she was suddenly accepting, wise enough to know this would be it.

She was puzzled to be invited to drinks. He painted it as a courtesy, and this half worked, but he detected some reserve. They arranged a time, Michael noting his secretarial function. Somehow he'd been assigned the role of factotum, which meant that she had taken his report as definitive, but also that she was somehow at arm's length from him. Drinks with the author would be fine, but it was not what she had come for.

Michael wondered whether she would renew her offer of dinner. The call was winding down, and as the final cadences approached he was tempted to prompt her. But Adela was the one who had made the suggestion, had insisted on it, and if she quite forgot when the time came, what was the point?

She thanked him, looked forward to seeing him at Hilldyard's, and then rang off. He replaced the receiver and gazed for a moment at the bedspread.

He eased himself into the bath. He wondered whether he felt used. He stared at the clammy ceiling and doubted whether he cut any kind of figure with women these days. He wondered whether he was bypassing women, or they were bypassing him. He felt it as a slight; but there was no slight. Nothing had happened. No expectations had been aroused. He had been nice to her, and she had been grateful to him, and that was that, and back to business as usual.

He felt the heat of the water bring tiredness around his eyes. He turned on his side, immersing a leg, the water lapping at his chin and mouth. He felt like a foetus in an enamel womb. He lay sideways in the bath with a melancholia that had touched him before, disappointment becoming torpor. It was a torpor that made him see the water with sluggish eyes, like an alligator about to submerge. He wondered, in this bathroom, who he was and what he would represent to a woman. There was the intimate sense of his own immersed body; but what was the body in itself, its limbs prone and unflexed in level water? Who would want this long-jointed shape in a bed, a body so similar to others in its properties and desires? Who out there would desire him in particular?

Desire was dormant in Michael.

In the past six months he had hardly looked at a woman. Erections had deserted him. The area between his legs felt fallow, bland, as if there were some deep recoiling of his potency. And he made the connection easily enough, because the slow collapse of his business, the out-of-controlness of debts, the meltdown of first this and then that project had deflated him. When Michael's company began to die, desire withered inside him. He could no longer project himself with any sense of fundamental balls. He had passed the age when good looks in a man mattered. He was thirty-five, and at thirty-five you had to be more than a set of sensitivities. Your antlers had to be locked with the world. You had to be alive with the current of applied values. Otherwise what were you that people could subscribe to? What sense of purpose, or mastery, or good terms with life could he present to a woman?

He had walked past the top shelves in newsagents', looking at the jigsaw body parts with a dim curiosity, vaguely hoping that the flesh cartoon would trigger some figment of lust. He had stared at bottoms and breasts and felt alien, not of this world.

Gradually, as work got worse, he stopped noticing the lack of lust. He noticed instead a more general failure of wit and acumen, a slowing down of essential reactions. He experienced psycho-motor retardation, the loss of spontaneity, memory lapses. Even conversation began to elude him. In his stew of worries he mislaid the ability to empathise, to think laterally. He was disconnected from insight. Exactly how he might 'be' with a woman deserted him. And of course, in this state, certain women were intrigued by his self-effacement – rare in a handsome man – which was actually despair on hold. Michael had not even been able to satisfy their curiosity, so that eventually they were bored; as bored as he was with himself.

He shut his eyes, feeling the soap bar melt between his fingers. When the phone rang he was already gone, asleep, and had to come back from a world away. He jetted out of the bath, took a towel and forced himself into wakefulness. He sat on the bed, blinked, grasped the receiver.

'Afternoon, Michael.' The voice from nine thousand miles away was loud and clear.

'Hello?'

'Have I got news for you!'

Adamson was talking from his LA office. He had a huddle with his partner at ten, a day of meetings beyond that. Speaking to Michael Lear was number one on his agenda.

Michael tried to interrupt. Adamson was on heat, flowing all over him.

He had done the research, found a mole in Coburn Agency. Paul Chapman, English, twenty-five, an aspiring screenwriter who subsidised his writing by penning reader's reports for Weislob's department. Chapman liked Adamson's girlfriend and was prepared to be bitterly indiscreet about anything to do with Coburn Agency. Chapman sucked up to Weislob for work, read nights and weekends covering literary material for him, and was in the loop on house projects. He loathed Weislob from the tips of his toes, and needed to discharge contamination by slagging him off when anyone would present a listening ear. He had done a report on *The Last Muse*.

'He's our stethoscope, Michael. Through him we can listen to the heart of Coburn Agency. The sound of atrophy, straining arteries, sclerotic valves. You're going to love this.'

He had asked for the information. For courtesy's sake he would have to hear him out.

Adamson set the scene with loving attention to detail. To appreciate the low-down Michael needed context.

'Coburn's like number ten in the charts, right. Not one of the behemoths. But dynamic. They want to break out. And now is their chance. Remember the plane that pancaked last year? Three honchos from Interstar. Three ten-per-centers slam into a mountain. Pilot sneezed. Heavy litigation. That was Interstar's chief exec Mart Korea, plus Abe Golden and Naim Johns, three lynchpins totally smudged on this low-grade mountain in Arizona. OK. And what's happened? Every agent in town is hitting on Interstar's clients because everybody in town knows that without Korea Interstar isn't Interstar. Nobody who's living in that agency can hold it together. A feeding frenzy. Talentscope is in there. Creative Artists Management are picking them off. The little guys are pitching in. It's like the baker's window's smashed, and there's tits and robins on the counter and fucking great eagles airlifting whole loaves. To begin with Talentscope had it pretty good. Fifteen of the top thesps at Interstar were biding their time, waiting to see how the balance of power moved. Interstar's strength derived from its packaging abilities, right, and the stars on their list didn't want to fragment the powerbase by leaking all over Hollywood. But they had to go somewhere. Well, Sam Calloway signed with Talentscope. He's big. With him you'd expect to get Michael Morton, cos they work together. And Morton is friends with Rex Polanski, etc, etc, a fat string of sausages crossing the road to Talentscope. But Calloway split after six weeks. He fuckolaed them, slouched off to his manager, and God in Christ knows what's happening, because if those bloodsuckers at Talentscope couldn't keep Calloway sweet, why would Morton and Polanski and Dolores Black sign on? Hammond repeated the formula. He signed with Talentscope and pissed on their chips five months ago. There's a bad smell in that agency. Dog turd in the boardroom.' He cleared his throat. 'So Hammond pulls out, Calloway's in limbo, and apart from a few B-string defectors Interstar's intact. This is like six months ago. Before Thinking Time. Before Hammond was in the top five. Enter Frank Coburn.'

Michael lay in his towel on the bed, powerless to interrupt but strangely fascinated.

'Let me give you Coburn. He's a middle-aged guy with a strong jaw and a bald head. He wears a walrus moustache and a string tie. He's one of the most physically arresting people you've seen. Hypnotic. Oozes protective power. The guy mesmerises talent like headlights freeze bunnies. Somehow Coburn got to Hammond. And he didn't do a one-man pitch. He co-presented with Tom Mahler, who's like number four in the pecking order. Mahler has perfect manners, he's literate, wears a tie-pin. He reps Clarice Burnaby, and if the man can eat her shit he's gotta be good. What Coburn was proposing was total service: packaging, tax advice, estate agency, procuration, you name it. Three agents for the price of one. Three disciplines: Mahler as lead agent, attorney Gloria Sabbatini for deals, tax; and our favourite person in the world Rick Weislob on project co-ordination, script shit. Meanwhile Coburn does the politics, the overview, the Caesar thing.'

Michael arranged himself for the elongating monologue.

'Now see it from Coburn's perspective. Hammond's friends with all kinds of talent at Interstar: Vidal Sorenson, Jasper Phillips, Barry and Omar Cazenove. Same tune. If Coburn can get these guys under his wing, he can begin to crank up for the big time. It's a confidence trick, a momentum thing. It's not going to happen tomorrow, but if just one fish stays hooked he can reel in plenty more. And don't think he hasn't started. His footsoldiers are out there tickling people's balls. They're saying, We got Hammond. We want you, too. Meanwhile, suck on this. Mahler is learning Shakespeare by heart – to pillow-talk Hammond. And some cute secretary is doing Hammond's shopping for him.' Adamson whooped with laughter.

'First months went well. Hammond's a loner, aloof, morose. Mahler reads his moods, listens for the subtext then feeds it back to the star. So Hammond lays a project on them. *The Last Muse*. He wants to act and direct. Can they set it up? Well, let me tell you, those geniuses went out and collared twenty million dollars on the strength of a letter from Hammond and their in-house coverage. Champagne all round. That was tiptop professional stuff. Except for a minor misunderstanding. When Hammond presented the project they thought he controlled the rights. How they got that thought, whose thought that was, history will decide. Maybe Curwen gave them the glad eye. Because it wasn't hammered down. It was an elementary question, a spec of detail that escaped three pairs of eyes. Sabbatini has sweaty sleepless nights. Somehow Mahler contained the embarrassment, turned fallibility into a bonding opportunity. The agent serviced his client's dismay. What he couldn't service was measle-spot Weislob calling Hilldyard and doing the hard sell.'

'Why did he do that?'

'Weislob is totally LA. He talks like a gangster and gets foul-mouthed under pressure. But the guy has an English parent and he did some postgraduate bullshit at Oxford.'

'Oxford?'

'Probably Keele. Anyway, he thinks he can schmooze Brits and when Curwen gave up he tried to sweet-talk Hilldyard.'

'Curwen gave him Hilldyard's number?'

'So he must be persuasive. But not that persuasive. When Hilldyard told him where to get off, Weislob said he could stick his MS where the sun didn't shine along with the prickly-pears, pomegranates and other bits of Mediterranean fruit he was swivelling on.'

'God!'

'Which was premature. Because however intransigent Hilldyard seemed it wasn't Rick's call to blow him out with a stream of abuse. That was a tactical error.'

'And has Hammond quit?'

'Let me tell you, he's cheesed. If it weren't for Mahler he'd've walked. Mahler is trying a high-level approach to Hilldyard via an eminent Italian screenwriter-stroke-novelist. They have absolutely no choice but to redeem the situation. If Hammond walks, it'll be all over *Variety*. And Hammond will only stay if they collar the rights, which is looking like mission impossible. Weislob and Mahler are sweating like pigs in a Jewish sauna. If they lose Hammond, the whole agency will take a slug in the pips, everybody's careers'll be mauled shitless. That place is crapping itself.'

There was a lengthy pause while Adamson let the news settle in.

'Interesting situation, eh!'

Michael remained silent.

'You see the opportunity?'

He had some idea of what was coming, but he said nothing.

'Whoever gets those rights has Coburn over a barrel.'

Michael held the phone to his ear and felt his heart beating.

'You can negotiate anything. All you have to do is get between them and the film rights in *Last Muse*. Then you take them.'

Adamson allowed the line to remain open, as if to make way for Michael's thoughts.

'What exactly do you mean?'

'You option the rights off Hilldyard, then force yourself into their film. They'll hate it. Tough shit. They have to deal. You control the rights. Man, you're hijacking on to a pre-financed twenty-million-dollar flick starring Shane Hammond. You get a producer fee, front-end credit, but more important, you dictate the creative approach. You beat them with the Hilldyard stick. Make sure it's his kind of picture. And that's just for starters. The real steel is on their agency fee. Now listen to this, Michael. Coburn will be stiffing the budget for a ten per cent packaging fee. Two million dollars. One chunk of spons. You'll take half of it.'

'What?'

'They'll fucking hate you. They'll scream and yell. But they have to keep the client. Either they accept your terms, eat doodoo, or lose Hammond. And if they keep Hammond, they're going to be coining it back.'

Michael could not help chuckling. Adamson's chutzpah was out of control, his opportunism so disconnected from reality.

'You're looking at one point five million bucks.'

The computation was enthralling, meaningless. 'I don't think so.'

'Seriously.'

'Seriously, Nick. Hilldyard won't grant the rights.'

'That's where you come in.'

Michael shook his head. 'No I don't.'

'Have you asked for an option?'

'Of course not.'

'Then you don't know his response.'

'I do.'

'You can't know that.'

'We've discussed it!'

'What you're dealing with is a man's state of mind. Opinions and prejudices. So get inside his head and press some buttons. Find out what makes the guy tick and give it back with nobs on.'

Michael sighed. 'He has very good . . .'

'Bend over for him. Go down on the bard. Whatever it takes, get your hands on that option. It's a matter of persuasion.'

He laughed out loud. 'I don't want to persuade him.'

'You don't want to persuade him?'

'No.'

'You don't want to make one spot five million bucks?'

'Not this way.'

Adamson's voice grew rougher, as though an escalation of force were required. His tone met the revelation of Michael's attitude with direct incredulity.

'What's so terrible? Where's the great ethical hang-up? We're making a movie not the H-bomb.'

He had no desire to convey Hilldyard's intimate reasons to

Adamson. There was no guarantee that the most personal and private scruples would register with him. 'I know his views and I respect them. If I attempted to hustle him I'd ruin the friendship.'

'What kind of friendship sets you back a million bucks?'

The question was too stupid to answer.

'If the guy rates friendship he'll loosen up. Fuck sake, this is just a book.'

'It's a novel and it's his lifeblood.'

'*Brief Encounter* meets *Love Story*. Wouldn't harm a fly.'

'He finds it painful.'

'He can take a pill. He can think seven hundred and fifty thousand bucks. For Christ's sake, he's got to be human!'

'He's very human.'

'This is not human. Some highly talented people want to turn his book into a film. The human thing would be to accept the money and enthusiasm with good grace. Jesus Christ, he should be so lucky.'

'Look –' He was feeling browbeaten. 'He's not a commercial animal. He's a novelist, and he's sensitive to things that don't bother other people.'

'Sensitivity's going to cost you an entry into Hollywood.' Adamson sighed deeply. He lowered his voice, appeared to calm down. 'I understand what you're saying.'

'No you don't.'

'What d'you want out of life, man? A few principles? Snow-white dealings with the nerve-endings of egocentric authors? Let me tell you. If this film is any good you'll be walking tall on Sunset Boulevard. You'll be right inside Hammond's world, rubbing shoulders with a braful of talent. The films you want to make will happen, and instead of being a UK indie pissed about by the BBC, you'll be cruising in the fast lane. You'll look back to the English days with total contempt. I mean, here's where it's happening, man. You want girls, the city is bulging with pussy. You want Beverly Hills palm trees and swimming pools, they are here for the taking. Because this is not a dress rehearsal. This is it. And if you throw away a chance like this you might have a nice life in Hampstead or Barnes, but you won't have happened. And I don't mean the money or the profile, I mean you. You won't have lived to the full extent of your talents. The current is strong here, Michael. It galvanises people. You could walk all over this town doing what you do best. Do you hear me?'

Michael had heard Adamson's creed. It appalled and fascinated him. 'Loud and clear.'

'And can you honestly tell me there's a principle at stake worth the sacrifice?'

'I can.'

'Think big, Michael. Seize the day. You throw away an opportunity like this and you've wasted your whole life.'

He rubbed his eye. Adamson could explain himself to Michael. He doubted he could ever explain himself to Adamson. Nick was a sworn enemy of that kind of thinking. It made the conversation one-sided, but in reality, Michael had no desire to convert him. It would take too long. 'What do you care, Nick?'

'Aha. Thirty per cent of your fee.'

He smiled: the shamelessness.

'You want to take on Coburn and Weislob alone? You'll be tucked up by the end of clause one.'

He adjusted the towel. There was gooseflesh on his shoulder.

'Twenty-five per cent up to a ceiling of three hundred K?'

He lay back on the pillow and allowed himself to think just once of his bank manager's face. All he needed to save his house was eighty thousand pounds.

'Opportunities are never handed to you, Michael. There's always a challenge. But you've put yourself in the right place at the right time. You've earned the chance. Don't let yourself down.'

He could sense Adamson's view of him: a slowcoach, a late starter, someone held up by his Britishness, a rookie in need of commercial hot-wiring; and he realised that in American terms he looked totally soft. American producers worked the system, operated in a meta-physical vacuum. That's why they were so good. They lived in a cold universe and respected its laws, money laws.

'All you gotta do is persuade one old man. It's not exactly building the wall of China.'

'Sorry, Nick.'

'You will be. If they option it without you. A total disaster.'

'Not for me.'

'Hey, Michael. You'd be sick as a dog.'

'Nobody's going to persuade him.'

'You'd better be right. Hollywood has a way of getting to people.'

'It's certainly got to you.'

'And if Hilldyard's principles change, don't be the only person

94

missing the boat. No point having more integrity than the author, eh!'

The remark disgusted him.

'Sleep on it, Michael. You'll dream sweetly of Shane Hammond kissing your arse.'

'Sorry to disappoint you.'

'I'll talk to Weislob in a couple of days. We need to open channels.'

'The matter's closed.'

'The matter is wide open.'

Michael held on to his temper. 'James Hilldyard's soul is not for sale to Tinseltown and neither is mine.'

'Fine. I'll call you tomorrow.'

'Nick!'

Adamson put the phone down, and for a moment Michael wondered whether he had misheard.

For several minutes he remained on the bed. He switched on the table lamp. It cast a parchment glow across his skin. The walls of the hotel bedroom felt cold.

He stirred himself to get up and dressed and moved around the room listlessly collecting garments. His shirts had been washed and ironed and hung up in the cupboard by the chambermaid. His underwear had been filed in separate drawers. Since Hilldyard's intervention the quality of service had improved and cushions had appeared on the chairs and shampoo sachets in the bathroom.

He sat on the edge of the bed pulling on a sock. It struck him as a curious thing to be doing after that conversation, drawing a sock over one's foot. He examined the white skin of his ankle, attention wandering to a point in mid-space. Adamson had contaminated the air, the room.

He decided to start writing. He took out a pad of writing paper from the desk drawer. He drew a pen from his jacket pocket and seated himself, forearm on the desk, his right hand suspended above the sheet. He was determined to concentrate. He wanted to return quickly to an earlier mood. He pushed aside all thought of Adamson and tried to remember an emotion that had come to him after lunch. Experience was vital in him now, gathered; he simply needed to lean into it and words would come, words that he had not sought before. He was ready to write down what had happened to him and to find a form for impulses of sentiment he had never defined. It was not simply that something had eased, enabling unaccustomed contemplation, the perspective of recovery, it was more a gathering of feeling, a ripeness, an urgency, as if he were too full and needed to get this out because whatever it was, this need, it was too important to be wasted. It had to be harnessed and set down, formed, saved, because suddenly the thing that he might write, the cluster of promptings coming at him from every layer in memory, could redeem what had been lost.

He rubbed his eyes. It was 7.30 p.m., and the hotel was silent.

Later he lay on the bed and gazed unblinkingly at a white ceiling lined in the centre by a plaster crack. He had written three paragraphs in two hours.

He was quite stricken when the telephone rang. It went six times, and he stared at the receiver without moving.

He saw his hand reach out. He put the phone to his ear. 'Hello?' he said.

Michael sat upright as if to protect the receiver. Adela apologised for disturbing him.

'Not at all,' he said, not quite in his own voice.

There was something she wanted to mention when they spoke before; it slipped her mind when he told her about Hilldyard. The following day she was going to Capri. There was a boat and then a hydrofoil; one came back about four o'clock. She had no special plan, just a stroll around the island, a snoop in the shops, lunch somewhere. Would he like to join her?

He was surprised, almost taken aback. He accepted quickly. They agreed to meet at the dock at a quarter-past nine. Adela rang off, and he slowly replaced the phone, bearer of all manner of tidings.

He pulled himself up, displacing his energy with a stride around the room, until he came to the mirror. He stopped to consider his face as another might see it for the first time.

In due course he put the paper back in the drawer and decided to slip downstairs for a drink on the terrace. He would sit on an easy chair and think things over.

He collected a Cinzano from the bar and wandered out on to the terrace and felt as he sat down and gazed at the fading light on the peaks of the mountains that he was getting to know himself at last. Things were settling.

In staying on he had done the right thing. Now that he was here, safe from the world, he could see that what had happened to him was not quite accidental. Bankruptcy had perhaps been a choice, the wilful precipitation of a crisis, something that would force change. Perhaps he had not so much failed to make an accommodation with life as evicted himself from an area of meaninglessness. Everything had led, at least, to lunch with James Hilldyard and to the Cimbrone belvedere; and a life which led to such moments could not be without purpose.

Chapter Nine

ADELA STOOD ON THE deck of the hydrofoil, one foot before the other, hand on the rail, her streaming hair aloft in the wind. She leaned as far as possible over the rail to feel the spray and to see foam jetting from the craft's sides. Her cardigan was billowing, her summer frock flapping; she smiled at the rush of wind on her skin, at the surly sea, the ghost of Capri on the horizon.

The day was febrile with light and vapour; translucent mist rose off the waters; spokes of sunlight developed patches of colour on ochre cliffs. The air was heady with sea change, mercurial weather that might mellow and maintain the placid autumn warmth or wipe the haze with bright skies and strong winds.

They began the journey in the cinema seats of the passenger lounge. The windows were the colour of orangeade, the seats uncomfortable, and when the craft got up speed they went out and gave up conversation to the blast of air and the roar of the engine. Adela was fascinated by the diminishing sight of Positano, suddenly enclosed by a magnitude of scenery that slowly reduced it to a smudge on the coast. It was strange to watch the halcyon town dwindle into the great reaches of sea and sky, and curious to follow the great backdrop of the mountain extending along the coast for miles. One could lose all sense of the modern staring at that band of rock.

Michael caught her smile from time to time, and when Capri approached he joined her on the port side to watch the striated cliff rush up. The craft throttled back and they saw its wash twirling over the surface of the water and slapping on the rocks.

They were a little uncomfortable at first, as if it were slightly false to be so exhilarated by the voyage before they had got to know each other. But the premise of the trip was adventure, and he could tell she was hungry for first impressions. He sensed that she had been restless and her restlessness now had an outlet. The wide horizons of the sea and the spectre of Capri met something acquisitive in her imagination. By the time the craft was moored in Porto Turistico, and they had exchanged the sway of the vessel for the solid flatness of the jetty, she was beaming with excitement.

They stood on the jetty and gazed at the backlit mass of the island. The marina was cluttered with yachts and sailing boats, masts rocking and cockeyed, a lattice through which came the subdued pastels of the waterfront buildings, and above the harbour frontage, terraces of olive and orange trees clambering up to the island's saddle, Capri town, where in due course they would recapture the sun.

After gliding up the hill they emerged from the funicular into the bustle of the *centro*, a tourist current leading to the Piazza Umberto, with its four hundred wicker chairs and beer tables. The instant convenience of the Piazza was a little premature, and they pressed on away from the German beer signs and credit-card stickers along ancient streets, narrow and smelling of stone. They walked past the palm-court entrances of grand hotels, around the porticoes of churches. They wended their way looking for a *caffè* that was perfectly situated in relation to all the picturesque elements, a place that would reward anticipation with culmination; but such a spot was hard to find, and none of the smaller squares exceeded the touristic apotheosis of the Umberto with its celebratory atmosphere of efficient profit. And although it was fun to explore, Michael soon felt disheartened, as if famous Capri were no longer real. On corner after corner stood perfunctory restaurants, over-sponsored bars, hotel porches, forbiddingly deluxe. They searched hard and found little to their taste, a negative consensus which was subtly bonding. After strolling past a monastery and sitting in the Giardino di Augusto, they discovered a trattoria on a side street. It had a balcony enfurled with wisteria and a steeply priced menu in a glass case by the door.

Now that they were seated Adela's inquisitiveness seemed to turn on him with full energy, and he quickly sensed that, although she was an actress, magnetic in limelight, part of her charm was her power of attention. She was relaxed, pleased with the setting, and yet extremely careful to listen. She picked up all tones, all gradations of seriousness; she let her companion know that she wanted to do him justice. She had expertise in this realm, knew how to encourage. She followed his face when he spoke, looking at his eyes, his lips, taking his meaning from all sources of expression. And although she was less professionally poised than on their first encounter, when she had so much to convey to a stranger, her relaxation today made it easier to see the reality of her talent. She was facially compelling, possessing features that were not only fine in themselves, but imbued with intelligence. Her gaze held a quickening intensity, as though she were of superior stock, had something special or marked about her which commanded attention, an energy of interest she was able to repay.

Michael felt he could confide in her. Not because she seemed discreet, but because something about her insisted on substance, and to serve her up anything less than one's best material was to risk seeming dull. She presupposed seriousness. She offered it herself. And this generosity of response was the quality that convinced him Hilldyard was wrong. She was not merely plausible, she was stimulating. She was not simply genuine, she was frequently outspoken. Though she had expressive resources and could doubtless project the most heroic emotions on stage, it was the latency of this power he found beguiling. And although she was sensitive and fine, Adela was not precious. Her eyes could glitter with irony, especially when the subject of her parents came up; though even here the irony was kindly, signifying a private perspective rather than a hardening of feeling.

'They've seen me on TV and still think I should marry a merchant banker and have a dozen children. They want happiness through me, and my being an actress spoils that.'

'Aren't they proud?'

She looked blankly at him. 'Dad thinks theatre is something laid on for the middle classes by travelling minstrels, people, you know, from outside society. It's lovely to go to Chichester on a summer evening, but God forbid one's daughter should go on stage and make an exhibition of her feelings.'

He frowned. 'So what do you talk about?'

'With Dad?' She was amused by the question. 'Oh, driving routes. How to get from Wokingham to Croydon when the M25 is down.'

'And your mother?'

Adela contemplated the question with an abstract look. 'She wants things to be "nice".'

Michael nodded.

'She doesn't want me to sleep with bisexual actors and says so a lot.' Adela's brow was knitted: the injustice of it. 'I'd love to if I could just find one.'

He laughed.

'I do my best. Honestly. To be a good daughter. But both my parents have set the limits of their life and feel threatened by my independence. I love them, but mentally we're on separate planets. Besides, they think I'm highly-strung.'

'Are you?'

She shrugged. 'I'd call it temperament.'

He raised the glass of wine that had succeeded his lager. 'Let's drink to temperament.'

She smiled, raising her glass.

Michael gazed at the peaks of Anacapri and felt the full warmth of an October sun on his face. They were having lunch on an island in the Tyrrhenian Sea and talking about people who lived in Croydon.

He was curious. 'Do you like being an actress?'

She knew the answer instantly. 'I love the art and hate the profession.'

He was intrigued; she was after all very successful.

'One's creativity is so dependent on luck,' she continued. 'I can't just get out there and act. To do the thing I want to do I need the patronage of casting directors, TV producers. My livelihood is down to their whim. Whoever you are it's a cattle market. Which means rejection and more rejection, and although I've had some breaks I'm sick to the back teeth of bloody rejection. Because what gets rejected is the whole you.' She gazed at him earnestly, inviting him to encompass the reality of that.

He nodded readily.

'A writer can write. A painter can paint. An actor is the one artist who has no creative self-determination. We're dependent on forces beyond our control to be able to express ourselves.' She looked askance. 'Which is why I got on a plane and came out here. For once in my life I thought I could influence my own destiny.'

Michael blinked, almost embarrassed. He showed his sympathy by not saying anything.

'One has a gift, something that feels quite valuable, and to get it across you have to give everything, every last drop. Which you do, and they love you for it, but in the end we're all dispensable.'

'But you love the art?'

'I feel a better person when I act.' She brightened. 'Noble.'

'Noble?'

'Only when acting.' She smiled to reassure him. 'But yes. There's something purifying about giving over everything you have to another character. It's an act of self-effacement, of discovery. Does that sound absurd?'

Michael looked exceptionally grave. It did not sound ridiculous. What she said had a strange effect on him.

'No . . . So how d'you cope with the crap?'

She took in a breath. 'By trying to respect myself. Whatever quality I have it's not going to vanish overnight. And if I can just focus on developing and improving and forget about trying to impress people, I'll be all right. I mean, I've been lucky so far. I just don't want to do rubbish. That's why I admire you.'

'Me?'

She fiddled with her bread. 'You only do the top stuff.'

He did not know whether to be puzzled or flattered.

'Basil Curwen thinks you've got real integrity.'

It remained unconvincing to hear praise from that quarter.

'He says you dazzled him with your knowledge of Hilldyard's novels. And he told me about Intelligent Productions and *The Other House* and that play by Mike Summers, which, by the way, I saw last year and thought was brilliant.'

He was pleased to hear late acclaim for his only TV drama. 'Thank you.'

'Oh God—' She was almost distressed. 'It was for grown-ups. I mean subtle.'

'He's a very good writer.'

'You're a very good producer. Every time I see something like that I think a miracle has happened. I'll bet *The Other House* is going to be fantastic.'

It seemed a shame to disillusion her.

'Well, actually, the Beeb canned it last month.'

'Oh!' It was almost a personal blow. 'Why?'

'I expect they're clearing the decks for a bonkbuster.'

'Oh, miserable!'

'Developing quality drama is a short-cut to oblivion these days.' He shrugged. 'Nobody stands up for it any more.'

'That's so depressing.'

'What I was interested in producing the system didn't want.'

'But you'll make other things?' She was concerned.

He wanted to announce his failure, to proclaim it, almost as proof of his values; but Adela had rekindled some of his old pride and that warranted a more careful response than the bitter cry that the system had failed him, that he had gone bust, and it was all the fault of the philistines.

'I don't know.' He did, of course. 'There are other things I might want to do.'

'Oh please!'

'Television is no place for passion, you see. If you care about things passionately don't become a producer, because a producer is a mule of compromise. And compromise is all very nice for business, but it detaches you from what you love. And eventually love has little to do with it. You do the work, but without conviction.'

Michael pushed the stem of his wineglass along the cloth. Adela was listening carefully. He was feeding himself out to her and she was reeling him in.

'I've had an awakening here. Talking to Hilldyard makes me feel that up to now I've wasted my life. I've been struggling to idealise the process whereby something precious is simplified for public consumption. I've turned what I love into career fodder. Become a dealer in the commodity of culture. I haven't contributed to culture. Intelligent Productions has diluted the arts. The arts can't be mediated via television or newspapers. They have to be encountered directly, one to one. The only authentic exchange. All the rest is background noise, the babble of other people's careers, colour-supplement verbiage.'

He frowned and sipped at his wine.

She seemed struck, almost disturbed.

'I knew that in being a producer I was losing my integrity. And if one wants to live according to some kind of self-truth I suppose it's inevitable that you become an artist.' He looked away. 'I've started writing. Nothing ambitious. Just to help make sense of things.'

He sipped at his wine again. He was sounding very earnest. Saying to somebody that you had started 'writing' was about as thrilling for them as declaring oneself vegetarian or Christian.

'What you say is very interesting.'

To Michael she looked more worried than interested.

She drew a strand of hair over her ear.

'Badly paid,' he said.

She looked at him with her green eyes, her features carved in seriousness. 'D'you mind if I tell you something?'

He was suddenly hooked on her parted lips, as if seeing them for the first time.

'You'd have been the ideal producer for this film.'

What held him was the depth of the upper lip, the way it adhered in the corners to her lower lip, two cushions meeting.

'You'd have been brilliant.'

A warm sensation spread through his chest.

'You're not wowed by Hollywood. I mean, you would have made the right decisions.'

Michael blinked, passed a hand across his mouth. He caught what she said; just. 'I've never made a feature film.'

'But that's your strength. You could walk away from all the bullshit. Oh, how frustrating!'

He wondered what to say. He could not share her view of him, though her faith was touching. He could only register the intensity of her disappointment.

'I hope that when you meet James you'll feel less frustrated.'

'Don't give up producing!'

'Right now my only concern is to work with Hilldyard.'

'You'll stay here?'

'For the time being.'

'Won't you be lonely?'

It was an odd question; it had never occurred to him.

'I feel less lonely now than I have in years.'

'Oh gosh.' She put her hands to her lips.

He smiled, raised his eyebrows.

'It's all so extraordinary,' she said.

'What?'

'Your incredible friendship.'

There was a note in her voice of warm-hearted envy, which made him realise how much she understood.

'Perhaps you should stay.' He was light. 'This place would do you good.'

'You could indoctrinate me. Cure me of my worldly ambitions.'

'I don't mean that. I could show you around a bit.'

'I'm serious. I'd give anything to stay. This is so much what I need.'

'Then stay.'

She shook her head.

The expression on Michael's face concealed his disappointment. 'You probably need a holiday.'

'I'm up for jobs on Thursday and Friday.'

'Come back afterwards.'

She frowned thoughtfully, and he wondered what she was reckoning. Her commitments were unknown to him.

'I don't know. There are things and things.'

'Don't let them get the better of you.'

She snorted. 'They always get the better of me.'

He had the apprehension suddenly that she was attached and that her warmth was the warmth of a woman on leave from a complicated and consuming relationship. She had glanced to the side, as if alluding to a certain aspect of her life, and the glance contained a fondness for that aspect.

He managed a half-smile.

'You could be my mentor, I suppose.' She was amused. 'I've lots to catch up on.'

He had found himself presuming that anyone so open, so interested in the progress of her life, would be unattached. She had spoken to him as if freshly created herself.

He was serious in response. 'What have you got to catch up on?'

'I've no personal philosophy. I haven't thought things through like you.'

'Then you must come back.'

'D'you do a crash course?' She laughed.

'That depends on the student.'

'Oh, I'd be a very good student.'

'Two weeks should do it.'

'You'd keep me company?'

'Of course.'

She raised her eyebrows in appreciative amusement. 'What an offer!'

He smiled. 'It would be nice for me.'

She stretched and inhaled, binding her arms tight behind the chair so her frock became breastful. 'Oh the life of the mind,' she hummed. 'All very tempting.' She straightened up to her full seated height, squaring her shoulders, in good posture. 'Shall we go for a walk?'

They paid the bill, rose from the table and made their way out of the restaurant on to a quiet road that ran in the direction of a belvedere under the muscled boughs of a eucalyptus tree. Adela seemed dreamy, taken by the smell of fallen leaves, the gated drives of monumental villas, the luxurious foliage around half-hidden hotels. She was happy to glide on the atmosphere, as if letting Capri into her system with the special openness of a person doomed to go home. She gazed up and across, stood under a tulip tree that rose in chapters of magnitude to a filigree summit against the sky and made sure Michael followed her gaze to the swaying silhouette of a bird that suddenly scattered itself with a screech from the upper branches.

Adela's behind view, the lilting shoulders, the falling arms, the horsey twitch of her frock fell on his eye with a musical smoothness, as though an extra sensuality accompanied vision. He could almost feel the dappled light running across the nape of her neck as she halted and turned, waiting for him to follow.

The path started to descend, and soon they were tripping off steps, gathering speed. Michael was drawn on by the desire to look beyond. Adela bumped along, hand grazing the rail, sharing his anticipation, as though they both wanted to make the discovery first. The path brought them out from under the trees to a railed promenade, and to a wide view of the sea and sky divided by an immense spire of rock.

They slow-motioned on to the promenade, the view hitting back on them until they stopped at the edge, palms on the rail.

'Excellent,' she breathed.

Behind them was a circular bench with a strawberry tree in its middle. After walking the promenade like the edge of a stage, Adela doubled-back to the bench. She sat there and slid down on to her back, hair spiralling over the wooden slats. She lay prone, one foot on the ground, one on the seat, and let the decorated leafy altitudes play on her eyes.

Soon Michael was by her side, sitting contemplatively, palms pressed together between his legs. Without moving he could see everything from the far horizon to the topsy-turvy features of her face. He could see the lineless dome of her forehead, the fine-stitched eyebrows, the lashes of shut eyes resting on a cheek. Her mouth was peacefully closed. She seemed to be listening to the birds and the breeze, almost unaware of him. He tried to claim his own concentration, to receive the spirit of the place and the moment, and not to disturb her reverie.

'Tell me,' she said presently. She twisted round, expelled hair from her face. She looked at him, wanting eye-contact. 'What did you think of that book?'

He frowned at the suddenness of the enquiry; it seemed to come at him from another side of things. 'Oh, I thought it was marvellous.'

She hesitated, pre-mouthing the words. 'What about the theory?'

'The theory?'

'The theory of love?'

He nodded.

'The lurv theory?' She hoiked an eyebrow. 'I mean . . . you know.' She sat up properly. 'The idea that true love is unimaginable until it happens, and that even if you think you're in love with someone, it's always possible that real love will come along like a revelation, making you realise that everything else has been a kind of half-life.'

He looked at her.

'And that is your chance, and you have to take it. In fact, you have to realise it first. And if the chance passes by, that's it. You've missed the opportunity to be happy. The chance of a lifetime. Whoosh. Gone.' She was more than hypothetical, she was assertive.

He shifted his weight. The précis was interesting, and it was interesting that Adela should be so definite about reading the book in this way.

'D'you think that's true?'

He was not ready to venture an opinion. He smiled. 'I'm no great expert on lurv.'

She produced a bent-faced look. 'You've been in love, I hope?'

'I have been.'

'When?'

'When I was married.'

'You were married!'

'Not any more.'

She was utterly astonished, then amused by her astonishment, the suddenness of it, which raised her colouring.

'When was that? Sorry! D'you mind me asking?'

'Eight years ago.'

Adela's eyes were unblinkingly fascinated by the idea of Michael's marriage. 'You seem so unmarried!'

'I am.'

'I mean ever.'

He did not know what he seemed or how he seemed it. She was

looking at him for more signs, her irises switching like searchlights over him. She leaned closer, collarbones against neckline.

'So what happened?'

Michael felt disorientated by the frankness of the question. He had no answer that was quite right for someone like Adela.

'You know, on a postage stamp.'

He looked at her lightly.

'Am I being nosy?'

'She was killed in a car crash.'

'Oh!'

'It's all right.'

He could see her embarrassment transforming into a complete readiness of sympathy that almost overflowed from her eyes.

He was always self-conscious about the effect of this disclosure. He did not want Adela to feel sorry for him. Telling people often doomed him to a kind of loneliness. But it was time that she knew and it was necessary to be open.

'I fell in love with Christine on my first day at university,' he began. 'We got married when we were twenty-four. She was a painter. We lived in a flat in Brixton.'

Adela's eyes were still full of surprise.

'She fixed herself up with a studio and did commissioned work, plus her own stuff, mainly landscapes. I loved her ability to express what I could only perceive. And she was beautiful. And of course living at a certain pitch made her irritably perfectionist about things that didn't always matter. She needed space. She needed a structure around her. But when things went well she was pure delight. My better half.' He paused and shrugged. 'When she was twenty-six something snapped. She couldn't paint for a few months, was depressed, prey to strange ideas. I found out then that there was a history of mental illness on her mother's side and before I knew what I was dealing with, before anything was diagnosed or explained, she had got herself killed in a car crash.'

He cleared his throat. He had begun the story and had to finish it.

'For a year I felt like lying down and dying. That was stage one. Stage two was about guilt. For not saving her. For being less gifted than she was, less fine as a person. One tortures oneself mercilessly, and then the rage kicks in. She had ruined my life by getting herself killed. She had taken me with her. Cheated me of my life. All this pain runs through you, and all you can do is hope that tomorrow will be better. For three years I just dragged myself into work. I honestly thought that was it. That was my allocation of happiness in life. I trudged on, numbed one day, distraught the next, and one morning I noticed that whilst all this was going on I had allowed nothing else to count. And the idea that work might count again, that was a turning point. One comes out of the tunnel, if one comes out, with a vengeance. I remember feeling that having been through hell I wasn't going to compromise about the future. I was probably manic. I left the Beeb, set up on my own, tried to put passion back into my work, and discovered that when you have conviction you're a bloody nuisance. In a mad kind of way I needed to go down guns blazing. I needed to purge myself of all cynicism. If that meant taking risks and saying no, and going out on a limb, I had to do that. Perhaps my mother was right when she said that my business problems were self-inflicted, that I was carrying the cross of my grief as a kind of a militant integrity, which alienated colleagues and cost commissions, but which was actually a failure to cope, or depression. But to me it seemed . . . Well, like the start of a recovery. I was rediscovering what I'd learnt from Christine. That art is part of life, and if you trivialise it, you trivialise yourself. Better to give up producing than hack on compromising the best of yourself: the thing you love.' He looked down. 'I was beginning to have strong feelings again. I wanted to hold on to that.'

Adela held her chin in her hand, fingers overlapping her mouth.

He could see at a glance how much she had taken in, how her sense of him had gained depth. But there was nothing she could say to such a speech. No response could strike any kind of note.

'I do believe in true love,' he said, returning to their earlier subject. 'A birthright you encounter by pure serendipity.'

She was happy to take the hint. Her eyes widened. 'But how d'you recognise it? What is it?'

He placed his hand on the seat between them and swung round to face her. 'Knowledge and illumination.'

'Knowledge?'

'When two people complete the best in each other.'

She was eager. 'You believe that can happen?'

'One can only go so far on one's own.'

'That's true.'

Adela seemed troubled. She leaned back against her elbows, pushing forward the swell of each breast.

Michael cupped his mouth.

'It must be incredible,' she sighed.

He swallowed, opened his mouth to speak.

'But suppose you hold out for something better,' she said, 'and it doesn't come along?'

He took in her expression, but then was suddenly mauled by her loveliness, blissfully molested.

She held his gaze.

'There's no alternative,' he managed.

'But what about compromise? One can't expect perfection.'

For a pure moment he felt the unfiltered impact of something unbearably exquisite. He was caught in her mouth's magnetic field, was weightlessly susceptible to iris and eyelash.

'Don't you think?'

'I . . . compromise?'

'Realism.'

'Realism?'

'Not expecting too much of other people,' she said. 'Especially men.'

He hesitated. He knew for a fact he could love Adela. 'You shouldn't expect less from others than you expect from yourself.'

'I know,' she sighed.

'Otherwise it's just a diary entry.'

'Oh Christ,' she wilted. 'Don't!'

Her eyebrows were knitted, her lower lip hung, but she managed a rueful half-smile.

'I've had relationships like that,' he said.

She looked at him directly. He wanted to kiss her. She seemed to read his mind.

'I'm having one.'

'You're having one!'

'Yes,' she said.

The first sensation was of leaning too close to her, and he drew back his hand from the seat between them.

'Damn! You're the only person I've said that to.'

Michael did not blush, but his embarrassment was intense.

'What I can't believe is that this whole thing has been an illusion.'

The admission cut him away from her. He was suddenly relegated, his intensity marooned. He felt peculiar, though not surprised, and slowly, as conversation rambled on, the shock became sorrow.

She sprawled back against the tree, chin on chest, immobilised by confession. She was prey to private thoughts.

'Is that why you have to go back?' he asked eventually.

She hummed softly. 'He's moving to New York for two years and just assumed I'd up sticks and come, as though I have no career, no roots. Which I certainly have. And I'm beginning to think my career is an abstraction to him, which means he doesn't understand me. Which means the relationship isn't real.'

Michael nodded slowly and thoughtfully, and felt a certain coldness enter his heart. Beyond the overhanging leaves stood the Kodachrome picture of a distant sea with its saturated royal blues and horizon of endless promise, and its dazzling stack beating back the afternoon sun, and he felt that his sudden loneliness was unbearably heightened by the crushing beauty of that scene.

He glanced at his watch. Four o'clock. They would meet Hilldyard tomorrow; on Friday she would leave.

Traipsing back to the funicular, he was wryly curious at how suddenly, how steeply, he had succumbed. He had actually had the impulse to kiss her, felt it gather, rise up, an appallingly strong urge. She had sprawled back so fetchingly that he was immensely relieved not to have embarrassed himself.

They cornered through the narrow streets, re-tracing their outward walk with more knowledge of each other and less energy flowing between them, and he wondered about her boyfriend, and what kind of a man he was.

Later, on the hydrofoil, the wind buffeted his face and purged his disappointment. Ahead of them Positano was slowly reborn, its cluttered terraces and shanty villas gradually emerging from the skirts of the mountains, its harbour lights ushering in the dusk. He felt the pull of a homecoming. He could look forward to solitude again, to more reading and talking with the old man, and to Positano's autumnal sanctuary, its gorgeous mornings and ethereal light.

And anyway, he rationalised, as they clambered off the boat on to the quay, glancing over the beach to where he had first seen Adela in her bikini, he had no evidence she liked him in that way. Her friendliness was probably non-exclusive. She was used to delighting people; that was her job. She was personable and attractive and she knew how to make of herself a proposition that was conceptually pleasing. It was her gift to be lovely, and her duty to be generous with that gift. He had succumbed to an allure that doubtless afflicted many intelligent men, men who liked to be engaged intellectually before submitting to the trauma of physical desire.

She was tired, flushed by the sea air, and he escorted her at an easy pace up the twisting Viale. The street was busy with evening traffic, Piaggio scooters, Ape vans, lively children.

He brought her to the hotel, where he gave her a squeeze and they managed a kiss.

'I can't believe I'm going to meet him,' she said.

'I'll call you tomorrow.'

'I'll keep myself free,' she smiled.

He hesitated.

'I won't mention the book,' she promised.

Michael made his way up the winding road, joining in with the six o'clock *passeggiata*. He took a seat at a bar and stared at the sombre reaches of the evening sky while couples drank beer and smoked cigarettes. Three teenage girls with tousled manes of chestnut hair sucked Orangina through straws. A young man placed his car keys on the next table and shouted across the street to a character in jeans and cowboy boots. The evening was just beginning.

After a last swig he went back to his hotel, where he took the unusual and unsatisfactory step of dining in the restaurant. By the time he slipped up the marble steps to his landing he felt dull and drowsy; and, when he twisted the lock and pushed into the trapped air of his bedroom, the dim light conspired with tiredness to draw him in a headlong slouch to his mattress and to a slow undoing of buttons and shedding of clothes.

He sat for a while on the bed. And then he rose for a last look through the shutters, and found himself drifting on to the balcony and into the cool air and standing before the night and the sea.

Later, he sat upright in bed.

He sat waiting for a moment, his hands flat on the bedspread, while something collapsed within him, some force of resistance that had run out, as it did from time to time, leaving a vacuum in his heart.

It came suddenly, the familiar spasm: a wrench of despair. He lay there, looking to the side, strangely grimacing; and then he tried to move, as if to pull away from the epicentre of the feeling; and as he reached the edge of the bed he wondered if this returning stab of sorrow were the memory of his love for Christine welling up and attacking him from within, like something to be set free.

He bathed his face in his hands and reached for the glass of water on his bedside table. Tomorrow, he thought, he would try to do some more writing.

Chapter Ten

'I'VE SEEN YOU ON television.'

'*Gwendolyn*?'

'With Frank McCallum?'

'That was me.'

'Is he really that handsome?'

'Oh, sure. And very gay.'

'Oh darn! D'you hear that, James? Frank McCallum is gay. Must've been jolly odd doing the sex bit with a gay person.'

'It was only my character that did the sex bit.'

'But your character kisses him!'

'My character kisses his character, and in the film his character is straight.'

'Oh, I see! How ingenious!'

'It's called acting.'

Frances trilled laughter. 'James, can we go somewhere decent for dinner? I'm absolutely famished and I refuse to eat another pizza. Rome pizzaed me out.'

'Conserve calories by talking less.'

They walked two by two along the road, Frances and Adela ahead, Hilldyard and Michael a few yards behind. To their right Positano glimmered in the dusk. For an hour they had strolled around the back of the town, under the overhang of the mountain. The evening air was savoury with woodsmoke. On the far flatness of the sea the lights of boats pricked the gloom.

Hilldyard was not happy. He gazed at his niece, as if to check that she was really here, in the heart of his retreat, like grit in the eye. Michael walked uneasily by him.

Frances Rampton was a sharp-faced, brilliant-eyed girl with a short haircut and a stick-like figure. Her accent was affected, her laughter shrill; her wiry form bristled with energy. She talked out all her ideas, however tangential, and had latched on to Adela with a hundred personal questions.

Frances, it transpired, had descended on Hilldyard without notice or apology. Whatever excuses he made on the phone she had brushed them aside as if sensing their falsehood or deeming them false. She had arrived at lunchtime from Rome, presenting herself with a suitcase and promising that she would stay only two days unless he was 'horrid', in which case she would stay for a month. Hilldyard spent the afternoon flappishly procuring a spare mattress from a neighbour and clearing a space in his study. He made her a sandwich and listened to her report on Rome; and when she crashed out in his study, he crept to the balcony with a tense face and a stiff drink.

Michael had spent the afternoon writing. He moved the desk in his bedroom on to the balcony and sat wearing dark glasses, one hand on the pad, one hand dangling in the crook of his thighs, his feet pressed together, a position of comfortable equilibrium that helped him burn away three hours whilst his pen travelled back and across, ceaselessly animated by a flow of ideas that rushed to be connected in his mind, ideas that the pen itself seemed to twirl out of focused recollection. He wrote about the trip to Ravello, his hour in the garden with Hilldyard, starting in the centre of things and working concentrically into the past and back again, and as the words and phrases came more fluently he wrote a purer and more concentrated version of himself, in a tone that had propulsion behind it, the pressure of backed-up experience; and Michael, rubbing his eyes at five-thirty and sipping water from his hotel toothmug, realised how daunting was the question of form. How could he frame his own experience? How could he organise the material of his inner life, the sensations and ideas that crystallised only under intense concentration, into a form you could share with other people? He was exhilarated and tired. After the release of writing there was a residue of strangeness, as though he had lost the sense of his own personality. He began to get ready for the evening, and noticed how remote Adela seemed, and how odd the prospect of their drink with Hilldyard, as if social reality were now insubstantial. As he shrugged into his jacket his anticipation sharpened. His nervousness about Hilldyard and Adela returned.

*   *   *

He arrived at her *pensione* and was sent up to her room. He found her struggling with hairpins in the bathroom. She was flustered, nervous, unhappy with each side of her face in the mirror.

Adela wore a strapless green cotton dress, tightly waisted and kneelength, with a sculptural *décolletage*. Her hair was up, ears delicate and neck slender, and although she pouted against lipstick and grimaced in distress at her reflection, she looked extraordinarily enhanced. She was notably shapely in this outfit, a very professional creation of slants and lines.

'Crikey,' he said, nervousness coming back.

'I'm suffocating.'

'You look tremendous.'

'Don't use that word.'

'Why not?'

'It means "huge".'

He laughed. 'Not at all!'

There was something spirited in her approach. She was asking to be taken on her own best terms. Such panache might well win the day.

Adela took a wrap from the bed, wound a choker round her neck and asked him to carry her wallet and lipstick in his pocket. She grabbed his arm and with a certain awkwardness he escorted her along the corridor and down to the lobby.

Hilldyard was to be encountered on the veranda of the villa, as though hiding from the clamour of Frances's welcome. Michael went through first and saw the trapped look of pain in his eye, as though he were pleadingly unequal to the effort of socialising; but then Adela came in, and Michael saw the author clip to attention, manners plucked from his terrible mood by the shock of the vision before him. There was a tableau transition in which everyone was introduced, Adela presented and received, Michael told to pour drinks and Hilldyard became the official host. Michael let the formalities play out, hoping that something polite and anodyne would soon establish itself whilst Adela admired the view. Frances nattered at his side as he thumbed ice and cut lemon, and Hilldyard's demeanour was transiently suave. For a while it seemed like an ordinary evening drinks party, except for the fact that James and Frances were flabbergasted by Adela's dress.

She sank into a wickerwork chair. 'Oh dear,' she smiled, looking around at the author's turned-up jacket sleeves and Frances's cardigan. 'I've rather overdone it.'

116

'You are elegant,' he bowed. 'We shall have to be witty.'

'Such a beautiful dress,' mused Frances. 'I'd kill for your cleavage.'

Adela blushed and managed a smile.

'Frances is outspoken,' said Hilldyard. 'It gets her into trouble.'

'What trouble?'

'Trouble with discreet, well-mannered people.'

'James, I'm thirty. I say what I like. When I like.'

'Of that I have not the slightest doubt.'

'If you had any so-called manners you'd have asked me to stay.'

'My dear, I'm busy.'

'So I see.' She gleamed mockingly, raising her glass to the others.

Hilldyard inhaled theatrically, though Michael saw the beginnings of a genuine unease.

Now, on the walk, Michael noticed how irritable Hilldyard had become with Frances's harmless chatter, as though he were dealing with a person ill-bred. Frances was eccentric and lively, and Hilldyard could neither out-talk her nor entirely encompass her. Michael saw his chance to relieve Adela when Frances stopped at a bride-shop window. He took her elbow in his hand and propelled her along the street, leaving Hilldyard to his fate.

'I feel a right twit in this dress.' Adela was gliding along in her shapely frock. She took his arm. 'D'you mind? I'm being boreholed by lots of Italian males.'

Attached, they deflected the men and attracted the attention of elderly women, strict buzzards who stared first at the excellence of Adela's *bella figura* and bridesmaidenly chignon, deeming her acceptable to Italian standards of daughterliness, then drove their dark eyes through Michael, shoes to shirt-collar, to see what measure of a man such beauty had won. He was pierced with scornful looks, an aquiline perusal of his worthiness as lover and breadwinner. He gave himself no airs but felt under the scrutiny the kudos of a real boyfriend, in this way tricking himself into the illusion of being that person, an odd sensation, a breathtaking split second that flashed back strangely when they descended the steps to the open-air restaurant, where her lush entry and his imposing height caused a waiterly flurry, as if, in a stroke, they had made the place fashionable. Chairs were pulled out, Italian spouted. Candles were lit and back-up summoned. Other guests took in the duo with more than routine interest, watching them cross the restaurant floor and noting the arrival of their more ordinary companions.

Hilldyard came to the table with non-aplomb. Whatever airs he had nurtured for the evening, he was now preoccupied by Frances. He sat down heavily, a template frown on his face.

Michael placed Adela opposite Hilldyard and put himself firmly in Frances's sights. The social combination was too intractable to fuss over. Everyone held their menus, as if in defence, and before long Hilldyard was peeking at Adela over his. He seemed to realise she was a personage, someone whose appearance suggested mastery in other worlds. He glanced at her, took careful note of her face and cleavage. Her bosom intrigued him. He gave it a good look before switching back to his menu, forefinger sliding like a cursor down the lines of *antipasti*.

Adela remained mild and still, as if co-operating with the process of assessment. Whilst Hilldyard was adjusting she could be scenery, known by her looks alone. She had the poise not to rush in. The group did not need animation forced on it. She had done her duty with Frances and it was now time to be demure and composed and let Hilldyard get used to the presence of a professional actress. In an awkward situation time was on her side. She was tactful and well-spoken and not unconfident in her evening dress.

Michael did his best to project the elation of someone relishing the evening air and the dramatic position of the restaurant. Before long he was talking to Frances about Rome, the places she had been: Trastevere, Campo di Fiori, the restored Sistine Chapel. She and a friend called Melissa had done the nightclub circuit: Danielli's, Captain Jack's, Bop Opera.

'What's a grand tour without a grand pick-up?' Her eyes glittered.

'Any luck?' he asked irresponsibly.

'One waiter got very lucky.'

Hilldyard groaned.

'James, you always said a love affair was the best way to learn a foreign language.'

'Is there a language you haven't learned?'

'Swahili,' she guffawed.

Michael smiled politely.

'What happened to Melissa?' asked Adela.

'She's staying at the Ambassador's, poor lamb.'

'Poor lamb?'

'Our man in Rome is *boring*.'

Further questions revealed that she lived in a mews flat in Marylebone and had dreadful money problems. She proclaimed she was unemployable and unmarriageable. The future was a blank page to her and she was quite sure that before long she would commit suicide in the messiest way possible. Having settled that she was out to enjoy herself, determined never to suffer the agonies that led to her overdose earlier that year. 'There's no point in suffering before you kill yourself. That's a waste. No. If I ever do away with myself, it'll be because nothing new can happen and I'm bored.'

Michael listened carefully. Frances's eyes were full of high-strung mirth. She knew how to seize hilarity, how to discharge her little gay mad moments. He carried on asking questions but was conscious of Adela by his side. He could sense her attitude of quiet respect, as if Hilldyard's prerogative were to talk and hers were to listen. The author's bearing had softened, too. He remained keen to embody in this first contact with an actress the probity of a literary novelist, but was clearly fascinated by Adela's glamorous comportment. His senses were encountering the very pulchritude he had sought for Michael: the attentive eyes and fine lips; the sympathetic gaze of a good listener.

'We're taking stock, I suppose.' He cleared his throat, looked around lightly. 'It's a good place to sit and think. One's history dribbles back, you know.'

She nodded fractionally, a lift of the chin.

'I find it killingly beautiful, of course.'

'Oh yes.' Her eyes widened.

He took her in directly, noting her sincerity. 'Landscape does me in. I've often wondered why. Probably I'm over-sensitive.' He frowned. 'My emotions get raided by the details, the symphonic simultaneity of the colours. Like a wine that brings out feelings. D'you know what I mean? And that's very important because then I can reach into things.' He seemed absorbed, ruminant. 'Beauty is a starting point for me, and here we have it all about, and actually, to tell you the truth, it makes me feel odd. I must say, it's quite uncomfortable being unlocked. At my age. I find myself thinking about everything, and not everything is easy to think about.' There was a pause. 'Michael's been marvellous.'

'What d'you think about?' she asked.

He stared at her. 'The war.'

Michael listened.

'Did you fight?'

'Round the corner. 1944.'

There was silence. Michael had not known this.

'It was interesting to see what they'd done to the most civilised place in the world. And what we did to get them out. It made me determined to hold on to the past. To keep life civilised you have to hold on to the forms, keep on retrieving every granule of civilisation to remind us what we are. The war cut across our lives, cut across the century and infected me with a passion for what is best in man. I mean, I've never written directly about it, and I don't talk about it, but the pity of it is always there and is a goad to one's best efforts.' He cleared his throat. 'I turn that over, and of course I think about the terrifying possibility that all this feeling won't find a form.' He looked at her from under his eyebrows. He was laying it on rather thickly. His sincerity came across like that.

She nodded.

'One has to get that piece of saved existence on to the bookshelf. Turn the miasma into sentences, paragraphs, a novel, an entity that seems so obvious to the reader and is so utterly mysterious to the writer. To answer your question another way, I come to Positano to ponder what on earth a novel is, what it might be. I've read and re-read novels to discover what they are, because their form tells me how to construe reality, and if you're an author, how to live your life.' He raised his eyebrows. 'You see, I believe in the novel quite religiously. It has occupied my whole life.'

Her lips were parted, her forefinger set on the stem of the glass. She was held by his candour.

He continued, aware of his audience, which now included Michael and Frances, and in doing so allowed Michael to realise that this monologue was an appeal to Adela's understanding of him as a man subject to the most precious, the most absolute imperatives. He was treating her as an equal, as someone in whom he could confide. It was his way of explaining his stance on the option, by going to the heart of things, declaring his commitment to the art of the novel, and implying that such commitment was opposed to adaptation, not as a matter of prejudice, but as an article of faith, against which there would be no argument.

Michael was pleased. Hilldyard was being kind to Adela. And he was speaking up for literature.

'D'you like James's writing?' said Frances.

Adela was thrown by the directness of the question. She glanced at Hilldyard, who looked down at his place-mat.

'Oh, very much,' she said.

'What've you read?'

Michael listened expressionlessly.

'Oh . . . Well, *Italian Murder* I've read three times. And *Arcadian Dreamers*. And . . . um . . .'

Hilldyard nodded and frowned, as if Adela were being put through an unnecessary test.

'It's a great privilege to meet you.'

'Thank you.'

She smiled. 'I think your books are marvellous, actually, but it sounds so glib just saying that.'

'It sounds very pleasant.'

'James never listens to praise,' said Frances. 'He's too much of a perfectionist to bear it. If a book's good enough for us, it can't be worthy of him.'

'I love praise, Frances. Of course it's usually too little too late.'

'I praised your last book, and you wouldn't even publish it.'

Michael was not sure where to rest his eyes.

'Which one was that?' asked Adela.

'I'm starving,' said the author. 'Can we get a waiter?'

Michael turned strenuously, raised his hand.

'The one he dedicated to me, of course.'

'I'll dedicate the next one to you.'

'Thanks a bunch. Just stick my name on anything.'

Michael had nowhere to look but at Frances. He was surprised to hear she had read the book, was its dedicatee.

The waiter arrived, his smile widening at the sight of Adela.

'James, see what Michael says. Let him read it, please.'

Hilldyard flinched. 'Come on, order.'

'You'd love it, Michael.' Frances was perfectly sincere. She seemed unaware of the delicacy of the subject.

Michael caught the look in Hilldyard's eye. He wanted nothing said.

The waiter raised his pen.

'We've both read the novel,' said Adela.

Michael glanced at her sharply.

'Really!'

121

'Yes. Really.'

Frances lit up. 'What did you think?'

'It doesn't matter,' said Hilldyard.

'What!'

'I don't want to talk about work. I want to enjoy my dinner.'

Michael could tell from Adela's bearing that she would not be warded off. She tossed her head, took a glass thoughtfully and then addressed herself directly to Hilldyard. 'If you really like praise you won't mind me saying I thought it was superb.'

Hilldyard rewarded her declaration with silence.

Michael fluffed his napkin. He was helplessly embarrassed.

'I told you so,' said Frances. 'What about you, Michael?'

He could hardly lie. 'Oh . . . I thought it was good.'

'Merely good!'

He blushed. 'Very good.'

'Then shouldn't it be published?'

'That's for James to decide.'

'Hang James! He's just an ego attached to a talent.'

'My reason in coming here—' began Adela.

'I know about that.' Hilldyard was quick. 'The less said the better.'

It seemed too peremptory.

'Oh, really, James!'

'Let's order,' said Michael.

They took note of the waiter, patiently waiting, and rechecked their menus. There was a moment of concentration.

'If I'd known you were against any kind of publication or adaptation I would not have presumed. We only ever wanted to do something serious, really worthy of the book.'

Hilldyard shook his head, as if nothing had been said.

Adela was surprised by the non-reaction.

'Was it going to be made into a film?' asked Frances.

'No,' said Michael, foolishly.

'Only with James's permission.'

'Marvellous!' said Frances. 'Who'd play James?'

Adela was forceful. 'We wanted to be absolutely faithful to the spirit of the book. This was never going to be an American film. The agent was completely out of line.'

'It isn't me.' Hilldyard winced. 'Josh is Josh. An invented character.'

'With an astonishing resemblance to James Hilldyard!'

Michael's heart subsided.

'Shane Hammond wants to play Josh,' said Adela.

Frances's palm banged the table. Her eyes were iridescent with joy. 'Uncs. D'you know who Shane Hammond is?'

'I'll have the calamari and then lasagne,' said the author, folding his menu shut and looking at the floor.

'He's a mega star.'

'Shall we order,' said Michael, who then ordered, and was followed by Frances and Adela. He caught the old man's eye, felt the pressure of Frances's tactlessness crossing the table like a line of incipient pain. Hilldyard's sensitivity showed in his bloodshot air of being annoyed and hounded at the same time. He was quite incapable of rehearsing the reasons he had given Michael; quite unable to change the subject, and was stewing in his powerlessness and embarrassment.

'What's going to happen?' said Frances.

There was cautious silence.

'How long were you in Rome?' asked Michael. She had already told him.

'They'd pay you a bomb.'

'Three-quarters of a million,' said Adela.

Michael nudged her with his leg.

Frances was open-mouthed. She looked at James in astonishment. 'You turned down three-quarters of a million!'

'I'd turn down more.'

'You're not serious!'

Michael saw Frances's shock, a look of incomprehension, almost of anger.

'I'm always serious.'

'You think that's wise?'

'It's a matter of principle.'

'What bloody principle?'

Hilldyard frowned uncomfortably.

Michael took the bottle. 'Wine, James?'

The old man set his hand on the glass, seeking composure. 'Do we have to rehearse this in front of other people?'

She scowled at the put-down but was instantly tart. 'I haven't a clue why anybody in your straits should turn down money.'

Adela sat rigidly, alarmed at what she had set off.

'If you don't want the cash you can bloody well give it to me.'

'Oh, you know why.'

'I know a lot of things.'

'It's none of our business,' said Michael.

'It's my business.' She was resilient. 'I'm his niece. Nieces have interests.'

'Because of Joan,' he said quickly, almost into his sleeve.

Frances raised her chin grandly. 'It's a bit late to be considerate of her feelings.'

'It's never too late,' he said softly.

'Shame you weren't then.'

'Which is why I'm repentant now.'

Frances stared over their heads at the night sky, as if divining her next rebuke. 'You always said she was dull.'

Michael was staggered.

'I never said that.'

'Whether you said it or not we all thought so.'

His voice was tight. 'You were a teenager.'

'Ah, but you confided in me.'

'I shouldn't have done.'

'But you did.' There was a flint-like hardness in her eyes. 'I mean, if Joan was so bloody marvellous, why did you have an affair?'

'It was wrong of me.'

'But you enjoyed it.'

Hilldyard shut his eyes.

'I don't believe in your repentance,' said Frances.

Michael's stomach tensed at the confrontation.

'Just think what they'd do to it!' said Hilldyard suddenly, his eyes watery with indignation. 'They'd make it into a bite-sized lump of formula emotion. A Big Mac plop of Hollywood sentimentality. A piece of corny tripe like *The Bridges of Madison County.*'

'Not at all!' said Adela, hands on the table's edge.

'They'll turn Josh into a down-home guy you can identify with, make his wife a manipulative *Dynasty* hag, throttle the script with wishfulfilment and cliché and probably add on some rock soundtrack to pacify the eighteen-to-thirty audience of candy-floss-sucking morons.'

'No, no, no.' Adela was vehement, both hands raised and fisted. 'How can you think we would do that?'

Hilldyard looked at her sternly.

'Excuse me,' she said, flattening her hands on the table and tossing her hair back. 'I'm not about to throw away my career fluttering eyelids in some corny American film. This is an art-house movie.'

'An art-house movie!' He was contemptuous. 'What the blazes is that?'

Frances watched with distempered interest.

'We are your readers,' she pleaded. 'Shane Hammond is an RSC actor. A literate man. If someone like that has the impulse to make a film of the book it's honourable. Sincere. What more could you hope for from a reader! A genuine creative response.'

Hilldyard gazed at her with dark assessment, needing a moment to absorb the challenge.

Michael felt compressed, on the edge of peril. He had created this scene, and its energies were out of control.

'Shane loves your writing,' Adela said desperately. 'He knows the book inside out. God, he's called me in the middle of the night to talk about it. This is not about money. It's about an actor's love for a fine novel and about wanting to realise a vision of it as a film. He would bring the best talents in the world to the project. He wants the most faithful adaptation.'

'Then why in God's name has he asked you to play Anna?'

'Are you playing Anna?' Frances was delighted.

'You're twenty years too young. What token of fidelity is that?'

Michael buried his face in his palms.

Adela took breath, was palely dignified, her seriousness fronting up to the challenge. She cast around, as though listening out for something, the recall of first impressions. 'Perhaps . . . maybe Anna's age is not all-important . . .'

'Oh really! Tell that to the author!'

'What about the reader?' she said. 'The book lives in the reader's imagination, too.'

'That's where it should stay.'

'You've created something that already exists for me. I mean, if I can feel that character, perhaps I can bring something. Maybe what you've written is an aspect of womanhood at any age.'

Hilldyard was beleaguered. 'There isn't a line on your face! You've never had children!'

'Neither have you. But you wrote this woman.'

'I've observed such a person.'

'And understood them by the same kind of artistic sympathy I employ as an actress. I have an imagination, too.'

'Adela!' He was fatigued now, but he came at her once more, with grave perseverance. 'Tell me honestly. Have you ever really been in love?'

She was startled, taken aback; her eyes flashed.

'D'you really know what love is?'

She shook her head in contempt of the enquiry.

Michael looked at her sideways. Frances hovered in fascination.

The question had impaled her dignity, and she came back tonelessly at first. 'I beg your pardon!'

Hilldyard held her gaze.

She stared back at him with inflamed beauty, scorning his challenge, demanding respect.

'I've been in love!'

'You'd be superb,' said Frances.

Hilldyard was expressionless.

'I understand your book, thank you very much.' She was galvanised now, revved up to maximum. 'I understand Anna's feelings. She feels love. But she's not going to be a man's salvation in some dated way. And no man is going to be hers. She'll experience love and life on her own terms and what is so compelling is the separateness of those realities.' She hesitated, seeing Hilldyard cup his forehead and look away. 'And Shane—' She was proving herself now, driving home what she knew, what she was worth. 'Shane understands Josh's character. Oh yes. The pathos of missing out on the great love, the person who makes you into yourself. Love is exactly what we understand this book to be about. And at a time when the identity of the sexes is changing, and the whole assumption of enduring relationships seems challenged by everything going on around us, your novel is like an experiment with the condition of love in modern times. There's no reassurance, no happy ending, no boy-gets-girl structure, and if that's a reflection of a modern reality, then the only way we can ever get something that subtle and true on the screen is to tell them, "James Hilldyard wrote this. Don't mess with it. It's the world we live in." That's what Shane wants to do. Make something unique. Something that you've given us.' She grappled with her napkin. 'And I admire him for it. I think it could be an overwhelming film.' She looked sideways, something vital discharged. She had said what she wanted to say and her expression now was of a nature opened out, fully evoked, glowing with adrenalin. She had done justice to herself, whatever the consequences. She had not surrendered.

Hilldyard was crumped down, mouth behind hand, eyes veiled, as if Adela had been addressing someone else. What she said had not revived him. He was deflated by the energy and sincerity of her speech.

Michael was demoralised by the sense of having no grip or purchase on the flow of things. He looked on as Hilldyard drew himself up from the chair, bringing his elbows and the whole forward weight of his authority on to the table, as if in a final settlement of the matter. He gazed heavily at Adela.

'I acknowledge your enthusiasm.' The voice was colourless. 'I credit you and Shane Hammond with the best intentions. I am prepared to concede that something of the book might translate if your aspirations were magically converted to celluloid.' He coughed lightly, drily. 'But I know about films, Adela. Yes, I do. A few years ago a book of mine was murdered. Mutilated. By very good people. Talented people. And I learned then that between the initial "passion"' – he spoke the word distinctly, deliberately – 'and the final cut come a sharp-suited throng of execs and marketing ghouls and other busybodies whose job it is to make money for the money by planing off every nob and barnacle of originality until the film is a synthetic unit of product fit for consumption by some normative cinema-goer, some bland, average, plastic non-person they call their audience.' He splayed his palm on the table, pressing the point down. 'Your best intentions are worth nothing to me.'

'We've more than best intentions,' she said tumultuously. 'We have Shane Hammond, who has good taste and incredible leverage.'

'An overpaid actor.'

'Who can get the best scriptwriters and directors,' she pleaded. 'Who has script approval on every movie he does. Whose judgement is so good people trust him implicitly.'

'How can I rely on the taste of a man I've never met who owes me nothing?'

Adela hesitated. She was astonished by Hilldyard. He seemed to offer no good faith, no trust in others. His scepticism was unmannerly.

She glanced at Michael, then back at Hilldyard. 'You want insurance?'

'Insurance! I want to burn the blasted book.'

She blinked. 'Option the rights to Michael. Let him produce the film.'

'Michael!'

Michael felt blood rushing to his face as if he had been in some way compromised.

Hilldyard showed the horror of total astonishment.

'Michael's a producer,' she said quickly. 'He'd be perfect.'

'Adela . . .' Michael sat up. He was completely unprepared.

'Michael?' Hilldyard's expression demanded an immediate denial.

'And he knows your writing backwards. He's the best person in the world to develop the film. It strikes me as obvious.'

Hilldyard was scrutinising his reaction, as though Michael were involved in a pact. 'Is this your idea?'

She kicked him under the table.

'You want to adapt my book? You want to go to Hollywood?'

'I'm sure he does. This could be Michael's big break.'

Michael laughed, blushing again. 'I've never even considered it.'

'Consider it now,' she said.

'You don't seriously believe in adapting my work for the screen?'

Michael could not catch up with himself except to realise that Adela's nerve was incredible.

'I haven't thought about it.'

'D'you need to think about it?'

They stared at each other in a crisis of misunderstanding.

'I wouldn't contemplate anything without your approval.'

'D'you want me to approve? Is that what this is all about?'

Hilldyard had made a false connection.

'I don't . . . It's not about anything.'

'Isn't it?' He nodded at the actress.

'Michael loves the book. He's a distinguished producer. And if somebody wants to finance a film with top casting he's the best man for the job.'

'Let him speak for himself, please.'

He was being tested on a question of principle, a test he had not invited, had no preparation for.

'Michael would be terrific,' she said.

It was almost as though Hilldyard had caught on faster, seen into the possibilities for him, was already abreast of his feelings and wanted to ward him off.

'You wouldn't consider it?'

'It's not a taboo,' said Adela.

Hilldyard's eyes glimmered with resolution, the desire to influence, to counteract.

Michael scratched his head, felt Adela all over his face, latched to him. 'I'd do whatever's in your best interests.'

'Don't equivocate.'

He would not undermine her completely. He had his own stance. 'A good film could sell millions of copies.'

'Of a book I don't want to publish!'

'Well . . .'

'This your recommendation? You, of all people?'

'James, please. I . . .'

'Ganging up with that lot?'

He was mortified. It was like a slap on the face.

'I'm trying to see it from every angle.'

'See it from the angle of taste and say no.'

He had lapsed unforgivably, had shown doubt when he should have been certain.

'Then, no.'

'Taste,' said Frances, 'has nothing to do with it.'

'I entirely respect your feelings. You know I do.'

'What about morals, James?'

A look passed between author and niece. Hilldyard's expression was electrically serious. Frances had said enough and he wanted her to shut up.

'Our great novelist is a coward who can't bear to think the world will find him out.'

He was opaque, expressionless.

'But people will find out. Sooner or later. You can't escape from your own life.'

'Be quiet!'

Frances smiled across the table.

'I'm not interested in producing this film,' said Michael. He looked at Adela.

'The trouble with James is that he wants everyone to believe in the moral superiority of the novelist.'

'Nonsense!'

'But it's a little difficult to be this exalted, elevated figure' – Frances addressed the others, eyes bright with mockery – 'when your private life's a scandal. That's the only reason you won't publish. You're worried about your reputation. You are a fraud, James.'

The blow of her rudeness left a hiatus of shock.

Frances caught Michael's eye as though she were inspired. 'All your aesthetic ideals would sound a bit hollow if people knew what you'd been up to.'

'I've never set myself up as . . .'

'Quickly! Publish before the newspapers find out. Then at least you won't be accused of hypocrisy.'

Hilldyard gave her a glinting, sidelong look. He had lost all authority.

'Somebody'll blag. You'll be written up as a Graham Greene sex-fiend.'

His cheeks reddened. He was lost for words.

'It's worth good money,' she said, puffing on a cigarette, her sharp elbows on the arms of the chair.

Hilldyard was silently appalled, and averted his eyes from any contact with Michael's or Adela's as the first course arrived on the arms of two waiters, and suddenly bread-baskets were swapped, wine bottles exchanged and a conjuring of arms brought seafood and salami, and the embracing warmth of Italian service, all eyelashes and teeth and quick glances at the voluptuous miracle of Adela, sitting with swirling hair and ripe bosom before her place-mat.

'Go and make the film, Michael.' Hilldyard bumped the table with the edge of his fist.

Michael's hairline retracted.

The author turned on him, confronted him across the table, his energy repossessed.

'If that's what you really want.'

He did not understand, could not grasp it.

Adela seized his arm. She was stiff with excitement.

Hilldyard had not defended himself. He had collapsed prematurely.

'I didn't say I wanted it!'

'It's yours for the taking.'

Frances's eyes glimmered victoriously. She clutched her cigarette in the steepled fingers of both hands, a spasm of self-applause.

'I wouldn't go against your wishes.'

'Forget my wishes.'

Adela squeezed his arm, holding him in place.

'Think about it, James.'

'It's your turn to think.'

'Sleep on it!'

'You sleep on it! You're taking my life in your hands.'

'Let's order champagne,' said Adela. 'I've got an Amex.'

Michael held the author's eye and felt the transmission of something cold, as though, suddenly, they were strangers.

Chapter Eleven

'WELL . . . ?'

She was inflamed, radiant; her eyes glittered excitedly.

They had been walking, it seemed, to her hotel, but had drifted through the piazza with its taxi rank and *cambio* sign and lamplit streams of bougainvillaea to the Via dei Mulini, which took them down to the bottom of town, to its basement of steps and narrow passages and the harsh brightness of shops, restlessly open.

He had managed the odd tight remark, holding himself in until he knew what to say. Adela walked ahead with all the pride of a woman in a beautiful dress, alive to the fragrance of night and the special romance of a Riviera town.

'Well!' She turned to face him. A flight of steps ran down to the restaurants on the front: Chez Black's, Da Peppino, Tre Sorelle. 'Fancy a drink?' She let down her hair, shaking it loose on her shoulders.

'Adela!' It was almost a shout.

She was startled.

'You had no right!'

Adela frowned at the harsh loudness of his voice.

'What were you doing?' he said.

She was shot up, panicked by his anger. 'I thought you'd be pleased!'

He was possessed by an almost uncontrollable indignation. 'Pleased!'

'I'm sorry!'

'Adela!'

She had come between them, he realised.

'You never even consulted me!'

'It was only a suggestion.'

132

'Only a suggestion! Only a suggestion! Are you really that desperate?'

Her pleading expression clouded and she turned away from him suddenly.

'Yes, probably.'

'Oh God!'

Hilldyard had gone quiet for the rest of the meal. Afterwards they had shaken hands, but without warmth. The author had turned away with old man's eyes.

It had never occurred to him that Hilldyard might be Adela's victim, rather than she his. And what maddened him was that he had sided with her, or seemed to. Something had prompted him to support her side of the argument, to strike an independent note for the sake of debate – a terrible mistake.

'What a bloody mess!'

She caught his sleeve, made him look at her. She was abruptly determined. 'This bloody mess could be your big chance.'

He could smell her perfume, her make-up.

'This could be so good for you.' She held him, shaking the point in.

'How would you know what's good for me?'

'Let's find out. Let's talk about it.'

She was suddenly vulnerable in her low-cut dress, out here in the cool and the darkness, her skin exposed to the night.

'There's nothing to talk about.'

She tugged his arm. 'Come for a drink!'

'I don't want a drink!'

'Walk with me!'

She squeezed hard, a pleading pressure. She brushed hair off her face so he could see her properly, the eyes looking up at him, the raised chin. She was almost courageous, standing firm and braving his anger head on; though in her look of determination he saw something frightening. Only he stood between Adela and the film.

'Can we talk about it, please?' she said.

'Forget it.'

'Just walk with me.'

She took his hand and pulled him in the direction of the steps.

He followed reluctantly down the steps and along the concourse to the edge of the beach and the fairy-lit pines. The night gathered over them, taking off into limitless black from the line of restaurants on the front. The sea continued its lull of white noise, a subdued roar and crash that mingled with the voice of a singer in Chez Black's.

They walked past fishing boats and harbour lanterns and found themselves rising on a ramp that led away from the beach to the cliffside walkway. The sea spread its docile murk below. Trees braced the path. Night came down to snaffle the weak bloom of an iron lamp, and soon they were walking through a tangy, moist darkness, behind coastal turrets and wind-worn pines.

Adela stopped to sit on a parapet, inclining her ear to the sound of the sea. Her arms were luminous. She hummed a tune caught from Chez Black's.

He stood back from the ledge, keeping a distance. He was unsure of her now. Adela had changed.

'You know . . .' She faced him in the darkness. 'I really want to get in that water.'

He shook his head.

'We could swim out and see the lights.'

'It's October,' he said tightly.

'Skinny-dip.'

She went on ahead and he followed her reluctantly into the darkness of crowding trees.

They crossed a creaking bridge and went past the restaurant on stilts, a wooden structure, exposed to the heavens, deserted. Soon they were on jingling pebbles, treading across the long crescent of the beach. The waves broke on the ledge of wet stones, making all their daytime sounds, but seeming ominous now, as if the water at night were something alive, restlessly active under the cover of darkness. He had no idea where they were going, except away from the lights and the restaurants.

She dropped down on to the shingle, arms bracing legs, moonlight touching her brow. 'Are you going to talk to me?'

He stood with his hands in his pockets, gazing into gloom. He was still angry, but his anger took a different tack – contempt for her naivety, her childlike optimism.

'OK, great. So what happens when the film is crap?'

'The film will be wonderful.'

Hilldyard would never forgive him, he thought.

'It'll be your creation. Your movie.'

He laughed harshly. 'Adela. I've never made a film.'

'Believe in yourself, Michael.'

134

He did not believe in himself remotely, but that had nothing to do with it.

'How on earth could a first-time film producer hold out against people like Shane Hammond and Frank Coburn and all those Hollywood shysters? I couldn't promise James anything. It would be a double betrayal. Producing the film at all and then losing control of it.'

She was calm. Her voice was placatory. 'Shane needs you.'

'Oh, please! Shane Hammond doesn't need me. No movie star needs Michael Lear! Don't be ridiculous.'

'Nobody else can get the rights. Only you.'

She turned, and although her face was shadowy in the dark, he could feel the intentness of her regard. A notion was growing inside her.

'You're in a strong position.'

Michael said nothing. He could hear her breathing deepen.

'Michael! You're in a position of incredible leverage.'

The echo of Nick Adamson. At first he did not follow her line of thought. He kicked back in reflex.

'I don't want incredible leverage.'

'Michael! Concentrate!'

He stared at her, his heart racing.

She was realising the logic of her own suggestion, catching up with Adamson's assessment, lapping it.

'Shane will be eternally indebted to you. You can dictate your terms.'

'Oh, money . . .'

'Creatively! This could be your film.'

He laughed again, this time warmly. Adela was losing the plot. The idea was degenerating into farce.

'Hey, movie stars don't really dig ultimatums.'

She cocked her head – special insight. 'He doesn't have the choice.'

'What!'

'If he wants the film.'

'He'll run a mile if I . . .'

'You're not going to betray Hilldyard. That's a given. Shane's only chance is to get the book on your terms. He'll accept because he'll understand you won't compromise. Your position's non-negotiable.'

He stood on the pebbles, tensely poised, the sea wind in his face.

'Michael, I know actors.'

Her voice was gently insistent. She believed what she was saying.

'Shane's . . . quite isolated.'

He sat down on his own patch of pebbles, put his hands on his knees.

Her hair was being lifted by the breeze into a flickering taper. Moonlight caught the edge of the arm she was leaning on, the planes of her cheek and forehead. She was sculptural in profile, shoulders contoured in light and shade.

'And he's pragmatic,' she said firmly.

Her insight arrested him. She saw more deeply into the situation. He wondered for an instant whether she had pushed him by chance or cunning into the centre of her plans. She was perceptive and quick and may have followed the logic of the situation intuitively.

'He belongs to the big, bad world, Michael. But you have nothing to lose. There's nobody else in Hollywood like you. He'll have to compromise or walk away from the project and I don't think he could bear to do that.'

He gazed at the sea and suddenly he was tired, as though the momentous opportunity she had put before him were at last real, there to be grabbed by someone with enterprise and nerves of steel. She had seen into the future for him, made him its centre, and the idea would seem ingenious to her, a great way for them both to get ahead.

'I have Hilldyard's friendship to lose,' he said, after a while.

She was thoughtful for a moment. 'Doesn't he want to make you happy?'

The question unsettled him. She was scrutinising his relationship with the author.

'My happiness is my business.'

'It could be his gift for everything that you've done for him. How could he deny you that? It's only a film, Michael. Keeping your friendship surely means more to him than keeping the film rights!'

He stared at her. Once again, she reprised Adamson, but in her own commonsensical manner. And common sense could always maintain, in the nicest way, that Hilldyard's objections were ill-founded, aesthetically prim, that turning books into films was no great moral question, and thus the onus was on Hilldyard to be reasonable and accommodating, or forfeit his entitlement to respect. Why should not great writers be subject to the same standards of reasonableness as the rest of us?

He said nothing.

'He can't expect you to stay here for the rest of his life holding his hand.'

'I'm not holding his hand!'

'Don't be offended. I don't mean to offend you.'

He was upset to be depicted in such a way.

'I've told you what we're doing.'

'What are you doing?'

He felt the dampness of the pebbles under his trousers and began to wonder wearily whether he and Adela had anything in common, whether she was challenging him to define himself in terms that she could understand, or subtly undermining his commitment to Hilldyard. He wondered whether the things he cared about could really interest her. She had seemed to be an artist.

Above all he wanted to be understood by her. He clasped his hands together.

'What are we doing?' he repeated. 'We're being true to ourselves.'

'What then?'

'I'll tell you when I know.'

'What will you know?'

'The future.'

She turned to face him in the darkness. 'Well, maybe this is it.'

'This?'

There was a peculiar silence. She was looking at him, but he could not see her clearly.

'What's happening now,' she said lightly.

'Now?'

'Right now.'

He felt something stir inside him.

She inhaled and turned, looking out to sea again.

There was too much silence.

She suddenly turned back and gazed at him. 'Michael . . .'

It sounded like a plea and it made his heart race.

'Listen, will you. You know what?'

'What!'

'You don't . . .'

'Don't what?'

'You don't have to be tragic,' she said.

He was stunned by the word. 'Tragic!'

'Come on. Come with me.'

She reached for a clasp. He heard the zip pull, saw the triangle of skin enlarge as the material divided. She rose quickly, sent the dress to her feet, unfastened her bra, shimmied off knickers. 'Don't look,' she said, making her bare way over the pebbles.

The figure dropped away, a monochrome sylph, intrepidly descending to the surf. He heard a gasp, almost of pleasure, then a splash. She was up to her thighs in water, wading in deeper, moonlight all around her.

He sat, heart racing. The impulse rose and fell.

She flipped and dived, soaking her hair through, twisting and turning in the water.

He pulled a shoelace, gripped his heel.

'It's lovely,' she called, her voice small and clear. She was facing the beach, the twinkling lights, the serrated mountainline way above Positano.

He could see her scooting sideways across the bay, relishing the element, its warmth and buoyancy. She inhabited the water easily. He felt a tingling at the thought of her body, a heat in the heart.

She had changed the subject, all right.

He turned a pebble over in his hand.

The situation, it taunted him, mocked seriousness. He was spare, marooned. It congealed inside him, the ache moulding him. Strength was to feel like this and still carry on. He had nothing to cling to but his unknown destination.

He looked at his hands, joined together, and knew he must not produce the film. He was on a different course, drawn away from such distractions. He saw all that as the outside life, a remote state of being, worlds away from the heart of things.

He pressed the pebble in his palm, glanced at the dark puddle of her dress.

He heard the cry faintly at first, like a seagull's. The surf muffled hearing, was softly deafening.

He rose tentatively to his feet. She was nowhere to be seen. He strained his eyes to see through the darkness, seeking information.

He started off, walking over the shingle, checking the waters to his left. There were no lights, no points of reference.

'Adela,' he called. His voice went into blackness.

There were marks of white and other flecks on the surface that held him up as he scanned across the sea. The pebbles made a bright jingle underfoot, and he halted to hear better.

The beach curved round to a point several hundred yards ahead and Michael found himself attacking the distance with a nauseous sprint that jarred his joints and bruised his feet. He was running too far, not far enough, haring off in the wrong direction.

He heard it again. Cut down to size by distance.

His shirt came off, then shoes. She called again, and the screech in her voice infected him with terror as he tore off his trousers and staggered down the slope to the water's edge. He inhaled violently, bracing himself against the shock, and plunged into the foam, beating out a crawl that smacked into the waves with all his might. The coldness forced air from his lungs, scalded his face and his eyes.

It took him a nightmare of striving to fight through the water's moving mass carrying him back, overthrowing efforts. She appeared, disappeared, vanished into darkness, bobbed up again, not seeming closer.

When he reached her, she grabbed him and he went down under her, mouth and nose filling with water as she threw her whole desperate weight on to his shoulders, her knees hitting his chest, her foot on his shin; and he barrelled and overturned, lungs breaking, and felt a gigantic spasm of terror as if he too would drown, and somewhere in the graspless water found the strength to kick up, breaking surface as she slipped under, lost for a second until his arm caught her and he pulled her to him violently.

She choked up water, and Michael took in great gasps, beating with his legs till they ached. He held her to him, arm around neck, chest heaving beneath her.

An age passed as they fought back against the current. Slowly, he recovered the control of his breath; strength went back into his arms and legs. She spluttered and coughed and clutched with both hands to his forearm, allowing herself to be towed.

They reached the shallows, and he gently released her. She found her depth and coasted in on the tide. He moved to help on the stones but already she was rising from the water. She wanted to be out of the water.

He followed hesitantly. She turned to face him. She was shaking, chin wobbling, teeth chattering.

He flung her his shirt, searched for his other clothes. He patted the pebbles, found one shoe, then another; hopped into trousers.

She wriggled into his shirt and stood there, waiting.

They made their way back across the beach. He took her hand

from time to time, whenever she lost balance. She was hunched against the cold. When they reached her clothes, he looked the other way. He was all shaken up. His legs felt like jelly.

'Michael.' The voice was plaintive. She was coming out of shock, returning to her senses.

'Sorry.'

She stood there in her green dress, her hair long and slick. He moved towards her, receiving his shirt. She flopped on to his shoulder, and he allowed himself to embrace her.

'I don't know what happened. I . . .'

'It's OK.'

She was shivery.

'Come on,' he said. 'Let's go back.'

Beyond the boarded hotel was a short-cut up to the Viale, a zigzag of innumerable steps. They rose gradually above beach-level, looking down on the roof of the hotel, and were soon in the region of orange groves and eucalyptus trees, panting in the spicy air. On the higher flights Michael became red-faced. His thighs burned. Adela trailed wearily, hand on rail, her dress hanging less immaculately than before.

They gained the top and made their way through narrow alleys towards the Viale. From there it was a short walk to her hotel.

Michael slowed his pace, heard her coming up behind him.

She stopped suddenly, looked across the ravine. With her hair damp and drawn back she seemed more vivid, her eyebrows clearer. She was back in possession of herself. An exerted body stood next to him, exhaling vital energy.

He could think of nothing to say. He was not sure where things stood.

'What time is your flight?' he said.

'What flight?'

'Your flight tomorrow.'

She leaned over the rail, gazed into the ravine. 'Three forty-five.'

There was a silence.

'I'm not going back,' she said.

'You're what?'

'This is more important.'

His chest went off in alarm.

She tilted her head. 'This will be the making of Michael Lear.'

He held her gaze; and then smiled uncomfortably. 'Why should you want to make me?'

140

She looked back at him serenely. 'Well, you saved my life.'

He shook his head, would not take her meaning.

'I need your help with those Hollywood shysters.'

They regarded each other closely. There was a pause.

'Aren't I enough as I stand?'

She seized on the question. 'Enough for what?'

His jaw moved. 'Enough to be going on with?'

She raised her eyebrows. 'Going where?'

He exhaled away the tension.

She placed a hand on his forearm, applied soft pressure. 'You could be wealthy.'

His eyes were vacant for a moment.

'Money would give you the power to do what you believe in.'

'I can do that here.'

'Hilldyard's successful,' she said. 'There's no harm in success.'

Her upturned eyes were so close, so eloquent. He looked at her breathlessly.

'Michael.' She said it with feeling. 'You have so much potential.'

He stared at her lips. He could not restrain himself; he had earned the right to say this. 'You're beautiful.'

There was a flicker in her eye, of surprise.

She released his sleeve but held his gaze.

His heart rushed away with itself. He cupped a hand to his face. 'You appreciate my dilemma?'

She knew more than she could say. He followed the calculation in her switching eyes.

'I haven't decided, you see.'

She nodded, mouth corrupted by concentration.

'I might not get involved.' He shrugged.

Her eyebrows sailed up vulnerably. 'It can't happen without you!'

'But . . .' He was determined. 'You'd appreciate my reasons?'

She frowned.

He had to be explicit. To care about anything was to be explicit. 'I don't want to be dismissed from your life just because I won't produce this film.'

She looked at him in surprise again, as though the phrase revealed new things. 'But you would have dismissed me!'

He shook his head, denying it.

She looked as though she wanted to hold on to something, the essence of the point. 'I'd have to go back.'

He sought her out; tested the eyes. 'Would you?'

'I can only stay on if this goes ahead.'

'Well . . . I see.'

She blinked. 'Why should I stay otherwise?'

He would not say.

There was a silence of seconds.

'I mean, it's lovely here, but I'm trying to have a career.'

He understood this too. It was becoming clear now.

'You won't detest me then?' he said.

She looked painfully askance. 'I won't be around to detest you. We might never meet again.'

'Can we meet in London?'

'Oh . . . maybe . . . If fate decrees.'

'Would you decree?'

She gave him a look. 'I'd always be interested to know how Michael Lear was getting on in his parallel universe.'

'I'm not in a parallel universe!'

'You're in another world!'

'No!'

She looked at him curiously and then incredulously, her loveliness affected by an emotion she could not conceal. 'Then where the hell are you!'

He took her hand, pressed it between palms and looked at her before he kissed her.

Her lips were dry.

'You know I've got a boyfriend,' she said tonelessly.

Michael enfurled her in his arms, and this time their lips parted as they kissed, and he could feel the softness and fullness of that mouth, a luxurious sensation. He put everything into his hug, a big squeeze that went into the soft pad of her front.

He released her, and she gave him a look, then sidled around him.

He came after her, wanting her lips again.

She responded consummately, as if passion were ready, taking his face in her hands, kissing him with all her mouth then sending him back with a twisted, lovely smile. 'Good-night.'

He held her hand for a moment.

'I'm off tomorrow.'

'Adela!'

She pulled her fingertips across his outstretched hand.

'Call me.' She was sliding away.

'Don't go.'

'Thank you for rescuing me.'

She drew off down the passage, spinning on her heel, all waist and derrière, a brisk clip past the sleeping houses and shuttered *pensioni*.

'Oh,' he said softly, to the disappearing figure. Soon she was gone.

Chapter Twelve

HE SAT OUTSIDE ON the terrace of the hotel. He felt trapped, as if held in check, everything but his pulse frozen into a position of sculptural fixity.

He stared at the necklace of lights on the mountain opposite and felt a craze of sensations.

She had attacked his mouth, a cannibal kiss, a flesh-eating kiss, all lips and juice, and the squeeze of her hand on his cheek was tight as a prayer. He had felt all the desire in her.

He exhaled jaggedly, letting out steam into the autumn air. He had the peculiar sense of being askew to everything, in a strange relation to the chairs, tables, the flowerpots, the local darkness, the ambience of a place he had previously worn like a coat. He could not begin to think.

Michael released a soft vibrant little moan, the fragment of a tune. It was strange to discover what lay beneath his sensible surface. The trapped ardour scalded him.

In his hotel room he was surprised to see a fax from Adamson on the bed; and a message that Rick Weislob from Coburn Agency had phoned him and would call back.

He read the fax with curiosity. And then the phone rang.

Adamson had already contacted Weislob. He had tried to draw him out, offering open-palm discussions on the project. In the fax he proposed that Michael touch base with Weislob as a prelude to formal negotiation. At all events he was supposed to phone Adamson before taking Weislob's call. They needed to shape tactics.

Michael was astonished.

He picked up the receiver. After the click there was an American voice on the line.

'Mr Lear, I have Rick Weislob for you.'

He frowned.

Rick Weislob: the turd bullet.

Shane's agent.

'Hello,' he said.

There was no doubt about it, the man on the line was pure agent, absolute agent: the token preliminaries, the pressure of time in the tone, the asides to people in his office, which failed to distinguish between the immediate realm of his will in LA – where he could kick ass personally – and the ear of a man thousands of miles away. Weislob was used to the long-distance business call; used to cutting deals and inflicting pain across time-zones. One heard the hard drive of a man committed to seventy calls a day. He was on the line, in the line, leaning into the call. He needed to make deals and get results and lived acutely in the mouthpiece of the present.

He had a seesaw, airy tone well cadenced with false reasonableness. He could wax predictable for a couple of sentences, striking easy notes of concern and common sense, and then go hard, control the call.

'We have ears,' he was saying, 'little birds that tell us things, and we've heard about you and your company and your conversations with Nick Adamson.'

He was still arranging himself, getting a pillow between the small of his back and the bedstead. He had been intercepted by a total stranger.

'Nick has spoken to you?'

'Oh sure.'

'You know Nick?'

'We know everybody. That's what we do here. Know what's going on.'

He had taken Weislob's call in spite of himself. He did not need either Rick Weislob or Nick Adamson in his life.

'Can I be straight with you, Mr Lear? Your enquiries on *The Last Muse* are causing a little concern over here.'

Adamson's overtures were represented as Michael's enquiries.

'My enquiries?'

'I think you know what I mean.'

He sensed what was coming. He was fascinated.

'Seems your a ways behind on the history of the project.'

There was a pause. He felt his heart beating.

'I don't think so.'

'Let me tell you. *Last Muse* is under confidential submission to Coburn Agency. We have a six-month first refusal on the movie rights through Curwen Associates. During that window no other entities have right of access to the manuscript. This novel is absolutely not in the public domain.'

'Just a minute . . .'

'Anything you say in relation to that title is bonded by confidentiality. Don't read it. Don't copy it. It's not on the open market. Michael, I want you to erase *Last Muse* from your mind and not discuss it with anyone. We have rights and we are going to protect them with whatever it takes and then some. That's what you need to know.'

Michael scratched his leg. His skin was salty and dry. He needed a bath.

It was strange to be lied to outright by a man he had never met. His response was impulsive. 'My information is quite different.'

'Then it's wrong.'

He hesitated, swallowed. 'Adela Fairfax told me your agency failed to acquire the rights.'

Weislob snapped out a laugh. 'She told you that?'

Michael looked down at the bedcover, at the pattern on the material. 'And so did Basil Curwen.'

'Michael, listen.' The tone was patronising. 'Adela is a wonderfully enterprising gall and I think she's a swell actress with a beautiful body and a great future, but the babe is not state of the art when it comes to movie deals.'

'Yes, well, maybe Basil Curwen knows a thing or two about movie deals?'

'Baz and I talk daily. We're doing the deal right now. This is a very complicated financing structure, and he's hanging in there for his client's best interests. Off of the record I'd say we'd be signed and notarised in a week. We have no need of other partners.'

He had certain knowledge of the truth, a sense of it being pushed around, the swell of indignation.

'Hilldyard told me! He turned you down personally!'

'False.' Weislob was hard, buzzed up. 'Hilldyard vetoed certain elements but has not categorically blocked the project. He's a talented man, and we respect his views. This is a collaborative process and there's nothing you can add. Like I say, this is a totally go project.'

Weislob had his story worked out and Michael was stunned by the mendacity of it. No way could Curwen bind Hilldyard without consent. He had never consented to a six-month 'window'. The agent was daringly and assertively lying.

He clenched the phone, hardly believing the exchange. 'Why are you calling me?'

'Courtesy. I'd hate for you to be misinformed or waste your valuable time in any way.'

'Courtesy?'

'Hey, Michael. Private function. No crashers.'

There was a pause. They measured each other's silence.

'If you guys are trying to get rich on this movie, forget it.' His rudeness was confident, brinkmanlike, right in the face.

Michael let the breath come out of him slowly. He looked around at the bare hotel walls, at the wardrobe and writing desk.

'I want you to call off Nick Adamson. Tell him there's a mistake. Tell him to, like, lose it.'

Adamson had put Weislob in play, and Weislob had shown his hand to Michael. Beyond the smokescreen of legal rights was something harder, more determined: vested interests, territory. Weislob was drawing a line.

'You there, Michael?'

It came to him as he sat with the phone on his cheek that things had changed. Things were re-aligning.

He blinked, a heart flutter. 'Who's attached to this project?'

'Uh?'

'Who are your elements and financiers?'

'You don't need to know that.'

He looked at his hands. He had held her waist in these hands.

'Michael, I'm going to put this in writing. I want this conversation on record.'

He thought of the expression on her face as she turned. Everything he might feel was contained in that moment.

'I'm asking questions because I think you need help,' he said.

'Wrong again.'

'Hammond won't appreciate a second fuck-up.' His anticipation hovered over the line.

'Excuse me?'

'You'd lose your job.'

There was a theatrical gasp, then a professional silence. Weislob's tone was measured. 'I don't think you're getting the message here.'

'The message is bullshit.'

'What!'

'Your clients are interesting. Your tactics are crap.'

The agent was loud-voiced. 'I'm pulling in our attorney. Janine, conference Gloria. We'll spike this right now.'

'I'm producing this film.' He was bent over the phone, wrestling into the call, fist tight on the receiver. 'I'll talk to you about casting. I'm interested in actors and directors, certainly, but I don't want to hear any more shite about your so-called rights. You have no rights.'

His heart was pounding. Through the riot of adrenalin he could sense Weislob's confusion.

'You can skip the pressure-silence, Rick.'

'I'm . . . This is unbelievable. Really! I'm appalled.' The voice was trumpety, strident. 'This is one hundred per cent my baby and there's no way, José I'm letting some small-time British producer leech on to it. This is a done deal. The fees are designated. Budget's closed. We have a producer. We have all the elements. There's no fat on this picture. No pickings for late-comers . . .'

'Make some.'

'Hey! Who d'you think you are, bozo? A no-credits no-track get-out-of-our-faces nonentity. From where I'm standing you're totally invisible. We don't need you. We don't want you. Keep your head down and step out of it, because Frank Coburn is not into jerking off Britpack wannabes.'

'Take it or leave it.'

'No, sucker. You clear out.'

'I'm not clearing out.'

'Don't fuck with us. We'll freeze your company. We'll injunct you off of the fucking map. Take on Frank, he'll rip your cock off and shove it up your ass. You got nothing!'

'I've got the option.'

'What!'

'Signed.'

Weislob was mute. Michael could hear him breathing through his mouth.

'Don't believe you.'

He had put himself in play, and the implications were proliferating.

'An option agreement. Signed today.'

The agent could neither believe nor ignore such a statement.

'What is signed?'

'An option agreement.'

Weislob took a moment to file his response, a hiatus in which the call seemed cut off. Michael waited, tongue behind his teeth. He experienced direct power over a man five thousand miles away.

'Basil Curwen has not confirmed this.'

Curwen would need to be squared.

'Basil's in London.'

There was a gasp. 'You went behind the agent!'

'I have a close relationship with the author.'

There was another pause. Weislob was thinking on his feet.

'Can you fax me the agreement?'

Michael sucked his teeth. He felt dizzy. 'Confidential.'

'Then fax it "in confidence".'

'I don't think so.'

Weislob needed to adjust before he spoke. Instinct would have told him to close the call, to duck out and regroup; but he was too far in. When he spoke, his tone had softened. 'Michael . . . you're like talking to a guy who's been negotiating those rights every day for two months.'

'You don't believe me?'

'Seeing is certainly believing.'

He let the line run silent for a while.

Weislob laughed nervously. 'Man, wanna come to the table, gotta play your hand.'

'I don't want to come to the table.'

His statement was so stark, so upfront, such bad news for Weislob.

'You can't dig twenty million out of the UK.'

It was a weak point for him to make.

'It isn't twenty.'

'Sure it's twenty. This is a locomotive A-picture. What you doing? Cramming it with a wad of Blighty thesps, some kind of limited-theatrical-release deal?'

'I didn't say that.'

'Michael, we have a package of elements that'll kick this movie's ass into worldwide distribution and heavy box office. It's a custom-made love story for the big screen. Not some fringe festival bullcrap.'

Weislob had decided to believe him. There was a short interval of resolution before 'belief' registered pragmatically.

'Would you consider a buy-out?' He was open, unabashed. He was not wasting time. 'Want me to pitch you some figures?'

'The author's overriding concern is fidelity to the letter and spirit of the book. If I have a better chance of achieving that with European partners, I'll go that route. If your team can make the commitment, let's talk. I'm not interested in an Americanised version of the story.'

'Oh absolutely,' he rallied. 'Like, this is cross-over art house. Totally. I have no problem with that, and come to think of it, I can't imagine an actor of Shane's status thinking any other way about the project. This is a book that's dear to him. And, you know, James Hilldyard is like the Big Cheese.'

Michael said nothing.

'He's the Dean.'

He was calm now. 'When you packaged the money, did they read the book?'

'Well, to be perfectly frank, with Shane attached we got a green pretty much off coverage. Reader's report plus director's notes.'

'Could you fax me them?' Already, he was thinking ahead.

'I'll trade the notes for the option agreement.'

The option agreement was essential to them. Michael could accept that.

'Let me give you a fax number.'

He was committing himself to Hilldyard's signature. To be a player one had to gamble and take the risk of one's negotiating stance.

Weislob read off the numbers. 'Know what, Michael? This is good development. I'm sure we can do some talking. I'd like to turn it over here with Frank and Tom Mahler, who are keenly involved in this project, bring the guys up to speed and get back to you tomorrow. I'll fax the notes, you do me the option, and we'll talk soon.'

'I'm glad we've spoken.'

'You bet.' He sounded bright, bushy. He had an urgent need to speak to his superiors. 'Ciao, my friend. Take care of yourself.'

He sat still with the telephone in his hand, noting a coldness in his frame of mind, as if he had become someone else. He wondered what he had done. It was certainly done and in full consciousness, and as he rose from the bed and walked around the room, he held on to an executive mode of thought.

Hilldyard would need to sign tomorrow. He needed to talk to Adamson, get a deal structure; he needed to brainstorm the film, have a vision, define parameters. He needed to evaluate the elements and consider the relationships. He would have to shortlist screen-writer alternatives and get wised up on production procedures under the American system. He would have to be different with these people: Hammond and Coburn, the financiers. In this line you had to have more energy than the people you were dealing with.

He sat down on the end of the bed. He had surprised himself. He had followed an impulse. He was held by the thought of it.

Later, he stepped out on to the balcony, reintroducing himself to the night air. Somewhere over the hill, beyond the lamps and window lights, she would be fast asleep.

While the bath ran, he regarded himself nude in the mirror, returning a self-portrait stare emptied of expression, as though in the mirror might be seen, almost by stealth, the person she had seen, looking back at him, reflecting his essence. And for a moment it seemed like the man in the mirror was staring back at him: staring him down.

Two calls.

The first in the night:

'Frank Coburn speaking.'

The voice was thick-cut and deep over the long-distance line. There was gravel in the back of it, a huge resonance on the phone.

'I'm told we have a problem.'

Michael's astonishment caused a hard beat against his chest. He pulled the sleep from his eyes.

Coburn had the voice of a god, tarry with authority. 'Either we dump the project or cut a deal.' Steady breathing. 'I kinda prefer the latter.'

He wanted to say something, assert himself.

'You're in Naples?'

'This . . . this is Positano.'

'Rick and I fly Naples Thursday. Friday we untangle this mess.'

'You're coming here!'

He pushed away the sheets, tried to quell the panic.

'You got the rights, buddy, we'll fly to Timbuktu.'

They had believed him outright. They were acting on his say-so, as if they understood the strength of his position better than he did.

'It's a long way to come for a conversation.'

'For a conversation, yes. For a deal, no. My secretary will call your secretary. Have a nice day.'

The line closed like a softly shut door.

The clock read 2 a.m.

The second interruption of sleep:

'What does this interminable number mean? The Caribbean? Grand Canary?'

His brother's voice resonated with full professional pomp, as though he had the ear of a junior clerk or instructing solicitor and were bringing to a perfection of articulate sonority the essence of his own greatness: a tone of inextinguishable confidence, of stealth and snobbery intermingled, of position self-regardingly won by guts and graft.

'Positano. Italy.'

'Very cultured. Where are you staying?'

'In a hotel.'

'A room with a view, no doubt.'

In London it was 7.30 a.m. and Cassian Lear QC was pushing another day forward with his entourage of case files and law reports. His face would be sallow, eyes drawn. But the voice was secure, and that was the noise, harshly incarnated in the earpiece of Michael's phone, that had jarred him awake with the edge of a fire alarm.

'Have you emigrated?'

He moaned at the shock of awakening. For a moment he was bleary, disorientated.

'Your mobile's dead.'

'My answerphone . . .'

'When was the last time you checked this answerphone of yours?'

'Is this early-morning cross-examination practice?'

'You seem unaware of developments.'

He said nothing.

'Michael, I don't understand how a managing director can be out of the country ten days after receiving a statutory notice.'

Michael, alone in his room, blushed.

'Who from?'

'You don't know?'

'Ah . . . yes . . .'

'Oh good. You recall owing somebody ten thousand pounds? That's marvellous. But you're unaware of the letters from a debt-collecting agency?'

There was silence.

'And the solicitor's letter from Customs and Excise? And the registered mail from NatWest. Well, you may be in blissful ignorance, but I'm not. I've had a four-hour meeting with your accountant and I've been through your office with your so-called book-keeper, and apart from the fact I'm distressed at the state of your business I'm quite frankly at my wits' end to know why you're holidaying at a time when your affairs are in a state of total buggery.'

'I'm not on holiday.'

'Michael, you've been on holiday for years.'

'That's not true.'

'You're down a hundred and twenty K and the plug is pulled by NatWest. Bang goes the house. Fancy doing that, Michael. Your one asset. Fool. And now there's this statutory notice, not to mention other creditors. You've got VAT arrears, unpaid instalments on service contracts, HP standing orders suspended, unpaid writers' fees, debt interest, accountant's bills. There are invoices going back to March in your file. And what are you doing? Cavorting on the Continent as if this disaster did not exist?'

The humiliation process had begun and he had to brace himself against the shame of it.

'That's why I'm here. I'm trying to do something about the situation.'

'Tell me about it.'

'I've been living with this nightmare for months.'

'So you're going into voluntary receivership, and we're folding the company with a debt position of 125 K plus costs. Bank gets your house, leaving fifty to sixty unpaid and lots of purple faces. You need to get out now in a responsible way, put your house in order and make it look more like a wind-up than a right royal fuck-up. Michael, d'you read me? Get the next plane back.'

He edged to the end of the bed and opened the window shutters with his free hand. Light cut diagonally into the room. A heavenly blue sky waited for him outside. He felt the day's brilliance on his cheek and it seemed to remind him of something.

Cassian had been supercilious at first, but now his anger was strong. The plumminess had fallen away. He sounded less like an advocate and more like an overworked civil servant in the middle of a departmental balls-up, unafraid to scatter copious expletives behind closed doors. He lived with pressure and it expressed itself through him.

Michael felt his own needs now, resistances that would meet Cassian head on. He had no desire for a clash; but no ability to back down, either.

'I can't come back just now.'

'You must.'

'There's something important . . .'

'What's more important than going bust arse backwards?'

'I've been meaning to call and explain what's happening.'

'Oh, here we go . . .'

'Listen!'

'Michael, I'm in court at ten. Cut the cackle and get back here.'

'Not possible.'

'For pity's sake.'

'Hear me out!'

He did not want to modify or edit what he had to say for Cassian's ear. He said what he said out of self-consistency. He expected nothing but resistant silence from his brother and that was what he heard as he explained the relationship with Hilldyard.

'What's that got to do with independent production?'

'We're talking about a major novelist.'

'Fuck that! I'm a major creditor.'

Cassian, too, had lent him money.

'An opportunity has come up.'

He tried to explain – simplifying for Cassian's sake – the extraordinary fortuitousness of his position, Adamson's input, the names of stars, Hollywood agencies, the call from Coburn.

'I have to see these people.'

'You can't go on pretending, Michael.'

'This is my last chance, for God's sake.'

'Your only chance is to come back.'

'Jesus, Cassian, will you believe what I tell you?'

'I'm not your bank manager. I don't have to believe a sodding thing.'

'Look, I've had a lot of bad luck, but now I've had some good luck.'

154

'Michael, I've been at my desk for half an hour. You're still in the sack in an earlier time-zone. How can I take you seriously?'

'You never understood how this business works.'

'Nobody gets rich by hanging out with novelists and feeling arty.'

Michael wanted to ring off, but was not the ringing-off type. 'Unlike you, I have to create opportunities. I'm not spoon-fed by clerks.'

'Spoon-fed! I'm in demand, you fool!'

'This is going to be a twenty-million-dollar movie. Shane Hammond is on board as director. I've got a chance to produce and I'm not walking away from an opportunity that can settle my debts and save my house!'

'Frankly, Michael, the Irish have more chance of building the H-bomb.'

In the beginning Cassian had been supportive. Showbiz had secretly appealed to him, and he doubtless enjoyed bragging to lawyer friends about Intelligent Productions, his little dalliance with the arts. But when the going got tough he was bound to weigh in heavy-handedly, becoming harsh, and blunt, so that Michael could be in no doubt of the low esteem in which his brother had always held him.

'Michael! Just for once, consider that I'm a barrister. I know a tad or twain about matters legal. You'll hate me for saying so, but I'm in a good position to advise you. Now, just think upon this. When your company goes into liquidation, either by means of a winding-up order or voluntary cessation, which I urgently advocate, you'll be doorstepped by a horde of indignant creditors who'll want to sue you personally. The assets of the company are negligible, future income nil and creditors like Grossman will get very few pence in the pound. Your chief source of liquidity, an overdraft facility disproportionate to cashflow expectations, is secured by an asset mortgaged to a bank. Nobody but the bank'll see a penny of it. That leaves a line of angry creditors baying for your blood with only the diaphanous veil of limited liability hanging between their eye-teeth and your balls. And if those guys can get it into the liquidator's head that you were in business running up debts and liabilities when you knew or ought to have known they couldn't be met, he'll shred the corporate veil and sue you as a director. And if, indeed, they plead wrongful trading, you're dead meat. Why? Because your accountant warned you both orally and in writing that at the time of the *Western Canon* negotiation you were way overextended. You ignored him, and it has taken him another two months to bring his worries to me. Michael, unless you return now and make some semblance of responsible management you're a sitting fuck. You'll be financially poleaxed, barred from credit for years, barred from the directorship of any company. Everyone will know you're a bankrupt. Lenders will shun you. Your funds will be controlled by a trustee so that any serious money you earn will be hived off to creditors. You'll be a complete pariah with a certificate of incompetence and a ball and chain around your goolies, and you'll be eyed with suspicion because wrongful trading smells. Is that enough, or shall I continue?'

'I need to think.'

'Don't think. Pack your bags.'

Michael held the receiver to his ear and gazed at his bare foot on the floor tiles. He was crouched forward, the forefinger of his right hand pressed to his lip. He gazed vacantly as the unpleasantness bore down on him. Cassian's words drummed at his person and he felt as a kind of sickness the pass he had come to; because, even though he believed in his new life, he had a kind of fierce pride still, which converted Cassian's picture of him as a fly-by-night incompetent into something utterly mortifying. He would not be written off. He would not be bankrupted. He realised the violence of his need to show the world he could succeed. He wanted to defeat Cassian with his success, to repel and diminish him and crush him.

He sat in the bed, his anger hardening.

'I'm not winding up.'

'Michael, you've got to come back!' He was desperate now. 'I'm a co-director. I'm statutorily liable. Your creditors can come for me. Don't you understand? And I've got assets. I'm a bloody sitting target, and Christ alive, the money's bad enough but d'you think someone in my position needs litigation? Like a hole in the head. I've just taken silk! The last thing I want is wrongful trading action boiling over in the High Court before my bloody eyes. You've got to get back here, please, so we can sort this thing out. You help me and I'll do my damndest to help you. Is that a deal?'

Cassian was pleading with him. He felt a wave of pity for the man, for the limits and conventions of his life. He did not deserve embarrassment. He had worked hard and played by the rules.

'A few more days.'

'Please!'

He put the phone down on his brother. He was becoming quite tough.

Chapter Thirteen

HE HELD THE DOCUMENT in his hands, caressed his upper lip and read slowly through the clauses. He had successfully printed an agreement on his inkjet.

He would acquire an option to purchase film and television rights in Hilldyard's novel. On exercise the author would assign all rights to adapt and exploit the book as a motion picture or TV mini-series, and thereafter to produce sequel and remake films and spin-off series. Michael would control merchandising, soundtrack and book-of-the-movie rights; plus the unfettered right to alter or adapt the novel in any way, subject only to author consultation without veto. Hilldyard would experience three-quarters of a million dollars on exercise and, when the film got made, a single-card front-end credit in a lettering three-quarters the size of the director's.

There was a space for the author's signature.

It struck him as curious that the imprint of a name, the motions of ink on a page, could change everything.

He tucked the document into his pocket carefully.

Today would not be subtlety day. He would aim to get things done, so that other things could happen. First this, then that, a practical progression. Not everything that Hilldyard might feel should trouble him now; a certain withdrawal of empathy was inevitable, a certain narrowing of concern for the author, and, if it disturbed him to contemplate such efficiency, he told himself that Hilldyard had been persuaded to change his mind, and that he had changed his mind, too. He honestly wanted to produce the film. It was now his wish, his ambition, and where there was honesty there need be no embarrassment. Self-knowledge was proof against bad conscience.

His preparations were cool-headed, even dextrous. He dressed, shaved, and after a moment's preparation dialled Curwen's office in

London. He was not decided on the degree of misrepresentation required to prepare the agent for the Americans, but he knew that something subtle would occur once they were talking. Curwen, it turned out, was ill, off for a day and possibly longer. There was no contact number and thus no risk of the Americans reaching Curwen before Michael did. He rang off thoughtfully.

He dialled Nick Adamson's Los Angeles number, not fearing to wake him in the middle of his night. The voicemail cut in. He deposited a résumé of developments and asked for a return call p.m. Adamson would be excitable, venally strategic. Once briefed he would shift into download: the shape of the deal, the theatrics of negotiation with Coburn, the body language and opening gambits and deal breakers. Michael needed that. He was reliant on that.

Adela had asked for a decision. He rang her hotel as though it were another business call. Her line was engaged and he left a message with reception: 'Shane's agent arrives tomorrow. With Hilldyard now. See you lunch.'

Enough to make her stay.

He descended to the lobby and asked the *Signora* to watch out for an incoming fax. Weislob had not yet sent the coverage.

He patted his pockets, composed himself. It was a ten-minute walk up to Hilldyard's villa and in that ten minutes he needed to become solid, dense with purpose. He inhaled resolutely and went on to the veranda where the day's light was captured in a thousand particles of colour.

Michael blinked, fetched out his sunglasses, waited a moment.

He made his way up the road, pushing himself to achieve clarity of thought. He needed to prevail. For once he was at the centre of things and the forces gathering to his person, of hazard and chance, would give him strength.

A wash of nerves hit the pit of his stomach, almost lifting him off his feet with exhilaration. He was dizzy for a moment, the screen of his mind clearing, losing colour, as though he could be anything, anywhere, was no longer fixed.

The figure came from a side-alley, catching his arm with a hard down-clasp.

Michael shrieked in surprise.

The writer recovered at the roadside. He held on to Michael's arm and glanced about, catching his breath. They had nearly collided. The old man was shaken.

'I was coming to see you,' he said at last.

Michael concentrated. 'I was coming to see you.'

They stood there facing each other, opening moves accomplished.

Hilldyard got his breath back, made a gesture. 'Frances has gone on a jaunt.'

'Has she?'

'Sorrento.'

Michael slowly nodded. 'Shall we go up to your place?'

Hilldyard looked over his shoulder. 'No. Come to my room.'

'Your room?'

'I have a room.' He produced a key from his pocket.

Michael looked at the key in surprise.

There was a flicker of insomnia in Hilldyard's eye. His jowls were rawly shaven.

'Go on.' He pointed the way up the narrow flight of steps. 'Up there.'

Michael pressed on ahead, putting some energy into his upward climb, as if he were his own man.

Hilldyard followed behind, one hand on the rail. The high walls on either side were crumbly, unrendered, host to spumes of weed and grass, and gloomy, like the sides of a dungeon. Halfway up the old man coughed violently, a catty spasm. He hauled himself on, watery eyes glinting behind Michael.

160

Chapter Fourteen

HILLDYARD UNLOCKED A TURQUOISE iron gate in the side of a powdery wall and they passed into another alley, a narrow cement path inlaid with blue tiles here and there. Terracotta urns were set in niches at intervals and fronds of vine overcurled the top of the wall. At the end of the path a row of steps led up to a door in the side of a whitewashed house. Hilldyard turned the key and pushed the door open. It swung into a sunlit room perhaps twenty feet in length. Light ran into the study from a sea-view window and raised the pattern of a faded rug and the crammed elevations of a bookcase. A thousand volumes were distinct, spines articulated in the wash of sea-light: Penguin oranges, Pelican blues, Italian whites, calf-bound reds and tans, antiquarian golds, a vivid density of paperbacks and reference tomes running floor to ceiling on two sides of the room. On the wall by the door a pine shelf held a still life of ceramics: jugs and vases in corn yellows and sky blues, and a tray of sea-hazed bottle glass – jade and amber lozenges culled from the beach. Above the shelf was a painting, a rendering of the view from the window: the timeless prospect of a green pine against vivid blue sky.

Facing the window: a wooden table. A chair with struts at the back and a fading cushion on its seat stood by. On the table were an old manual typewriter, ribbon sagging, an electric typewriter with a sheet under its roller, and a computer screen and disconnected keyboard. These machines had been shoved together to make room for a mug with a maroon cockerel design in which jostled pens and pencils, and an extraordinary whirlpool of pages, spiralling on to the floor and surrounding the legs of the table, smattered with writing, Hilldyard's rapid hand, sketchy jottings, bustling paragraphs, a teeming of words around a central pad and cartridge pen.

Michael averted his eyes from the desk. He glanced at the hundreds of books towering over him. He was walled in by a lifetime of reading. Hilldyard's life; Hilldyard's reading.

The air was dusty and warm. Hilldyard unlatched the glass door, sliding it open. He stood for a moment with his hands on the back of a wickerwork chair and gazed at the sea with professional discernment.

'My ivory tower.'

Michael nodded slowly.

'Not much ivory, but some good books.'

He had to concentrate now. He was not yet ready to speak.

'Try the writer's seat.'

He did so. The swarm of words came closer. The handwriting was messy, energetic, spermatozoically thriving on the page, as though the life of a novel were teeming into being from a million impulses of thought.

'Suits you.'

Michael looked about him.

'I started in this room. I wrote three novels here! I used to rent it from a painter who lived in the villa. That's his picture. We became good friends and when he retired he sold me them both. Gad, what a festival! Italian conveyancing. Paid everyone twice, of course. A dozen bureaucrats, some kind of mayor, two or three Armani wearers from Mafia head office and a lawyer with an eye-patch and two missing fingers. A delirium tremens of hitches and set-backs overcome by a fiesta of bribery and more talking than I've ever heard in my life. Struth, these folk! They're gifted in that way. A beautiful babbling race.'

Michael nodded, feeling for the option agreement in his pocket.

'But now I own it. No doorbell. No phone.' He turned to face Michael. 'Absolute solitude.'

'James.' He stood up.

Hilldyard raised a hand.

Michael reached into his jacket. 'I have something for you.'

'I won't grant the film rights.'

His face gave him away. He could not manage the first response.

The author waved a hand, acknowledging the element of surprise whilst brushing it aside.

He had miscalculated. He was seized with panic.

'Sorry, Michael.'

'I thought . . . Adela converted you.'

'Really?'

162

He hesitated before lying.

'You thought that, did you?'

He smiled back desperately. 'You changed your mind last night.'

'I was evidently drunk.'

'You weren't, James.'

'Wish I had been.'

'It's a sensible idea. Look, here's an option agreement.'

'*Last Muse* into Hollywood won't go!'

'If that's the only reason . . .'

'I don't need any reason!'

Michael swallowed. Hilldyard was forceful and impatient, and, whatever had made him cave in the night before, he had shaken it off. Michael hesitated nervously. He had expected weakness, resignation. He had misread the situation.

He clung to common sense, the bluff of reasonableness. 'You didn't listen to a word of what we said!'

Hilldyard caught his tone and gave him a suspicious look. 'I heard it very well.'

'It's gone in one ear and out the other.'

'Rubbish does.'

'Frances and Adela will be heart-broken!'

'You're the one that's heart-broken.'

Michael steeled himself, fighting back. 'You can't be afraid of the publicity!'

'How can you ask such a question!'

'The world won't condemn you for being unfaithful once. Actually, the world doesn't care.'

'Oh God.' Hilldyard was horrified. 'Where is your imagination? Did you leave it in bed this morning?'

Michael shook his head. His palms were sweaty.

'Why should everything I feel be translatable into reasons? I don't have to justify myself to the ordinary consumer.'

'I am not the ordinary consumer.'

'Then stop acting like one. Snap out of it, for pity's sake!'

Hilldyard turned irritably and crossed to the far end of the room. He pressed both palms to his cheeks. An explanation was evidently required of him and he could not bear the effort of it. 'You know that I loathe adaptation as a matter of principle!'

Michael's chest was tight, and he stood speechless.

'Let me ask you, where do they come from? All these incredible books? From the minds of men and women who have spent years crafting their perception into the rigours of a form. Who have polished each phrase, wrestled with their senses for the best word here, the lightest touch there, brought every cell of these extraordinary organisms into being by a huge effort of imagination, and left us records of human consciousness that add to the wealth of our lives and are the essence of civilisation. The idea that these marvellous constructs of language should be hacked down to ninety minutes of cinema entertainment so that paraplegic consumers can be drip-fed the world's literature without making an ounce of mental effort I find too awful for words. It is so contemptibly uneducated. Adaptation of any decent novel is vandalism. It mutilates the integrity of the original, misrepresents the truth of experience. It is an attack on the word, a violation of the selfhood of writer and reader! It cheapens the subtlety of life as recorded by the best minds! What you propose is an assault on all I have lived for and I cannot abide it!'

Michael stood his physical ground, but in his heart felt humiliated. He kept his hand on the back of his chair, struggled to think clearly. He had no choice but to contest the issue, to go against the grain of Hilldyard's absolute conviction. There was something here, a chink. Hilldyard had made no exception for him. His relationship with the author had been overlooked. He was being given no credit for the special nature of that relationship, and this was something Hilldyard could not deny.

'I have great respect for the integrity of the novel. I hoped for respect in return.'

Hilldyard frowned.

'When I offer my services as producer, I'm offering my own integrity. Isn't that worth something? Given the chance?'

Hilldyard's eyes burned brightly. 'Is this your chance?'

'I think so.'

'My God, you're easily tempted!'

'What?'

'Film producing?' He was scandalised. 'It's just hustling.'

'In a true cause.'

'The producers of this world are not carriers of the cross! You said so yourself.'

Michael brought his hand down on the chair. 'Can't you accept that I'm unusual?'

Hilldyard's eyes glittered. 'You're unique!'

'Then give me a chance!'

He shook his head violently. 'You're unfitted for such work. It's false to you.'

'Why on earth?'

'Because you like my writing! Don't you see?'

Michael's bafflement was total.

'The only reason you want to make this film is because you feel guilty for having failed as a producer, when failure is the very proof of your having something more special to give. You are sacrificing yourself to the standards and expectations of inferiors. You're accepting their canons of success when you should be determining your own. You want the money and recognition for the proof of something to others. You want that girl because she is out there, in the limelight, and the thought of possessing her reassures you that you are a person to be reckoned with. But who's doing the reckoning? Enter Hollywood as a man of integrity and you'll find the room empty. Those guys aren't rated for their sensitivity to literature. They're rewarded for the ability to suspend personal taste in the interest of market norms and audience research data. The original men with no face. Is that you, Michael?'

He gazed blankly at the author.

'Is this what your great love of literature has come to?'

He felt brittle now, dispossessed of resolve. He had been seen into and he stood back from the chair.

In a few hours Frank Coburn would be boarding a plane destined for Naples; Adela had delayed her return. Out there people were still living in the false future he had lied into being. Stress condensed inside him. He could pull the plug on the Americans. Adela could be apologised to, said goodbye to; but to halt these developments was just too painful. Oh yes, he wanted the film all right; he had wanted the symbols that would attach to success. He wanted power and control because without power he was a ghost in the world. But more than that, he wanted redemption from failure. He wanted to be successful, effective, passionate, and through Adela he had seen those things as possible again.

He sat down by the desk, the pangs of resolution and despair blending indigestibly. His chance had been crushed, and for a moment he savoured the bitterness of that.

'You think I've sold out?'

Hilldyard looked down into his hands. He could endure other people's suffering as well as his own.

'You were on the cusp.'

'I'm falling below your very high standards?'

There was silence.

'Life won't allow me your standards.' Suddenly, it was clear to him. 'I'm not a genius. I'm an ordinary mortal who needs to work and have a future.'

The author stroked his forehead, soothing himself. He had many distractions but his main concern now came into focus and he rose from his chair and strolled across to the writing desk where he leaned forward, setting his palms on the edge of the table-top, and presented to Michael a look of intense determination. His lips moved prematurely.

'Michael. Take this into your heart.' He drew into himself the thread of the younger man's concentration. 'When I look at you, I am looking at an artist. I am looking at a man who will only be fulfilled as an artist. I see a person who lives on the finest, most felt responses. And I know in my heart that the key to your life is not public success but intellectual integration. You have yet to find the way of being true to yourself. And when you find it, your unhappiness will cease. Suddenly, you'll be here, dense with purpose, driven to produce the thing that your intelligence tells you is an inexorable response to life. Integrity will be a physical sense of well-being. All this film talk will seem peripheral. Because you are more intelligent. And intelligence that has spread its wings soars over the world of commerce. It is my utter conviction that your happiness lies in this direction. Life hasn't brought you to my doorstep by accident. As for genius—' He squinted. 'Genius does not make a life. Whatever your measure of talent, it will be more than some and less than others, and what matters really is courage. You need to believe that what you think and feel can count. That you can remake the world in your own terms. The important thing is to live and work to the breadth of your unique faculties, and I have no doubt that when the courage is granted you you'll do that. That will be your redemption. Nothing else.'

Michael sat with crossed arms and the author leaned towards him, knuckles on the table. Hilldyard's certainty ran against his astonishment, ran around it, the force of it baffling him as though he had been told something true but incomprehensible.

'You honestly think I'm a writer?'

'A novelist, a biographer. It hardly matters.'

166

The men faced each other, gazes locked.

Michael laughed oddly. True, he had started to write. He had wanted to capture something. He concentrated on this thought but somehow could not link up with the side of himself that had sat on the balcony, scribbling feverishly; that self seemed airy, unreal.

'How could I be a writer and not know it?'

'That, my dear fellow, has been your whole problem.'

He looked into the author's grey eyes, mirrors of himself. The remark caused him turmoil, as though he were stuck outside self-knowledge.

'I'm thirty-five!'

'Writing is a means to live one's life. It is never too late to live one's life properly.'

'You're making me into an author!'

'I see you becoming one.'

He was desolate. 'But how?'

Hilldyard was vibrant. 'By discovering the courage to express what is positive and beautiful as though your life depended on it.'

Michael crushed his face into his palms. 'I'm not that good!'

'You wouldn't be here in this room if you weren't. I'd have got rid of you.'

He looked up in surprise at Hilldyard's face.

'You need insight, Michael. Insight will come.'

He shook his head. He was aware of his weakness now. 'I need a bloody epiphany.'

Hilldyard stood up, nodded slowly. 'In your case certain things must be burned off.'

Michael clenched his hands together. In every direction so much effort was involved and all the time he was becoming smaller, weaker.

'It's me that'll burn. I'm going bankrupt.'

'Bankrupt! You'll discover an immunity to that kind of loss.'

'Actually—' He wiped an eye. 'I can't bear it.'

'Whatever, you'll live. And having life, you'll keep the only thing that matters. Compared to the eternity of oblivion in store for us the simple possession of consciousness is a miracle. Against that blackness everything we endure, every loss, every sorrow is a kind of asset. So you have to write, because writing is maximal consciousness, maximum life. That alone is the secret of a writer's self-sufficiency.'

The agony seeped through him, squeezed his heart.

'This is your crisis. Have it. Survive it!'

He was nothing, he realised. There was nothing beyond himself.

'It is your bearing as a man, your moral centre, the one thing you can fail or fall short of. Not to develop the unique instrument of your talent is the one cataclysm that awaits you, a failure you might never perceive because perception would be its first casualty.'

His head swung back as though he had been struck. He tried to hold in his mind the sense of himself as a writer and immediately weakened. He believed in the value of literature, had sustained himself for years with a love of poetry and drama, had often experienced the heightened perceptions of this novel or that play and regarded such moments as something essential, sublimely human; but when challenged to express his perceptions, and to become himself a creator, he felt drained to the core. Something was demanded that he could not supply. He was challenged to be of the best material and felt himself lacking.

He needed, he realised simply, to exist in the dimension of ordinary reality before submerging into the virtual domain of art.

'I believe in you, Michael, because you have inspired me. How many men does one meet these days of such fineness, such sentience?' He laid a hand on Michael's shoulder. 'What is essential in you is innocence.'

He sagged.

'Your painful life has turned you into something precious. You writhe, but the writhing won't overcome what is true in you. At heart I think you're incorruptible.'

He shuddered with embarrassment. He was offered sympathy and kindness and could do nothing with them.

The author stood behind the chair, fingers pressuring his collar-bone, as though to press in certitude and self-belief.

'Don't take this in the wrong way,' he said softly, evenly. 'You've become for me a kind of muse. Thanks to you I've been given another book to write.' He hesitated, realising something afresh. 'You've given me a character.'

Michael felt the fingers on his shoulder squeezing gently.

'Someone I hardly dreamed could exist any more.'

It came as a double-take, astonishment suspended. 'You're using me?'

'Someone like you.'

He turned in his chair and looked at the fragile old face.

'As a character in your book?'

'As the first impression, the kernel.'

Michael was overwhelmed by a sense of irony. He was going to enter fiction when he had barely existed in life. Hilldyard was using him, taking him, syringing him out of life into art.

'Don't . . . you mustn't spoil yourself . . . You give me the current . . . I mean, there's work to be done. This is a declaration, you see. Of my great fondness for you and a love for something you have kindled in me. I need you to stay.'

Michael consulted the open palms of his hands in a trance of wonder. On top of chagrin came a new emotion, a kind of apathy, as if to be told such things was to receive a burden, and to stand for something valuable which he could not enjoy in himself. He felt, bitterly, as though he could only exist for other people's benefit.

'We can help each other,' said Hilldyard, standing behind him. 'I mean, before you came along, I was a decaying geriatric. But now' – he smacked his palm on the mess of papers – 'I'm off again, feeling, thinking, writing, and if you can do that for me, I can do something for you. You're at an age when great things are possible. I want to see you through to the next stage. And this is the place to do it. Away from distraction.'

It flashed up in his mind and before he could stop himself the words were out. 'You want me to sacrifice my life to your novel?'

Hilldyard flinched. He was quickly dignified. 'If you believe in anything, you believe in my writing. And you believe in it because literature is an absolute. That's why you came here. And you know that I have only ever written for the kindred souls who believe that all this' – he glanced at the books – 'matters supremely.'

Michael made a gesture, a wave of apology. Even shame felt numb.

'And in your heart you want to help.'

Hilldyard hovered, patting his shoulder again, then trod discreetly over to the window, to the sweltering blueness of sea and sky.

Michael covered his brow. A course had been offered to him, an alternative way. It was the final draft of their previously vague collaboration and on the face of it he was offered extraordinary tuition in becoming an artist. He tried to fasten on it. There was nothing to grasp immediately, just the conception of something he could not feel from inside. The one thing he needed to do he had not the strength to believe in, and this failure was the cornerstone of other failings: a weakness his father had probably despised.

Hilldyard's presence sat on his freedom of thought. His omniscience was suffocating.

He pondered his change of heart. After he had kissed Adela everything had become gathered; a hard energy came up from way down, passion and ambition wound into suffocating need. It was a need that knew the desperate importance of its own fulfilment and which eclipsed the artistic self. One kiss sent stabs of yearning through his heart. For the first time in years he felt emotion as a positive energy. It was like a natural resource that had to be exploited. The raw painfulness of containing such regenerative desire was almost unbearable. She had been sent to him. She was compensation for a ruined life, for the loss of Christine, and she had arrived at a time when he was ready. He clutched his head in despair. He could not say this to Hilldyard, but it agonised him that Hilldyard could not understand his need, and would not help his return to normal life by giving him the one thing he required to secure Adela: the film rights. If Hilldyard could not understand the pain of Michael's necessities, why should he nurture Hilldyard's?

The misery of the situation gave him weary strength. He knew where he stood now. He would have to go back and the reality of that was worth stating bluntly.

'My brother called this morning.'

Hilldyard nodded attentively.

'I have to go back to London.'

'Oh!'

'This film' – there was no harm in candour, now that it would get him nothing – 'was my only hope.'

Hilldyard shook his head. 'Go and come back.'

'Perhaps.'

'You must come back!'

He slouched, eyes down. 'I have no free will any more.'

'But . . .'

'I have to face the music.'

'My boy, it's only music!'

He grew pale. 'It is devastation.'

'Companies come and go,' Hilldyard waved. 'People live their long lives.'

'You see—' Michael wiped his nose. 'You do see, James.' He

would not get another chance at happiness. 'Your scruples are standing between me and survival.'

'Oh really!' The author was fraught. 'Don't torment me. My scruples are my religion, my faith.'

'A little mercy could save my home, all the money I have in the world!'

Hilldyard squinted in sympathy.

'It's in your gift,' Michael said, all-earnestly. 'Just a signature. A gesture between friends.'

'I can't.'

'You want me to stay?'

Hilldyard was distressed.

'James.' He grabbed the author's hand. The fingers were thick, soft, firmly responsive. 'I'll make the film and come back. I'll set up an office here. I don't have to be in London all the time.'

The author grimaced, squeezed tight. 'I cannot believe that.'

'Let the film be a tribute to our friendship.'

'Oh God!'

'Please!'

Hilldyard shook his head, eyes glistening.

'James!'

'I . . .' The old man's breathing was stertorous. He sighed profoundly. 'The essence of being an artist is a terrible loneliness precisely because there are certain matters on which one cannot compromise.'

Michael withdrew his hand and crossed to the window: the bright view, the coruscating sea and emerald pine. He felt ashamed to the core of his being. He had jettisoned dignity. But dignity was void now. Dignity had lost the argument and Michael, suddenly feeling that the truth was obvious, turned to Hilldyard and said, 'Does it matter what they do to the book?'

Hilldyard scowled.

'Let there be a film,' he said flamboyantly. 'Even if it's crap, does it matter?'

'It matters to me.'

He raised his voice. 'More than the welfare of another human being?'

Hilldyard coloured brilliantly.

'You don't know what I'm facing!'

'What are you facing?'

Bleakness swept over him like wind.

Hilldyard caught him by the arm. He brought his face up to Michael's.

'What have you done?'

He could not speak for a moment.

Hilldyard followed first one eye then the other, testing and penetrating, waiting and seeing, watching out the crisis. He put his hand under Michael's jaw, touched the flesh of his cheek.

'My only chance. My last chance!'

Hilldyard regarded Michael passionately, with declaratory fire. 'The beginning starts now.'

'Help me!'

The author went white.

'Give me the option.'

There was a silence and then something queer crossed Hilldyard's face, a shadow of fear.

'James . . .'

'Frances and I were lovers.'

The author seemed to shrink, a fairy-tale reversion into toad-like form.

'"Anna" is Frances, you see.'

He did not understand.

'She was fifteen years old. Joan died, and Frances went mad.'

Michael received the author's stare like a sheet of ice-water.

'The book is tainted, Michael.'

His thoughts tripped over each other, could not catch up. He was winded by surprise.

'There's your "reason".'

'Frances was fifteen!'

'Don't judge!'

He frowned with a sense of the bizarre, the uncanny. 'You had sex with her?'

Hilldyard's face went an ecstasy of red.

Michael could not contain the idea. 'You told me "Anna" was middle-aged.'

'"Anna" never existed.'

'But you told me . . . ?'

'It was a lie!'

Michael was shaken.

'So that you wouldn't hate me. So you wouldn't desert me.'

172

Hilldyard took his forearm. 'You see, I had to write the book but its contents are a lie and a cover-up and pray God some day you will understand why it is a betrayal of myself and of Frances and Joan and must never be published or filmed, and that is what I have to tell you and that is an end to it!'

Michael was suddenly overcome, as if run through.

Hilldyard squeezed his arm.

There was a hard locking of eyes.

He pushed away and got his hand to the door handle.

'Michael! You wouldn't sell your wife's memory.' Hilldyard aimed a finger at him. 'I won't sell mine.'

Chapter Fifteen

TWO GERMAN GIRLS, BUSTS expressed by the straps of their ruck-sacks, stood outside a *pensione*. The windows were shuttered but a side-door was open and the travellers pondered their choice. A cat came past on the road, stretchily satisfied by board and lodging.

Michael emerged from a passageway and slipped between two parked cars, lips moving as he reset his sunglasses.

He stood by the parapet at the road's edge sightlessly gazing at the terraces, at the tapestries of vine falling between them.

He walked, not to her hotel, but high above the town, on a road that wound round gorges and under the branches of walnut trees.

It was only lunchtime but already the sun had passed mid-point in the sky, lowering its angle and casting an afternoon lustre of mellow gold on the distant buildings near the beach; deepening shadows in the cleft of the town, so that an entire hotel was immersed in shade, and, higher up, raising whitewashed walls to a dazzle. Rooftiles became crimson, the soft-hued washes of innumerable façades lit up, window glass refracted slivers of blinding light.

The air up here was fresher, sharp-scented with pine resin. Great jigsaw clouds hung in the blue. A gentle wind ebbed in from the wide plate of the sea, which caught the light in a million places. From way off bright items of sound reached his ear as he stood and gazed at the view. There was something both vivid and placid about the squeak of a scooter, or dog-echo, or men shouting their salutations in some far corner of the town, as if nothing could escape, however remote, the ravine's transfiguring acoustic.

He sat down on the verge. The sea seemed serene, limitlessly incandescent, but in the far distances of the day a storm was brewing. Along the coastline the sea's blue had turned to a rage of white surf against the cliffs. Rollers were polevaulting high against the spits and stacks, lingering in a zenith of foam and freefalling back into the swell.

The weather would soon change. Rain and thunder would sweep in. The glinting town would be lost in mists and drizzle for days, possibly weeks. The sea would become dull, the beaches bare, the restaurants empty.

He held his knees and gazed with the bleary fixity of a drunk at the hairs on his forearm. Hilldyard's revelation made vision seem skew-whiff, and Michael was too shot-up and knocked off to understand where it left him. He was exhausted by the unknowability of human beings. Frances and Hilldyard were an uncanny proposition, bizarre, beyond his ken. The idea mildly disgusted him. He did not yet know what to think, but knew he was shocked. The information was disappointing, morally disappointing; but then he had been morally disappointing, too.

He was relieved to have escaped the scene of his abasement. All that humiliation blew one's fuses.

He clutched his knees and thought of Adela down there some-where. She was waiting for him to arrive with good news.

Without the option he could not have her. He knew that for sure. All he could do was cup his chin and reflect on the bitterness of this.

They had only just met. He had experienced her ardour, but had no claim. They appreciated certain things about each other, perhaps. If Adela had been direct with her lips, she had been more honest with her tongue. She had come to an age when life and work needed to bind each other. She desired love, but wanted more. Michael as he stood was no use to her, though Michael as a producer in control of the film rights – well, that might be different. If he could get his act together (she had hinted) she might readily succumb to the attraction between them. She needed a person whose energy of becoming was as great as her own. She had ambition, immense talent. Her partner must aid, not oppose that. The right man needed edge, and Michael had no edge at all. He had nothing but himself.

He held his knees as though he were holding his unhappiness, embracing it. He was experiencing new physical sensations, chest pangs, muscular edginess, tingling skin, the ache of repressed energy, as if something were trying to get out of his body. His feelings were on the move again. Frozen matter was being called into life. He realised that he was, quite simply, ready for a relationship in a way he had not been since Christine's death. He was able to fall in love. He was dying to be in love, and the strength of the urge magnified Adela's appeal into something almost unbearable.

He sat with his hands on the grass, and felt sorrow glutting up. Everything was mad. Everything was skewed for maximum pain and disappointment and this had always been so with him. The chance of a second life had come along and he could not take it.

Chapter Sixteen

ADELA'S *pensione* was in the heart of Positano, at an X-junction of restaurants and shops, opposite the post office.

The small man at the desk rang Adela's room, but her phone was engaged. He shrugged, thumbing a number on the key rack and directing a hand upstairs. Michael went up the steps, past skew-whiff pictures of lurid sunsets and snow-white villas and a model of the Madonna on a ledge.

He found the corridor and walked along to her door, ajar. He could hear a bath running, the plumbing working up a din, and could just hear her talking on the phone. He entered the hall and was about to knock when her voice became clearer, and he was struck by the sound of it.

'Oh very beautiful. The apex of two-star.' She laughed. 'About ten by six. Jack would laugh. It's quite a joy, you know, Sarah . . . the bohemian life. Yes, I know . . . Did he? Well, there's nowt wrong with a bit of winking cellulite at the Cottesloe . . . Darling, he wouldn't ask you if you weren't gorgeous. You are! You're beautifuler than me. Tell Bernie to sort him. God, these directors are shameless!'

He stood against the wall.

'At least Jack carried cash. What! Diz hasn't paid for a drink in living memory. Not hard up, Sarah. Very mean. He's chucked and he should stay chucked. Say what you like, Brand, he was never mean! . . . Yes, we met yesterday.' The tone lowered. 'One hopes one wasn't too unmemorable in one's strapless cocktail frock . . . Michael . . . yes . . . He did. No, but Frank Coburn's flying over, which is . . . Yeah. Fingers crossed and everything . . . Look, call Bernie and ask him to phone Tucker and tell him to stick the nude scene down the front of his very sweaty Levi's . . .'

He was about to enter when her tone changed again.

'Brown eyes. Intense. He needs this as much as I do.'

He breathed in.

'Don't give me advice, please . . . Is that your latest phrase? You didn't!' She shrieked. 'The Semen Demon! God . . . Abominable harlot! . . . What? . . . It doesn't mean anything. It means I don't want to talk about it. And that doesn't mean anything. Or that.'

He eased himself backwards, but then couldn't hear.

Her voice was soft now, as though she were talking half into her pillow.

'Anything I tell you, you'll tell Jack . . . So what you don't know you can't pass on. You can't read anything into what I say. Truly, no comment.' She laughed, a snugly girlish laugh. 'Well, do give my best regards to your super new dish of a man and don't forget to call Bernie. Bye, angel.'

He moved swiftly back into the corridor and heard her banging through the inner door into the bathroom. Her phone rang again.

'Damn.' He retreated back down the corridor and from the top of the stairwell heard the hotelkeeper say 'Visitor'.

She was expecting him now, and Michael went back again, a leaden arm rising, a rebellion of nerves in his neck and chest, until his palm hit the opening door and there beyond it, framed by window-light, she stood in a satin robe, her hair pinned up and her eyes wide with surprise.

'You're here?'

He waited on the threshold, amazed by the sight of her.

She reversed through the door, spun into her bedroom.

'Come on in.'

'Sorry to . . .'

'God, the bath!' She brushed past him, a hairpin in her mouth.

The bed was exuberantly unmade; a chaos of bags and clothes and open wardrobe doors crowded the room.

'Hi!' She was bouncily back.

He smiled involuntarily.

'So?'

'This room's tiny.'

'Minute! The bed's like a sandbag.' She clapped her mouth. 'Believe me, I'm not this messy in real life. I can't be. Sit down.'

He walked to the small balcony, leaned on the grille, felt her coming up next to him, sharing his view of the square. He could feel her suspense. She was all nervous energy and her skin creased around the eyes as she resisted the brightness.

'You're very calm and collected.'

He was spaced.

'I've had an interesting morning.'

'And?'

Her uptilted face was searching him; all its beauty, its smoothness, fairness and fullness was aghast for his news, as though it were a yearning for him; as though the news he would bring were like a kiss.

He glimpsed the alternative future.

'Michael?' There was alarm in her eyes.

Something like the tip of a blade ran through him, sectioning his heart.

'You've got the rights?'

'The rights?'

'Did he agree?'

He took in her opalescent eyes, the petal paleness of her throat, the palmable swell of satin breasts.

'Well, anyway . . .' he began.

'You've got the option?'

It sunk inside him, a release of dead weight.

'Are you OK?' She touched him with both hands.

'Yes.' He smiled suddenly.

'The option!'

'The option is signed.'

'He signed the option?'

'Absolutely.' He kept smiling. 'It's signed.'

'Oh God,' she yelled. 'Man of genius!'

He succumbed to the collision of a hug and the impact of a kiss, followed by the heat of her breath. 'What happened? Was he OK?'

The lie clotted inside him. 'Yeah . . . Yes.'

'Incredible.' She bounced back against the end of the bed, her bathrobe riding up. She had the thighs of a dancer. 'Tra la la. When do the agents get here?' She put a Scarlet O'Hara hand to her bosom, touched off her hair.

'Tomorrow.'

'D'you know what? You're my saviour.' She sprang off the mattress towards him. 'Can I call Bernie?'

'No.'

'OK, OK. My friend downstairs will bring us a bottle. I've got him

. . .' She made a sign with her little finger as she went to the bedside phone, smiled violently as she dialled, with cat-like delight.

Michael gazed over the balcony into the street below. He could feel her through thin air, the imminence of her touch, the scent of her skin, the shapeliness of elbows and shoulders, chin and cheeks, the tensile backs of her thighs, her calves, the gossamer all-overness of flesh as if it were enveloping him.

'Ah!' She was pressing her palms to her face. Her body wilted with the abjectness of relief and when he turned to look at her, she smiled at him through tears. 'Thank God, Michael,' she gasped. 'Oh, thank God!'

Chapter Seventeen

THE 'CHAMPAGNE' WHEN IT came was, indeed, Asti spumante. The crisps on the tray were also Italian. Michael answered the door and received a smile from the hotel-keeper before taking the tray back into the room and putting it on the dressing table.

He looked around for somewhere to sit.

Adela lay in the bath, listening to the radio.

The bedroom was alive with street sounds. The shutters were half open, casting diagonal lines on the rug.

He cleared a pair of embroidered slippers and a make-up bag off the chair and sat down. He considered the room from a sedentary position, the spectator of his own predicament. He had lost control, and now he felt experimental and on borrowed time, and weird, as though he had crossed to the other side of things.

His mouth tasted queer. Something was turning his breath.

Her bathrobe had pleased him: a gorgeous piece of silver-screen satin, a coming together of sex and luxury and womanly self-love. Adela's body deserved sensuous adornment. Like any actress, she knew the secret of her comeliness, its magical allure and special effects. And for a moment back there she seemed like a hologram of ideal beauty, something unbearably lovely, projected from the needs of overwrought nerve-endings.

She came out of the bathroom wrapped to the armpits in a towel and rubbed at her neck and ears with a hand towel. Standing perceptively before her image in the mirror she threaded back wet hair with fine fingers. She was self-possessed, relaxed, abundant. Things were now on course and she could prepare to flourish. She gave a quaint glance at the Asti spumante and then sashayed past to the wardrobe. 'Excuse me,' she said, bending forward by his side and drawing out on the flat of her hand a folded shirt.

He smelt the almond aroma of hair-conditioner.

'Would you like a bath?' She smiled.

He cleared his throat.

She stood over him and let the shirt unfold, as if she were about to put it on.

'Or would you prefer a drink?'

'I'll take a drink.'

'Shall I wear this?'

'You're staying, then?'

She glanced at him and then sat down on the bed, hand cupping the inside of a thigh. 'I'm staying.'

He took the Asti bottle and wrestled off the cork. The fluid fizzed uncontrollably as he poured, cheap foam overflowing the glasses.

She placed a crisp on her tongue and lolled sideways on the bed. Michael looked at her softly, a long moment.

She took the glass and played it between her hands and the look she gave him then made him blush.

'What happens now?' she said quietly.

His heart rushed. It seemed like an invitation.

'Oh.' He suppressed the hot air bubble in his chest. 'Um . . . The mother of all negotiations.'

'Shall I call Shane?'

'Too early.'

'He'll talk to Frank.'

He shut his eyes as though reading the words off the back of his lids. 'If we play Shane, we play him as a trump card.'

She drew a hair from her cheek. 'Isn't your trump card the option agreement?'

'I'm a one-card player.' He was bluffing on no cards.

'Shane's on our side.'

He looked at her absently.

'I need to square the agents first. They have to swallow the fact I'm producing this film and it's my baby not theirs.'

There was hesitant admiration in her eyes.

'I'll call Adamson tonight.'

'Adamson?'

'Hollywood contact. He'll give me language.'

'God.'

'Yes?'

She did one of her three-quarter-profile poignant gazes. 'I can hardly believe it's true.'

He looked away. 'Nothing's true, yet.'

She sighed with total relief, as though the tension were still escaping in surges. He had brought about the consummation of something she desired with every sinew of her being: the role of a lifetime. Now that the goal was achieved she was relaxing into herself properly. Her aura had changed. He saw in the colour of her skin and the warmth of her smile just how much one lie had done for her.

'Michael?' The towel had ridden up her leg to reveal a line or crease dividing the upper roundness of her thigh from the muscle underneath. 'Will you sit next to me?'

She was ahead of him. He leaned forward.

'Come.'

He moved from the chair to the edge of the bed, bringing his wineglass, too. He sat by her side in appreciative compliance and she turned a holding look on him that let him see at close range the green filaments of her irises, the delicate lashes.

'Cheers,' she said, over her glass.

He could feel her readiness. His closeness was acceptable to her. She knew what he felt, what he might intend, and her easiness encouraged him. He looked at her collarbone, at the cream beneath it.

She placed a hand on his leg.

'Hello,' he said, setting a hand on hers.

'I've taken advantage of you.'

Her hand slid away.

'I've led you on, I think.'

His heart raced.

'There's a problem, Michael.'

He could not think what to think, except that the moment was ghastly.

'I'm in turmoil.'

'What!'

'Oh . . . Jack.'

'Jack?'

'My . . . my boyfriend!'

He waited for more than the repetition of a name, directing all his nerve endings to what she would say next.

183

'The . . . He called, and . . .' She craned her neck, inarticulate for once.

He had been a fool to ignore this.

'Right now I don't know what to do. I suppose things aren't quite over. He's got his hooks in me somewhere . . .'

She sat in the limpness of her shame, and he saw that all this 'boyfriend' might stand for had crept up on her and seized her in a way he had not witnessed before; it had taken this moment to bring it to the surface.

He placed his glass delicately on the tray and felt desire curdling in him. He had lied his way into nothing, a double humiliation, and the disappointment was merciless.

'I need this project so much, you see . . . I desperately need a gig.'

He heard this from a distance.

She remained still by his side, as if reckoning the consequences of admission.

He scratched his chin. The first impact was like a burn or cut, a nasty moment followed by numbness; misery later.

'I like you,' she said. 'I do like you.'

He was able to foresee sorrow. Although he had lied to her and had given himself a false opportunity, the true thing, the spur to his deception, was that he honestly wanted her; and what he felt, as he sat like a statue, was the immensity of that need. He would have to pack the thwarted force back into himself. The need of years.

'I just don't know what would happen.'

'I see.'

'I want to be honest with you. You of all people.'

He sighed at the dull compensation of honesty.

'What I probably need is an affair.' She avoided his gaze. 'Not what you need. I think you deserve something nutritious.'

He grunted, incredulous.

'You're very serious, Michael.'

'What sort of "affair"?' he heard himself asking in a strange voice.

'A means to an end,' she said quickly.

He rubbed his forehead.

'I have no idea what I would feel at the moment.' She chucked up her chin.

'What end?'

'Getting over Jack. Or getting him back.'

'You want him back?'

184

She was half playful, half serious, a victim of her own uncertainty. 'I don't know what I want!'

He nodded, understanding nothing.

'I don't want to use you.'

'Who do you want to use?'

'Nobody! I'm not like that.'

There was a silence in which he felt racked by jealousy.

'You need love, I think. And whatever I could offer, it might not be that.'

Her honesty pained him.

'This is a weird conversation. I mean . . . I mean, nothing's really happened.'

After a pause he stood up and walked to the balcony. He noticed that the light outside had changed. Foreshortened figures crossed the road. One of the restaurant owners from the upper town was snatching out gesticulations before an elegant woman as she moved a display rack into her shop.

He should not have let his hopes run high. Life was not like that. His big chance had been a delusion. Michael bit his lip and felt all hope subside. He must come clean with her. He had a duty to own up, even though it would mean the end of their relationship.

'We must talk to Shane,' she said.

He turned.

She rose to her feet, cradling her arms, throwing her hair back.

'He should know what we know. He mustn't hear it from the agents or he'll think we've been manoeuvring behind his back.'

Two half-drunk glasses stood on the tray.

'Now you've got the option, you're in a very strong position and I don't want to alienate him. Without him we're nothing. We've got to be smart!'

He was struck suddenly by the memory of Hilldyard's confession. The truth was so much stranger than one imagined; shocking. And it came to him then – that Hilldyard had wrecked everything. There was no fall-back now.

'Michael.' She drew closer.

'What?'

'Are you OK?'

He allowed himself a laugh.

'What's wrong?'

In the mirror he could see the slant of her neck half draped by hair.

She hitched the towel over her bosom with a hooked finger. She was a picture of thoughtful concern.

'We have to be honest with each other.' She came towards him, to give him her face close up.

He nodded.

She touched his forearm. 'Do you really want this film?'

Her touch had its own special current.

'Do you?'

Her eyes searched him for an answer, plumbing his reticence. It was the most important question and she had asked it pleadingly, as though she were really saying something else.

He frowned.

'I must know.'

Her finger moved on his arm.

'Do you?'

It was a caress.

She was intense, almost hypnotised.

He understood now.

'Do you?'

He leaned towards the uplift of her mouth which grazed his lips, pausing and pressing, darning out a slow kiss, her hair on his cheek. And when he grabbed her, the towel slipped and her breasts were full in his hands as though she had put them there. He was taut with the shock of her nakedness, everything for the taking, Adela full on, gasping as he clutched at her.

On the bed she was forceful and tumultuous and freely possessed of her own choreography. She crawled on the mattress in a mobile swoon, hair everywhere, everything on offer as a present to pleasure, which he could not begin to consume with kisses and caresses. And as they manoeuvred around each other's bodies, Michael's edginess turned to relief, the deep relief of making love to someone whole-heartedly, without guilt, without doubt, in a blaze of arousal, as though Adela's lovely body were a temple in which could be worshipped the best of her, and the best of himself.

Chapter Eighteen

HE WAS SUMMONED AT nine o'clock on Friday morning. The call came through to his hotel room and he was told by a candy-voiced American girl that he would be collected in thirty minutes. 'We're a short ways out of town. And Mr Weislob asks would you please bring the option agreement, sir. Uh huh. Thank you so.'

He waited in his room, standing by the shutters before a grey sky, until a suited Italian chauffeur with shades and moustache hopped up the steps on to the hotel terrace and made his swift way to the lobby entrance.

He took a notepad and calculator and was soon descending the steps behind his escort. The man was courteous and quiet and gave off the aroma of macassar and starch as he led the way, natively indifferent to the view that opened out at the foot of the steps as they passed the ravine and encountered the steep set of the town.

It was a black Mercedes, cumbersomely parked across a snake bend in the road, and Michael fell into the back seat with a solid sense of impostorship. He wore a blue suit and a lilac open-necked shirt. His black shoes were polished to a gloss and he felt poised as the big car turned and made its cushioned ascent of the Viale.

The agents were not staying in central Positano, but out, along the coast road, and he noted with curiosity the number of twists and turns that elapsed between the receding town and their destination, as if he were being driven to a villain's hideout. The coastal slopes became steeper, the mountain more lowering. Small villages stuck in coves or on outcrops veered by and the glare in the sky was complicated by a storm cloud. The sea was lead-like, sharp against the horizon.

The hotel was perched, like a Riviera fortress, on a promontory of cliff that in times past had flaked great facets of its mass into the sea.

They swung into the drive, and Michael saw to his right the jaws of a cove suspending a swimming pool at one level, a tennis court further down, and right at the bottom, for use in finer weather, a concrete beach clamped between cliffs.

It was international luxury-class inside, with much glass revealing the coastal view, and marble floors and statuary and deluxe imperviousness to external weather conditions. He was presented to a handsome male receptionist in a blue tunic and directed to a seat in the lobby while his arrival was confirmed.

'Hello,' said the candy-voiced girl.

She whistled across the lobby like a game-show hostess, all fresh and clean in belted hotpants and augmented sweatshirt, which sported the legend 'Coburn's In Town'. Her thighs were honey brown, and her bare arms hung in listless innocence.

'Hi,' she said, cutting the word off brusquely.

He rose to a handshake and curtsy, just a kink in the legs.

'Nice to meet yoooou.' The lip gloss glimmered as the eyes sparkled.

He nodded.

'I'm Bambi.'

'Hello, Bambi.'

'Will you come on in?'

She smiled over her shoulder and kicked off in front of him through the lounge of the hotel.

'You're from England, right?' she said as they entered a lift.

'I am.'

'London is neat.'

He cleared his throat. 'You're from LA?'

'You got it.'

The lift led to an inner courtyard of sprinkling fountains and wrought-iron tables laid for breakfast. With a gazelle hop she took him up a run of flagstone steps leading through a portico to a wide corridor. Rugs led the way over terracotta tiles and by malachite side-tables and the architraves of apartment doorways.

'Frank and Rick'll be right along.' She brought him round a corner through an open door into a suite with a head-on sea view.

'Can I fix you coffee?'

He could see through an archway a vista of white walls and marble floors.

'Make yourself at home.' She smiled.

He nodded and positioned himself in a chair with a view of the sea. Bambi clicked her heels and swept off through the annexe, and then there was silence.

They had isolated him.

He remembered Adamson's advice from the night before.

'Be as Jewish as you can.'

'What the hell does that mean?'

It had been an hour-long call, a deluge of angles and conjectures, projections and weavy second thoughts.

'Talk a lot. Show them you're not afraid to spiel the hind legs off a pregnant cow. It's the international parlance of negotiation. Means you're flexible and undeceived at the same time, cos it mirrors the lip-service platitudes they'll be churning out. If they're philosophical, be more philosophical. If they're warm and human, let them see teeth, open palms, the twinkle of a cuff-link. Grease for grease. That way you'll lull them. I mean, man, these guys are going to be very fucking edgy. You've got the option, and they've got jetlag. If you go cold and English they'll freak. Don't confront. Describe where you're at from an enlightened Jehovah-type perspective. Wisdom of the ages.'

'Is Coburn Jewish?'

'Nope.'

They had decided to dub the packaging percentage a finder's fee.

'Control the agenda. First the picture. Then the deal. It's easier to agree on editorial. Non-contentious semantics. But you can be articulate, real. Besides, you'll have the upper hand. You've read the book.'

'Surely they've read the book!'

'Hey! They've read coverage. Weislob has probably flicked the manuscript on the jet. If you're lucky they'll know the author's name.'

Adamson's advice had been purchased for ten per cent of Michael's fee, and ten per cent would buy calls and contractual overview, a full behind-the-scenes consultancy. His aspiration to produce the film had been guillotined, and Michael had him where he wanted him. Adamson was the third person he had lied to about the option.

He watched over himself now. He was at the centre of events. In the past twenty-four hours he had become disinhibited and could meet things head-on.

'Would you join us, Michael?'

She beckoned him from the next room and he followed her leggy beeline to an inner door, which she knocked on before opening for Michael's admission. The room beyond was wide and bright and gave directly on to a courtyard swimming-pool area like an atrium, all ferns and hanging baskets, stone seats, mosaics and frescos, an emperor's bath in mock-Pompeiian style.

Weislob stood by the patio door, wearing wrap-around shades and talking into a mobile phone. He was small against the open length of the room, his black suit and slick-cut hair seeming miles away. He turned when Candy knocked but made no response to Michael's arrival. Instead, he rocked forward and incised the air with his hand, pushing a deal point.

'Hi, Frank,' said Bambi. 'I have Michael Lear for you.'

The room shrank when Coburn came in, as though five-star luxury could not compete with so purposeful a tread.

'Bambi, I want to conference Meyer Obermann and Phyllis Cheatham at midday and Zike Weinberg at two-fifteen. Tell Marian at Zike's office we're gonna talk schedules on *Red Devil* p.m. Hope Freeway can call me any time about Barbara Brindisi for *Ghost Town* but I don't want to hear a damn thing about Chum Nasser. Will you fix those London meets and tell LA to e-mail the call checklist through to the portable here and Maximilian Durnhauser. Everything goes to Max, right. And honey, tell these guys we're in the bunker till whenever. No interruptions. No faxes. Zero antipasto. Do Rick, then join us.'

Coburn was shiny bald with a wrestler's crease at the back of his neck. His shoulders were broad, kegged in muscle. He wore a kimono, track-suit bottoms, pumps. Like a frontier cowboy, all thew and moustaches, he carried himself with equestrian energy across the room, not offering Michael a hand or nod, or the security of a glance, but making him feel somehow included, as if his buffalo might were a shield to the near at hand.

Weislob snapped off the phone and came into the room. 'OK, let's go.'

'You got anything for Bambi?'

'I got everything for Bambi.'

Coburn turned to greet Michael, as though he had just come in. There was no pretence at familiarity, only a handshake, the glare of assessment. Coburn knew human nature. His eyes were disarmingly brown, containing surplus personality.

'Rick Weislob.' A big hand ushered in a short associate.

190

Weislob without shades exhibited no friendliness. The face was sour, usefully mean. He did not look like his voice. His hard blue eyes regarded Michael unflinchingly, as though the telephone call between them had never happened.

The 'bunker' was an empty bedroom, with wall lamps set into a panel either side of where the bed would have been. The hotel staff had brought in a conference table and four chairs for the purpose of the meeting and provided water in a jug and glasses.

Weislob sat down at the far end of the table, his jacket buttoned, shades pocketed, fingers conjoined. He had the bottled quality of a man who has had to eat shit and is heavily unpleased, tight-faced with the anger of it.

'Real pretty place,' said Coburn, coming away from the window and leaning against the wall.

Michael hoped that their flight had been OK.

'Flight's a flight.'

They had tried to intimidate him. He was unimpressed. He was not going to be bullied.

When Bambi arrived, Coburn averted his eyes. She sat opposite the boss, legs crossed, pen and notepad ready.

For a moment there was a curious silence that rehearsed all that stood between them, the incongruity of the situation, its uncustomariness and gravity.

'You got the option agreement?' said Weislob.

Michael shook his head.

'Bambi, did you ask Mr Lear to bring the option agreement?'

'Yes, sir.'

Weislob was unblinking.

'You never faxed the coverage,' he said.

'I faxed it Wednesday.'

'Didn't arrive.'

'I have fax confirmation.'

'Not received.'

'Talk to your hotel. You got the option?'

'It's in my hotel room.'

Weislob gasped, unable to conceal impatience. 'Michael. We fly from LA. Ten hours. Six thousand miles. Meanwhile, you leave the contract in your hotel room.'

'I didn't ask you to come.'

'You agreed to show us the contract! You made a promise!'

'Bambi.' Coburn leaned forward, rubbing his eye. 'Have reception call Mr Lear's hotel. Mr Lear can authorise the hotel staff to collect the agreement from his room and give it to a messenger.'

Bambi rose questioningly.

Coburn humped his shoulders.

There was silence.

'Thank you, Bambi.'

'It's a standard agreement,' Michael said quickly. 'You've seen hundreds like it.'

'There's agreements and agreements.'

He drew himself up. 'I'd hate to waste time on small print. This discussion might go nowhere.'

'You got sequel rights?'

'Yup.'

'Merchandising, CD-rom.'

'Sure.'

'Option renewals?'

Coburn came towards him rapidly, placed hairy hands on the table, leaned forward on thick arms. 'We're in this town for forty-eight hours, pardner. My attitude is that when we leave we have a deal.'

He was like a Western sheriff, but real; as though he had gone through things to make him real; fights.

'I hope so.'

'Not hope. Know.'

'I can't . . .'

'Michael!' There was dark energy in Coburn's eyes. 'The situation is dangerous.'

'Because of you,' said Weislob.

Michael frowned away his annoyance. 'For me it's not at all dangerous.'

'Legally it's devastating.'

He flinched.

'We're saying be real!'

'Is that a threat?'

Coburn sat down hard. 'Leave the room, Bambi.'

She made a dignified exit.

Two pairs of eyes came at him.

Coburn dropped a forearm on the table. He drove a tongue into the pouch of his cheek. He shut his eyes meditatively before swinging a slow, sleepy gaze at Michael. 'I can see you like her. Most everyone likes Bambi. Rick here sucks her tits in his dreams.'

'The babe's a breast mountain.'

'Know what, Michael? This business of ours is crammed with shitty people. A flakefest. Hanging out with wannabes, coke crazies, lots of weavy crap, lots of talented furkin people going nowhere, and we get sucked off with all the fringe trash. We're businessmen first and foremost; technicians of profit. We see a market, we make a product, we go straight to the money. Sometimes . . . manners are useful.'

'I don't do manners.'

'Rick is a specialist in non-manners. He's too small to be nice. And the reason Bambs so kindly left the room is cos I want to protect the meek and the innocent from the sight of this thing.'

Coburn leaned to the side and produced an object bound in cloth. He set the bound lump on the table. With a forefinger and thumb he pulled away the material to reveal a hand-gun.

He revolved it on the table's surface, then swept the thing with the edge of his palm towards Michael.

He had never seen a hand-gun before. For a second he felt strange.

Coburn sat back, arms crossed, a biceps in each hand. 'We're LA people. Frontier folk. I've always had a drawer full of metal. I've done Kalashnikov courses. Shooting-range promotions. I got a diploma in gunge. Rick here does martial-arts classes. Like running between punks' legs and biting their balls off. And sure, if some scumface Hispanic pulls a tool on me I'll shoot him. No problem. Squeeze the trigger like taking a piss. Cos I believe in democracy and I believe in a man's right to defend his property. Like if you came into my house' – he pointed at Michael – 'and you laid a finger on what I own, I'd blow you in half with this here gun.'

'You took the option, Michael. You stole property.'

'I keep what's mine.' Coburn lurched towards the gun, grabbed it back. 'I wanna piece through customs, favours are called. You know. Bambs there, great at favours.'

'Two of the biggest alibis in the business.'

'So let's cut the fuck and get to the point.'

Michael scratched his neck, displacing astonishment. Coburn was stagy and grotesque, and he had not expected anything like it.

'We ain't the suave charming guys we seem.' Weislob's eyes were crystal blue, the skin sallow. He had eaten his jetlag and digested it in one.

'OK, dear.'

Bambi returned, resumed her seat, and waited with parted lips for the discussion to continue. She gazed expectantly at Michael.

'You got the option?' said Weislob.

The gun had disappeared.

'Just a minute, Rick.' Coburn was on his feet, stroking the back of his neck. 'Michael says he's got the option.'

'Maybe Michael's lying.'

'You lyin', Michael?'

He made no response.

'We have a lie detector here.'

For a moment he was checked, as if they knew something and were psyching him out. But they could not know anything.

'This discussion proceeds on the basis that you have the rights, that your attendance here represents you have the rights, that we are here in reliance of that and that you'll give us the agreement at' – Coburn checked his Rolex – '3 p.m.'

'If you want to talk, talk.' It was time to dig in. 'I'm not accepting conditions.'

'Don't hardball us!' Weislob hit the table.

'Rick, slow down.' Coburn wandered towards Michael's end of the room, clapped his palms together. He was suddenly different. He had given his mood a makeover. His eyes glittered with theatrical anticipation. Suddenly, he pulled the gun from his pocket and clicked the trigger. A tongue of flame shot up from the barrel. 'You got me a smoke, Rick?'

The short agent took a cigar tube from inside his jacket, put it flat on the table.

Coburn smirked at Michael, a hillbilly smirk full of childish mirth and sophisticated gamesmanship.

'Maybe later. When Michael's a little more relaxed.'

Weislob grinned for an instant.

Michael let the air out of his lungs. His expression remained blank but he was physically relieved, which meant that he had been successfully toyed with.

'Michael, we got something you want.' Coburn cleared his throat, replacing the lighter in his pocket. 'We got Shane Hammond rolling up his sleeves to do a part. We got green wave on a movie called *Last*

Muse, which you're going to associate produce for the biggest cheque you've ever banked. We got a case of money for your option expenses and legal costs, plus a sweetener and then some. Bambi? Thank you, honey.'

Bambi came to the table with two separate attaché cases. She sprang the catch on each opening them wide.

Michael was surprised to see what he saw. The dollar wads were neat and fresh, toylike.

'You're looking at thirty thousand bucks which will be yours when these discussions are over.' He winked. 'Plus a roll in the hay with Bambs. OK, Rick?'

'My pleasure.'

Coburn laughed. 'And that's just howdy-do money.'

She was looking at him. He averted his eyes. They were an act, experts at bluff, menace, disorientation.

'You get associate-producer retainer during development. Ten thousand a month, plus expenses. Then a production fee in any tax shelter of your choice on first day principal p. One hundred thousand dollars.' He walked behind him. 'I repeat: one hundred thousand dollars. One more time, Rick.'

They both sang. 'One hundred thousand dollars.'

'You're looking at one fifty plus grand and you haven't said a word. You haven't had lunch. We'll give you points, we'll give you onscreen credit, single card, letters not less than seventy per cent bullshit and major paid advertising. Welcome to Hollywood.'

'Welcome, Michael.'

'Rick's got paper. We can sign off now. Your signature buys those greenbacks. Our signature gets us that option. How's about that?'

'Speak your mind, Michael.'

He pressed the fingers of both hands into a steeple. His heart was racing. His first realisation was that Coburn had blown his cover by advancing a deal large enough to suggest pragmatism and therefore flexibility, but not large enough to reflect the leverage causing that pragmatism, Michael's leverage. His second thought was that Coburn had calculated he could be bought. If that assumption were true, it would explain Coburn's confidence, his routine with the cigarette lighter-cum-gun prop, his gamble on the offer. But it was not true. His heart quickened. There was an opportunity here, and Coburn had just confirmed Adamson's most bullish predictions.

'Interesting.'

'We think so.'

'The offer is made in good faith?'

'My friend, we did not come here to procrastinate. We are businessmen and we are busy men.'

'The figures you mention' – Michael waved his hand – 'I had numbers in mind.'

'I'm sure you did,' said Coburn.

'Different numbers.'

'Hey, bud.' The American was all smiles. 'We'll pay less if you want.'

He smiled back. 'I'll tell you what I want.'

Weislob was poker-faced.

'I'd like to touch on the creative aspect.'

Coburn blinked.

'I have a vision of the film.'

There was silence.

'And it's important to myself and the author that this thing is done properly.'

Their faces were expressionless, shadowy with reserve.

'Unless I can meet Shane and establish that we want the same film . . .' He shrugged. 'No point in talking further. You see, we're dealing with an important novel, and the development should not go forward without your team being clear about the type of film I want to make. A film that is dramatic, cinematic, but true to the book. If we can come together at that level of aspiration, I'm happy to continue discussions. But I won't let the tail of the deal wag the dog of the film.'

He was conscious of having spoken in a firm tone, of having conveyed a little of his metal to the Americans in a different language to their own. The agenda had moved on.

Coburn gazed at his lap and rotated his thumbs; the window light caught the scimitar whites of his eyes.

Bambi was jotting rapidly, turning Michael's sub-clauses into shifty shorthand.

'What d'you say, Frank?' shrugged Weislob.

'How many films you made, Michael?'

'I haven't made any films.'

'You want to make a film?'

'Not any film.'

'You want to get a movie scripted, cast, financed, produced and exhibited once in your life?'

He said nothing.

'Get some perspective, Michael.'

'Shane Hammond is the money, right. Guy pulls twenty million like picking his nose.'

'Shane's big, Michael.'

'You're invisible.'

'Baggage.'

'No track.'

'This is not your film, never was, never will be.'

He was hard. 'It's mine for three years.'

Weislob grimaced. 'What you got is not yours.'

'It's ours,' said Coburn.

'You stole confidential information, read a confidential manuscript. You've acted in gross bad faith and have no right to call this your picture.'

'You've heard my terms,' said Michael.

'Don't bluff.'

'I don't need to bluff.' He held the table-top, fending the pressure. 'I can go elsewhere.'

Coburn rose bearishly. Michael sensed the anger-point had been reached.

'We've checked you out,' said Weislob.

'Due diligence,' added Coburn.

'Intelligent Productions is a blown-out piece of garbage, no revenue, no capital, big debts. Won't be around by Thanksgiving. See, we've totally researched you, Michael, and we see the logic of your hijacking this movie cos you're up shit creek without a hank of rest-room paper.'

Coburn rounded boomingly. 'You're opportunistic and desperate, and frankly, my friend, I raise my hat to you readily, because you got our arses out here like greased lightning. But, *amigo*, if you really think a star like Hammond is going to sit round a table listening to a chicken fuckin' word of your so-called "vision", you're out of your jock-strap.'

'Wise up, Michael.'

'Sell out, Michael.'

He caught Bambi's eye and spoke mildly and abstractly. 'The option's in my name. Not my company's.'

'Your name is bullshit.'

Coburn hovered above him. He heard the big man breathing.

Michael looked at his hands in self-consultation. This was the crux moment and he fought against chagrin.

'Would Shane prefer to wait three more years or talk to me now?'

'Don't try it,' said Weislob.

'We do all the talking. Till the deal is sealed and signed.'

'Shane's time is money.'

'He'd talk to me.'

'He's cute with old folks and bums but he doesn't like wannabes.'

'Stars aren't into speculative de-scussions about the nature of the universe with industry freshmen.'

'Hilldyard wants to meet him.'

There was silence. It was a strange thing for him to have said.

'I think you should inform Shane.'

'Shane is not sociable.'

'Why don't you ask him?'

'Ask him what?' whined Weislob. 'Audition for some pesky old author?'

'He should be so lucky.'

'Fuck.' Weislob's palms hit the table. 'Shane Hammond's way bigger than Hilldyard. Hilldyard's just another bookworm scribe. Hilldyard should be touching the hem of Hammond's jacket if he could get within a mile of a man that famous.'

It was an insight to hear what these men really believed. They spoke ugly words, said crude things and believed them implicitly.

'Hammond winks, there's twenty, thirty, fifty million bucks on a plate.'

Coburn shook his head. 'Hammond does not need James Hilldyard. He has the pick of the best Hollywood scripts and can work with anyone he chooses, including authors a lot more visible than Jimmy-boy.'

Michael's heart was sinking in his breast.

'Fact is, Hilldyard needs Hammond, being as right now our scouts say the bard ain't shifting them stateside.'

'I'd say in the US market James Hilldyard is not only not visible but a complete lemon. Where's that Pulitzer? Where's that Nobel? Right out of sight. What the good man needs is a big, bruising movie opening on twelve hundred screens with a Universal or Sony on a major-spend advertising campaign.'

'A humungous tie-in.'

'Get the people readin'.'

'Bums on seats. Paws on pages.'

'Not some squirty little English producer trying to play off his literary status against a major Hollywood star.'

'Won't work, Michael.'

He was subdued, hemmed in.

'Take the ransom and sign.'

He had played it too straight, too respectably, and he wanted to leave them now, leave behind the whole monstrous situation that was as dismal to him as it would be horrifying to Hilldyard. But he had no choice. There was no backing out now, not until all the cards were played.

'*Variety* would pay more for this story,' he said, turning an eye on Coburn. It was important to hold his eye.

'I didn't hear that.'

'*Variety* would pay me more,' he said.

Coburn blinked, came round and sat right before him. 'Dumb, Michael. You'd lose thirty thousand bucks now. You'd lose more later.'

Balls was what you had to have, he thought. *Cojónes.*

'Want to hear more?'

'Some things I don't hear.'

'Then read about it. How your agency lost Shane Hammond! Full-page feature. Your face. Hammond's. Hammond's new agent. The screw-up on the option. Hilldyard's views on Rick. Your sweaty trip halfway round the globe and failure to close a deal. The trades would lap it up. Not great for business, but no publicity is bad publicity!'

Coburn tongued his cheek. His eyes were neutral.

'Are you blackmailing us?' Weislob was sharp. 'Make a note, Bambi.'

He saw the cold disgust in Coburn's eyes.

'We can play it that way.' Michael stood up.

'Sit down.'

'You're not leaving this place till the deal's done.'

'Or we can have a civilised discussion.' He went around the table to the door.

'Don't move.'

'I'll be lunching at the Marinella restaurant. On the beach. If you want to talk on my terms, I'll see you there. Otherwise, give my regards to Tinseltown. Pleasure to meet you, Bambi.'

Coburn rose violently.

Michael grabbed the handle, pulled the door open.

'Big mistake, Michael.'

'We'll see.'

Coburn let him leave without another word, but in his expression Michael saw a strange absence, a moment of non-being.

Weislob picked his nose; and then the door was closed.

Chapter Nineteen

THE DRIVER DROPPED HIM off at the snake bend in the road. He sprang out of the car and walked downhill, towards his hotel. He had promised to call Adamson. He needed more than advice. On the drive back revulsion had expanded inside him. He felt as though he had stepped out of a bad-trip parallel reality that one shuddered off with every turn of the road while feeling simultaneously exhilarated and hardly able to believe he had threatened them – the audacity, the machismo of it – as though at last he were kicking ass for every rotten thing that had happened to him.

He sprang up the flight of steps to the hotel thinking of the chaos he had stirred up. He was light-headed, coked up on hazard and impulse, and he came on to the terrace almost too speedily to notice the raincoated back of James Hilldyard, standing on the veranda by the hotel entrance. Michael braked hard, stood staring, then reversed along the terrace and slipped down the steps again, glancing as he went to see Hilldyard's face sweep like a searchlight across tables and chairs to a point above his head.

He dropped into an alley, fetched his breath back, stared vacantly at two cats eyeing a lizard at the base of a wall. Soapy water slid down the cement path. He had not stood here before. It was not a good place to stand.

He had arranged to meet Adela at noon. She had wanted first news of the Coburn meeting.

'Shit,' he said.

Seconds later he was slipping up the steps, nerving himself to have another look over the stair rail; but on the way he glanced through the weepy remains of an autumn walnut tree and saw Hilldyard at the veranda's edge. Even at ten yards the face was visibly distraught. Hilldyard was staring at the view, hoping for Michael's return.

He could feel the need in the old man's eyes, and it was with a betrayer's knot in his stomach that he descended the steps and decided to stay in the alley for as long as it took him to lose heart and clear off.

He went further up this time, stared at the cats, regarded the textures of dilapidated plaster with unfamiliar nervousness and made himself bide time while the old man waited. The minutes dragged. He drew a hand over his face, to clear thoughts. There was nothing to think, actually.

He could not keep still and walked on, following the alley along its winding route, which he hoped would lead to the Viale. The alley forked and climbed and levelled, produced lampposts, tresses of creeper, and the impassive backs of shuttered villas with their marble steps, entryphone buzzers and associated cats watching his shoes as he passed; and in due course he returned to the second path and went past maritime façades and pots of cactus and geranium to a point where the track ended in grass and he was looking, suddenly, at the back of a girl painting a picture. She stood with her easel at the edge of the terrace. Michael stopped dead in his tracks. She was almost camouflaged by the similarity of her hair to the reddish colour of the vine. She was motionless, brush poised.

He trod closer, drawn by the glimpse of a flight of steps to her right and then by a need to verify the spectacle of a woman he had never seen in Positano. Quietly, he approached, gaining the sense of what she was intensely regarding as she held her brush aloft. He saw the sea through branches and leaves, the twisted stem of an olive, the facets of a shoreline turret, parting the tones of light and shade, and then her billow of auburn hair, her Doc Martens and dungarees, and when she turned, the calm brow and fine mouth, and the feral way she bared her teeth to bite on a roll.

She saw him but said nothing. He passed her with a nod and made his quick way down the steps, his astonishment complete, almost frying him with a sense of the nervously unexpected, until a cross-roads of alleys approached, and just as he turned, the figure appeared, and he flung himself into a doorway and listened to the shuffle and smack of shoes on steps, and waited an agonised eternity for the old man to pass, which he did, touchably close, with a hand on the rail and his raincoat belt dragging behind him. Michael held his breath and watched Hilldyard sink down the remaining steps. He had soon reached the bottom and turned out of sight.

Up on the hotel terrace he rubbed his eyes and wondered whether to call Curwen or Adamson. He had to get going again, apply the engine of his mind to the next stage, though the prospect of Adela's arrival sent the distraction of slide-like thoughts across everything, the view, the next telephone call, as though to hold down all that with tight control while anticipating her company was impossible. He sat down hard on a seat. He could not properly visualise Adela; and not being able to picture her made it hard to prepare for her. She brought an energy that worked on him, changing him, making him into someone different. He bit his finger, enjoying the agitation, and thinking that in all probability love had dropped on him out of the sky.

She had liked him physically; he was sure of it. No first lovemaking was ever solid in memory; too many things were lost in the shock. There had been the uncanniness of flesh, her sharp intakes of breath, the way she moved on the bed, supply voluptuous. In return for his losing control she had granted him all her sexiness. She wanted to be memorable, threw herself into the role. But then things slowed down, the first energies subsiding into entwined reliance. He had his moments of worship and wonder. Their caresses became more personal, as though touching were now a means to locate the emotion of the encounter. He brushed her hip flat-handed, stroked the soft underside of her jaw. And she nuzzled his hand and became collapsible in the crook of his arm, trying to let herself go, striving under his touch. Lying next to him Adela seemed fully possessable, and, as she stiffened around the tenuous thread of excitement, he felt the tension in her desire, the swell of what she was able to summon up, as if she could treat arousal with the unabashed force of a maturely sexual being. And when she came, she rolled on to him to conceal the intensity of her relief.

She was used to making love, of course, had grooves accessible to Jack and to some extent transferable to a new body. And Michael later wondered whether he had stolen Jack's show or Jack had stolen his.

When her turn came, she wanted to do something for him and seemed conscious of differences. There was less expertise in her touch, even shyness, and that was more personal. A man had to be satisfied, yes, and a man had to take satisfaction, too, and Michael's responses were unknown to her, as they were unknown to himself in this situation. His long ascetic body had not been offered such luxury in years: the syrupy ardour of her kisses, the plump comfortable lobes of her breasts. He could not really believe it, and the disbelief held him back for a while, until gradually the flowing hair and upturned face and the plush cladding of her arse when she turned rewired desire and soon enough they had before them the coalition of his stiff cock and her dreamy smile. 'Exercise your option,' she had said, adding wit to provocation, and with reverent control and due sense of occasion he had taken some exercise.

Afterwards, she lay on her front, face away from him. She was silently wondering how much self-control had been leaked.

In due course she made a comic groan that brought her back into full daylight. She drew up, hair crossing her breasts, and came down with a mattress-creak face to face; and then her look was neutral, as if closeness needed no expression. Her lips parted, hair spilled away from her temple and she gave him the benefit of wide eyes, enormous on the pillow, and boomerang brows. Between them lay the sense of an event having taken place; she sought its implications in his eyes. He gazed back into hers. Before long, he decided to kiss her, as if a kiss would cast light. His lips connected with her passive mouth. She received his gaze unblinkingly; and this restraint, he thought, was her invitation to stay alert and see beyond the moment – which he did not care to do. He ran a thumb across her lip, drove his fingers into the thickness of her hair. She let this pass. He was welcome to see how beautiful she was. Her loveliness went out to the appreciative man, was available to him; and Michael reciprocated with his own intensity of aspect. He was so struck by her, it was too much. She read it in his eyes and laughed softly. She had landed this brooding specimen of a man on her pillow, a character with beautiful dark hair and serious eyebrows, a man of high literary taste and principled feelings, and suddenly it amused her. She smiled brightly.

Later, when he had returned to his hotel and started to prepare for the Coburn meeting, he could hardly believe he had made love to her. The memory dissolved in his hands, was part of sliding off time, and this seemed to evoke still stronger feelings, as if emotion could substitute for the material presence of a person and thereby keep alive the reality of what had happened. The lid had been flipped and there was extreme urgency in his desire to confirm the miracle, to go through the threshold again and be on the other side of things, naked in her arms, basking in the plenitude of her body. He was terrified by the thought that what happened to them was an accident, a sexy one-off, caused by things that would not be allowed to run out of control again – a prospect as unnerving as its opposite: namely, that he now had a lover in the person of Adela Fairfax.

He reached for his room key over the concierge desk. Hilldyard's note came back between fingers from the pigeon-hole.

The old man had written one page in an italic hand of tattered distinction.

Dear Michael,

I beg you, as soon as you get this letter, give me a ring or come to the villa. I came this morning in the hope of finding you because I am frankly miserable at the unfinished state things are in with regard to our last conversation, which must have left you with some awful thoughts about me, and which I am most keen to counterbalance and explain to the best of my ability, and of course I would dearly like to see you for your own company. I am not an unfeeling old man and I do understand the nature of your difficulties and I would like to help in any practical way other than to grant the option, which I'm sure you finally understand is impossible for me, and I'm glad to have made a clean breast of that. There are, of course, more things I may tell you about myself, and in their general light I am sure we can remain true confidants and friends and colleagues, though of course what I have told and will tell you must seem very unexpected.

Unfortunately, Frances is now very upset about the film not going ahead, really quite frantic, and it may well be that she seeks you out as she thinks she has rights in the matter. If this does happen, I implore you to support me by telling her that this was not my decision, and I know this is a fib, but that the money fell through, or some bromide about Shane Hammond not being available. I know it is a terrible imposition to ask such a thing. Please help your old friend. These are difficult times for me, and it is a blessed relief to know that, after everything, I can call on your support.

Come and see me.

Trustingly,

James

Michael re-read the note and then jogged upstairs. He would now call Adamson or Curwen.

Standing in his hotel room, paid for by Hilldyard, and gazing through the shutters to the mountain, he sensed the deed ahead as a kind of revelation. The means were being offered to him, as if breaking Hilldyard was a necessary development in his knowledge of the man, the last stage in a unique interview.

He wondered how much pain Hilldyard could resist. The man had high thresholds. Pain was a writer's friend.

He did not brace himself much for the telephone call to Curwen, but just dialled away, heard the agent's secretary on the line and learned quickly that Curwen was ill. Joy was a little hushed, vague about when he would return and not responsive to Michael's urgency. There was no contact number. All calls were going through the office. His earlier message had been relayed, and, yes, the Americans had been leaving calls, too. She knew that a film was involved and was quite definite that Curwen, when he called, would call Michael first. Michael pushed for Curwen's home number, detected evasion, and became suddenly angry.

'He's in hospital,' said Joy.

The agent had collapsed at a drinks party, been driven by ambulance to the Brompton Chest Hospital, spent a wretched night on the ward before transferring to the oncology wing of a private hospital the next day.

'Isn't he taking calls?' It seemed impossible that Curwen would cease to operate from wherever he was based. 'Where is he? Which hospital?'

'He's not at all well.'

His lungs were dissolving, his heart was faint, there were advanced secondaries in the liver, his skin was covered in blotches, his eyes were sunken. Curwen the impresario was suspended by the thinnest thread of life.

'Who handles deals in his absence?'

There was something curious about the death of a middle-man, so pivotal in health, so empowered by the interests he brokered, so inessential on his demise.

'He's dying, Mr Lear.'

'He can get me on this number at any time.'

It seemed impossible that Curwen should cease to be; uncanny that he should time it so well.

206

Strange things were being given to Michael, implements placed just so in his hand. He had not killed Curwen, albeit Curwen's collapse played into his hands as though he had actually poisoned him. Curwen had to go some time, of course, and it need not make Michael guilty that he had chosen this moment of optimum convenience not to be around for the Americans' enquiries. The reverse, in fact. Curwen's withdrawal encouraged chance-taking. If the poor man was going to the trouble of dying, Michael had better make the most of it.

He stood on the balcony's edge, gazing at the sea and the mountains and the zigzagging houses dropping sideways across the ridge. Glassy light played on the lines and textures of things. The air was fresh, breezy. One became too easily fascinated by the plethora of forms defined by sea light, even in overcast weather.

The scenery clawed at him. The prospect was painful to behold. Every purity was out there in the uptilted mirror of the view showing him his better self. He was keyed up, now, leaking with feeling. It seemed as though all beautiful things were in sympathetic vibration with his inner self.

He felt pity for Curwen. Curwen's life had been meaningless.

He shed a tear and rested his eyes on the terrace's chairs and tables. Everyone was level before a view, he thought. One busied oneself with daily things, schemes and ambitions, money and love in some convolution or other, and all along the view was there, waiting to be noticed, offering to steal you away from the hours and minutes of a busy life and reveal what it was you had for a soul.

One took in the scene like pure oxygen. Its purity stung the inner eye. He could drag in everything now, the chairs and terracotta urns, the blue awning running from the wall to the balcony posts, and the head of hair at the end of the terrace, rising up the flight of steps.

Adela waved at him, walking swiftly, carrying towards him a sense of energy and freshness which spun up his excitement. And as she sped across the terrace, he saw again the immense system of delights she offered and thought it impossible that anyone so consummately pleasing to every nerve in his body could not be destined for him.

She had waved a bunch of flowers at him, and he had gone down to join her on the terrace.

She was striking in jeans, sweater and lipstick, and all-welcoming as he approached her. She wore her variety well, showing herself lovely in different clothes. Her smile and colouring and mouth softened all resistance.

He kissed her lightly and received the bouquet and stood there as she went to the balcony. She was happy today. She sensed her future and it made her exuberant. She had a springiness on her feet, a readiness to run and jump. Her hair smelled of blossom.

He put the flowers on the table and joined her by the balcony. At first he kept his hands to himself. Restraint was dynamic. She pointed at this and that, held it all appreciatively in an open gasp, as if to show that she had taken in essences to do with where he was staying and what he had come here for.

She faced him suddenly, drawing back a strand of hair. 'How did it go?'

He shrugged and smiled. 'Fine!'

'Really!'

'They bullied me, and I blackmailed them.'

'What!'

Her beauty was exhilarating, especially when stirred by indignation.

'Coburn's a gorilla.'

She was taken aback. 'But why should he be? You've got the option.'

'That brings out the gorilla in him.'

'Michael!'

'Don't worry.'

'Are you sure?'

'We're having lunch on the beach.'

'They shouldn't be nasty to you.'

He took her hand. There was no virtue in coyness. His feeling for her was true. Everything was being swept along and there was no time to tarry. Why not show feeling? Show her what he could express?

'You look lovely today.'

He kissed the knuckles firmly. She watched him execute the kiss with due sense of occasion, following Michael's style in these matters. It was one style amongst many; a perfectly good one.

'Don't let them get to you. They're only agents.'

'I'm not letting them get to me.'

He encircled her waist with his hand.

'Michael.' She twisted out of his clasp, keeping hold of his hand. He nodded.

Her face was set. 'D'you want the good news or the bad news?'

His heart leapt and that was proof in itself.

Her lips were parted. She looked at him directly. 'I think you ought to know.'

He tried to cover his alarm.

'Listen here,' she said, patting the rail. 'The good news. You have a movie star on your hands.'

'What!'

'I called Shane last night. He's in Paris this morning but is flying here this afternoon . . .'

'Here?'

'Naples, then coming for dinner.'

'He's coming to Positano?'

'Yes, Michael!'

He tried to control his panic. 'Why?'

'Why d'you think?'

'What did you tell him?'

'Like I said, we have to be straight with him. He knows you have the rights. He wants to sit down with both of you.'

'Both of whom?'

'You and Hilldyard.'

He missed a heartbeat. 'We can't inflict James on him.'

'He has to see your relationship with James.'

He shook his head. 'That's not easy.'

'Nothing's easy, but everything's got to happen.' She held his eye, checking his nerve.

'Does Coburn know he's coming?'

She frowned, summoning calculation, not achieving it. 'Shane was completely gobsmacked when I told him about Coburn.'

'Do they know he's coming?'

'He doesn't want them to know.'

'What!'

'So don't tell them!'

He was very disconcerted. 'Don't tell the agents who say I can't meet their client that their client wants to meet me?'

She shrugged.

'Are they still representing him?'

'I think it depends on this deal.'

No wonder she was tense. Reality-levels were increasing. All elements were in play, and he felt his own nervousness rising and sinking in waves. Time was now short.

'Great! So what's the bad news?'

She closed her eyes first then took his sleeve. Her jaw came forward, an actress's tic: the jut of courage. She struggled to find the right terms.

'Oh, I think he's a little bit interested.'

'He?'

'Shane.'

He did not follow. 'Meaning what?'

'Meaning lots, I should think.'

He shook his head. 'What are you talking about?'

'I think he's interested in me.'

He started. 'Shane fancies you?'

'Possibly.'

Something subsided within him: the sense of limitless complications.

She gave him a look of veiled concern.

'I thought you should know,' she said.

He was lost for a moment.

'We'll deal with it,' she said.

He nodded. They would deal with it. Yes. He realised that.

'Come to my hotel,' she said.

'Your hotel?'

'After your meeting. I'll tell you about things.'

'What things?'

'Things you need to know.'

Michael stared at her, his mind racing.

'When is your meeting?'

He glanced absently at his watch.

'Do the meeting. Then come.'

Chapter Twenty

HE WAS VISIBLE NOW, fully in view, and he felt like a high-noon cowboy striding over the beach towards the wooden stilts of the restaurant. The sky was grey, the sea dark. There were no witnesses, just a deckchair that some optimist had abandoned, an overturned fishing boat, and way off, in the shrunken distance, the crow-black figure of Weislob doing calls on the beach. Michael pressed onwards, his heart in his mouth. At least they had come, and as Adamson said to him during a fast phone call, that was proof. They *had* to do business; their mere attendance gave him the edge. Though now, of course, Frank Coburn knew his man, had taken stock, and would be super psyched up. Michael had meanwhile realised that to have any honour in the matter he had to control the film artistically. An impossible condition for Coburn.

Adamson was pleased by the venue. 'What is it? Shanty caff, bare boards and chemical toilet?'

The Marinella was a platform of wood extending on struts to the water's edge. It hugged the boulder that stopped the beach, and its planks and bamboo canopy were cured by the salt breeze and summer sun; as was the owner, a rough old boy with a maestro's glower and an artificial leg that he cranked around tables as he took orders and brought food. He would lay out a tablecloth, clip down its corners, and recite in a drone the meal of the day, as if satisfaction were simply unquestionable if you went with the flow and let him get on with it. Michael had lunched there before, once on his own and once with Hilldyard, and had sat each time on the deck, mesmerised by the sea light and the taste of parsley on sardines, and the coppery rosé in his glass.

'Eat well,' said Adamson.

'I'm not hungry.'

'Be psychological. Nothing you can say will make a bigger statement of control. You'll need a main course, two side orders and a glass of wine. It's the European mode: business as a subset of lifestyle.'

It was 4 a.m. in Los Angeles.

He mentioned Coburn's toy gun.

'No bite, loud bark.'

'I think it's pretty tasteless.'

'Coburn is a player. Players play with you.'

'You don't think he was trying to tell me something?'

'Look, he's steaming because you nicked the rights and dropped him in the shit bucket. He's going to use every prop in the book before taking the strain on your position. Insult, intimidation, flattery, menaces. You put a top agent on the warpath.'

'I've certainly fucked with his pride.'

Adamson hesitated, computing pride. 'Coburn's bottom line is keep Hammond, and the route to that is bend over.'

He could hardly believe this. 'I just force the deal?'

'Like nutcrackers on a cashew. He'll fume and rant, but it's soundtrack, because you've got one mother of a crow-bar under that guy's butt, and without the authority of a client behind him he'll come off his position like a hinge out of balsa.'

Michael had not been reassured, because Adamson had no certain way to know Coburn's resourcefulness at full tilt. If Coburn was good, it was because he thrived in tight corners.

'Michael, you've got him cheeks wide over a barrel and you can cram every clause in the book up his bottom line.'

'It doesn't feel like that.'

'Hey, you're in hell's kitchen with a mad butcher.'

'I think he takes it personally.'

'He hands it out. He can take it. These guys swivel on client shit all day. Their sphincters are Teflon-plated.'

Michael laughed unhappily. 'So what do I do?'

'Coburn's come to hear terms. Soften him up. Don't go between him and the client. Be his solution to a client problem. Stress collaboration, shared goals.'

'Then rip off his packaging fee?'

'It's your greed versus theirs.'

'I should be taking the moral high ground!'

'Do unto Coburn what he'd do unto you, and do it sooner.'

Michael was going to ask Coburn for five hundred thousand dollars. That's what he was going to do unto him.

The restaurant seemed empty from a distance. The season had come to a close; perhaps this was its last day. He wondered whether the owner would be there, waiting to serve whatever solitary diners presented themselves at half-past one.

The beach stones were hard walking, adding weight to one's feet, pulling on one's stomach muscles.

Adela's news ate into him. There was additional instability in the scheme of things, more variables to keep in control. Acute vulnerability went with high stakes. He was opened up inside, holed in some intimate place, had no choice but to push on.

Rick stayed on the beach as Michael walked up the concrete ramp to the dais of the restaurant. Up on the boards a tourist in a tennis shirt sat at a table, waiting to be served.

Coburn was sitting at the end of the platform. He had freed a chair from its table and placed it by the rail so that he could rest his arm and stretch his legs while looking out to sea. He wore a roomy suit and buckled loafers. A chunky watch dangled on his wrist. Even the smooth back of his bald head held body language: tough-guy forbearance.

Michael sat down at the next table. No pleasantries could be executed. The maestro came out of the kitchen cabin and made his way over to the table. He brought cutlery, oil and vinegar and the morose disposition of a man who lives only for the changing light and a few bikinied bodies (in short supply today). Michael listened to the menu whilst regarding the agent's profile.

Coburn sat in bulky self-containment. He gazed into the distance and allowed the energy between them to purify and condense, as if he were testing certain instincts for manoeuvre or attack. It was impossible to read him. He had the advantage of such self-knowledge in the realm of brinkmanship that his every move scrambled prediction.

'Hello, Michael.'

The tone was concessionary.

He stood up suddenly and swung his chair over to Michael's table. 'Mind if I join you?'

Coburn was massive across the table, bull's shoulders and neck filling out the view. He smiled with his eyes, smoothed his moustache thoughtfully.

'You're a great poker player.' He nodded. 'Rick and I dig your style. Ballsy English types are rare.'

It was a man-to-man approach and it explained Rick's demotion to the beach. 'We've shot a few rounds into the sky, checked each other out and, from where I stand, you got what it takes.'

He raised the flat of his hand, a cease-fire gesture.

'Let me give you a perspective. If Shane Hammond, bless him, wants to leave us, he'll go. Clients come and go, and that's the reality of agenting. We've been in business ten years before Shane, and I figure we can stay afloat with or without him. He's a star. But we have our pride. And we don't believe that if Shane quits folks are gonna think the worse of us. Let me tell you, Hollywood is a psychological war zone, a crucible of total competition. What counts in the end is not this deal or that deal, not execution on any terms, but the humane way of putting talented people through the grief of Tinseltown. That's as much as we can do. Luck makes the rest. Everybody knows that. Say this here deal flunks, and *Last Muse* ashes out, I don't think Shane's gonna walk on us. He knows we're doin' our damnedest. Hey, we're right here, talking to you. And if we can't fix it, nobody can. See, I'd tell him the facts. Like Michael Lear's a man of taste and manners. But Shane's a star, and stars need to move with senior talent, not rookie producers. And when Shane tells me you got the rights, I say not because you want to make the film, because your company's going bust and you're desperate. And when he says Michael Lear's a friend of Adela Fairfax, I say Adela's great at socialising but she's not a qualified head-hunter. And when he says he's unhappy, we say here's a ninety-million-dollar movie for him to walk into and while he's doing that we'll talk to Ike Petersen and Felipe Garcia Gonzalez about creating another vehicle, for him and Adela, which he can direct. And if he says something else, we will too, because actors are our business, and we can make them listen to their own best interests.'

Michael nodded neutrally. Coburn's depiction was not unsustainable. Things could be made to look like that and it was in his interests to know how an agent might report the situation to a client.

'So maybe we can forget the coffee break this morning and talk business?'

He shrugged assent. Silence was his ally.

'Michael, this is one hundred per cent good faith.' He raised a finger. 'You'll not get a better deal this side of Hollywood. And I think you deserve it. One: "Produced by" credit. Two: a seat at the table. We'll consult you on script, cast and other creative decisions. Three: real money. We'll arrange thirty thousand dollars to assign the option and assume all financial responsibilities to James Hilld-yard. We'll get you a retainer payment off of the development package. Forty thousand dollars phased to the script schedule. We'll give you two hundred thou bucks additional to the option budget and retainer. You're looking at a round trip of two hundred and sixty K, which for a first-time Hollywood outing is rich in the extreme and damn near guaranteed. You want the bad news? You're not the only producer. You got an exec, Babe Hogan, client of ours, and a co-producer, Jonathan Drake. Babe controls the money. Drake is boss on set. Without this support, the bread won't touch you. But, you get visibility and kudos. You learn bags from Babe and Drake. And you're in great money for less sweat.'

Coburn looked at him far-sightedly as though the deal he had sketched would be music to the ears of Michael's agent, if he had one. When the trance was over he cocked his head and pouted realisti-cally. 'Hey, I never say take it or leave it, but if you turn that one down, there ain't much I can do.'

Michael gazed into the agent's brown eyes. The offer was now balanced, rounded out, calculated to seem reasonable to a party acting in good faith. It was a deal generously proportional to the role he would have played in ordinary circumstances and a wise man might be grateful for that much concession. He almost wanted to please Coburn by accepting and reward him for the respect he had shown. Coburn, once co-operative, was the kind of man you wanted to appease. Honour was involved and to say yes was to endorse Coburn's assertion of good faith. Here was a Hollywood player paying his dues and stretching his pragmatism to the absolute limits.

'No thanks.'

Coburn inhaled deeply, against the surprise.

Michael felt a line of power, as if it were something he could hold on to.

'Not in the ballpark.'

'Michael!' Coburn raised imploring hands.

'I'd like more money and more control.'

'You got lots of money and lots of control.'

'I have terms to suggest.'

Coburn exhaled, shaking his head. 'My friend, be real!'

'I'm feeling dead real.'

'Rick,' he shouted.

There was a moment.

'Would you like to hear my terms?' he said.

Weislob was in position in seconds, chair drawn up, mobile on the table, palms wedged between his thighs. He looked around and about him, all eyes and ears for the state of play. He was ready to ride in on the details of tense argument.

Coburn barrelled forward. 'You're seeing one and a half per cent of final less contingency out of a zero-slack budget. We're jammed on money, and as for control, not even Shane caps out on that.'

'D'you want to hear my terms?'

It was necessary to do this, he thought.

'Why should I hear your terms?'

'Because you want to close the deal.'

He received Coburn's anti-British look.

'You're in good faith, Frank?'

'I'm up to my neck in good faith.'

'Good faith listens as well as talks.'

Coburn shook his head.

'Let him shoot, Frank.' Weislob had the adolescent baritone of the eternal shorty.

The waiter approached, tray in hand. Weislob watched the array slide on to the table, tomatoes and mozzarella, white bread, red wine.

'Would you care for some lunch?'

Coburn's eyes were flat.

Earlier, Michael had noticed that they were sitting at the table where, only a week ago, he and Hilldyard had lunched together. They had tucked into a plate of *fritto misto*, and Hilldyard had talked about Italian light and the quattrocento sensibility of landscape whilst attentive Michael had raised morsels to his lips and gazed at the sea's fluttering aquamarine and the cathedral of a cliff at the end of the beach and tried to pinpoint the centre of his unearthly elation. And it came to him then, in the listening trance, that consciousness held infinite connections, was woven in dimensions of time and space radiating from the sensory present. One lived on a meniscus of experience, one thrived on subjective flux, and yet this kaleidoscope of transient life, the more one submitted to its vivid beauty, the more depths were stirred, connections realised, as though the absolute present contained the code for all layers of meaning;

216

layers which Hilldyard automatically perceived because his channels of experience were so extraordinarily dilated. And this thought, of the latency of revelation, its immanence in the palpable present, had moved Michael. Everything was there, if one cared to look: all explanation, all meaning.

'I want full producer status. You can give me back-up. Call it what you like. Everybody in the food chain defers to me. I account to the money. I argue with the money. I call the creative shots in collaboration with Shane. If Shane and I see eye to eye, his authority will pass through me to everyone else. If we disagree, the project won't even start. I asked you to give me your coverage on the book but so far haven't received it. As far as I'm concerned any deal is dependent on there being an overlap of approach to the task of adaptation and that's something that has to be squared with Shane as a pre-condition to all this.'

'We haven't given you the coverage because you haven't shown us the option agreement,' said Weislob reasonably.

Coburn sat with crossed arms and dark eyes.

'If you're still hung up on the option agreement, call Curwen.'

Rick hesitated.

'Go on.'

'Frank?'

'He'll tell you. Call him now.'

Weislob picked up his phone.

'Go ahead.' He was not himself. 'Double zero, double four . . .'

'What else, Michael?'

Weislob held the phone aloft.

Michael gazed hard at Coburn. 'A hundred thousand dollars on signature.'

Coburn scowled.

'Plus five hundred thou or half your packaging fee.'

There was silence.

'Whichever is the greater.'

Michael looked at the dead quick of Coburn's eye. 'On first day.'

Weislob seemed not to hear the figures. His face was mild, almost abstract, as if nothing of significance had been said.

Coburn's face had creased up with distaste. Now he shrugged, shook his head. 'No can do.'

'Think about it.'

'Nothing to think about. It's not right you should have that money. And there's no packaging fee on this pic.'

'Then add one.'

Coburn laughed harshly. 'If only movies were like that.'

'It's a budgetable item,' said Michael coolly.

'Oh yeah. But this film's different. This money's tricky money.'

'You better talk to the money then.'

'Michael, you're in over your head. Take the offer while it lasts.'

'Those are my terms.'

'Hey.' Coburn was sudden. 'Don't hardball me!'

Michael held his eye.

'Easy, guys.' Weislob raised a hand.

There was a curious pause.

'Michael, if we stand up and walk, that's the last you'll hear of *Last Muse*.'

'You can't afford to walk away.'

'That so?'

'You have to deliver.'

'You're stopping us delivering.'

'Hammond won't believe that.'

Coburn's face masked hard feelings.

'Go on then,' he said. 'Walk away.'

Coburn exhaled harshly; his voice was like gunsmoke. 'Don't push me.'

'Unless you deliver, Hammond'll quit your agency.'

'OK, Rick. We're out of here.'

'What's a client worth?' He was getting into it. 'Two hundred? Three hundred? Half a million?'

'Rick and I are cabbing to the airport right now.'

'Don't lose the only star you ever had!' His heart pounded.

Coburn leaned on the table. 'Thanks for your time, Michael. Sorry we couldn't close a deal.'

Weislob rose, too, fastened the button of his jacket. 'Best of luck with the movie.'

The agents exchanged glances.

Coburn took off first, gliding past tables and chairs towards the steps at the back of the restaurant. Weislob attached his wraparounds, took the mobile and gave Michael a goodbye nod. They gathered at the back near the cash register and then pushed off up the ramp.

He watched Coburn's meaty fist progressing up the banister and Weislob's dorsal profile rising in its wake.

'I'll give Shane your regards,' said Michael.

His heart leapt. He tensed in his seat.

The agents stood on the ramp, staring at him across the length of the restaurant.

'When I see him tonight.'

Coburn maintained an expression of scepticism for a second longer than disbelief might suggest. Rick clutched the mobile in both hands, as if compressing the truth of Michael's statement from its shell.

'There'll be a message at the hotel,' Rick told his boss.

'Call the hotel,' said Coburn.

Rick stood aside, dialled, waited.

'I know more about your client than you do,' said Michael.

Coburn's eyes were bruised with ire.

'Hey, Frank! You're on the way out.'

'You're on the way out, motherfucker!'

Coburn covered the ground fast and his fist came down hard on the table, bouncing wine out of the glass and cutlery on to the floor.

'Nothing at the hotel.'

'If you're lying you're so fucking dead.'

Michael hated these men; he hated them with rich anger. He wanted to see them go down, as he knew they would, because he had the leverage and it was only a question of nerve.

'Shane's coming because he'll deal with me.'

'We'll tell him not to.'

'If he wants your opinion, he'll ask for it.'

The rage in Coburn's eyes was fathomless, helpless, and Michael saw instantly the glaze of tactical confusion.

'Shane likes results, not opinions. He wants to believe that when big Frank Coburn gets going deals are cut, not fucked up.'

'You trying to blackmail me?'

'Cool it, Frank.'

'You fucking jerkoff!'

Coburn lunged at him, pulling a handful of air from in front of his face. Michael lurched sideways. A fist came down on the side-rail, sending a vibration around the edge of the structure. A finger came up like a blunt spike.

'Listen, cocksucker. I busted my guts ten years turning Coburn Agency into a top-talent outfit. I spent six months on Hammond's ass persuading him we were the best place in town. We hooked Grade A talent because we're a fucking Grade A agency. And for longer than you can imagine we've been everywhere trying to raise twenty million dollars of very oh-so complicated weirdo money to let Shane make an uncommercial movie that no friggin' studio would touch with a toilet brush. If there's a packaging fee on this film we earned every cent of it and we are not going to be ransomed out of nothing by a free-loading limey cunt.'

This was it, Michael thought, the distance, and he knew he had to go it. 'You raised the money but blew the rights, Frank. You can sweet-talk fund-holders, but when it comes to writers, you're grease monkeys. And that's the truth about your agency. You don't have the class to handle real talent, because if you did you wouldn't ask turd bullet here to hustle Hilldyard. Oh sure. Rick blew your deal right out of the water. You didn't have a prayer after that.'

Coburn glanced at Weislob.

'No novel, no package. No packaging fee. You can bribe and bully with the best of them but you can't understand men of genius like Hilldyard because, bottom line, you've no respect for writers. And when Hammond quits, Hollywood will know you can't handle thoroughbreds. You'll be written off as boutique merchants. Little Caesars doing movie-of-the-week deals for superannuated starlets. Fringe hucksters. Showbiz parodies. If that's what you want, fine. Otherwise, put your brains back in and think this through. I've got the rights from Hilldyard. I've defused the anger he felt on dealing with Rick. I'm bringing to the table the last link in the chain. If you agree my terms you can take the credit for resolving the problem. You can portray yourselves as white knights. I'll back you up. But, gentlemen, if you think I'm going to do all that for less than top dollar, think twice.'

Coburn raised his eyebrows in ironic appreciation of Michael's sang-froid. Anger still lurked about his broad mass and heavy hands, but the anger was not directed.

'Frank, those allegations are totally false.' Weislob crossed his hands, licked his lips perfunctorily.

Michael could feel the give now, the hinge raised and loosened. Coburn had heard him and there was a sense of completed exchange in the air, all rhetoric spent. He wondered how Coburn might shift gear without losing face.

Rick watched his master with apprentice curiosity. He had seen him confronted, faced up to, coolly countered. He must have wondered what extra resources Coburn would summon.

Coburn flexed his fingers and turned round to face Michael.

'Make a note, Rick.'

Rick produced pen and pad.

'I want a deal memo for tomorrow. Memo to include Michael's conditions. Michael to fax us a résumé of terms. Two fundamentals. That you and Shane are in synch. And that we have sight of an option agreement by eleven tomorrow morning. The option assignment will not be operative till Michael's received one hundred thousand in a designated account.'

Rick dotted his pad and replaced it in his pocket.

It was Michael's turn to look admiringly at Coburn. These agents were extraordinary. Huge, puffing pistons of theatrical rage one moment, glib pragmatists the next.

Coburn held his stance. His face was empty-eyed. 'Before we split, one thing. We sign off tomorrow and the lawyers'll draw long-form. That's the deal. I'd like to shake on something else.' His eyes were dead. 'If Shane leaves us now, I'm makin' you a promise.'

Michael waited.

'It's like this,' said Coburn, raising his hand as if to shake Michael's.

'Bye bye, my friend.'

Coburn pushed his hand forward.

Michael could not refuse the gesture.

The grasp was forceful, sudden, a consummation of hatred, horribly personal; and in his palm when Coburn let go was a bullet.

Michael regarded the thing coldly.

'When you least expect it.'

He set the long, bevelled shell on the table. He felt a thud of fear but knew the threat was theatrical, a cowboy bluff for Rick's benefit. Coburn could not lose face.

Coburn nodded actorishly. The hate was real but not of the moment. He had lost the plot of his own machismo and was now wiped and lumbering, an American agent pitted against uncool dynamics in an uncool environment.

They took leave of the restaurant unmomentously. In Weislob's eye there was the parting look of reproach for Michael's attitude and the unfairness he had inflicted on professionals. Coburn strode lightly, his bearing watered down by defeat. He did not look over his shoulder but walked up the ramp that joined the restaurant to the footpath along which picturesque and overgrown seaside route the two men would return, no doubt silently, to the first beach, the restaurants, the domed church, the tessellated paving of Via Murat with hibiscus peering down at them through the overhead trellis.

Michael nodded at the proprietor, secreting the bullet in his fist as the weathered man approached to clear the table.

He asked for the bill and resumed his seat by the rail. While he waited he tapped the bullet on the table. The metal was smooth, pleasant to weigh between fingers, the point nicely tactile, like an executive toy. He squinted at the white light of the sky. It was good to put oneself through these moments. Daring gave one edge, renewed daring. Men were designed to do battle and exert nervous energy. That's whom Hollywood was for: acrobats of chance, men of rapacity and wrath, scurrying overlords of the animal kingdom. The rage of it might be addictive, a person's way of clambering above the froth of anonymously competing lives and trouncing one's rivals.

He drew fingertips over his eyesockets, rubbed the stubble on his jaw, and grimaced all-achingly at the blanched band of the beach and the inexorable press of the sea. The form of the mountain, treading into the water from on high, occupied vision so completely that, when he stopped thinking about everything and looked at what lay before him, it sent through him a surge of joy which raked his tear ducts.

He knew he could do it now. He had the passion of his own identity. He would push that all the way against Adela and Shane Hammond and whatever problems came to him next. All this, tightly seized, would get him a life back.

He paid up and made his way as fast as he could across the lurch and crunch of the pebble beach. Exhilaration powered him up the zigzag of steps so that soon, without pain, he found his throat throbbing and skin moist. The metal tube rail vibrated with the force of his grasp. He came on to the alley near his hotel and did not think of the place where he and Adela had kissed for the first time.

The banked levels of the town were like a citadel of villas, linen white against the grey sky. The houses rose in shuttered somnolence above the street on which he walked, so electrically full of his future. Positano moved around him as he strode down the road past the stores and bars and the tourists taking their seats outside the *caffè*, adjusting sunglasses and looking up at the afternoon sky.

According to the waiter a storm was coming in.

Chapter Twenty-one

HER ROOM LOOKED DIFFERENT. The shutters were wide open. The bed was neatly made. The carnival of her dressing-table possessions, her shoes and clothes and clutter, had been swept clean off the table and floor and everywhere was kempt and bare, and on the luggage-support two shoulder bags were stacked, and Adela, as he entered, was kneeling on a suitcase and tugging around its edges a reluctant zipper.

'Perfect timing,' she said rather breathlessly.

The room was full of her energy and efficiency. Michael had no idea what was going on and stood there openly surprised by this woman who rose to her feet, dusting hands on jeans and flicking hair over her ear.

'Are you leaving?'

'I've been upgraded.'

She sashayed around the suitcase and came up to him. She looked into his eyes with her usual directness, preparing him for the next revelation.

'Shane wants me to join him at the Sirenuse.'

'Join him?'

She smiled. 'He's booked me a room.'

'Why?'

She heard the dismay in his voice. 'Oh.' She shrugged. 'Because he probably thinks an actress of my standing shouldn't be obliged to stay in fleapit hotels.'

She heaved the suitcase on to its wheels, took lipstick from her pocket, presented her mouth to the wall mirror. 'Would you pass up two nights of five-star?'

He walked quickly towards her. She turned and looked at him before he kissed her, a quick, possessive kiss.

'I like it here,' he said.

'Michael.' She touched his chest, intimate but restraining. 'I don't have the choice.'

He hesitated, struck by the tone.

'Shane wants me there because he can't move around freely.'

'He can wear shades! He can wear a baseball cap!'

'He's a very private man.'

'Why should that affect your sleeping arrangements!'

She pouted, topped up the colour of her lips. 'He's a night owl.'

Michael walked across to the window, drawn to daylight. He knew that he was being jumpy and assuming things; and that he distrusted the invigorating effect of Shane's visit on Adela, as if it were more than she could do to conceal her own nerves and was annoyed with him for forcing her to do so.

He had liked it here: the Bohemian quarters above the noisy square.

Her coolness was ambiguous. Perhaps she meant to show that this sort of thing happened in her line of work. She was resolute because she wanted to get a job done. And while it might be presumptuous of a film star to summon her to his own luxury hotel, Adela was too determined to let presumptuousness inhibit her. Michael knew that she had many resources and many imperatives and would handle each new development with tact and charm, and little could be concluded, if he would just stay cool, from the nervousness that a movie star's imminent arrival created; though, looking at the room's newfound order, he saw how powerfully Hammond's stellar magnetism affected other heavenly bodies. Hammond's presence was a lot more irksome than the use of his bankable name. His fame and power gave him rights over people, an edge in personal matters that could not be resisted by those he privileged with his company.

He turned back from the window. She was attaching a slide to her hair, lifting it away from temple and ear so that one saw the soft curve of her jaw. The lipstick anointed her mouth, gave a concentrated stab to the pleasingness of her looks. Even in a sweater and jeans she was fluffily feminine; competent, too. She was very aware of the architecture of her face as it might now be presented to the desk clerk of the Sirenuse, or to the hotel's rich patrons, or to Shane Hammond himself.

He remained by the window as she attached earrings to the picture of her face. He was unused to the hazards of submitting to feeling. He had allowed passion to escape from some inner hiding place and was now vulnerable to anything that might thwart it.

'What were you going to tell me?'

She glanced at him acutely. 'Do I look OK?'

'Of course.'

'How was your meeting?'

'I cut a deal.'

'I'm sure there won't be any problems.'

'There were loads of bloody problems!'

'But with Shane behind you . . .'

'I've never met Shane!' She was trying to take his achievement away. 'He doesn't give a shit about me.'

'You got the deal, Michael!'

'Not on a plate! Those hyenas want my blood.'

She stood up, cradling her arms. 'They're powerless.'

'I had to fight.'

'OK!'

He stared at her. He had endured an ordeal by fire for her benefit.

She returned the look, duly corrected. She had got the message. She raised her eyebrows to move the subject on. 'So it's in the bag unless you blow it with Shane.'

'Blow it?'

She nodded knowingly.

'Am I auditioning?'

Adela was rock-like. 'We are all auditioning.'

He swallowed. He did not like this. He could not endure the idea of being a supplicant, especially to a movie star, however bankable.

'What were you going to tell me?'

She came towards him, bringing herself to the window. She was composing herself; formulating various points, which she would need to state carefully. She had information and wanted to share it for the sake of completeness.

'I've told you my suspicions.'

He watched her closely. Anything she might say about Shane would be an indirect way of saying things about himself.

'When I was understudying at Chichester, Shane was aloof. Pleasant but aloof. He was like that with everybody. There were several fine women in that production, and he was spoilt for choice, but he seemed . . . uninterested.' She raised her eyebrows. 'I thought he was gay or on sabbatical. But then somebody told me he was

226

dating the daughter of a Labour peer, Carlotta so-and-so. End of story. The next time I saw him was in New York, with Jack, at a party. Jack was embarrassingly thrilled to meet him and did everything possible to get in the way until an American casting agent yanked him off for a dance, and I had Shane to myself, and Shane was asking questions about the BBC and all things British, and running a big spiel about the horrors of Hollywood and laughing at what a cliché he must seem. He told me actors were a fucked-up bunch and that he loathed Hollywood and would be glad to return to the RSC if he could only break the habit of earning multi-million-dollar fees. He really rolled back the frontiers of self-indulgence. I did my incredulous "Haven't you got everything?" bit. And then Jack made his way over, and Shane took my hand and said, "You're very beautiful, but don't marry that man." Which I thought was extremely rude and very perceptive.' She glanced frankly at Michael. 'To tell the truth I liked the idea that he could read my mind, because I knew at that party Jack was history.'

He was half puzzled to learn Jack was history then. That had not been his understanding.

'Next time I heard his voice it was 4 a.m. He was very cocky. But of course he made up for it nicely by offering me a part. The implication being that from just one meeting Shane knows I'm right. And he's marvellously low-key, as if the film he always wanted to make would happen as soon as he chanced on the right actress, and now he's found me and, bingo, we're off.'

Michael had so little of the initiative that he thought it better to retain what little he had by saying nothing.

'And then' – she smiled with lovely, candid irony – 'I read the novel and discovered about my character. The love of his life. The woman who teaches Shane what real love feels like.'

'Shane?'

'Shane's character.'

There was a pause.

'Which means, I guess, that he thinks I have a quality which would make me convincing to an audience in that role.' She looked at him flatly. 'And if the audience likes that quality . . . maybe he does, too.'

'Your quality as an actress?'

'What I can do,' she said. 'What I can project.'

'You?'

She looked at him for a long moment. 'Yes, me.'

He let out a long breath. 'Is there no difference between you and your acting?'

She paused a moment, before coming out with proud tranquil assurance. 'I can't put across what I don't feel.'

He nodded, saw the reflection of her back in the mirror. He wanted her to discriminate between appearance and reality, between personal feeling and histrionic effect. She had not answered his question.

'He called several times after that. Usually with a pretext. Maybe he was reassuring himself. Or rehearsing. He's very method. And every time I try to be as relaxed as possible. The funny thing is, when we have these conversations it's like I'm the only person in the world he can talk to. When he heard about the problems with the option he was stricken. He's so determined to make this movie. So fixated. The story is a personal thing with him. Love and impossible love and, well, he's going to be very bound up with whoever plays Anna.' She cast her eyes down and then aside. 'That actress has to do it for Shane.'

He was immersed in the implications. All this uncertainty stemmed from his decision to lie, from his desperate neediness, more desperate than ever.

'Do what?' he said, softly.

'Oh.' She shrugged. 'Make sparks. Be his idea of a perfect woman. You see, he's discovered me. He thinks I'm it. No one else in Hollywood is going to offer me a movie like this because nobody else believes in me on the big screen. I have to live up to that.'

He nodded. That much was intelligible, though he wondered where acting stopped and life began. Perhaps a man like Hammond made no distinction between the emotions of living and performing, but Adela should. She was intelligently self-aware.

'So you see, there are two angles here.' She looked so furtive, so thorough in her sounding of the matter before them. 'Either he's just intense, the great thespian brewing up vibes for his next star performance, in which case I play my part and keep my job. Or—' She turned towards him, tossed her hair back, parted her lips in high oral coquetry. 'He's using the film as a pretext for something more personal.'

He looked at her. What gave him most pause, the thing that checked his response, was that Adela had kept this information to herself from the day of their first meeting. And while that meant her depiction of Hammond's interest had been economical, it also meant that his 'encounter' with her had managed to happen despite her little secret, suggesting that she was not entirely consumed by the idea of Hammond's interest.

He went across to the bed and sat down; allowed a tired sigh to escape from his body. 'You think Shane needs all this pretext to make a pass?'

Adela was silent for a moment. 'I don't think there's too much difference between how he feels about work and how he feels about life. A romantic, I guess.'

'He's a star, for heaven's sake. He can have anyone!'

She was grand. 'Oh, not anyone!'

'Why doesn't he take you to an expensive restaurant?'

'Screen gods move in mysterious ways.'

He was forlorn. 'You mean he's playing some kind of game?'

'He's rich, famous, probably miserable. How am I supposed to know what's going on in his mind?'

'It's you that talks to him!'

'Yes, and I'm telling you my hunch!' She frowned. 'After all, he's coming to Positano!'

Michael took this in slowly. Things were cast now in a queer light. The information he had received, it was so very unrelaxing.

'Why are you telling me this, Adela?'

She raised her eyebrows at his tone. 'Because it's going to have an effect on things.'

Michael waited, heart beating hard. He never knew quite what it was possible for her to say next.

She came towards him, rested her delicate hands on the strap of a bag.

'I'm going to have to be charming, you see. You'll have to let me play my part.' She watched him closely.

He laughed nervously. 'What does that mean?'

'Oh.' She widened her eyes. 'That you make allowances for me.'

He was transfixed.

'I must live up to Shane's expectations.'

The emotion he felt was very unpleasant.

'It wouldn't do to be indiscreet.'

'Indiscreet?'

She was not untroubled. 'We have to keep mum. If what I say is

229

true, we can't let Shane see that his chosen actress is' – she raised her eyebrows – 'you know . . .'

He made no reaction.

'We can't risk alienating him.'

He nodded, beginning to doubt her integrity. Such tact was no more than deception. He spoke gently. 'But nor should you risk alienating the producer.'

She frowned. 'I'm telling you so you won't be alienated!'

'Adela!'

'I know it's awkward!'

'Awkward!' The word did not go far enough, not by a long way, was completely inadequate.

He looked at the floor. This conversation was absolutely not to his taste. 'What will you do?'

Her face lightened and she strolled across the room as if dress-rehearsing the idea. 'The obvious thing is to say I'm still in love with Jack.'

Michael recognised the excuse. 'Which he knows isn't true.'

She turned and came back the other way. 'It's a neat way of not rejecting him.'

'He'll like the challenge.'

'It buys me time.'

'A day or so. It won't get you through the shoot.'

'And it has the advantage of mirroring the story in the novel.'

'Until the characters elope.'

She was thoughtful.

'And have their love affair!'

She seemed absent-minded, distracted.

He rose from the bed and moved towards her. He placed a hand on her shoulder, looked feelingly into her eyes.

'It needn't be complicated. Be up-front with him. Let him know about us casually.'

'Us?' It was less of a question than the voicing of a vague notion, the sense of which she could not fully feel.

'You know what I mean,' he said experimentally.

He saw that she did by the sudden steadiness of the look she gave him, offering her honesty, full access to the conundrum as it struck her. She breathed in and squeezed his hand.

'Inadvisable.'

'Isn't it better to be honest than to play out a charade?'

'And risk losing everything?'

'If Shane has any class he'll respect your feelings.'

'Shane's class is one thing. It's his ego I'm worried about.'

He was impatient. 'Either he wants to make the film or he doesn't.'

She stared at him with sudden, terrible anguish. 'If I reject him, he'll cast someone else!' She bared her teeth and looked away, almost devastated by the thought.

Michael was shaken. It was as though she had revealed herself.

'He has absolute power over my career. My only power is over his emotions. That,' she said vehemently, 'is why he wants me. Why he's prepared to make me. Because at some level I've got something he wants, and this film is a route to that!'

Michael paled. She had spelt it out.

'Michael!' She grabbed his hand, brought herself tightly into his clasp. 'I have to carry this. Trust me to do it for both of us.'

He felt something precious slipping away from him.

'You mean sleep with him?'

Her breath was hot on his skin. She squeezed his hand between the prayer of her palms, urged it against her breast. Her eyes scan-searched his face, seeking him out, as though his response were the only one that mattered. 'It won't come to that.'

He gazed into the depths of those eyes, unable to believe his relationship with Adela had reached this point. There was yielding and pleading in the cast of her upturned features, a loveliness in the rounded cheekbones, forgiveness in the lips, conscience in the wide openness of her brow, youth in the natural, abundant hair. The nape of her neck was silky warm to his fingers.

The silence that surrounded them was void of forward momentum. They had reached a centre-point, a moment that was still. He held her close, felt the fluff of her jersey on his palm, breathed in the exhalation of scent from her skin. He had become too quickly attached to Adela. Circumstance had accelerated their romance beyond the normal speed of development, heightening chemistry and complexity, intensifying emotions before it was possible to resolve the ambiguity about whether the film was an excuse for an affair, or the catalyst for true love. Michael craved for the latter to be true though it was too late to judge and too soon to know.

'What if I fall in love with you?' He was surprised to have said it.

For a moment she was strangely absent. 'And what if I fall in love with you?'

He was almost moved, though possibly he was meant to be moved. 'Why would you?'

She did not catch his meaning.

'Date Shane and you'll be at all the right parties. You'll be on magazine covers.' He could not restrain himself. 'And where your career is concerned you have to be smart.'

'I have to be smart,' she said angrily, twisting away from him, 'because I've got no heart, no feelings. I'm just a desperate actress ready to shag anybody who'll put me up for a job. Is that what you think?'

He absorbed her anger, wanting to believe it.

'D'you know what it's like being an actress? D'you know what it's like being sized up by directors and then passed over, auditioned and rejected, patronised and sexually harassed, made to feel like you're meat on a hook? You have no idea what we go through! What we wouldn't do to escape the cattlemarket soullessness of being in competition with thousands of other talented good-looking women, struggling for a living. Don't you see what a break this is for me? It's divine intervention. The chance of a lifetime! And what I need from you is a little understanding and flexibility about what I need to do for both our sakes. God, if this film gets made I don't want an egomaniac fucking actor on my hands. Give me a break. I don't deserve your moral superiority. I'm trying to make something work.'

He was always impressed by her when she was pushed to the limit, as though it were her fate to be unfairly suspected by people and her burden to have to defend her integrity with outbursts so forceful nobody could doubt her.

'And what about him?' he said, on top of it now. 'If he's serious about you?'

She screwed up her face. 'Would you rather I deceived him or you?'

'I'd rather you deceived no one.'

She hesitated for a second and then found the answer. 'We don't have the choice.'

This was it, he thought. His feelings were the best thing about him, not to be trammelled or squandered. He hesitated and then came out with it. 'If you are prepared to deceive one of us, why should either of us trust you?'

She frowned, as though she had not foreseen the angle and it checked her.

'How do I know,' he said, his moment of truth come round at last, 'that you aren't playing me along till the film deal's signed?'

She crumpled on to the chair in the corner, legs drawn together, head flopping on a hand.

He felt that he had betrayed her trust but knew the feeling of unkindness was the only alternative to suspicion and anguish and he was not deterred by the awkwardness of it.

There were glittering tears in her eyes. She shook her head slowly. He pitied her; but even her silence was ambiguous.

'You don't know you're born, Michael Lear.'

'I know one thing. If Hammond's after you, I'm not producing this film.'

Her face was so pained.

'Somebody else can have a go at Hilldyard.'

Her hair wept over the chair-arm. 'Oh, I wish I hadn't told you!'

He sat there, gaunt with sorrow for himself, for Adela.

'Christ, we've only slept together once. How can you load me up with all this obligation?'

It was a fair question and he could not help seeing things from her point of view. The perspective changed things, required honesty. He spoke quietly because he wanted to sound definite. 'You're my redemption, Adela.'

'What?'

His heart fluttered with the nearness of confession.

She rose forward in her chair, curious and distraught at the same time.

He felt overcome by the need to be honest, because honesty would shed light over everything, and Michael was exhausted with the murky and uncertain and it struck him with an adrenalin twist in the heart that he had no idea how she would react.

'What are you talking about?'

He adjusted his position so he could look her straight in the eye. He wanted to make his confession as a gesture of trust, to show her that they both deserved honesty. The words would be simple, would go to the heart of the matter like the edge of an axe.

'I haven't got the rights.'

Her eyebrows sailed up in unconcealed astonishment.

'He changed his mind.'

'Oh my God!'

'Nothing I could say would persuade him.'

She shot to her feet, electrified. 'You lied to me!'

He flinched at the accusation.

'After all this talk of deception you lied to me about the option!'

'You gave me no choice.'

'To get me into bed!'

'To stop you leaving!'

She had the tempestuous colour of an enraged heroine, as though she were throttled by impossible confusions of feeling. And yet it was not rage he saw, but overwhelmed horror.

'Oh fuck! Oh Jesus!' She pounded the travel bag. 'Michael, you are utterly insane!'

He flinched again but honesty had given him strength and he made no half-hearted attempt to cut in. Her panic was the fright of an actress whose great chance is threatened. He expected as much and would let her burn off the shock before calming her down and moving her into the reality of the situation.

She subsided on the edge of the bed in a hair-torn weep of anguish. 'Shane will go ape.'

'Not if you don't tell him.'

'We can't not tell him!' Her face collapsed with the awfulness of it. 'Oh Michael, what have you done!'

He rose slowly. He was ready to tell all.

'I've organised the elements. Bluffed and lied and done a deal with the agents. Shane's coming, and I'm about to find out whether this wonderful project is for real. If it is, I'm lined up for three-quarters of a million dollars and a producer credit.'

'You what?' Her jaw dropped.

'If Shane and I agree.'

She was delirious. 'You don't have the rights!'

'I'll get them.'

'What?'

He had the initiative now and he could see in her eyes a total dependency on what he would say next.

'I've learned something about James.'

There was a pause. She seemed to respond.

'You have?'

He frowned.

She came like quicksilver off the bed, stood before him. 'What?'

'You don't need to know.'

She was instantly fascinated, her mind grappling with the implication. 'You wouldn't?'

She had understood instantly.

He gave a half-nod. 'It would be the end of our friendship.'

Adela averted her face, shocked by the realisation of many things. Michael could tell that he was being re-evaluated and that she saw what he proposed from his point of view, even from Hilldyard's. She would also sense that if Michael proposed something like this, he meant to execute it; though with no certainty of success. Of one thing only could he be certain. The endeavour was unconscionable, steeped in betrayal and dishonour.

'I owe Hilldyard everything.'

'Yes.' She was almost depressed now.

There was a pause and he saw her brow tightening. She knew what was coming.

'I can only sacrifice his commitment for yours.'

Her features were in shade now, and the light through the window was tinted with blue.

'I can swap his love for some kind of chance with you. But to betray him just for . . .'

She captured her face in her palms and sat liquidly down on the end of the bed. He remained standing, watching the effect of his words.

She looked up at him with piteous incredulity. 'You'd do it for me?'

He knew what the answer was but his certainty seemed strange. To say that he was in love with her was to say nothing. Adela was his salvation, although it was not a salvation he would have on any terms. But he would do surprising things, and what he needed now was a view of her hand. He wanted the truth in so far as the truth could be compressed from his relationship with Adela. That would be his only insurance.

'For you, yes.'

'But, Michael.' She laughed nervously. 'How can you be so sure about me?'

'It's proving to be hard.'

'How can I . . . I can't make promises.'

'I don't expect promises.' He was soft. 'But if you think there's nothing between us, what I have to do would be on your conscience.'

'Oh.' She drooped.

'He's an old man.'

She sighed deeply.

'I'm asking you to be frank.' He realised he was calm.

'And if I leave you in six weeks?'

He looked at her keenly. She was open, natural. It was an idea she could contemplate generically.

'Then we'd better part now.'

She caught his eye. She saw that honesty had given him power, that he had entered into the situation on his own terms and that it was for her to meet him on the terms he sought. For a moment, she looked as though she had no choice, but then seemed to understand what that would mean. He saw her examining her conscience, as if there were too many feelings to be sounded, as if this final question eluded calculation and Adela could only respond to the challenge by impulse.

'I won't leave you,' she said.

'Come tonight.' He swallowed.

She was unprepared.

'After your dinner with Shane. Come to my hotel.'

'Michael, don't be silly! I haven't seen him in ages! He'll probably keep me up all night.'

'Come when you've finished.'

'It's far too risky!'

It was the only proof he could think of.

'Make an excuse.'

'Don't you trust me?' she said.

'I will then.'

She looked about her, filled with the drama of it, as though the moment of truth were something one had to endure whatever the consequences.

'I'll keep the option agreement until 2 a.m. If you haven't come by then, I'll tear it up.'

She looked at him in a certain way. She was learning new things about him. For a moment she simply digested the ultimatum, taking in its pressure and adjusting to the new demands on her resourcefulness. And then she tossed her hair back and started gathering her things.

Together they hefted her case and baggage and made their way along the corridor and down the stairs.

Outside it was dusk, and the hybrid illumination of the lanterns and the failing sky cast a strange light on the street.

He dropped her case inside the porch of the Sirenuse Hotel.

'I'll see you later,' she said, deferring the kiss but smiling. 'With the option agreement this time.'

Chapter Twenty-two

THE RAIN HAD STARTED at five o'clock, well after sundown, and the black mantle that hung about the town, the smothering of mountain-side darkness, was suddenly alive with windless rain falling heavily and spatteringly on roads and terraces, hard on roofs, mercilessly on passing unfortunates caught in the downburst. The weather collided with Positano, as if Positano were too high on the hill or too close to the sea to dodge punishment. It took the teeming brunt face on: a frigid rebuke to the sunshine hopes of a thousand seaside villas.

Raindrops crackled on the windy road, water glazed the tiled patios of boutiques, weltered off awnings, dribbled around car wheels. As he climbed the medieval cascade of steps, hiking from the Viale to the alley by Hilldyard's villa, he took shelter from the walls and the overhanging trees, though his jacket was soaked and his shoes squidgy from the plaited rivulets that swizzled down the steps. A sopping cat puttered by, lost for a hideout. A saucepan on a back-door step was brimful.

He had bathed in his hotel; then tidied the surfaces in his room and arranged his shirts in a drawer. He placed Hilldyard's manuscript on the desk, in parallel with the laptop. And then he lay back on the bed and reclined with his hands together and thumbs conjoined and waited for certain sensations to settle. On his return he had found another note from Hilldyard. He could delay no longer.

Outside the rain played wet havoc.

The door opened almost immediately, as if Hilldyard were waiting in the hall.

'Have you seen Frances?'

His thin hair was ruffled, almost rakish, and his eyes held Michael's without the ceremony of a greeting. 'Get inside.'

In the hallway, under light, he saw Hilldyard's high colour. His cheeks were flushed, his eyelids sore.

'I thought you might be her,' said the author.

'Where is she?'

'God alone knows.'

'Shall we go in?'

Hilldyard clutched his forehead with childish perturbation. 'She's messed up my front room.'

'Frances?'

He seemed feverish.

'James, let's get a drink.'

'I can't endure this.'

'Endure a drink.' Michael got his hand to the door.

'Don't go in there!'

The door swung wide, revealing the living room.

His first impression was that the room had been ransacked by burglars, everything strewn around in the search for valuables. The sofa was on its back, the side-tables tipped over, the rug ploughed up by the passage of a *chaise* she had driven across the room. Pieces of crockery and broken glass, and cushions and periodicals lay on the floor. She had cracked a reproduction picture over a chair; swept clean the bureau so that notebooks, a glasses case and the telephone lay scattered on the floor by the window.

The author shuffled by him. 'Let's get a bottle and get out.'

'It's pissing.'

'We'll go to my room.'

Hilldyard put on a coat, and Michael took an umbrella, and they made their exit into the rain, and made their way across slippery stones, and down the steps and through the door leading to the private passage and along to the author's den, and as Michael crossed the threshold and Hilldyard switched on an Anglepoise lamp and fumbled two glasses off the shelf, he could not believe what he had come to do.

He stood by the shelves and saw the blocks of Thackeray, Dickens, Trollope and Hardy, editions of poetry by Longfellow, Yeats, Words-worth, William Cowper, paperback troves of Graham Greene, Virginia Woolf; essays by Strachey, lectures by Nabokov, French editions of Stendhal, Balzac, Proust, Apollinaire. He saw the manuscript paper on the desk, the bifocals and coffee mug, the cuneiform handwriting that marked the papers with fresh jottings, the DNA of a new novel.

They could hear the sound of the rainfall.

Hilldyard gave him the whisky bottle so that he could make himself useful. He bent down and switched a bar heater on at the wall.

'What's the matter with Frances?'

Hilldyard answered him with a drained expression and took his glass to the wicker chair and sat down in front of the window. He gazed through the blur of his reflection into the night. His breathing became thick and slow, as if the impact of events had passed its crisis and left him exhausted but calm, in post-operative stasis.

The writer had no ready means of expression. In due course his attempt to answer the question failed completely, and Michael was left with the sight of a man chewing his forefinger.

'That bad?'

He left it a while. He had to go slowly.

'What's she going to tell me, James?'

Hilldyard closed his eyes.

'We're all human,' said Michael, dry-mouthed.

There was a grunt.

'You're close, you two.'

Hilldyard's face seemed to crack with pain, not private pain, but the agony he could now offer up to Michael's regard, as if, feeling so monstrous, he could no longer control the sense of his plight and had to make it over, inflict it on someone else.

Michael saw the puckered brow and pleading eyes and felt suspense lurch into pity. Hilldyard was experiencing an internal débâcle. Something long suppressed came out in his queerness of expression.

Michael feared what he might learn. He was about to become a man's confessor and wondered if he had the nerve to hear him out and still stick to his plan.

Hilldyard stood. He laid thick hands on the cool window. His breath condensed on the glass.

What he had to say was gathered.

'I have never told a single soul because I could never believe anybody would forgive me. I have never forgiven myself.' His voice was thin, light and frail, though the words found their way with steady release. 'I can only try to explain how the thing that happened took me over.'

There was a lengthy silence.

'When Joan fell sick, to begin at the beginning, I did everything I could not to show my fear. She was heroic, not showing hers. We had doctor's orders, a medical regime, things to do and not to do, and the hopes one clutches on to with that kind of illness, which came from nowhere and might as well go to nowhere. I tended her, read to her when she was bed-bound; and when she was stronger we'd drive across the hills, which seemed more immediate in those short months than ever before. She wanted open air and birdsong. She wanted to see it all exactly as we had loved it, and we'd find new places, heaven-sent views and rolling Tuscan fields, knowing that each day was the last of its kind. The last May day. Oh yes, the last green gauze she would see on the trees; the last bright spring warmth she would feel on our terrace. And each night, I lay in the room with her on the bed. And I would listen to her deep-breathing sleep knowing this innocent rest was a prelude to oblivion and that one day soon she would be sleeping for ever.'

Hilldyard turned from the window and faced Michael, his hand raised and softly clenched.

'Frances wrote to us from England. Offered her services. The kindest letter. She was at that certain age, bright and selfless, with an English schoolgirl's complexion. One feared for her future because she seemed perfect then, like a magnolia flower. Joan, of course, wanted to see her niece, and Frances would only come if she came for a while, and privately I was grateful to have the support. We had our locals, the village, but I never came to Italy for friendship, and if there were people to tend Joan, there was nobody to put up with me in the way I need putting up with. I think she was with us for a couple of months. She was a help, brightened the place up. She could cook and clean and iron. Not that we asked her to. She seemed then a remarkable, strong girl, a fine young person with none of my brother-in-law's cantankerousness. And then one day . . .' He caressed his forehead. 'She and I were sitting on the terrace, Joan was resting indoors, and I quite forgot that I was talking to a fifteen-year-old girl. Oh . . . she was abreast of it all. The dear thing had taken it all in. Our situation. She was full of the gentlest awareness and yet, somehow, not heavy-hearted or intrusive. She was spring-like, a new season coming into being surrounded by a real season unfurling colour all over the landscape. And I realised then . . . it appeared to me . . . I was . . .' He paled. 'I had been living with death, and here was life.'

There was a peculiar silence, as if he hovered above memory.

'I was fifty-nine, you see, and I knew that a portion of myself would depart with Joan. How vividly I saw loneliness from the near side of her death. Because although we all have our time on this glittering earth the mortality business is so wretchedly sad. You look away from it, you come to terms with it, you ignore or suppress or challenge or defy it because the thing itself is too miserable for words; and the sadness lives for ever, flows around and beneath our daily lives. Joan became worse after her bursts of energy, and Frances and I spent many hours together, going to the village, buying food, talking about books, the teachers at her school, her sprightly view of the world, and Joan was quite relieved I had a companion to spend the hours with when she was too tired. We were finding our separate ways to cope, she and I. There were so many hours. I could hardly work, although I fooled around in my study.

'To begin with she might sit against my legs on the rug when we watched television. I would pat her head or grip her hand remonstratively if she teased me. When we strolled along, she would link arms with mine, like a loving niece. And then what happened developed so gradually that there was no moment at which I could say I had transgressed. We cleaved to each other, in my case because I was escaping death, in her case because she had, I suspect, a peculiar desire to lose her virginity to someone safe. Even then poor Frances was adrift. To think that fragile wisp submitted to my stale old body . . . It fascinates me to remember what we did, where we did it, because it is so unthinkable I wonder sometimes whether it really happened. We were utterly split between the pains we took for Joan, the love and care we cocooned her with, and this Pentecostal copulation, so soaked in sin as to be almost cleansing. I have never done anything so wrong and yet never felt more impelled towards it. In late middle age I had become concupiscent, and the more we did this dreadful thing, in odd hours at odd places, the less it seemed to have anything to do with sex. For me, it was just the wolfing of another's aliveness, an almost mechanical passion, confined to the ravenous instant. We put ourselves so far out that guilt was unfeelable. Our secret was hardly spoken. What could we say to each other? If the rest of the world could see us we were damned. The great writer in bed with his girl-niece! It was too stupefying to contemplate. I felt washed along, driven by nature, and everything else carried on around our madness. Doctors came and went. Joan's sister visited. We made trips to the hospital. I fed the cats, shaved in the bath, read the local newspaper to my wife and felt no detachment or reserve. Everything that might be felt was simmering away. Only, deep inside I realised I was recovering.

'Joan fared better through the summer. A remission of sorts took the pressure of a deadline off our backs because I suppose I thought that, although the prognosis of her illness typically included a false remission, the remission itself was so positive, so miraculous that anything seemed possible again and for once we all felt light on our feet, heady even, as though inevitability had taken a holiday. It was around then that I started to work again. My concentration returned. I was propelled into the idea of a new novel and left the women together whenever I could and even wrote during the night. What had come to me, what had exploded in my head, was the idea that this situation, the demented contrast between love and rich leave-taking and the long togetherness of a married life, and the Dionysian cleaving with a teenager was the most complex thing that had ever happened to me, and that in its contradictions so many things were wrought that if I could just find the form and the arrangement, I would pour into this book something more powerful than I had ever generated before. An energising obsession. It took me over completely and for a fortnight I steamed out the pages, almost a novella, forty thousand words produced under white heat, which I then reworked, revised and rubbished and then began again. Some kind of fission was taking place. Or melt-down. I was burned up by the intensity of the subject, and yet unable to transcend its personal nature, as if everything that went on at that stage contained me in it and was impossible to objectify. It was so damnably about me. I could not create a character for myself; could not formulate a type that would work convincingly. The more I thought about it, the more difficult it became to frame my experience in terms that were morally intelligible. And yet the material kept flowing. I had put myself on heat.

'Joan was curious. And Frances, to whom I confided, was queerly flattered by my new productivity. When Joan asked questions I dissimulated. I had no intention of telling her what was going on in my study in case such activity appeared to be stealing energy from her. To balance things I redoubled my attentions and did what I could to play down the excitement.

'Frances began to sense my withdrawal. I think she saw I was tending towards self-sufficiency. And even though I went to her room at the appointed time when Joan was asleep, I was beginning to fear the limpet strength of her attachment. She yielded her body like a sacrificial offering to my good will. Everything in her was confused. And I knew her behaviour was a hopeless mix of filial need and sex, and that I was in the paradoxical trap of being her surrogate father and illicit lover, the guarantor of love for the privilege of abuse. And I wondered whether it was I who made her thus, or whether she had come to us out of a disturbed impulse to find in the nearly bereaved attentions of a famous uncle compensation for an unloving father. I asked myself these questions. I began to see that my behaviour was an adjustment. That hers was sickness. I had corrupted her and would inevitably betray her.

'Joan deteriorated. We reeled back into suspense, endured the tests, had our half-sympathetic, half-scientific nods from doctors. And as the prognosis darkened, she was struck with woe. Her courage deserted her. The end was drawing near and the poor woman was raging to be alive, to be well. She was distraught, ghastly with anger. She was so jealous, she said, of me and Frances with our health. She was furious that I could still write, that nothing could stop me; and in desperate remorse I threw myself into the task of a homage to our time together, to what she had given me. I wanted to inject her with every last fulfilment. I wanted her to see and accept the end and feel the round fullness of her life. I wanted her to commemorate, not despair; to give us the best of her remaining days. And slowly she softened and subsided into mild new restfulness, and somehow the pain eased, and I saw then that she had loved her lot in some way, the writer's wife, her long toil of support, and that my achievements were her doing, and my output was her gift to the world, and that she had made my life perfect and that I loved her in and through my work, that she was its muse and the garden of my happiness, and this, I believe, she took to herself and in the worsening hours seemed comforted by. And as she sank, my agony returned. I was incontinent with loss. I slipped around the house like a ghost. Could not sleep. Could not eat. Misery convulsed me. One night, unable to endure her shallow breath and wan face under the low light, I crept from the room and stood in the corridor, struggling with short breath and a ridge in my belly, as if this were the worst stage of the process, and slowly, as the darkness thinned, I saw the aperture of Frances's doorway, and out of insomniac boredom I tiptoed along to

244

hear the sound of her easy sleep. And when I came to the door, I heard her call softly. She was wide awake and couldn't sleep and so in pyjamas and dressing-gown I went inside, into the warm air, and saw her risen up in bed, her white nightie vaporous, and before long I was lying with her under the sheets, clinging to her side with child-like shudders.

'We didn't do anything. We hardly moved. And yet something must have disturbed Joan. I heard her call for me once and as I eased myself out of the hug, drawing strength to go back, the door came open slightly, and there she was. She was over us in the dark. Could see everything. Took it in instantly. Her voice was so weak by then. She said, "Oh, God!" with a tone of frail surprise and resignation, as though she knew immediately that the wound was so deep that nothing anyone could say would heal it, and that she would not live to recover from the shock. And then she went, the light of the landing left in the door, and I lay like a stone as Frances dissolved around me.

'By the time I got to her room, she had locked the door. I knocked and pleaded, said everything I could think of through that silent door. Took a ladder to her window outside, also bolted. Sat weeping in the kitchen half the night, Frances's convulsions of guilt driving me mad. I knew that my life would not be worth living if I did not tell Joan everything as honestly as I could, throw my weakness on her mercy, and show her Frances's terrible contrition so that at least my dear wife would be spared the torture of her own imaginings, and God, how I struggled through those ghastly hours to find the right words, to frame the sense of what had happened, to find for myself an explanation that would not be horrible to either woman. I was gibbering with the fear and guilt of it. I was lost. Truly lost.

'And in the morning I tried her door again and decided to waste no time and smash the bloody thing down. It took three runs along the landing. Three runs. And on the third run I had the premonition as I shouldered through the splintering frame that she had crossed another threshold. I reached the bed and found her asleep still. She lay perfectly composed on her back and showed no trace of unrest or pain.

'I took her hand in mine and knelt down beside her and when I kissed her palm I knew she was dead.'

They sat opposite each other for an age of silence. Hilldyard had nothing left in him and kept his hands on his lap.

Michael was unable to introduce the sound of his voice into the air.

'Frances went back to England and was in shock for a year. Told nobody. She has never had a boyfriend. And no matter what I say, I can't make her understand a halfpenny of what I was going through, because her understanding has frozen at the age of fifteen. She is too disturbed to show empathy and thus has no understanding of herself, which means I'm only what she needs of me or hates me for. And however I try to show love as her uncle, it is either not enough or a parody of what happened back then. I have made her unreachable, and she blames me for everything, while detesting herself. The years have gone by and always I hoped she would settle down, find a man, a job, ease into normality, which she never does, will never do, and instead her anger grows.

'Her anger crucified me. She would visit me in Tuscany, and every time she would insist that it was I who killed Joan. And yet every time she wanted my love back, which I could not find to give. Those visits destroyed me as a writer, as did the certainty that love had vanished from my life. I had ruined the memory of my marriage, could get nothing from it, because Joan died without reconciliation; and what I had done to Frances was not love, so much as theft. I'd blighted her future to cure my sorrow and loneliness. I found myself isolated, unforgivable, corrupted. I could not shake off the contradiction between my achievements as an artist and my actions as a man. My life had failed. It seemed impossible to believe in anything . . . literary.

'That book was an attempt to bring love back into existence. An act of wish-fulfilment. Frances depends on it. She takes it as my homage to her and identifies with Anna, as if Anna were the woman Frances might have become and Josh the man who would have loved her. I created Anna to prove I could express love if not in memory then in imagination, and to show in some self-deluding way that Joan made me unfaithful, when what really happened was much darker, a complete singularity, which I could never treat fictionally because I refuse to promote such unspeakables and because literature does not need them. All the beauty, all the moral care one puts into a novel cannot co-exist with that.

'There were times when I thought the book should be published. It was what I had done, for better or worse. So I gave the manuscript to Basil and immediately regretted it. To publish this lie was worse than

246

silence. I demanded it back. He held on, and you know what happened then.

'Bad times, Michael. I don't know what kept me going. Until you came along, trundling in out of the blue. You arrived in Positano, and quickly I knew something about you, which you wouldn't know yourself, but mainly that I could trust you, and that you liked the best part of what I could offer, my work. You reconnected me with this place. I was inspired by all the old things. I wanted all of a sudden to use my powers to return to the world the fineness I had subtracted from it. You were my inspiration and my subject: a sensitive young man in retreat, whose qualities had neither been effaced nor properly channelled. You opened up the future for me.'

Michael glanced away, resisting communication, hiding shame.

He stared at Michael, as if to prove the transformation, and Michael in his seat felt the energy of his gaze, like solar warmth turned on him, and saw the aspect of a changed man. Hilldyard seemed, for a moment, years younger, at the height of his powers, virile with talent, as though staring at him from a previous era.

'She's blackmailing me for the film money.'

Michael felt himself blush.

'I keep telling her there isn't going to be a film. She says I've got to sell the rights and pay her off or she'll tell the papers.'

He allowed the silence to endure as his skin prickled.

'I'm not sure which paper. The *TLS* or the *Sun*? You see there isn't a literary tabloid.' He looked down, his imagination defeated by the idea.

The words exhaled from Michael's lips like last breath. 'Call her bluff.'

'Can you imagine what it would do to me if this got out?' Hilldyard puckered his lips. 'I mean, what happened is not material for the public domain. It's a part of my life that nobody can understand. It can't be interpreted on the facts. Frances knows this. She knows how destructive it would be to tell anyone. She knows that it would injure my reputation as a novelist, disgrace me as a man, and still achieve nothing for her, except a spasm of power.' He looked up. He was pale. 'Talk to her for me, please.'

Michael recoiled inwardly.

'She'll listen to you. You can say the film fell through. You can vouch for the fact that I'm sorry.'

He blinked against the effort of dissimulation.

'For God's sake, help me, Michael!'

Michael stood up, unable to bear the tension. He walked around in a circle and came to a stop. For a moment he was checked, thought he could not continue. His tongue was dry.

'I've something to tell you.'

'You're not going away!'

'Not that.'

'Thank God!'

He raised a flat hand, compelling attention. 'I've done a deal to produce the film. The Americans are here. Shane Hammond is here.'

Hilldyard was silent.

'The film is set up. All I need is the option signed by you. They want to see us at the Sirenuse tomorrow, but I'll handle that. I know how you feel. Unfortunately I must insist.'

Hilldyard's astonishment spread like a blush through the skin of his face. He regarded Michael with the shock of total surprise, as if all his powers of insight had failed to prepare him for this moment.

'Insist!'

'Fate decrees.'

He scowled contemptuously.

'I've no choice,' said Michael suddenly.

'How can you insist?'

'I think you underestimate the desperate nature of my position.'

'Nobody in the world can be this desperate!'

'In the real world they can.'

'My dear boy.' Hilldyard was stupefied. 'You're surely not proposing to threaten me?'

There was a peculiar silence as the two men stared at each other.

'Sign these,' Michael said quickly, pulling the papers from his jacket.

Hilldyard registered the unfamiliar tone of voice with narrowed eyes, as though he were hearing for the first time Michael's steeliness, a trait he had not witnessed before. He gazed in scorn at the outstretched arm, at the blasphemy of an option agreement proffered in these circumstances.

His eyes were round with hurt and barely controlled anger. 'You'd throw me away just like that?'

Michael was rigid. 'All I ask is your signature.'

'Well, you know, you might as well ask for my life.'

'Don't exaggerate, James.'

'Oh Michael!' He shook his head with exasperation. 'Don't underestimate.'

'It's only a book.'

He smacked his hands in front of his face. 'Nothing is only a book!'

'It hurts no one to see this adapted.'

'You can't offer me that document without knowing you are hurling our friendship away, because if it means anything, it means not doing this.'

'I have no choice.'

'Except to betray me?'

It had come to this, and he looked at it barely.

He saw the effect of his self-possession in the author's stare. He was inhuman all of a sudden and Hilldyard was reckoning this against his panic.

'And if I say no?'

'I'll go to the papers.'

'You're possessed,' he shouted.

'Frances wants justice! Give her reparation and save yourself!'

'You'd be killing me. Because if this got out, that would be my end. Are you really prepared to contemplate that?'

The two men stood a few feet apart, the wear and tear of tension creasing their brows. Hilldyard's astonishment seemed to tie itself in tighter knots. 'You couldn't do that without dying inside.'

'Come on. Sign it.'

'I took you in,' he pleaded.

'To be your acolyte! So that I could sacrifice myself to literature. Like Joan, like Frances. We're all the servants of your immortal genius, and all around you people are dying or going mad, or broke, while you dream of new novels and new claims on posterity.'

Hilldyard was aghast.

'For once in your life, James, forget about books and do something for people!'

The shock of it spun him round, as though he had been dealt a blow from an unexpected source and was lost for a reply.

Michael stared at him squarely.

Hilldyard faltered, as though he had been told something that he could not believe.

'I can't survive this, Michael.'

'Sign the contract,' he said softly, 'and your secret is safe for ever.'

He raised the letter contract, the thin thread of his future, and saw it slowly taken by Hilldyard, who knew he was blackmailed and was for the first time in his life collapsing. And Michael saw in the author's shrunken stance that he lacked courage to fight back or face him down. His will had given way and he was shamed, weak.

The author sat on the wooden chair and laid large old hands on the white paper.

Michael could scarcely believe the sight of pen on paper, the casual artist's brush of a signature, making a mark where there was just a line. Hilldyard rested forward, elbows on the table-top, physically inert. He was silent with the vision of consequences; marginally aware of Michael standing behind him. His breathing rose and fell and his rounded back grew rounder. The contract lay under his hand.

Michael waited for a moment, and then he moved to the desk and took the contract between his forefinger and thumb, tugging it gently.

The clasp on his wrist was sudden. The old man's strength intense. But the face was distraught and the fingers slowly relaxed their hold, and, without pulling, Michael's arm was released, and the author's hand remained suspended, fingers outstretched, a weightless wave.

Chapter Twenty-three

HE MADE HIS WAY down the wet steps, fingers sliding along the rail. The rain had eased to an average drizzle that dampened his face and neck. He was sheltered between walls but a wind was kicking up, rattling the branches overhead and sending whistling gusts through the streets.

He kept the contracts pressed to his heart under a lapel and watched his feet on the slippery stone. The descent was slow, a dead tread with every sinking heartbeat, a trance of departure from that dim room with its bent-over figure and lowering bookshelves. He had not even closed the door behind him, as if so feeble a courtesy were now out of character, falsely considerate.

On the street he walked through puddles, under blurred lanterns and around cars beaded with wet. The town had vanished into shuttered darkness. Every building was opaque, eyeless, incognisant of his passing. Walking into the wind he felt the pull of his own gravity and then sudden weightlessness, as though his substantiality were tricked with by the lulls and gusts.

He had no desire to return to his hotel and carried on descending through the levels of the town, past the trattoria, the closed-up *caffè*, the clothes shops in the casbah, the alleys and dimmed restaurants at the bottom. He was numb to the cold and wet and the ghostliness of deserted streets and could only keep sinking down. He came past the church, high and massive above twirling litter on the piazza.

Out on the windswept beach he took the pungent salt air full in the face. He walked against the din of the sea to the harbour jetty, where cresting waves reeled in succession against the quay, smashing pyrotechnic sprays into the air. Gallons splattered on the concrete ramp, walloped the parapet, overflowed the jetty, which drowned in every succeeding roller.

The night was immensely black and charged with tempestuousness, deep reaches of dark energy transmitting agitation in giant shock-waves against the shore. Soaked and cold he chanced his way along the cliff-edge path. Pine trees creaked and moaned in the wind. The sturdy turrets took lashings of rain and sea-water, and Michael with an open mouth and dull heart kept going between the stony ground and the rampaging sea, as though nothing could stop him.

He came in time to a cove, where the waves broke less explosively, the water humping hard against a ledge of stones and receding flaccidly for want of real impact, and he felt himself drawn to the sea, and came off the path and lay against an upside-down boat and turned his face to the cold prickle of raindrops. And then his insides began to ache and he was inundated with heaviness, a pressure on his heart and lungs, almost suffocating, which he had to sit through. He closed his eyes and listened to the crash of the sea and the surf.

He had her now. The knowledge of it was dull. Anticipation was closed off by the heaviness, the aftershock. There was no hurry, anyway, to fuel with anticipation what would come back in her presence. He could wait for that. That value would reassert itself, when the heaviness wore off. Emotion would rise in him, his grievous need, the yearning that distributed its ache through his limbs would all come back and numb the terrible pain of what he had done.

Chapter Twenty-four

'COME ON, CHEER UP.' She slapped his haunch. 'You're soaked, Lear.'

He lay inert on the bed. His legs ached.

She kneeled beside him, unpinning her hair, which she had worn in a chignon for the Hammond dinner. He could smell the fabric of her tights near his face.

The Sirenuse Hotel had called a taxi for its guest, sending her uptown in snug insulation from wind and rain. She was dry and chic in a satin jacket and black frock. Her shoes, quickly discarded, lay on the floor mat.

'Let me tell you, partner, this is going to be a milestone movie. Think *Wuthering Heights* for a modern audience. The book needs opening out. I mean that's all right, isn't it? It has the potential. Shane wants a contemporary *English Patient*.'

She had slipped into the hotel entrance without being seen, and come along the corridor and into his room without knocking. She had the offstage aura of a woman acclaimed by applause, buoyed up and glowing, and clinging to the swell of success wherever she took herself. She entered stealthily and had the composure to offer through her nervousness a smile, a look of wholehearted directed beauty at the man on the bed, before asking her question. He gestured vaguely, and she found the contracts on his table. She was silent for a moment, respectful of the evidence. Her lips moved as she turned the pages and saw the signature, and knew at last her quest had ended. And then she collapsed on the chair with a gasp.

She sat open-mouthed, silvery earrings dangling against her neck.

'He's got flu. We drank Lemsip and champagne.'

She closed her eyes against the emotion.

He wondered for the first time whether Adela Fairfax was her real name.

'He's already directing the film in his head. He knows the look of it. Knows what he wants from me.' She drew forward, pushed herself up. 'Do I seem sort of mature?'

He could see her reflection in the mirror.

'I think I understand what's going on now. It's like he's an artist, or a sculptor or something. He knows how to work with faces. How to mould a performance out of material. Hey, something incredible. You know Cathy Astor? Twenty-one and annoyingly beautiful. Shane told me Keith Halliday's casting her as Anna Karenina. Can you believe it! One phone call. No meeting. Halliday thinks she's the next Vivien Leigh. Utterly nauseating if Shane hadn't told me that I had a quality of still passionateness, or something.' She checked her face in the mirror, imagining the 'something'.

She turned, suddenly seething with affirmation. 'It's nice to know one's not on the shelf in one's thirtieth year.' She cocked a hip, put her knee on the bed. 'You have to meet his producer. Does all Shane's films.'

She was kneeling on the bed and she could see his face for the first time.

His throat was dry. 'Producer?'

'Go with the flow, Michael.'

'Is he in love with you, then?'

She began to loosen her hair, unwinding it against a shoulder.

'Oh, don't worry about that.'

It did not seem to matter now. Things would take their course.

'You'll like him.' She released her earrings. 'He's actually quite real.'

She claimed the hotel room was a manners thing, a gesture of respect. 'He's saying, "I'm just like you guys but I've lucked into all this wealth and let's share the fun." His schedule's crazy. When he sees the people he respects, he gives it everything because normally he's surrounded by agents and managers, and the people who matter really matter. The hotel thing is just tact.'

He blinked. He was unwell. 'Do you fancy him?'

She pressed his chest with the heel of her hand. 'I'm here, aren't I?'

'Does he know?'

'Know I'm here?' She frowned disapprovingly. 'Why, he's dreaming of sore throats and blocked sinuses on the biggest bed you've ever seen.' She took his hand, squeezed the palm. 'What happened?'

He closed his eyes, could not answer.

Her hand reached his face, pushed back the damp hair on his temple. She traced his hairline with a fingernail.

He could hear her breathing as she dwelt on the sight of his face on the pillow, and touched his cheek, and the corner of his mouth.

'Beautiful man.'

Adamson had called. He had learned of developments from the agency mole, whom Weislob had phoned after Michael's meet with Coburn. 'Sabbatini and Mahler are on the way. Coburn's flying back. Jets'll swap sonic booms mid-Atlantic. Is the eleven o'clock meeting confirmed?'

Coburn's departure made no sense to him.

'He's invisible to clients,' Adamson explained. 'A God-like deal-maker, behind-the-scenes mystique and other clichés. Mahler does all the Hammond meets, and you're on to something weird here because Mahler is the one nice guy in Hollywood. Like, he's nicer than us. He's nicer than your mom. He'll schmooze you and Hammond through the agenda, and Sabbatini will ink the deal. Have Sirenuse fax me the contract. Don't care whether I'm sleeping, shagging or shitting. I'll comment by return.'

He had done it for her, too. She knew that.

'Take your shirt off. It's damp.' She leaned over him. 'Come on.'

He could not move.

She stroked his face. 'It'll do you good to tell me.'

'Is Adela Fairfax your real name?'

She laughed, a bright, ringing laugh full of nerves and music.

'What's your real name?'

'That's a secret.'

'Tell me.'

'You tell me yours, and I'll tell you mine.'

'You know mine.'

He lay on his side. He was unable to say anything more.

'Shall I go, Michael?'

He would not answer this.

'Shall I go or do you want me to stay?'

He looked up at her kneeling over him, her hair suspended above his face, lips ajar. Her eye was so steady, as if something were fast gathering inside her. He could only respond with the look of a man temporarily unable to express anything. His passivity misled her.

He could hear the bedsprings move as she arched forward, unzipping her dress and loosening her bra. She let the material fall around her shoulders, ran the straps of her brassière down her arms. And when she reached for his shirt button and he dared to stare at the woman on his bed, vulnerably undressed, but biting her lip with a gaze that was sexually clamorous, it was the strangest moment he had known.

Slowly, expressionlessly, she lowered her mouth and breasts around his face and neck, a compress of flesh and breath, as though trying to assuage his guilt with the comfort of a body that wanted him to know he was desired.

He was in a wilderness, and she was spilling over him, drowning him.

'I'll tell you,' he gasped.

She breathed hard, erotically fastened.

'Adela!'

'I'm here . . .'

'Listen!'

'Listening.'

'Please!'

Her hair confused him, blinded him.

'You want to know?' He pulled back, pushed away.

She was open-mouthed.

'I'll tell you!'

Everything that tormented him should torment her. On what other terms could they touch each other's bodies.

'Michael!' Her eyes went round with the sting of rejection.

'This is not a stage play. You can't perform your way through what's going on!'

'You wouldn't tell me!'

'But do you really want to know?'

She leaned on one hand, angry and hurt.

He realised with a pang that there would never be anyone else he could tell and if he must tell her then she must want to know for his sake.

'Look at me,' she said tremblingly.

He stared at her. She would never be able to absolve him. What he had done to Hilldyard was not hers to forgive.

She half covered herself, looked at him with indignant beauty. 'What more do you want?'

'I did it for your sake!'

'And here I am!'

She had to enter into the awfulness of it and know what had been done and take into herself everything he felt, because one conscience alone was insufficient. He had to trust her, to grasp it, to tell no one. It was the only bond they could have.

It took him fifteen minutes to get it out, beginning to end, the mess in Hilldyard's living room, the retreat to the study, the confessions and revelations, the confidences, the moment of treachery and the final bitter exchange, and as it poured through him he felt swollen with guilt. Necessity had made him behave in the most unconscionable way and he could no longer understand the necessity. He was not hardened. She had to take on board what was happening to him, because Michael did not understand it himself.

She lay on her side as he spoke, hand on brow and finger in the corner of her mouth.

He felt sick, and sickness was a kind of selfhood. It proved the existence of a moral nature, and he could turn the pain of it on to his sense of Adela. She became defined against this.

'And now you tell me Shane has a producer and wants to fuck with the book.'

'He wants to open it out.'

There was a long silence.

Now he had told her, he realised that she could not easily speak. So many things that one might try to express cancelled themselves out. They had done wrong and there was no simple way of living with the knowledge of that.

'So he's gay, or what?'

'Gay?'

'In love with you, obviously.'

The deduction struck him as perverse.

'You're his muse.'

'Is this all you have to say?'

'Well, frankly, I'm absolutely thrilled.'

He looked at her in consternation. 'Have you no conscience?'

'If I had a conscience I'd send Frances to Scotland Yard.'

His heart failed.

She was upon him suddenly, pinning him to the bedstead.

'He's got a crush on you. It's obvious. Any woman could see it. But don't confuse the dotage of a homosexual sugar-daddy with the esteem of a great novelist.'

He looked her hard in the face, as if double-checking the intention behind the words.

'He wants you to be his beautiful manservant. And you fell for the muse routine because it's so flattering.'

'You really believe that!'

'It's wonderful to be told you're inspiring. Specially if your career's in a mess.'

'He rescued me!'

'Ha!' She grasped his neck victoriously. 'I'm the one that's rescuing you.'

He realised suddenly that she was not acting. This was Adela. Or whoever Adela was behind her name.

'No woman's going to share you with him. He knows it and he's fighting his corner, guilt-tripping the hell out of you. It's just a book, for God's sake. And if you wanted me, you had to get the option and lose him.'

He smiled bitterly. She had described it exactly.

'Look at me.' She spread her arms gloriously. 'Aren't I worth it?'

Something inside him coagulated.

'I am.' She grabbed his shoulders. 'I am.'

'Nothing's worth this feeling.'

'Stop feeling and start fondling.' She laughed. 'Take it out on your wicked mistress.'

Quickly, she had her hands around his trouser belt, was pulling his fly.

He clasped her wrists but she broke free and with one hard tug had him uncovered, naked to his thighs, and the look in her eye was such that he could not move. 'I'll suck you,' she said.

He felt through his coldness an involuntary displacement, control deserting him, a removal of will from his head to his nether regions, a tingle through chest and belly that he tried to withhold for fear of complicity until the truth was out, the incriminating flicker beneath her triumphant green eyes, which she saw and he saw her seeing.

'Oh.' He felt a hot ache, almost a nausea of desire that had no choice but to enfold in its pangs the spice of guilt, making desire more piquant, and the union of her mouth and his penis self-consciously wicked and ultimately lustful; and as he went under, into the pit of his neediness, taking and then giving, and his agony converted and swelled to a storm of copulation in which Adela became rudely abandoned and completely herself, he knew she was only acting in the one sense that this was a scene of her making, because she had found in him something that she wanted, and that in such collisions of dark energy he possessed her, too. This, then, was Adela.

They lay panting on the floor, Michael a dead weight over her, her throat still rising with the last strains.

He saw the iron leg of the bed and the floor tiles close up.

He had touched the point he was aiming for.

'Michael,' she said softly. She held him in her arms. 'I'd better get back.'

Chapter Twenty-five

HOLLYWOOD AGENTS STOLE EACH other's clients, and when they pounced, swooping on a star on holiday in Hawaii, or helicoptering on to an actor's yacht, or presenting a chauffeur-driven Rolls-Royce for use on the set of a film packaged by a rival, it was not the ethically free stealth that awed Michael when he read of the stories in *Variety*, but the gung-ho commandeering of expensive transport. Jets chartered, helicopters hired, yachts and speedboats jumped on so agents could be seamlessly in place around someone else's client. Steroid representation meant showbiz gestures, a blank-cheque attitude to making the pitch, and it struck Michael as hair-raising that Coburn Agency were propelling another two agents around the earth's curve so that Hammond could be assisted to meet him on a Saturday morning in an Italian town. Such supersonic ubiquity was the index of a client's power. His agents were on twenty-four-hour call, could be airborne any moment, made to move like pinballs across continents. They were the suits and the suits did not have private lives or suffer jet-lag. They were simply units of representation who could take their Hollywood functions to any venue, beach or rain-forest, protecting a client's interests without deviation or regard for local scenery. Coburn had scrambled Sabbatini and Mahler, the humans in his office, to fly through nine time zones, hard-drive against their body clocks, in order that Michael, when he arrived at the Sirenuse Hotel on a Saturday morning, could be greeted by the gentlemanly Mahler as a long-lost friend and guided through the foyer to an equally personable handshake with Gloria Sabbatini, Coburn's in-house attorney, wearing white chemise and power-jacket.

Michael was almost soothed by Mahler's good-guy smile. Here was a man well-adjusted to celebrity management, the nerves of demanding stars and the trepidation of ordinary mortals. He could handle the vibes with the alert gentleness of a trusted uncle. They sat down on the foyer seats, a huddle of three, Mahler extolling the Amalfi coast, Gloria explaining her Italian roots, as briefcases were opened and documents withdrawn. Michael twice checked his jacket pocket, feeling for the option agreement. He was soothed by Mahler's dapperness, the signet ring and French cuffs; the tan suit on white shirt; the perfectly knotted tie, nice teeth and *cappuccino* complexion. This man had played golf with studio bosses and corporate honchos, had attended the birthday parties of movie stars' children, was that mildly phoney but essentially welcome thing: an American gentleman. He had one gold molar.

Gloria kept the remains of a New York accent, a bold, masculine, husky sound that went well with a rippling laugh and quick hands. She placed the documents on a coffee table before Mahler. In Coburn's absence Mahler was the senior agent. He wore his authority lightly.

'Thank you, sir,' he said, taking Michael's option agreements and passing them to Gloria.

'Gloria's the legal eagle. Don't look too closely, hon. I want to hit the pool before Yule.'

'Three-page deal memo,' she said neutrally.

'Short and sweet. Just how I like 'em. Say, Michael, can I get you a drink?'

He declined. 'Where's Rick?'

'Poolside with Adela and Shane. Hey! How'd that happen?'

'He gets the real tough assignments,' sighed Gloria.

'Myself,' shrugged Mahler, 'I find it so terribly arduous talking to extremely beautiful women.'

'She's gorgeous,' said the lady attorney, her voice unnaturally deep.

'You'll want to check these out.' Mahler passed a draft agreement and side-letter across the table. 'Shay's on a pretty tight schedule. When you're happy with the black and white, and I've read it myself and it looks great, maybe we can mosey down the terrace and get everyone introduced.'

He explained about faxing his colleague. Mahler took him to reception and left Michael to it. He watched the pages slide through the fax machine. Over his shoulder he saw Gloria conferring with Mahler about the option agreement. Her hands made three points.

Mahler tongued his cheek, nodded knowingly. The document seemed to pass muster.

When the fax had gone he stood by the reception desk scanning their three-page agreement and side-letter. The first agreement was with a company called Cine Inc, the entity Hammond was using for the project. The second was with Coburn Agency. The Cine Inc document contained the terms of his producer deal, exactly reproducing the figures he had demanded from Coburn. The side-letter detailed Michael's cut of the packaging fee. He read quickly. Everything, to his astonishment, was included, sums doubled in words and numerals. The shortness of the agreement and the simplicity of expression was final proof of Adamson's assessment: the agents desperately wanted to close the deal. Long-form contracts might follow, but on signature of these pages he would receive one hundred thousand dollars and further unconditional undertakings.

Michael was relieved, and he could tell from the way Mahler smiled that Mahler expected him to be. They had not fought. The agent could afford to be generous.

Without mentioning Adamson's name, he explained the procedure. Mahler nodded graciously. If necessary they could amend in ink. The crucial thing was to sign before Shane departed.

'Ready to meet the star?'

They descended a flight of steps, went under arches along an arcade that was spaced by huge urns and the vista of a bar with white piano and glass-polishing waiter. An elderly man in bathrobe and raffia sandals crossed their path. A chambermaid disappeared into a lift. The establishment was quiet, in late-October lull, but eternally tuned to a five-star pitch of presentation and service. A moustached manager in a double-breasted suit met them with a smile and enquired after their happiness as they arrived on the terrace like long-standing guests. The view from the terrace was spotlit, like a painting in a gallery held up to the satisfaction of the hotel's guests, as though the Sirenuse, so well placed to behold the town from the superiority of its position, purveyed the full Positano experience to guests who might not wish to venture beyond the complacence of poolside sunbeds. Patrons could swim and sip long drinks in the knowledge that a masterpiece was before them, its colours palpitating beyond the balcony rail. At the end of the rail, at a discreet point beyond the pool's far corner, Michael saw a cluster of figures: two white-coated waiters bent over a trolley, bright-haired Adela, the figure of a man wearing sunglasses and lying back on his deckchair as if determined to imbibe every beam of the sun's good will. And Rick Weislob.

As they cornered the pool, closing the gap in space time between himself and Shane Hammond, Mahler prepared his cuffs, and Gloria set her best smile. Meanwhile, Hammond watched them approach without making any physical preparation for the imminence of Michael's arrival. Michael was knotted up and pale-skinned, in no state to impress movie star or shop assistant.

The introductions were a haze. Hammond sprang to his feet with last-minute energy, giving Michael a sharp handshake and a firm look, immediately conveying authority. Mahler's hands directed other introductions and reacquaintances. Adela's cheek came forward, her husky 'Hi' breathing through scented waft. Weislob swiped his hand and grasped his elbow and conducted him with a shoulder pat to a seat near Hammond. Gloria and Mahler drew up chairs and Mahler sounded pleasantries and requested the waiters to serve coffee whilst Adela repositioned herself in draped elegance behind Hammond, as though she planned to be more of a talented spectator than an active participant.

Hammond was shorter than Michael expected, neat-figured in chinos and white shirt. His sleeves were rolled up revealing good forearms and strong hands, and it came as a shift to see the famous face in three dimensions, something you could walk around and check from all angles. He seemed little more than thirty-five or -six, though he must have been forty. His hair was short, well kept, his demeanour high-tempered, royal.

Mahler made jokes about Italian paparazzi and Italian film distributors, eking joviality into the gathering, and Hammond kept his mouth shut and listened to the prelude with tolerance.

This quietness later seemed like deliberate poise, a reticence that kept him in the centre of attention whilst others were being listened to. The Englishman's worldwide success allowed him new economy of output and expression. Meetings had to be efficient. Meetings were not an actor's métier. They were a necessary imposition on scarce time and private moods, and Michael suspected, through the blur of his nervousness, that this American servility might even be embarrassing to an RSC actor. Hammond was famous. He needed top agents. But he was also British.

Michael had been terrified since he woke. He had come out of sleep suddenly, lurched forward and remained transfixed in the mess of his sheets while the tank of his mind filled with its slow, corrupted fluid, consciousness discoloured by guilt. His shame was greater in the morning than in the misery of the night, because the intervening hours had surely worsened things for Hilldyard, and improved nothing for Michael. What he had done would have sunk in now, progressed from shock to an established bruising or rupture; and every successive waking moment would indict Michael further, time itself cementing Hilldyard's despair, his sense of violation.

He had dressed like a man preparing himself for an ordeal. He found an earring of Adela's, held it to his lips, put it in his pocket. It was hard to think about her. She had derailed him from a sense of self, and yet he had followed her, gone with her, wherever that was. She had prised him away from his centre and he had no idea how to construe such an experience. It left him numb, motiveless as far as she was concerned. Adela, he realised, made love in a value-free zone. That's how she liked it, and she liked it because everything else was so stressfully calculated and intelligently strategic, and she liked it hard and lithe and brazenly carnal; though nothing had been possessed by feeling.

He needed to talk to her now; see how she felt about things, was affected. He needed the reassurance of a conversation that had nothing to do with Shane Hammond.

He had no idea how to impress Hammond. He had his wits but no certitude, no integrity to fall back on. His moral pith was extracted. And yet today was his day, and he found it completely strange to know that in a few hours he might consolidate his power by signing a deal. That would be final. He had it in his control to damn himself, an important opportunity which he must seize with determination. Retreat was impossible because on that side of things he had left nothing. The logic of peril forced the next stage, gave desperate necessity, and the manly thing was to get on with it. Then at least he would have objective strength – whatever the condition of his soul. His soul might wither and die. But so it could, if he had the money, and a hook into the future. And then, perhaps, his love for Adela would redeem the inner man, if she would let him love her as he wanted to.

Time to call Adamson.

Where he was it was late. He was audibly tired, though with the steady tone of a man using his last push of concentration to get a deal closed. Adamson did not let go. His sense of detail, his foreshortening of problems, the long-distance will-power he threw at Michael – these qualities were the essence of his being, making him endlessly high-concentrate. Phoned-out by a day in the office, his normal weavy spiel was slowed down. He took longer to collect the points.

'Say something nice about one of his films.'

'Yes.'

'*Thinking Time.*'

Michael hesitated. 'I never saw it.'

'Say you admire his work.'

He let out breath. 'OK.'

'Shake his hand and say it. Right off. First thing. Listen, this man's a rich, famous actor. Unlike other rich, famous people, he's insecure, paranoid and petulant.'

'Are you sure about that?'

'Eggshell time. You can't over-stroke an actor's ego.'

'He'll be relieved, surely.'

Adamson laughed wearily. 'Shane Hammond relieved? From where he stands, you just pulled a fast one.'

'I've got him the rights, Nick!'

'But he wants the project. So he can't be rude. And, likewise, you can't imply that you have him by the balls, or think you have. Sensitive. On the other hand . . .'

'He wants to do the deal.'

'He knows you can't back out.'

'What?'

'Your deal's too rich.'

'I can back out.'

'Unrealistic.'

'If I don't like his pitch I . . .'

'They'll know you're locked in. Coburn's not stupid.'

'But . . .'

'Which means you can be marginalised.'

Michael was behind, his intuition adrift. He panicked. 'It's a situation of complementarity. Of mutual interest.'

'Your so-called editorial control means Jack-shit unless Hammond buys the Hilldyard veto.'

'Hilldyard doesn't have a veto.'

'You'll get no respect from Hammond unless you stand up to him.'

'I'll stand up to him.' The words sounded hollow.

'If he thinks you've ransomed him, he'll know you're buyable. If he knows you need money, he'll realise that, eventually, you'll cave in on everything. And he'll make the film he wants to make.'

'Surely he respects Hilldyard?'

'Hey. Don't believe what you read in women's magazines.'

These equivocations weighed on him. 'I'm not prepared to just make any film.'

There was a pause.

'Perhaps we'll see eye to eye.'

Adamson started up slowly, framing and phrasing the presentation in its best light; and as he spoke, Michael felt a terrible longing for his words to be true.

'Your leverage is that you own Hilldyard. You have the relationship, and no matter how cynical Hammond feels, that relationship he has to respect. Like Hilldyard's major. Huge. A great living novelist. And you're his special friend. Now take that proposition one stage further. It's as if you are Hilldyard, an apostle of his taste. He's selected you to defend the . . . uh . . . keynote themes of the book, whatever they are, against false adaptation, development hell and blah-de-blah . . .'

'It's just that I know' – he had no one else to tell this – 'Hammond wants to "open it out".'

'And it's your God-given job to ensure fidelity to the . . . whatever . . . of the book. That's your role. Without that role you're just a man to pay off. Michael, you have to go toe to toe with him, or he'll know your ligging, and your control will end when you sign on the line.'

'Right.'

'It's a gamble.'

He realised that he was too far in. There would be nothing left for him if Hammond pulled out.

'Make him respect you.'

'Yes.'

'Be yourself. Say what you believe. Think about the book's bottom line.'

'These things are so subtle.'

'I mean, don't fucking blow it!'

'No.'

'But don't let them think you're a patsy.'

'I'm not.'

'Sell the Hilldyard pedigree.'

'Right.'

He could see it now. Nothing he said would be true any more.

He was politely listening to Tom Mahler. The longer Mahler spent recapping the situation for Hammond's benefit, the more oppressive Hammond's silence became. His brow was furrowed against the glare of the light and the gist of gathering issues. He was not handsome in a notch-jawed, straight-nosed way. Rather his face held intensity, like the young Orson Welles; the cheeks were broader, the mouth tighter-lipped, and the eyebrows capable of an ironic setting within an essentially serious demeanour. Hammond was more masculine than beautiful, though the eyes, when they flashed sideways, were surprisingly fine, unexpectedly so. An actor had to have natural attributes as well as talent.

He was still, listening to Mahler.

Michael swapped flat looks with Adela from time to time. She was neutral, of course. He felt the impulse to reassure her, to let her know he was OK now and that she could ignore his anger of the previous night. She did not need to worry about that. He would handle that; his problem. He looked at her miraculously incarnated yet again and found it impossible to believe he had had the luck to touch and kiss this woman, impossible to think she was still his. It lifted his yearning, and once raised, he found the desire to love almost unbearable. Such precious sensations needed a haven. They were the best thing left in him.

'Gentlemen, Michael has done us a great favour in making of himself a kind of link, if you will, in the association between Coburn Agency and James Hilldyard, and I think we now appreciate that in our previous design for the project there was an element missing which he has provided. Certainly there are details to finesse. Every movie has a one-off dynamic. But Michael will correct me if I'm wrong in saying we have a way forward on the commercial terms and will be in a position, with Gloria's permission, to sign off this morning, if that is our wish. Michael, we sincerely appreciate you, and I'm sure you respect the impact on any project of Shane Hammond. This man you see before you is one of the most important figures in contemporary cinema. He has great achievement behind him and a golden future. I'm here to ensure that his interests as director and star of this film are protected, and that any new element coming to the mix synchs with his vision of the film. We cannot paper this over. That's why we're here and I want us to dwell on it carefully. The agenda is simple. Gentlemen, how do we envision this movie?'

Michael finished his coffee and was available to speak. The important thing was not to dive in.

'Shay, d'you want to lead off?'

The star rubbed his eyes, hung his head. 'Can we back up a mo?'

Mahler raised palms. 'Please.'

Shane cleared his throat; his sinuses were heavy. He spoke in a low-toned voice of gravelly resource, which tended to a drawl, as if he were trawling for the essence of his concern. 'I'm sure I should be grateful to Michael . . . for his intervention. You know . . . I'd written this project off. So . . . Great. Congratulations on your no doubt considerable persuasive skills.' He coughed. 'What I don't get, and pardon me if I'm being a bit fluey and thick, is the exact difference between the kind of film the author thinks Michael would make with his blessing, and the kind of film he wouldn't let us make.' He squinted.

'Michael, that's a key question.'

Michael hesitated, remembering himself. He faced Hammond's inquisition directly. It was a direct question, and a direct answer was in order. There could still be integrity on this matter.

'He trusts my judgement.'

Hammond did not experience this as a *sequitur*, but took up the point.

'What did he think was so wrong with my judgement?'

There was a pause. 'He has no personal knowledge of your judgement.'

Hammond kept the sun out of his eyes. 'I've done some pretty good films.'

'Of course.'

'I don't think my image is particularly lightweight.'

'Shane has an Oscar,' said Mahler. 'Literally countless theatre awards. You should see his CV. It's gold-plated.'

'I'm not boasting.' He smiled falsely. 'I'm just not clear what values you stand for that I don't.'

Adela moved to the edge of the chair, bit her lip.

Michael was taken aback by the hostility, not foreseen on this point. It had never occurred to him that Shane might have taken Hilldyard's rebuff as a personal slight.

'I've done Shakespeare, Chekhov, Strindberg . . .'

'You stand for a lot.'

'Yeah, but you stand for more.'

Adela caught his eye, saw him take up the challenge.

'I've worked with him,' he said softly.

'And what's the magic ingredient?'

'Oh.' It came easily. 'I believe in the integrity of his work.'

'You have a monopoly on integrity?'

He wondered if Hammond was always upfront, or whether he was just irked by Michael's presence in his life.

'I sincerely hope not.'

'As in we're peasants if we don't agree with you?'

Mahler intervened. 'With respect, Shane, Michael never said that.'

'Where is James Hilldyard?' Hammond blew his nose. 'I want his blessing.'

Michael's anger was rising now. Shane was overstepping the mark.

'Tied up.'

'He's tied up?'

He hesitated. 'He writes for a living.'

Hammond appreciated the dryness of the answer. 'So what are you? A quality monitor?'

It was a dangerous moment.

'Some kind of watchdog?'

'I'm the producer.'

'Who's never produced a film before.'

He checked himself, thought for a second. 'No. But show me an experienced producer who's managed to get the rights to this book.'

'I've got that.' Hammond shot to his feet, superbly volatile. 'But here we are talking about your combining with a team to whom Mr Hilldyard wouldn't sell the rights, and what I don't get is why you think you can do a deal with me when he wouldn't.'

Michael swallowed. 'I hope I can deal with you.'

'You hope so, eh?'

He glanced at Adela. 'Yes.'

'So what would you like to know? How may we satisfy you?'

There was no help to be had from Mahler. Nobody wished to go against the grain of Hammond's ill-temper. If this was how he felt, then that was the issue, as ungainsayable as crappy weather. Michael, in the depths of his chagrin, saw very well that Hammond's

269

benevolence was not stirred by Mahler's description of him as a white knight. His contribution would not be appreciated. His presence slighted Hammond's autonomy. He was an unwelcome reminder, perhaps, that Hammond's powers were not absolute. The actor had gone to Hollywood hoping to shake off this kind of literary middle-class Englishman.

How arrogant of Hammond to assume he had no judgement because he had not produced a film!

'Perhaps we should discuss the film,' he said.

Hammond stood by the table taking a replenishment of his coffee from the waiter.

'You want to vet the approach.'

'Shay.' Mahler extended a hand, like some intervening biblical figure in a Renaissance painting. 'Hilldyard's last movie was a box-office stinker. A total flop-out dodo. Without any disrespect to you, the author is jumpy about adaptation. In appointing Michael to safeguard his interests he's making a gesture of trust. Michael wants to help us, not hinder us, and it's in everybody's interests to do a movie that squares not only with our goals and ambitions but with the author's. It's a question of mutuality, not compromise. We have to respect this very fine novel, and Hilldyard, through Michael here, must surely respect our concerns. For sure, the movie concept must have integrity by all our standards. See, Michael, Shane is so committed to this project. He will star, he'll direct, he will live and breathe this project for one year, eighteen months and understandably he's protective of his baby. And Shay, I know I'm right in saying that Michael wants to help you do this. He sees it as your vehicle, will work to your ends, and enrich your ambition with very valuable consultation and advice.'

'Do I have to parade my vision of the film before you now?' said the actor.

The insolence was so personal, Michael had to manage his restraint. 'I'd love to hear your vision.'

Hammond came back to his chair, sat down and placed his coffee on the ground. His expression went serious, a shift of mode. He pulled his hand over his face, glimpsed around him with artistic pain.

'What can I tell you? This book hit me like a rabbit punch in the kidneys. It went off in my head like a rocket. I'm not sure why. The sick wife. Well, OK, my mother died of cancer. Wham. That gets you. That was one of the worst years of my life, and boy, does he nail that bad trip to the mast! The impossible affair, beautiful, forbidden, self-destructive. Tell me about it. Those two things together . . . one fucking great way into a character. I liked the domestic backdrop. So muted and familiar, cluttered with reassuring things, completely sterile. Not the habitat of a hero. This is where a weak, prematurely middle-aged man is dying away his life. His soul's in the fridge with the fruit juice and bacon rashers. Then wallop, he's in love. *Brief Encounter* with a catch. He goes the distance and when he gets there he can't do it. Can't commit. Blows the gig and then the gig blows him. The set-up is over his head and then things go really wrong. That's a love story with a sting. And maybe I'm revealing too much about myself if I tell you it hit me here.' He punched his chest.

Michael nodded.

'Your man can write the arse off a donkey. He's telling us a lot about ourselves. Stuff we may not want to hear.'

She was looking at him. Michael returned the look suddenly.

'But stuff that happens everywhere. Love and death is here in Italy, there in Greenland, alive and well in some kitchen sink of an American backwater town. The core of this book will travel. And I want to make a film that gives audiences everywhere that core. On screen.'

He cleared his throat, looked into the sky, tongue under lip. 'How to adapt?' Hammond seemed pained, as though bearing the weight of the world on his shoulders.

Michael nodded.

'The story drives a knife in and turns it. That's why I'm interested. What can I say? Either I connect with the material or I don't. Right now this story's preying on my mind. I want to lift that complexity and richness off the page and slam it on to the screen. How?' He bunched his fist. 'Is another matter. You've got to do things. Pull it apart. Knock it back together again. You got to strip out, add on, restructure. It's a fucking hassle. I've worked with screenwriters. These things don't write themselves. Forget that. That's donkey work. What counts is that we build it up in a way that's true to the novel. That's what I want. That's what I care about. That's why I'm sitting here.'

His hands remained aloft, waiting for further inspiration, and for a moment Michael thought he would continue. His vibrancy had risen quickly, and there was still a tremor in the air. Hammond had no conversational inclination, no social *élan* when surrounded by men

271

of business. What he carried with him was the handy volatility of the great thespian, the trained and channelled passion that could erupt at the press of a button, grabbing whatever rhetoric lay to hand, and impress executives and agents with the unquestionable thunder of talent.

There was nothing wrong with what he said. He had testified to his deep response, and that was his bond. He was a person wired to his own emotions, used to running on the force of instincts, and after the manifesto shock-wave of his first speech would recompose himself and check what else it might be necessary to say.

Mahler leaned forward. 'Does that make sense, Michael?'

'Of course.'

Hammond eyed him carefully.

There was a pause.

'How d'you see the adaptation,' he asked, 'from a director's viewpoint?'

Hammond was not enlightened by the question.

'I mean . . . do you think it needs opening out?'

'Michael, I'm glad you mentioned that,' said Mahler.

Hammond glanced at his hands, unready to commit further thoughts.

'How did you describe the film to your financiers?' Michael asked.

'Shay, d'you want to take this, or shall I?'

Hammond shrugged.

'OK,' said Mahler. 'Like you said. We've got to get this lovely book out of its covers and on to the screen. When we go to script, we'll go with a blueprint. We figure Shane needs to do this picture summer of next year. So there can be second drafts and third drafts, but we need to be on track with the first draft. To keep that schedule we've put Rick and the story department on to the project to brainstorm parameters prior to selecting our screenwriter. We've talked to the money. We've kicked ideas around with Shay, and we're trouble-shooting the problem areas down to a real tight brief. Can I be frank? It's a great book. But it's a book. To make this work as a Shane Hammond vehicle it needs opening out big time. Gee, the story department have come back with some very creative ideas. You know, the story's kind of bleak. It's grey-toned, almost *noir*. And the action is very talky, linear. We figure that to make this work you need to loop in a couple of extra sub-plots, and doctor the character arcs to make them less shallow-curved. Josh is a depressing guy, but it's his movie, so we need to shape up the backstory, and we need to surround this very domestic, private world with some parallel action.'

'That,' said Hammond, 'is the sound of the American marketplace. Fifty per cent of the world market, ninety per cent of our money. We can handle it.'

'Rick is story-editing?' said Michael.

'Rick's co-ordinating input.'

He gazed at the short agent.

'Shane's not a screenwriter,' explained Mahler.

Hammond swung around. 'Michael, we need to lift this project.'

'We have scenarios.'

'We need to find,' said the star, 'some real out-there penalty for Josh's infidelity to his dying wife. These guys call it jeopardy. In the book it's psychological hell. In a feature film the hell must be concrete, life-threatening. And that ties into Adela's character. Their affair needs to be more than moral torture. She needs to be connected with some unexamined part of his past.'

He was dumbfounded. The ideas were extraordinarily radical.

'What d'you mean?'

'I want Josh to have a dangerous past. Let's say MI5, counter intelligence, but a desk job. Other people do the dirty work. This is all way off backstory.' Hammond swished back and forth, shaving the air with his hand, as if paring out sections of the novel he did not want. 'The man did a desk job like Harrison Ford in *Clear and Present Danger*.'

'*Clear and Present Danger!*'

'Anna's father was killed in action. An old friend of Josh. In fact, Josh is Anna's godfather.'

Michael could hardly believe his ears.

'Anna is late twenties, say a journalist, and she wants to know how her father died and whose fault it was. Right.' He held the point like an invisible rugby ball, as though he would pitch it to Michael. 'She believes Josh holds the clue, even though he's retired and has nothing to do with the firm. Josh's wife falls sick. Anna hears about this and offers her services as nurse. After a decent interval of nursing she starts to probe Josh. What neither of them expect to happen is an affair. The affair starts and this sticks close to the book. Adela's character discovers she's fallen for an older man. So the motives are complex but the passions are real. Then the backstory kicks in. Anna forces Josh to make enquiries about her dead father within the service, opening a bloody Pandora's Box. Bad guys are put on alert. Josh is going through his wife's terminal illness, and then, I don't know, the IRA are coming over the garden hedge. Something like that?'

'You mean a thriller?'

'This is not an exploitation movie,' said Mahler.

He glanced at Adela. He wondered whether she knew all this.

'This frames the book,' said Mahler. 'A structural brace.'

Time slowed down for him. The agents leaned towards him, Hammond gaped at the sky, Adela folded her arms and raised her chin, as if half distracted by the sun's warmth. He was totally stupefied. They were utterly changing the story.

And then the pounding started. His heart resisting everything, pounding against the trap.

'IRA is dated,' said Weislob.

'Mafia, whatever,' said Shane.

This was the moment to speak out. This was the moment to dig his heels in, and it terrified him that there was so much he wanted to say and could not say. Their ideas were alien, at odds with everything he had found in the book.

'Whose ideas are these?'

'It's a working plan,' said Hammond. 'Is it crap?'

He looked at Adela.

'What about setting?' said Mahler.

'Try Michael.'

'I'd keep the English setting.' His voice was light, powerless.

'Agreed.'

'Shay!'

Hammond turned to Mahler.

'Money's on New England. What did we say, Rick?'

Weislob steepled his fingers. 'Josh is ex-intelligence. Now affiliated as an academic to Ivy League. He and his wife are Americans. Anna's the English Rose god-daughter. Finance really dug the transatlantic love story. For MI5 read FBI. For IRA, ah shit, Mafia.'

'That's the American version,' explained Mahler.

Michael could not conceal his reaction. Mahler picked it up.

'What Shay's career needs, Michael, is an American lead. We all know too many top British actors who never hit top whack in the States because they could not play an American hero. Brits tend to be

274

good villains, tongue-tied upper-class gooks, patrician charmers, and there's only so far you can go with mere good acting. Shay's already broken out of that. He's got the indefinable star quality and what we need is a vehicle to impact on a coast-to-coast American audience.'

Hammond frowned. 'Can we Americanise this story?'

'We need a character ordinary folks can relate to.'

'Well . . .'

'The story needs to position Shay as a loving man but a moral man.'

Michael could not contain himself. 'Who screws around while his wife is dying?'

Mahler shrugged. 'Shay, we need to talk about this.'

'That's the film, Tom.'

'Michael's put his finger on something.'

'The film is dark,' shrugged Hammond.

'You can't throw away sympathy for your character!'

'We'll fix it.'

'Easy,' said Weislob. 'The man's wife is bitch-city. Our hero has stuck in there through shit. Has tried to make the marriage work. But in his heart he's starved of love. The rest is bad timing.'

'This is what I'm up against,' said Hammond to Michael, as if he were no part of it.

'Does he reconcile with his wife before she dies?' asked Mahler.

Hammond referred to Michael. 'Does he?'

'Not in the book.'

'You know. That's kind of bleak,' said Mahler.

'These are just ideas,' said Hammond. He came back to his chair, sat down squarely. 'I'm not interested in making a Brit movie for the art-house circuit. I've done all that, paid my dues. I want a film that can open on fifteen hundred screens which isn't popcorn additive. Half the material's in the novel. Maybe more. The rest we have to find.'

Hammond had changed, Michael realised. At one point he must have been an artist, pure and simple, a man with a gift. Now he was an executive of his own career. His proposals were as pragmatic as his tone. And now he had relaxed Michael wondered if his initial touchiness were not the defensive pride of a man who knows he has sold out.

It was time for him to speak and yet, still, he had nothing he could say. There was nowhere to start. Their premises were incompatible, the Americans' too fluid, Hammond's too commercial. Anything he might say about the moral ambiguity of the book, its inconclusiveness and thwarted romanticism, its irony, its unhappy ending, its reality in his own imagination, would be meaningless to them.

He stood up. He felt dizzy. The light had got to him. The Americans' voices confused him. He looked across at the film star squinting back at him. He could not fathom how they expected Hilldyard to agree these suggestions. If Hilldyard would not agree them, how could he?

To deny Hilldyard's voice in the matter was to deny his own. He had denied Hilldyard and therefore had no voice. There was no part for him to play. He had no interest any more in these curious proceedings. He stood for absolutely nothing.

'What d'you say, Michael?'

He was a non-contributor.

'Any comment?' said Hammond.

He hesitated. 'I think we've got a lot of common ground.'

'Are we on the right track?'

Michael sat down. He wanted to say goodbye to them all. He needed but lacked courage.

Adela was waiting for him to speak. He looked at her blankly, wondering if she read his mind. This was what she wanted him to go through with.

Hammond caught Mahler's eye. 'Approval clause.'

Mahler nodded.

There were some whisperings. Mahler touched Gloria's sleeve. 'Contracts.'

Michael held his hands together and looked at the terrace flagstones. He would have to dig into himself to find what he wanted on the screen, and perhaps he wanted nothing more than the book.

'Are you happy, Michael?'

She was looking at him now.

He would not be producing this film, he thought. It would be happening around him, over him. Control would be meaningless unless he dug in now, and he could only dig in to say No, to say Ridiculous.

Weislob approached with his mobile. 'Need to call your adviser?'

Gloria sat at the second table, amending the assignment contract with her pen.

'One thing James Hilldyard can be sure of. If this film works, the book's going to be huge.'

Modesty was not Hammond's forte. Or maybe he knew enough to know that all great men are egotists, and that Hilldyard's egotism would take care of itself. It depressed him not to be able to speak his mind.

'Michael, you look fazed.'

He held the mobile phone.

'Press Call and then dial.'

It was outrageous, he thought, that they were so fearless of the book, so breezy about dismantling and dismembering it, as though stripping one art form for the benefit of another were a casual necessity, taken for granted. Their approach had no tact, no caution.

Mahler drew a chair across, sat near him. He laid a tanned, manicured hand on Michael's arm. It was a private beat, an inside-track moment for deal-makers.

'Shane has raised a very important point which we should address.' He spoke quietly. The others could not hear. 'He needs to have approval now.'

'Approval?'

'Of his vision.'

His heart sank and he laughed softly.

'Michael, I know the contract says script approval.'

'It does.'

'Can we make that vision approval instead? You've heard his ideas. They're great ideas. You know the way we're headed. What I would really like is for you to endorse the American-version coverage which we can annexe, so's right from the start we're on track.'

He spoke emptily. 'If I don't like the script?'

Mahler pursed his lips. 'You tell us, and we talk about it.'

He massaged his eye-sockets. 'Just talk?'

'Hey! You wouldn't tell Henry Ford how to make a motor car! Shay has to have' – he was hushed – 'approval over everybody. Because Shay is . . . the movie.'

Michael hesitated. There was nothing he could say.

Mahler patted his arm. 'Gloria will amend. Hey, chief, got your contract-signing pen?'

'Sounds good,' said Hammond.

'I think a celebration is in order.' Mahler turned to Adela. 'The lady is looking beautiful, and I have a thirst coming on.'

She smiled, took herself to the edge of the terrace.

Michael stirred himself to get up and walk around the pool and make his call to Adamson.

As the mobile processed the digits he gazed at the tableau by the pool. Hammond reclining in his bright white shirt; a waiter departing for champagne; Mahler by the table's edge, rubbing his hands and joking with Weislob; Adela in her blue, wind-wafted dress, leaning on the rail before the halcyon panorama, hair incandescent in the low light. On the pool's other side, an elderly German couple lay on deckchairs, fully clothed, eyes shut.

'Shit,' said Adamson, over the poor line.

That was it; they were defeated.

'Let's hope they make it.'

After the call, he drifted back. A row of champagne flutes was being filled. An ice bucket was on standby. Mahler had two chairs drawn up to the table, two sets of agreements placed on the cloth, two attendant pens, like cutlery, next to each contract.

'Take a seat, Michael.'

He wanted to say something, like a man in the dock, before going down.

'One swell place,' said Mahler, relief in his voice.

Hammond followed Adela to the balcony. He stood next to her, hands behind his back, falling into her scene as if for the camera's eye.

Michael raised his pen. He looked again.

'How about lunch?' said the film star softly.

She turned to him and smiled. Michael had seen the smile before.

'Sign here. Initial there.' Mahler's finger touched the page.

'That would be great,' she replied.

Hammond said something. He could not hear what. Soon they were talking.

He let the nib down, still waiting. Out of the corner of his eye he saw rising champagne bubbles. They trickled upwards from the bottom of the glass, gasped on the surface.

He signed his name carefully, laboriously, as though his consent were held back to the last letter. It was strange to be tied for ever in the loops of one's name to a company called Cine Inc; strange to become no more than a link in the chain of title, a channel for the passage of rights.

Shane strode back at Mahler's calling, made a performance of signing, grabbed a champagne glass for a high-handed toast and slapped Michael on the back *en route*. His signature had just dispatched a hundred thousand dollars from an account somewhere, owned by one of his companies – part of a tax structure that his accountants and lawyers understood, in the scheme of things now he was big. Such transactions were fiscally shrewd, for him to sign off on and for the suits to get right.

'This is the life,' said the actor, giving Adela a glass. He toasted her. 'Where is Positano?' he said.

She laughed. 'Italy, you fool!'

'I know that, ma'am! Where's Rome from here?'

'Behind you.'

He glanced over his shoulder.

'About two hundred miles.'

'By the way, you're looking very lovely today.'

She smiled.

He laughed heartily. 'Hey, Tom!'

Mahler was alert.

'Every single time we meet, you're drinking vintage champagne on expenses.'

Mahler cracked a smile. 'There's always something to celebrate when you're around.'

'Platinum-tongued Yank.'

Mahler laughed louder. Being with Shane was great.

'Beats Perrier in the Polo Lounge. I'm telling you, Adela, never have so many sharks drunk so much fizzy water. You guys should relocate here. Get some grappa under your belts.'

'Pass,' said Weislob.

'Really, Rick! You do surprise me.'

'Know what, chief, this place is like Deadsville.'

Hammond laughed. 'Adela, where can we go for a nice quiet lunch?'

Michael sat at the table, listening. He was cast adrift, inert, and then he saw James Hilldyard.

He wore a linen jacket, baggy trousers, and was being directed to their group by a waiter. He stood for a moment on the far side of the pool; and then he saw Michael and started making his way towards them. He moved quickly along, as though arriving late, and Michael saw him and the shock of it made him dizzy. He was caught at it, witless, unable to think.

Nobody else noticed Hilldyard before he passed the champagne table, and by then he was heading so quickly towards the man in the white shirt his intrusion was completed before it could be stopped.

The author stood there, vibrant with indignation. His eyes glistened as he spoke. 'Are you Shane Hammond?'

The actor turned. 'I am he. What can I do for you?'

Michael saw Adela's face.

'Excuse me, sir, this is a private gathering,' said Mahler.

'Fuck off back to La-La Land.'

Hammond's eyebrows skipped up.

She was speechless too long.

'Tom.' Hammond shrugged. 'Can we lose the stand-up comedian?'

'Sir, this is . . .'

'James Hilldyard. *Sir*.'

Hammond changed colour. 'Oh God! I'm so sorry. I had no idea. It's a privilege to meet you.'

Hilldyard looked severely at the extended hand.

Mahler was wide-eyed.

'I do not wish to be met.'

Hammond was open-mouthed.

'Shane.' Adela came off the balcony.

'How can you help me, indeed?' Hilldyard was precipitate. 'By removing yourself and your entourage from this town and understanding that you will never make a film based on my book, and that I curse any attempt to persuade me to grant an option, that I detest adaptations, and am horrified by the behind-the-scenes manipulation that has gone on around me and my guest. My head is not turned, and never will be, by the interest of famous actors or the wiles of young actresses. I hold Hollywood in contempt and regard this gathering as a disgrace. Is that completely unambiguous?'

Michael buried his face in his hands.

Hammond's confusion was undisguised. He glanced at Mahler and Weislob, sharing shock.

Mahler got moving, bringing himself around to face Hilldyard where his conciliatory body-language and sincere respectability could have its best effect. 'Mr Hilldyard. Please forgive us. I think there has been a misunderstanding.'

'There has. It is yours, and I have ended it.'

Hammond flinched. 'I'll be damned.'

'You will be damned.'

'Rick, get a chair.'

'Don't patronise me!'

Hammond swallowed his pride. 'Please . . . these are my representatives. Tom Mahler, Rick Weislob. This is my attorney. They've flown here from LA.'

'Not at my behest.'

'Excuse me! You've signed an option agreement. Tom!'

Mahler, like a clerk of the court, passed the option agreement to Hammond.

'Here it is. Signed in your own fair hand.'

Hilldyard did not react.

'Am I right or am I right?'

Michael boiled in shame. He glanced at Adela. Her skin was pale; her forearms were tense.

Hilldyard had absorbed the challenge and now stepped closer to the actor. He looked at him unwaveringly before he spoke. 'Which would you rather believe, the author in person, or a piece of paper?'

Hammond stared at the old man, an uncomprehending stare.

'Mr Hilldyard.' Mahler made his entry again.

'I don't need the agent when I can talk to the principal!'

'This is a binding document!'

'Would you bind me against my will?'

Hammond's expression corrupted as he registered the strength of Hillyard's feelings.

'Sir, your will is expressed in this contract. You know what it is to sign a legal document.'

'And if I signed the blasted thing by mistake—' He turned pained eyes on Mahler. 'Surely you'd let me withdraw from the agreement? Surely, Mr Hammond, you'd leave my poor book alone if I asked you politely?'

Hammond frowned. 'Politely? You just said fuck off!'

'I'll take that back.'

'Please note, Gloria.' Mahler cupped his chin. 'Signature admitted.'

'Yes, I do admit it.' He was vehement. 'I signed the thing yesterday evening at eight o'clock and since then I've had second thoughts and the law of contract is one thing but ordinary human decency is another. As far as I'm concerned the thing in your hand is morally void.'

'Michael!'

Hilldyard blinked, glancing hesitantly at Michael, and then looking away again.

'Can you tell us what the fuck is going on?'

They were looking at him now. He had no voice. He was paralysed. Hilldyard was defying him to lie before the others and betray him in public. He had second-guessed him, knowing his true nature, had come here with courage and resolution.

He felt Hammond's eyes drilling into him. Hammond had not backed down. He was standing on his rights, displeased and unbending. He refused to defer to a man who showed no respect.

He saw it now, everything.

'Easy, Michael,' Mahler dapperly interceded, palms pressed tight. 'Whatever Mr Hilldyard is alluding to, it is not in your power to revoke an agreement which has been assigned to a third party. Legally, we own the option, and Mr Hilldyard's change of heart is irrelevant to that fact.'

'Oh for God's sake, man! This isn't a game! The contract's totally void. Meaningless. Tell him, Michael!'

'Michael, I'd counsel silence, in your own best interests.'

Hammond stood straight, alert and inflexible. 'Michael can deny it.'

'You can certainly deny it,' said Mahler.

By the balcony, hands tight on the rail, she was intensely willing him to speak. Her mouth was ajar; eyes brilliant.

His mouth was parched. He tried to swallow.

'Void for duress,' said the author quietly.

Mahler theatrically turned. 'That's a very serious allegation. Prima facie slanderous. You wanna take it back?'

'Take back the truth?'

Mahler slapped his pants. 'Michael, you are being accused of unconscionable pressure in getting Mr Hilldyard to sign a contract. If that damaging assertion is true, and I sincerely hope Mr Hilldyard is mistaken, you are exposed to legal action not only from the victim of the duress but from the assignee of your option rights. I can't believe that a producer of standing and integrity would put himself in that position. Can you please give me reassurance that this is not the case?'

Hilldyard averted his eyes, as though he knew Michael's character and did not need to encourage a response.

'Are you going to sit there like a stewed prune,' asked Hammond, eyes bloodshot with flu, 'or are you going to put the record straight?'

Michael could not defend himself, and he could not speak against Hilldyard. He was dissolving.

She came across from the rail, walked between Hammond and Mahler, strode towards Michael, put herself between him and the others.

It was all falling through for him.

'Come on,' she said.

He gave her a look.

'Say something!'

He could smell the perfume in the folds of her dress.

'Michael!'

She would have him say what he knew, deflect Hilldyard with allusions to this or that, hints of exposure. She wanted him to use his secret.

'Michael has been defending your best interests right through this meeting.' Mahler raised a judicious finger. 'I'd like to record that.'

'And I'd like to erase you!'

'Jesus, Tom!' Hammond snapped. 'I thought this was sewn up.'

'Shay, for Christ's sake! This is news to me.'

'That's the trouble with you guys. You're always one step behind.'

Mahler gaped with panicky embarrassment, swapped glances with Gloria.

Weislob came over, face notched with anger, mouth stretching and warping around the shapes of unspeakable words.

'Come on, Mikey baby. We ain't wiring that hundred grand till you start telling the truth.'

'Easy, Rick.'

'Hey, man, say the words!'

'Michael's in a sensitive position. And we must be tactful in taking his loyal reticence as a polite denial of Mr Hilldyard's allegation. Mr Hilldyard, sir, if you hold a grievance against Michael, it is your right to have recourse against him. Meanwhile we, as bona fide purchasers for value without notice, own the rights, which we intend to exploit with or without your blessing. And frankly, sir, I don't see any court on this earth voiding a contract because of your indecision. This is the real world, and in the real world honourable men are bound by their signature.'

'I told him' – Hilldyard let the air run out of his lungs – 'personal

283

confidences which he threatened to expose if I didn't sign. The contract is void. He has assigned you a void.'

'You fucking little hypocrite,' Weislob hissed at Michael.

'This man is the hypocrite.' The author pointed at Hammond.

'Don't slander my client!'

He needled Hammond with a crooked finger half bent in Weislob's direction. 'This man represents you?'

'You were blackmailed, then?' said Hammond, with a raised eyebrow.

'Don't interrogate me! Who d'you think you are?'

'You're very rude, Mr Hilldyard, and I'm just wondering what God-given right you have to insult people you've never met before. You know, I'm beginning to think you're pulling rank because you've got no moral high ground to stand on whatsoever.'

'There speaks an over-priced actor. I'm no star-fucker, but I can tell you, go ahead and make that picture and the world will know how you and this actress preyed on this man, flattered, tempted and corrupted him with money and sexual favours so that he would put unbearable pressure on me to sign the option. If anyone has exerted duress it is you. It is your persistence, your greed and egotism that's caused this mess, and it's your image that will be ruined if you defy me.'

'You're blackmailing us!' She rounded on him, flaring with rage. 'You're slandering me! You have no right to say those things. I never corrupted Michael. I've never had sex with him. It's your imagination that's completely corrupt. And let me tell you, if it came to a contest between the world's good opinion of Shane and a man with your history . . .'

'Adela!' Michael rose suddenly.

'You wouldn't stand a chance.'

Hilldyard blinked. He realised that Michael had betrayed him a second time. He had not kept the secret.

She was flushed, hyperventilating, pent up with wrath.

'Adela!'

'If the world knew the truth about you, you'd be finished. About you and Frances. Talk about corruption. He fucked his fifteen-year-old niece on the bed of his dying wife!'

'Shut up!' screamed Michael.

'You filthy pervert. How dare you threaten us!'

'Michael!' Hilldyard stepped back, eyes burning with anguish.

'You have no respect for ordinary people. No respect for anyone but yourself. You're a monster, a sexual abuser, an adulterer, but you think you stand above us all because you write novels.'

'Oh God,' gasped Hilldyard, raising his right hand.

'Don't deny it. Michael told me everything. I mean, did your wife die of shock, or did she take pills? And what about Frances? How many suicide attempts have you inflicted on her?'

Hilldyard made a lunge, sending a hand through the air, as if to beat the sound of her voice, but groaned instead, clutching the back of the chair and looking at Weislob with an expression of agonised injustice. He held position for a moment, then flopped in a faint, gashing his head on the chair-arm as he went.

Michael dropped to his side.

Hilldyard's head rolled on the ground.

Mahler was on his knees. 'Loosen his shirt.'

The gash on his forehead was blue before it bled. Mahler pulled a handkerchief from his pocket, pressed it against the wound.

Hammond grimaced. 'Fucking hell, Adela!'

'Will you get some water, please,' said Michael, hands under Hilldyard's head.

'Ooh, nasty! Rick, hotel doctor.'

'Get some water, please!'

The face was a death mask, the eyes sunken, the jaw slack.

'Come on, old boy. You got a pulse?' said Mahler.

Michael wept as he felt under the sleeve, thumb seeking radial artery, skating on the feathery skin of his wrist.

Rick was shinning it round the pool, a short man in a dead-sprint.

'Michael!' She was desperate.

'He's breathing,' said Mahler.

The groan was ugly, inhuman, as Hilldyard gasped awake, rearing forward.

'Easy, easy.'

He touched his head, found blood leaking through his fingers.

'Don't move.'

Hilldyard struggled. He pushed Michael away, rolled sideways, managed to rise up. He got a hand to the chair but then his legs crumpled and his old shoulder went hard against the flagstones.

There were blood spots on Michael's shoe.

Hilldyard thrust himself up again, face contorted with effort. He panted as he rose, brushed his knees with a wince, stared at his palms. Then he turned and pushed his way through the group, staggering around the chairs and following the edge of the pool, heading out the same way he came in.

Michael caught up with him on the far side of the terrace. The author halted, eyes watery with pain, and thrust his hand against Michael's chest, knocking him back and propelling himself the final few yards into the building. He nearly smashed into an exiting waiter, averted, dodged a deckchair and disappeared through a doorway.

Michael paused for a moment, and then ran after him along the arcaded corridor towards the flight of steps.

Halfway up the steps Hilldyard turned above him. Their faces were a yard apart, the author's warped by distress.

'You've finished me.'

Michael clutched the old man's arm.

His skin changed colour, the shadow of premonition.

Abruptly, frantically, he tried to free his arm and Michael held on. The old man was right before him, but looking to a further point, askance, while his breath brushed Michael's neck.

'Now it's me that has no option,' he said, and twisted violently so that Michael lost his grip.

He made good his escape, forcing himself up the remaining steps into the foyer where he hurried on to the doors and the street without a backward glance.

Mahler sat in a chair and pinched the bridge of his nose. Hammond was a frozen bystander, champagne glass held loosely in hand. Gloria Sabbatini and Rick Weislob stood in conference at a distance and gave Michael Lear, when he returned, the briefest of glances.

He came back into the silent group with no care for their thoughts. Hammond did not see him, would not register his presence. Only Adela acknowledged his stare with an expression that was neither hard nor penitent. She had the look of someone exposed. She trembled still with the shock of what she had said.

'That went well,' said Hammond, knocking back the champagne.

The actor's interests had not been furthered. He was deciding what to do about it. 'Where's Frank?'

'Ahh.' Mahler checked his watch. 'He's in LA.'

'Fuck, this is uncool.'

Michael wanted to speak to her. Her look told him not to try. Her arms were crossed tightly against remonstration or appeal.

Weislob and Sabbatini wandered over. 'Relax, chief. We got the contracts. We got the rights. He fucks around, we ringfence him.'

'Are you totally coked?'

'Hey, this is a done deal. It's legally ours.'

'Rick.' Mahler's voice was tired, on edge. 'There's a duress point.'

'To prove which he has to crap on himself.'

Michael subsided in shame.

Hammond took up the point. 'You're saying he won't sue because we know he's a sex fiend?'

'He didn't hang around for second helpings.'

Mahler groaned.

'We just go ahead and make the film!'

Weislob jabbed away with his mobile phone, as if it were grafted to his hand. 'Listen, Michael did the duress. We're bona fide purchasers for value without notice.'

'We just had a faceful of fucking notice!'

'Suppose we lose the notice?'

Michael could not believe his ears.

'You mean we agree to lose the notice?'

'The old guy never came here. Our word against his. Six eye-witnesses never saw nothing. And if he wants to remember telling us duress, we get our memories back and remind him what Adela said.'

'Which was untrue,' said Michael.

She shook her head, shivering.

'What's the truth, Michael?' Hammond was cruel-faced.

'Chief, this isn't about truth. It's about the law of contract.'

He went right up to her. She could save herself now or be damned for ever.

'Tell them it was a lie!'

She raised a hand.

'Take it back.'

She fixed him with a look of plaintive intensity. Her frightened eyes begged him to be sensible, to go with the flow, to move with, not against her.

'Find her another role,' he said.

Hammond shrugged. 'Like they really grow on trees.'

'You can't make this film!'

'You sold us the fucking rights,' said Weislob. 'Who are you to talk?'

Michael wanted to touch her face. She wanted to let him touch it but her eyes said no.

'She was lying,' he said.

'Michael!'

'You can't make the film on the basis of her allegations. You can't blackmail Hilldyard with lies. Don't you understand? She wants the part. She'll say anything!'

She caught his arm and pushed him backwards, towards the balcony rail, shoving him away from the others, her lips drawn, wrists locked, revealing something unfamiliar to the men behind her. She stood with her back to them. Her eyes were jewel-bright.

'You know it's true,' she hissed. 'You told me!'

'In confidence!'

'He's admitted it!'

'He admitted duress! The rest you told them! You've got to take it back.'

She shook her head, almost smiling at the paradox. 'But it's the truth!'

On either side he saw staring faces, Hammond, Mahler, Sabbatini.

He looked at her again. 'Truth means nothing to you.'

He saw the reaction, the alarm of it striking her, as if honesty could compel something at last.

She endured his grip. 'You'll spoil everything, Michael.'

His fingers sank into her arm and with the pain of it she side-stepped, breasts jiggling. She widened her eyes in desperate appeal. 'For us, then!'

There was a depth of vulnerability in her look.

'I need you,' she breathed.

'Need me?'

'This is working!' Her eyes flickered.

'Are you trying to tell me something?'

'I'm trying to tell you . . .'

Her eyes spoke of something nascent, something mutual, some strange kinship caught up in the whole bad business, of two consciences in the same state of desire and disrepair and difficulty. In the hard look she gave him he saw her contempt for Hammond, and her knowledge of the risk she was taking in simply staring at him in this way when the others were so close.

'I want you,' she said, between clenched teeth.

It came to him suddenly. This was how her love would work. He hesitated, drew closer, inhaled the full incense of her nearness. 'Tell them it was a lie, then. Tell them for "us" '.

Something dark crossed her face: a lapse, an inward distraction. The moment had come.

She gasped, reaching out to him with the tip of her finger, which brushed his jacket.

'Michael . . .'

The connection was loosening, a thing stretching out, a grip sliding, sliding, until suddenly the hands parted and she was dropping away, her dress fluttering in the free-fall of separation.

'Adela!'

It hit him like a blow in the chest, something knocking him back.

She turned violently to the others, shouted at them. 'It's all true.'

'Despicable,' he yelled, a voice-ricochet around the pool.

It came across his vision like a whorl of black and it blinded him as he stood there, hands hanging, ready to drop, and through the dots he saw shapes, a wing or throbbing form that seemed to grip his throat and choke him until he felt the balcony rail in his back and the hard ground under his knee-cap and felt himself gasping and conscious again.

They stared at him as he rose.

It came to him quickly. The contracts were still on the table.

'Adela!' He took one of her earrings from his pocket, held it up, let it dangle from his fingers.

She could not hide her embarrassment, and when he threw it at her she fumbled the catch and dropped it.

'Now d'you believe me?' he asked Hammond.

The actor was transparent for a moment.

'She'd do anything.'

'It's not mine,' she said.

Michael saw the ugliness of her desperation.

'She'll fuck anybody,' he said, staring at Hammond, connecting the two of them, hot-wiring them together. 'Even you!'

He made it to the table in swift strides, gathering the two Hammond agreements and tearing them up, a crossways shredding and ripping into small pieces. He took his agreement with Hilldyard and stuck it in his pocket. And then Weislob came at him terrier-like, adding his hands to the tussle, and getting Michael's elbow on his cheekbone.

'Fuck sake,' said Hammond in the far-off background; Weislob was pulling weightlessly and deflectably, and Michael could see through the tunnel of his resolution that nothing was not torn or scattered and that he had in his hand the signature page, ripped in half, which he needed as evidence.

With heat in his eyes he turned for a last look at the actress, at the agonised stances of the agents, at the trumped face of Shane Hammond, and then made his way around the pool, away from the group, away from the five-star view of the town, the champagne buckets and parasols and deluxe recliners.

Chapter Twenty-six

HIS LIMBS ACHED THROUGH and through, muscles hurting with effort as he pushed up the third flight of steps.

He had started off walking up the hill, a hollow feeling in the small of his back, as though he were slow in gaining the necessary velocity of escape. When he passed the taxi-rank by Adela's *pensione*, impulse turned to panic, and he threw himself at the mile of road that led up to Hilldyard's villa. He ran with spattering feet past scooters and tourists and familiar shopfronts, and felt revulsion coming up in waves from his stomach.

His lungs gave out on the third turn, when Positano revolved on its axis and the sea flattened out like a bedspread, here and there pricked by an islet, and the twists of the road threw vista upon vista across his path. He panted along, unable to think, but knowing that he had been in the centre of something awful. What had happened on the Sirenuse terrace was perfidy touching down, like the snout of a tornado, syphoning away all human decency. He was the point around which foul winds turned, and now, as he ran again, he was running to shed contamination, flaring along in the dire fear that Hilldyard had collapsed in horror.

He lived only in the present now. He had no concern for what the author might say to him. He was ready to endure anything.

The front door was locked. He grabbed the handle, tried the key Hilldyard had given him. The middle of the door budged under the weight of his shoulder but the top was fastened from within. He knocked hard, calling loudly. He waited, panting, keeping nothing in reserve for the moment when the door opened. He knew what the look in those eyes would mean. He tried to get his breath back. The air was too thin. An old woman with stockings sagging at the ankle gave him a wide berth as she passed along the alley.

He was faint. The blackness came back, rising like water in a tank. He thought he would expire on the step and bent double, reaching for the wall and becoming for an instant so weak that he did not care if the door opened and Hilldyard found him in a heap on the ground. He felt the stone under his palm and allowed himself to collapse against the door.

Sunlight poured on to the opposite wall. The sun was full on from somewhere up there, and the sky royal blue. He lay back, sweat on his chest, the veins on his neck throbbing, and felt himself levitated into the blue above, sky-diving into azure; and as he swooned in the depths of its colour, adrift in its purity, he felt the ghost of his original self steel into him and for a second he was torn apart by the searing beauty of the blue heaven. The sun had set things ablaze, splashingly, dazzlingly, and he was part of light. Light caught his hands, smote lines along the alley. He gasped at the pain of a sensation which seemed to stave him in at the temples.

He dropped on his knees like a penitent, put his finger through the letterbox, and yelled into the hall. He knew Hilldyard was there.

Back in his hotel room there was a moment of normality when he picked up the telephone and dialled and pretended that it was an ordinary day and that, if the telephone rang, James would pick it up, and Michael would say something quick before ringing off but know at least that he was OK. The phone rang endlessly, so he dialled again, and it rang endlessly again. He smacked the receiver down with frustration and lay on the bed thinking that one hour had passed since he left the hotel. The uncertainty was killing him.

Lying on his back he was prey to thoughts which afflicted him as physical pain. He imagined Hilldyard's cold body, skin grey, the spirit no longer present, the capacities of a remarkable mind switched off for ever.

'It can't be that bad,' he said, rising up and standing by the balcony. The sea was sparkling; the roofs below were a glinting white. Bougainvillaea covered balconies and courtyards.

One could not be a high priest of art and a fornicator. No man could stand by his art demanding its importance to humanity and be known as an adulterer, a near paedophile, the proximate cause of his niece's madness and his wife's death. If you believed in the novel as Hilldyard did; if you set a standard of moral consciousness by which to regard humanity, then you had to be exemplary. Every writer wanted posterity on his own terms and, for Hilldyard, posterity had just gone to the dogs.

Out on the street, running again, he thought about climbing over a garden wall to gain access. He could go in through a neighbour's house. Worry was beginning to exhaust him. He was flagging. He went past the shops and trattoria like a jogger, ducking under awnings and dodging parked cars, fists bunched. And then, as he approached a hairpin bend, he thought he saw Adela through the rear window of a black Mercedes that was coming into the bend from the opposite direction. He stood transfixed, then hurled himself in its path, hands up, shins fearing impact. Rubber rasped, the bonnet skewed sideways, a car in the opposite lane screeched to a halt, its nose ducking on a handbrake. A woman screamed nearby, and then the driver erupted, yelling in soprano outrage, shaking his fists, and Michael reeled back like a madman, turning on his heel and running off in the opposite direction.

Hilldyard's neighbours were not in. He beat his fists red proving the point.

He decided to run down to the tourist office in the *centro*. He wanted an English-speaking person who would know what to do. On the way, he passed the entrance to the police station and felt unequal to the ponderousness of official help. Further down, the tourist office was shut. Exhausted and dispirited, he wondered whether the Sirenuse could help him. He imagined himself at the desk of the five-star hotel trying to explain the crisis but he couldn't bear the thought of seeing Mahler or Hammond again.

He went into the church and sat on a bench in the gloom, inhaling the aroma of brass polish and incense. The confessional boxes were spaced along the wall. Candles flickered before side-altars. In the next pew an old lady blubberingly prayed. He threw his head back and gazed at the dim frescos on the dome above, at the altar cross, and the painting of the hooded virgin, her face fallen in sorrow. He felt the urge to pray even though he did not believe in God. Soon he was outside again, staring at the piazza.

He decided to write a note on a scrap of paper and stick it through Hilldyard's letterbox.

Later, when he had pushed the note through the old man's door, and was wandering past vegetable stalls in the upper part of town, he saw a gate which snared his curiosity and drew him through an arch into the cemetery, which was perched on the edge of the hill and open to a view of the pink sea and the rosy yonder of mountainside villas. The stems of three pine trees divided the view.

He eased down on to a bench and gazed at the trees, letting his breath come back and his limbs solidify with exhaustion before noticing the girl he had seen before. She was right there, at the bottom of the cemetery, by an easel; dead still.

He started and missed a heartbeat as though electrocuted by the sight of her. It was a vision that returned to haunt him in the middle of the night when he lay on the bed in his stuffy room hounded into wakefulness by a dream of Rick Weislob and Bambi licking ice-creams, and Frank Coburn venting fire and brimstone from a cathedral pulpit in a sermon about morals and the Hollywood system.

He lay arms wide across the mattress and felt his heart accelerate from a dead beat into grim thudding. He needed to swallow air. He could not move, was stuck where he lay. Panic went through him as the day's faces returned to haunt him: Mahler and Weislob, Coburn and Hammond, Adela, who seemed sketchy, as though she were already fading into the past tense to which she now irreversibly belonged, until he smelled her scent on his pillow and recoiled from the shock of it.

And as the agony abated and he was forced to remember again her head in his groin and the golden sands of her cascading hair, he went on to think more easefully of the girl painter in the cemetery, a person unknown to him, but belonging to him in the way that images do when they fuse the uncannily familiar with the sharply unexpected.

He lay in darkness, cocooned by the night. He could not understand how he had come to be so bad. He marvelled at the awfulness of what he had done. He was responsible, he knew. That was the astonishing thing. Blame was inescapable. There was no coming to terms with that; merely the living of it.

He did not care much whether he lived or died.

In the morning he spoke to the hotel manager. She tried to call Signor Correggio using a number in the telephone book, but either the number was wrong or the solicitor was out; so he asked her to call the police. After a lengthy exchange that seemed to cover a number of other topics he was told that a police car would collect him from the bottom of the steps and they would drive up to Hilldyard's house.

The day was beautiful. The bonnet of the car shone as it approached. Even the moustache of the *carabiniere* seemed to shine as he rolled down the window and told Michael to get in the back. The car smelled clean inside, of after-shave and upholstery.

They drove to the top of the town. Michael directed him into the alley behind Hilldyard's house.

They arrived at the front door. The situation had been explained.

The policeman assessed the exterior wall of the building before stepping forward and knocking on the door.

They waited absently. Michael's throat was dry.

After a respectful interval the procedure was repeated, three sharp knocks followed by a smoothing of moustaches and a glance around the alley.

Michael felt the silence drumming on his ears. He began to feel weak.

It was now legitimate for the policeman to go to stage two. He raised his hand to the door knob and turned it.

The door opened.

Michael blenched with surprise. The policeman turned to watch his reaction. They stood outside looking in through the hall. Light flooded in from the living room.

He went in first, and the policeman followed supportively, removing his cap and brushing his feet on the mat.

His note had been picked up from where it must have fallen. He went through the connecting door into the living room as though for the first time.

The room had been cleared up, and the sofas faced each other again. The floor was tidy. Someone had shut the bureau, enclosing its chaos on itself, and replaced the lamps on the side-tables.

On the glass table he noticed a bag which made him think that Frances had come back and that perhaps the two of them had gone out. He saw his note. Maybe Frances had cleaned the place up. The kitchen door was open. The window in the bathroom had been put on the latch. Everything seemed in order on the balcony where the wicker chairs and geranium pots were bleached in the brightness.

He gave the policeman a provisional nod on his way back, showing that he was making good progress and grateful for his patience. It looked like Hilldyard had let Frances in after Michael's last visit. Possibly he had drawn back the bolt after reading Michael's note. Frances might have let herself in.

He entered the bedroom, hand reaching for the light switch, and saw a glint in the darkness.

He stopped. He was looking at an eye.

The eye was unblinking.

His chest tightened, and he felt strange as he pushed the door open and saw Frances on the bed. He must have gasped because the policeman was suddenly behind him and then the light came on, and Michael saw the short-haired girl with her head on the author's chest and her hand on his cheek and her body curled around the hump he formed under the sheets. She blinked as the light came on, fingers tightening.

He could not move so the policeman went forward and knelt by the bed, looking into Frances's eyes, as he checked her cheek with the tips of his fingers. He touched Hilldyard's forehead with his palm then searched under the bedclothes for a wrist.

The policeman crossed himself.

Michael saw the empty bottles of sleeping pills on the table, and the empty glass.

Hilldyard was gone, cold to the touch. He had put himself to bed and left his shoes in a neat pair on the floor.

Out on the balcony he shouted at the wide view and heard his cry echo back as he dropped to his knees. He grabbed the balcony rail and gasped in a heart attack of panic. He swayed around biting his fingers as the shock of it exploded, like thunder after lightning.

Soon there were people in the villa: a doctor, more police, an English-speaking Italian woman. He stood white-faced in the living room answering questions and looking through the bedroom door at a paramedic detaching Frances. When she came out she stared expressionlessly at him.

Beyond her he could see the author's hand resting on bedclothes, and a body bag being carefully unfolded.

Chapter Twenty-seven

THE SEA SPREAD WIDE and glinted in the hot light. Everything down there was picture-book tiny, little houses, squiggly roads, shelves of cultivation.

He pushed back and looked around the balcony like a weightlifter about to heave a deadweight, loosening his limbs and compressing his will for the final effort. Any second he would climb over and jump wide.

You had to gain momentum, a back and forth striding with clenched fists and set teeth, a surge of hate like a karate spasm to break through the barrier.

The day was vast around him, a cathedral ceiling frescoed with galleon clouds. The striped hills were soaking up the sea-light. Autumn never ended in this place.

He had checked out of Positano and come to Ravello and taken a room in a lovely hotel with huge bedrooms and Gothic windows and a maroon smothering of creeper on its stone walls. He wanted luxury and convenience for a couple of days.

He had his breakfast in the dining room and looked at the other guests as if through Plexiglas.

Once he was resolved, he began to feel numb. It was an unusual numbness, like an anaesthetic shot to a certain point of pain, leaving the mind free to plan details and make arrangements. For the past two days he had vomited every few hours, though there was nothing to sick up. His poor system was trying to expunge guilt, because guilt was attacking the body as well as the mind. Guilt was not content with mental torture. Guilt diversified into aches and breathlessness, heartache and giddiness, a poisoned gathering of self-disgust which would not stop.

Hilldyard's suicide destroyed all hope of forgiveness.

The Cimbrone Gardens were empty, and down below he could see neither people, nor cars. A nice day; the sun beamed.

The impulse was coming and going in waves, and he could tell there would be a climax or peak and that he had to ride its energy to jump the rail. He sat down on the bench to prepare himself.

In front of him, spaced along the balcony, were seven busts. They had been placed there by a former owner of the property: academic sculptures in white marble dividing the view like figureheads. They embodied what Hilldyard had proclaimed: the nobility of man before the vastness of creation, and, after every season's tourists had departed would remain, like sentries of consciousness. And when, in another year, the tourists flocked back with their zoom lenses and silk scarves, the statues would greet them, standing between the spaces of the view and mutely endorsing the peculiar rapture that attended that extraordinary prospect. And as he slumped against the bench, his heartbeat echoing in his head, the bars on the rail were like lines in which sight became trapped and compelled into blue heaven, and it came to him like a blizzard in the eyes that he was there again, seeing what Hilldyard had seen and loved, and feeling the old exaltation again, the view steeling into his soul, as though he were absolved by the will to die, were allowed to feel joy again, the joy of the dazzling sky and glimmering water and the cradled vastness of the Tyrrhenian Sea, an influx of happiness, his better self coming back, his bond with Hilldyard blessing him as he rose from the seat and crossed to the balcony, and put his hands on the rail and looked steadily at the drop, the universe opening for him; and he sucked in his breath, feeling the lovely heat of the sun, and raised a leg over the rail, hands tight, his foot finding a hold on the other side, swinging his weight around, so that he was standing with his back to the view, the snaking roads a hundred yards beneath, the garden ahead of him with its high pines and vermilion trellises.

Thirty, twenty-nine, twenty-eight, all calm, still calm, twenty-five, twenty-four, breeze around his ears, a cerulean wash in his eyes, twenty-one, fingers white-knuckled on the rail, goodbye fingers, familiar fingers, innocent fingers, eighteen, seventeen, not long, fifteen, halfway, fifteen, remember Christine, so clear, so present, twelve and eleven, joining you, my angel, a hot rush, like a gust of wind through the breast, ten and nine, yes, force down, force onwards, grit your teeth, eight, seven, oh God, bloodshot hydrangeas

298

and smeared colours, down now, six, fingers off, five, four, three, chest erupting, let drop, two, oh Christ, now, got you, goodbye, eyes shut and drop and what? The eyes, what? Claw back. Oh Christ, see her, see her. Ah, no, can't be. Not now. There she is. Oh God. Sideways. Christine, he calls. Christine!

A staggering half-run, hardly supported by his poor heart, down this path, that path, through borders, around bushes, across slippery grass, statues on his right, sundials on his left, shoe in mud, ankles in brambles, a headlong, helter-skelter shambles of a run to the place where he thought he had seen her. He stared with tear-smudged eyes in every direction, heart overwhelming him as though he would die of confusion. He stood at a crossroads in the path, a bedraggled scarecrow of a person, heard only birdsong, the grunt of a lorry in the valley.

He smothered his face and let out a gasp of tainted breath. Clutching his shoulder he stared back towards the belvedere. Agony ran through him like a poison, and for a moment Michael thought he would pass out.

Panting, he sat down on the ground, drawing up his knees, but the effort was too much and he fell sideways, resting his head on the ground.

She was forty feet away. Visible through a gap in the hedge. She had put her easel in front of an opening in the trees. He gazed at her and felt a tingling around his arms and the back of his neck. His hand when he raised it was shaking violently, and he let it drop, let it rest on his hip, let it alone. Behind him he heard soft, amicable voices, a man and woman.

Thick hair, a khaki jacket, jeans. She was painting quickly, before the light changed or somebody interrupted her.

He kept his eye on the figure and felt a limitless subsiding, a caving in, as though the shock of coincidence took the wind out of his sails. Drops of sweat released themselves from his hairline and slid down his face.

The image shimmered and fragmented, and then realigned into clarity: the figure of a woman, the easel, the looming sky and sketchy mountain, the population of leaves on the trees, a dense, swarming mass of greenery, surrounding her, muffling the air, colonising vision. It was all he could do to sit in a trance and stare at the back of a girl he had already seen twice in Positano.

He stayed for an hour on the ground, damp going through the seat of his trousers, pine needles tickling his bare calf, the smell of leaves and rotting cones investigating his lungs. Intermittently he would shake, little spasms. A headache came and went, and the pain in his shoulder seemed gradually to dim, and eventually he felt able to stand up, which he did very slowly. And when he tried to walk he was surprised that his body co-operated. He stretched, orienting himself. The sun had moved around the sky, pushing long shadows in front of the cypresses. The day was fading.

He went closer, and as he neared the flight of steps, the view opened sideways and he could see her dipping her brush and marking her picture and staring intently.

He gazed at her as though holding the thread of a memory that went back through the years, to something overlayed but gathering now, Christine in France, up in the hills, painting one fine summer evening a great, wide Claude Lorraine canvas of a view. He had sat on a hay bail and watched her from behind as she stood by the easel, working rapidly to catch the light. He was spellbound by the view.

The valley was dramatically sidelit, poplars incandescent, mown fields beaming Labrador gold, and yet amidst the brilliance night was gathering, a presentiment of darkness that slowly encroached on the hilltop blaze. One moment the landscape was a patchwork of greens, richly sombre, colours at the height of tone; the next a scene of dying intensity, distances merging, detail blurring. And as the sunset conflagration waned – the upper sky becoming nostalgic, streaked with russet and opal; a cloud igniting in final baroque splendour before the sun viscously sank into the horizon – the valley filled up with dusk, an inky mist that engulfed the foreground, engulfed Christine. Soon they were losing each other, losing themselves in the dark.

He helped her with the easel back to the car and before long they were driving through the lanes, Christine in the passenger seat, paint on her fingers, her eyes on the road, Michael exhaling cigarette smoke as he steered and changed gears, marvelling that she was his love and that they had been together before that transient light.

* * *

He lay on his back along the length of the bed, clothed. His hands were clasped together. Light from the lamp half-caught his face but he felt nothing of its heat. His breathing was slow, silent. His legs motionless.

A door banged in the hotel corridor, cutting off remote voices. Cisterns hissed, footsteps came and went. Downstairs in the dim restaurant a couple sat on their own, secretively talking. The man at the reception desk folded his newspaper and licked his underlip.

Outside in the street the air was still and cool, spreading its autumn dew on the bonnets of cars and the plastic seats by the *caffè*. Beyond the piazza, where an old man sauntered under lamplight, darkness crowded in. It was a moonless night, and the trees in the Cimbrone Gardens were lost, the bushes and flowerbeds invisible. Darkness dwelled over statues and pathways and out across the thick blackness of the sea. The trees were blind to the mountains and the mountains did not know they were there, and even the grunt of a car on a hairpin bend vanished into the folds of night.

Chapter Twenty-eight

HER FACE WAS DIFFERENT.

She was tired, of course, and guilty, and that left a mark. But there was something else, too, about which she could do nothing. Her face showed experience, the aspect of an older person – a kind of knowledge that affects the complexion, as though it were no longer possible to play certain roles. And, of course, she was nervous. Her composure was constantly failing. She had come on an impulse and to hell with the red eye and blotchy skin and wrecked composure.

There was a knock at the door.

He stood by the bed with his back to the door. He had been dressing slowly.

She half-entered, keeping the door as a shield.

'Michael?'

The sound of Adela's voice was so unexpected that he did not immediately turn.

She closed the door behind her.

'Your hotel told me you were in Ravello,' she said nervously. 'I've been everywhere searching for you. Checked every hotel.'

He did not know where to look.

She came further into the room.

His heart was beating hard; he turned to face her.

She returned his look searchingly, in fear of his reaction, which he could not conceal.

She had no right to be here. Her presence was inadmissible. Michael could not believe the sight of her. He stared at her, though as he stared at the familiar face he saw something new, and this held him.

Her countenance was somehow damaged. It was as though everything that had happened in the last few days had left its mark, worked through in her skin; so that she was disarranged, compromised; and all this she presented with an open gaze, as though it were a kind of evidence, and his reaction, which she would not miss, a kind of proof.

'Michael.' There were tears in her eyes. 'I feel so terrible. I can't believe what I did.' She wiped her cheek. 'If I hadn't said those things, he might still be alive.'

She did not move towards him. She understood everything Michael might think of her, had taken that as read.

He stood with his hands by his sides, and noticed the lines in her forehead and a strand of grey in her hair.

'Sorry,' she said, dabbing her eyes. 'I'm sorry.'

He had not expected to see her again, and now it was strange just to look at her.

She let him gaze at her for a moment, but then glanced away. Her hand fluttered, something she was not able to say, could not manage. And then she was motionless and silent.

Eventually she walked around the end of his bed, moving towards his window and its view of the mountain. She stood by the window and let time pass, as though by standing there and accustoming him to her presence she was referring to something. And when she turned and looked back at him, her expression had changed again.

'Why are you here?' he said.

There was silence.

She hesitated, and then she looked at him fearfully. 'Had you ever thought that now he's dead it doesn't matter? I mean, he's lost everything, but we don't have to.'

He listened sternly.

'I know it sounds awful.' She frowned. 'But the damage has been done.'

He was still dazed by an interminable sleep. He had decided to stay one more day. There were things to think about, processes to conclude.

She came back towards him, looked at him squarely. 'Have you torn up the contract?'

The contract was at the bottom of his case.

Michael shook his head.

'Why not?'

He stared at her.

'Why not, Michael?'

He was unable to say why, unable to speak.

She breathed out. The colour was coming back into her cheeks.

'Adela, please . . .'

'He's dead! Nothing you can do will bring him back!'

For a moment he was stunned, as though a gun had gone off, and he looked at her with a kind of fear. Her expression was incredible.

She came around the end of the bed, came up to him, gave him the look of an honest woman who will not be rebuffed. 'I want us to carry on where we left off.'

The proposition was deplorable, absurd. He shook his head. 'But you have no real feelings for me!'

'That's where you're wrong. I've all kinds of feelings for you. You wanted me to prove them with impossible conditions, conditions imposed by your unassailable integrity. You couldn't just let things happen!'

He shook his head again.

'Why did you betray him then? Was it a whim? I don't think so. It didn't feel like whimsy. It felt like passion. Uncontrollable passion. You did something wrong, but in the name of passion, and whatever happened afterwards, you can't undo that.' Suddenly, her voice was thick. 'I know how you feel. I know what you're up against. And I'm saying, please God, it doesn't have to be like this. Give yourself a chance. Let me help you.'

She turned away, almost humiliated.

It was strange for him to be the victim of her pleading again, to feel it coming in waves against him. Her stamina was incredible. She felt what she said absolutely, as though just by feeling it she could change things. And Michael realised then that he believed her, even when she lied. Her desire fused everything together, made one issue out of several things; and the fact she was here, running the gauntlet of his anger and incredulity, was a form of consistency. If her nature were different to his, she was at least true to it.

She moved to sit on the end of his bed. She gave him a tired look: the look of a person who has nothing to hide.

He sat down, too; rested his back on the pillow.

They stared at each other for a moment.

He had been at this juncture before; the point where some part of him collapsed before her insistence, as though he were always obliged to hear her out. Perhaps it was because he wanted to know her view of things, to see how she construed what had happened to them.

'What are you proposing?'

'That we get on a plane. Talk to Shane. Do what we were going to do.'

He looked at her starkly. 'Make the film?'

'You've got the rights. Your deal with Shane can be signed off again. He still wants to direct the film.'

'Have you spoken to him?'

She nodded.

It was weird looking at her now. Despite everything she was beautiful.

'I'd be marginalised,' he said in a thin voice.

'Marginalised, and a lot richer. Plus you'd have me.' She stated it as a fact, as though she were subject to some pre-existing agreement between them, a bond she implicitly accepted. 'Have you gone off me?'

He was still attracted to her. Nothing would ever change that. But that in itself meant nothing.

'You weren't so indifferent, I seem to recall.'

'I was never indifferent to you.'

She tossed her hair back, flashed her eyes at him. 'Don't freeze me out now.'

He looked the other way, avoiding her appeal. Then, after a moment, he said, 'What d'you really think of me?'

She frowned for an instant, trying to do justice to the question. 'There aren't many people like you, Michael.'

He spoke tonelessly, as if trying out the idea. 'We ignore what happened?'

She rose from her end of the bed and came closer. She sat down in front of him. She was wearing a white cotton shirt and jeans.

'Michael. We've been through hell. But it's a hell that nobody in the world knows anything about. Life doesn't have to be miserable. What's done is done and there's no sin in making a film and trying to rebuild our lives.' She touched his forearm. 'The future holds everything. There's still a chance for us both, you see.'

He let her hand rest on his forearm. It was not unpleasant to feel her touch.

'What else will you do? Go home to a repossessed house and a broke business and a lifetime of guilt? You don't need to suffer any more. You could use the money to pay off your debts and set up shop again. This is just the beginning. I'll take care of you. I promise I will.'

He was almost soothed by these words, and as he looked into her eyes he could see she was sincere. She was offering her support, doing her best to salvage things in her own way; and Michael could almost believe in her love for him, conditional as it was.

He squeezed her hand. The emotion was sudden, uncontrolled, and it hit him in the heart.

'You and I don't have a chance,' he said, 'unless I tear up that contract now.'

She gasped.

He breathed in heavily.

Her face was suddenly stricken.

'I can't accept that your feelings for me are dictated by a piece of paper!'

'Oh.' She masked her face with her hands. She was consumed with woe, had lost all control.

He watched the display with strange detachment. She was obsessed, he realised; had always been obsessed.

'I'm thirty-four,' she said, suddenly.

'What?'

'I've never had a chance like this and I'll never get one again!'

'Thirty-four?'

She nodded shamefully. 'And my real name is Sarah Fowl.'

He was stupefied.

'We actresses' – she shook her head – 'two a penny.'

'Sarah Fowl!'

'Why d'you think I came here? Why d'you think I went to such incredible lengths? This is my last chance before I'm over the hill.'

He stared at her, showing all his astonishment, and getting in return a vulnerable defiance, as if she were daring him not to be repelled by the truth. She wiped a tear from her cheek. It had taken everything to tell him this and now she was fragile.

It struck him as amazing that her strongest card was honesty. Because the truth about Adela was more stirring than the lies she had told him.

'What about Jack Brand?'

It was not the memory that distressed her, but the struggle of being honest. She shook her head. 'Well, anyway, he didn't want to marry me.'

He felt his heart leap.

'I lied to you about my feelings for him.'

He was tense.

'We split up two years ago.'

'Lied?'

'To protect myself. To test you.'

He wanted to stand up and walk. He needed to escape from the shock of her honesty. He went past her and around towards the window. He opened the window and breathed in the fresh air.

Michael stared at the distant terraces on the mountain, at the pale-blue sky. It was a fine autumn morning.

The information she had given him affected everything. He was contemplating new possibilities, strange notions, the bizarre idea that Adela might be vulnerable because of her age, might in fact be a different kind of person. The six years did make a difference, not to him, but to Hollywood. It was late to start in a system that demanded mint-fresh beauty from its stars. He could see that, and he could see how her insecurity would have been worsened by a relationship break-up. She had been deemed unmarriageable, and felt herself, as a consequence, professionally ineligible. And it made him wonder whether her amorous feelings for him, so apparently convenient, were actually based on self-knowledge. She might know the value of his strong feelings. She had been around long enough to judge what kind of man would be good for her. She had identified him, encouraged him, and by an incredible effort of will tried to co-opt him into her professional and emotional come-back. Hence the audacity of her original suggestion: that he should produce the film.

She remained seated on the bed, her hand plucking the bedspread into creases.

He took a sidelong view of her face, now meeting his gaze across the bed. It was a face that seemed more honest now, transparently paradoxical. She was defiant and rejected, appealing and resigned. The extra years had released themselves, developing in her expression a more complex loveliness than he had seen before.

He realised that from now on she could not pretend.

From the window he could see the southern reaches of the Amalfi coast. Beyond the mountains, Salerno; beyond Salerno, southern Italy. This extraordinary landscape he would leave behind. Soon he would be standing in a London street, wondering what to do with the rest of his life.

Her persistence was oddly magnificent. There seemed nothing more real than Adela's needs. She was the sum of those needs and she was remarkable, a great actress. She had captured his imagination and released his energy and desire. It was not his mission to disappoint her. He had no wish to emulate Hilldyard's insistence on art over friendship.

He went to the suitcase and sprang the catch. He worked his way through folded shirts and trousers, feeling for the plastic file in the bottom of the case.

The contract was still intact, albeit creased and dog-eared. Two signatures met on the final page. All was in apparent good order and he had no idea whether the document would withstand the scrutiny of entertainment lawyers, or executors, or whomever succeeded Basil Curwen.

He placed it on the bed and turned to face her.

He could see from her expression that she was moved. He hesitated for a moment, words not ready.

'Come here,' he said.

She rose from the other side of the bed and came towards him.

He took her hand, pressed it into his. Her lips parted. She breathed in deeply.

'It's yours.'

'What!'

'This contract.'

'Oh, Michael . . .' She wanted to fall into his embrace but he held her wrist tightly.

'I'll assign my rights to you. You can have the option. Whatever the lawyers need from me, I'll sign. Anything you like.' He swallowed.

She frowned.

'But I don't want to be involved and I don't want any money.'

He looked at her intensely.

There was a long pause.

He could not speak. Adela saw this and touched his sleeve lightly. He shook his head.

'Michael!'

The colour went out of her face.

Suddenly she gripped his arm, half smiled at him. She hesitated for a second, her mind racing. 'You can't turn me down just like that.'

'I would never turn you down.' His heart hammered away. 'I think you're marvellous.'

Adela was distraught and exhausted and wrung her hands in frustration. 'How could you inflict such a choice on me?'

'Because I have no choice.'

'You don't want me?'

'Oh, I do.'

'I'm nothing without this!'

He shook his head hopelessly.

'How could our relationship ever recover from your denying me this chance?'

'I won't deny it. It's yours.'

She laughed in rich anger. 'You're appalling!'

'I know what I am.'

She shook her head, incredulous.

He felt the emotion as a kind of spasm in his gut, as something inflicted on the body like illness, beyond control. He was opened up again, and he knew that he loved this woman and yet he would not go with her if she took the contract.

She stared at him.

The contract lay between them on the bed.

Adela's look darkened slowly, as if she had swallowed something terrible, were subdued by the outrageous effort of digestion, her cheeks becoming grey, her brow contorting; and for a moment he thought she would collapse. She was staring at nothing now, staring into some personal hell, envisioning the future, and her expression froze completely.

He touched her arm, and she looked at him and gradually the colour came back into her cheeks.

She took the contract from the bed and held it for a moment. There was an other-worldly strangeness in her eyes. 'Take it.'

'What?'

'You signed it. You destroy it. If that's how you feel. Why should I be the one to make the choice?'

'Choice?'

'A dead author or a living woman. A literary god, or the person you love.' There was fire in her eyes. 'Go on. Tear it up. Just kick me out of your life like worthless rubbish.'

'You'll lose the film if I do.'

'And you'll lose me, and your money. And your life.'

She had proved herself, he thought. Her fury was conclusive. She did love him.

'Don't go,' he said.

'You obviously have no feelings for me at all.'

'I do.'

'But you're not prepared to prove it, so it doesn't matter. I wouldn't ask you to throw away a chance like this.' She reversed back around the bed, straightened her shirt, looking at him with fierce pride. She made a move to the door, pulled it open dramatically. She was attempting an exit, hoping that he would relent, or think twice before she had gone. It was her last gambit.

He watched her standing there, her last few seconds in the room, conveying to him a look of pitiful emotion and controlled distress.

'Goodbye, Michael. I'm sorry I came to see you. Goodbye.' She raised a hand. There was a tear in her eye.

He nodded again, holding her gaze. 'Adela!'

She gasped. 'Yes?'

'Adela.'

She stared at him.

He held up the contract as if to show her something, a gesture of appeal, of self-doubt.

There was a terrible expectancy in her eyes.

'Don't go,' he said.

'Michael!'

She lurched forward.

He tore the contract before her eyes, two smart shreds back and forth, and let the pieces flutter to the floor.

She gasped and then gazed at him glassy-eyed, her look dimming.

'Don't go!' he said.

She stared at the remains of the contract, at what he had just done to her.

'Adela!'

She looked at him, but without recognition. And then she turned quickly and walked out of the room. He heard the sound of her receding footsteps in the hotel corridor.

*　　*　　*

He spent the morning in the gardens of the Palazzo Rufolo, strolling between parterres and gazing at the view to the south, the mountainous coastline that veered into a hazy distance. The air was soft and warm. The garden autumnally moist. He inhaled the tang of decaying leaves and the smell of stone in the courtyard. Under the trunk of a pine tree he stopped and gazed up into its net of green, looking at the twinkling light in its needles and listening to the birdsong around him.

Later, he went back to the hotel. He spent the afternoon at a table in his room. He had asked in reception for writing paper and was now self-contained, alone with his thoughts. At the top of the page were notes, half-sentences, ideas jotted down; and then a column of writing which grew over the following hours, a long paragraph, the words coming easily; so that Michael, as he wrote, forgot himself physically, his tired eyes and the ache in the pit of his stomach and his stubbly chin; and became fastened instead to what was in memory, the surges of it, like incoming waves on a wide shore, limitless, mesmerising, inextinguishably his.

AKNOWLEDGEMENTS

I am more grateful to Liz Calder and Arabella Stein than they will ever know.

I go down on one knee for my priceless agent, Felicity Rubinstein; and on the other for Claire Wrathall, rock-like editor. I go down on both knees and mabye even further for my wife, Fiona, without whose influence and support this book might never have been written.

I am also indebted to Evan Jones, Lawrence Norfolk, Katrine MacGibbon, Mark McCrum and Mark Roberts for sharp readings and timely encouragement; and to Mary Tomlinson for her flexible rigour.

A NOTE ON THE AUTHOR

Conrad Williams was born in Canada.
Formerly a lawyer, he is now a film agent.
He lives in London.

A NOTE ON THE TYPE

The text of this book is set in Linotype Sabon, named after the type founder, Jacques Sabon. It was designed by Jan Tschichold and jointly developed by Linotype, Monotype and Stempel, in response to a need for a typeface to be available in identical form for mechanical hot metal composition and hand composition using foundry type.

Tschichold based his design for Sabon roman on a fount engraved by Garamond, and Sabon italic on a fount by Granjon. It was first used in 1966 and has proved an enduring modern classic.